Substitute Angel

TIMOTHY BEST

TouchPoint
Press

SUBSTITUTE ANGEL by Timothy Best
Published by TouchPoint Press
2075 Attala Road 1990
Kosciusko, MS 39090
www.touchpointpress.com

Copyright © 2013 Timothy Best
All rights reserved.

ISBN-10: 0692024166
ISBN-13: 978-0-69202-416-4

This is a work of fiction. Names, places, characters, and events are fictitious. Any similarities to actual events and persons, living or dead, are purely coincidental. Any trademarks, service marks, product names, or named features are assumed to be the property of their respective owners and are used only for reference. If any of these terms are used, no endorsement is implied. Except for review purposes, the reproduction of this book, in whole or part, electronically or mechanically, constitutes a copyright violation. Address permissions and review inquiries to media@touchpointpress.com.

Editor: Nicole Gardner
Cover Design: Brannon Hall
Author photo: Brannon Hall and Trey Tomsik, photographer

E-book ISBN: 978-1-31020-454-8
E-book ASIN: B00GEH05B2
E-book BNID: 2940148193548

First Edition

Printed in the United States of America.

For my parents and sister, Jan. Angels all.

CONTENTS

Two Months Out Of Six	1
Anniversary	9
The Deer	21
Clair	27
Adjustment	32
A Little Help	40
Mrs. Huffman	48
First Impressions	55
Secret Ingredient	65
Two Days Earlier	73
The Mushroom House	77
Lunch	83
Progress	99
Invitations	106
The Dance	116
The Auction	128
Steps Back	136
Snowbound	142
Secrets Revealed	149
Astronomy Lesson	159
Later That Night	165
What God Does	176
Being There	179
Dinner	185
Into The Mist	194
Rescuer	204
Private Talk	213
Against The Odds	220
What's Owed	224
Sleep	241
Better Days	247

*Reputation is what men and women think of us.
Character is what God and the angels know of us.*
—Thomas Paine

TWO MONTHS OUT OF SIX

June

"She wants me," Doc Reynolds thought, catching the girl in the cotton sundress looking at him again. She was seated in a row of desks next to him and three seats ahead. There were only fourteen students in a classroom that held twenty-five desks. So the moves that students made, even subtle ones like over the shoulder glances, were noticeable.

Or, maybe the movements of other people were more interesting because he wasn't paying that much attention to the professor. He really didn't care about King Richard III and only took this class—Appreciation of Shakespeare—because he had to get one more elective out of the way before graduation. He thought the class would be easy. He was wrong. It was a serious dissection of the way Shakespeare wrote and why, the analogies he drew between the politics of the day and his characters, and the class had even debated about whether or not Shakespeare was one author, or a company of actors and authors writing under the same name, not unlike Monty Python.

Or, maybe he was easily distracted because it was summer—nearly eighty degrees outside—and he and his company of fellow Shakespearians longed to be anywhere but here, in the Quirk Dramatic Arts Building on the campus of Eastern Michigan University. Summer term didn't even feel like school. It felt like pretend school. He could hear the rhythmic buzzing of the cicadas outside getting louder, then fading, then getting louder again like an air-raid siren warning of cold beers and oiled bodies landing on the beaches. Then, his mind drifted to other classes, more serious pre-med classes where he still had pending assignments. But, then his mind boomeranged back into the cinderblock confines of the classroom in Quirk and England of the 1500s. He chewed on the tip of his pen as the girl in the next row over and three seats ahead tossed her blonde hair over her shoulder. He liked that she was wearing a cotton sundress. Most of the few girls left on campus were still wearing their baggy sweatpants leftover from the cold Michigan spring. They looked like they were constantly going to the gym, which did nothing for their figures.

"We've got an even number of students here, so I'm going to have you work in pairs," the professor announced. "You'll do a scene from one of Shakespeare's plays. It has to be a minimum of four minutes. You won't be judged on your acting, but I do expect some blocking, movement, maybe even a prop or two, and correct interpretation of the scene's importance to the play. You're going to tell me about this importance in a thousand-word essay that you will co-write with your partner."

The class began to groan in unison. "Take this seriously, ladies and gentlemen," the professor continued. "Your scene and essay will count as one-third of your grade. You have two weeks. Pick your partners at the end of class and submit your names and the scene you want to do next time we meet. If more than one team wants to do a particular scene, we'll flip a coin over it."

While everyone else was looking at each other, the blonde casually glanced over her shoulder back at Doc. He smiled his killer smile and half-gestured "You and me?" with his forefinger. That was all he had do. She smiled slightly, shrugged, and nodded.

"Oh, yeah," he mentally confirmed. "She wants me."

Her name was Julia Orton, and they talked a little after class that day, which was actually the first time they had spoken to each other since the semester had begun. Prior to the assignment and needing a partner, Doc had certainly noticed her and she him, but she wasn't pretty enough to merit any serious attention. Besides, he figured, he had assignments to finish up, medical school applications to fill out, and then there was graduation, although he was going to forgo the whole cap-and-gown bit. It was not a good time to start a relationship.

"Why are you called Doc?" she asked as he walked her to her car. She had a small, almost cartoonish voice, but he liked the sound of it. She was a commuting student, like him. Both lived with their parents. He lived in Ann Arbor, some seven miles away. She lived in Livonia, twenty-five miles in the opposite direction.

"It's a nickname from high school. I was the guy you wanted for a lab partner in biology. Matter of fact, I'm hoping for medical school after this."

She looked him over. "No. I'd say it's because you're such an 'operator' with the girls." She was referring to his obvious good looks. He was a hotter guy than she was a girl. She had also guessed correctly. He was used to and enjoyed the attention of the opposite sex.

"You already take your MCAT?"

"Yeah," he answered, impressed that she knew what the Medical College Admission Test was. "I'm applying at Michigan, Notre Dame, and Wayne State."

"Think you'll get in?"

"To Michigan and Notre Dame? I doubt it. But, my mom wanted me to go for it. With luck, though, maybe Wayne State, if I catch someone feeling generous."

She liked his uncertainty and hint of humility. She also liked that he listened to his mom.

"So what's your real name?"

"Wyatt, but everybody calls me Doc."

"And what scene do you think we ought to do?"

"What else? The balcony scene from *Romeo and Juliet*."

She looked at him a little teasingly. "That's pretty intense. It's going to take a lot of rehearsing."

"Lots," he agreed, thinking more with his libido than his brain.

She smiled, pleased that she was holding her own in the flirtation department. From her perspective, Wyatt "Doc" Reynolds would be quite a catch. He was twenty-two years old, an honors student, and the kind of guy that girls elbowed each other about if he passed them in a bar. He was slightly underweight for his height of six feet but taut from years on the high school cross-country team. He had dark brown wavy hair, that he wore a little long, and thick Adrian Grenier-like eyebrows that accentuated piercing blue eyes. A million-watt smile of perfectly straight teeth thanks to braces, when he was eleven, completed his presentation and had sealed many a date.

By comparison, Julia wasn't ugly, but she wasn't a beauty. She was pleasant looking when she wore makeup and anonymous when she didn't. She had a waif-like look. She was five-feet-two and also slightly underweight like Doc. She had straight blonde hair, pale skin, large blue eyes, a narrow, pointed nose, and a small mouth. She resembled a character in a Japanese anime movie, the beautiful heroine's best friend who wasn't beautiful but was earnest and sympathetic. Probably because of her plainer looks, she was a little more obvious in her attraction to Doc, but that was fine with him. She intended to be an elementary schoolteacher and had already done her student teaching the previous winter and spring. She already had several applications out to schools in the Livonia area. She didn't watch a lot of TV or listen to music, but she liked to sew. In fact, she had made the cotton sundress that she was wearing.

    A few days later, they went to the library to work on their scene. But that wasn't conducive for reading out loud. Then, they started having coffee in the afternoons at a local Starbucks. But that wasn't conducive for working on blocking. Next, they tried to rehearse a couple of afternoons in a local park. But they felt self-conscious about onlookers. Then, one night, over dinner, Doc joked, "We really ought to just get a room at the Huron Hotel. There's nowhere else to go and, at least, nobody will bug us." Even as he made the suggestion, he knew it was a thinly veiled invitation for intimacy. But, a little to his amazement, she agreed. What followed was a night of sensuous passion. That was how it all began. In fact, it was probably *because* both of them knew the timing was lousy to begin a relationship that they began it anyway. It was rebellious. It was naughty and exciting. It was something to do after acing their class assignment and graduation. It was something they could control at an in-between time in their lives, when they controlled little else.

December
    The first time Doc saw the Christmas tree, he was at Walmart to get some supplies for his father's lawn and garden nursery. The Plastic Ono Band was singing "Happy Christmas" on the store's Muzak system, while wide-eyed children tugged on their parent's coats and leaned toward the Toy Department as if being pulled by a magnet. It was December 17 and the kids felt both the excitement and the time crunch of the season. The artificial tree stood on top of an almond-colored credenza in Home Furnishings and was about three feet high. Attached to its branches was a string of thirty small multi-colored lights, although they weren't plugged in. It seemed to be in an odd place, as if the tree had been put on the credenza as a display afterthought. But it caught Doc's attention. Seeing a box of glass ornaments on a nearby shelf, he thought the items would be the perfect romantic touch for the hotel room he'd be going to later that night, when he rendezvoused with Julia. He plucked up the items and deposited them in his shopping cart, along with the light bulbs, coffee filters, and paper towels for his dad's business, where he had been working since

graduating.

Zipping up his coat and coming out of the store, the afternoon Michigan landscape seemed to be awash with a single color: gray. The clouds above were pregnant with snow and gray. The tall, dirty piles of plowed snow at the edges of the parking lot were also gray. Even the pavement of the lot, itself, was bleached out and gray. Such was a typical winter's afternoon in Ann Arbor. Pushing his cart across the lot, while the cold air nipped at his face and ears, Doc made his way to his maroon Ford Taurus also streaked with gray from the salt trucks and slushy snow. He thought about the evening to come. Tonight would be his last rendezvous with his girlfriend before Christmas. He had gotten Julia a sweater from Macy's, some Picasso perfume, a gift card from Barnes & Noble, and lingerie from a place called Marie's Boudoir that he couldn't wait to see her in. After making love, they could order room service. The Hyatt, where he had reservations, had room service until midnight.

That was one of the odd things about this relationship. During the past six months, he had learned more about the motels and hotels between Ann Arbor and Livonia than he ever thought possible. He'd also learned a lot about lying to his parents regarding his weekend nights. But he just couldn't help it. A little deceit was unavoidable. Julia was his love heroin—an addiction he didn't want to be cured from. He had dated better-looking women, but none so sexually uninhibited. He had to laugh at himself that this average-looking girl had so completely captured his heart. "It's the ones you never see coming that'll get you," his dad had joked. He'd given up buying music, books, clothes, and spending any disposable income so that he could set aside some of his savings and "rehearse" with Julia. That's what they still called their get-togethers.

As Doc's car crunched its way over the gravel drive of the nursery that sold Christmas trees, poinsettias, wreathes, and roping this time of year, he saw two unusual things. One was that his mother was there. He recognized her car and, since she was an accountant, it wasn't normal for her to be there during business hours. The other thing was that both of his parents came outside in the cold wearing no coats and sober expressions as he approached. Just about the time he assumed a close relative must have died, his mom flashed a wide grin and held up the sealed embossed envelope from Wayne State University Medical School. It was a business-letter-sized envelope, but was bulging with several pages of information. The kind of information a new student would need to know. If it were a rejection letter, the envelope would be thin and contain only one page.

Hours later at the Hyatt, a satisfied Doc rolled over in bed and saw the opened letter peeking out at him from the inside pocket of his winter jacket that was draped over a chair. Near the chair, on top of a writing desk, sat the Christmas tree he had purchased hours earlier. Its thirty lights and glass ornaments cast just the right combination of cheery, yet intimate, holiday illumination in a hotel room decorated in efficient-looking earth tones for traveling business people. Past a partially closed bathroom door, Julia stood naked in the bathroom brushing her blonde hair; the scent of their love making still hung in the air. Her hair fell five or six inches over her slender alabaster shoulders; long enough to cover the tops of her medium-sized breasts, but not long enough to cover her small, erect nipples.

Staring at herself and sighing a little as if she were disappointed with what she saw, she slipped on a black turtleneck that came down and barely covered her pear-shaped bottom. Wearing nothing else, she clicked off the bright bathroom lights and went back into the bedroom. As she did, she stepped over the white low-cut lace bra and crotchless panties from Marie's Boudoir that had been breathlessly stripped off her a half-hour earlier.

"Hungry?" he asked.

She climbed back into bed, but remained sitting up. "No," she replied in her small voice. She leaned back against the headboard and looked up at the reflection of the Christmas tree branches on the ceiling. "Thanks for bringing the tree, Doc. It was really thoughtful. But you spent too much on presents. You ought to take my stuff back."

He smiled at her warmly. "Don't worry about it."

"I'm sorry I didn't get you more," she said, glancing at a crumpled-up wad of wrapping paper and a Cross Pen and Pencil set he had opened earlier. "But you said to keep it simple, that we both needed to save money."

"No. It's great," he assured her, politely hiding a little disappointment.

She smiled slightly then turned her large blue eyes back to the ceiling and the reflections of the artificial pine needles. "You ever wonder where we're going?"

"Of course," he said, likewise turning his gaze to the ceiling.

"And?"

"And, this place is pretty expensive. So, next week, I think we're talkin' Red Roof Inn."

She rolled her eyes. "That's not what I meant. I was talking about the bigger picture."

"Ah," he said. He climbed out of bed and walked over to his jacket sitting on the chair. As he went, she couldn't help but admire his slender butt and hairy, muscular legs. He retrieved the envelope from the inside pocket and turned back to her, offering the correspondence as he approached. "Ask and you shall receive."

Only one page remained from the original fat envelope. The cover letter was all he needed tonight. She turned on a small bedside lamp and read.

"Oh, my God!" she said, now understanding. "You've been accepted to Wayne State!"

"That's Doctor Doc to you," he cracked, with an arched eyebrow.

She flashed a knowing smile and nodded. "I knew you'd get in somewhere. I *knew* it."

"Yeah? Well, *I* didn't."

He moved his pillow up against the headboard, got back into bed, but sat up like her. She turned off the bedside lamp, put the letter on the nightstand, then patted the top of his hand. "I'm very happy for you, Doctor Doc."

"Happy for *us*," he corrected. "This is a game changer."

"What do you mean?"

"I've got to get an apartment near campus. I'll be closer to your folks' house and closer to where you work. We finally *know* what we're going to be when we grow up, Julia, a teacher and a healer. That's a good combination. You want to know about the bigger picture? How about this: I can't imagine my life without you, and, now, for the first time, I've got something more substantial to offer than lingerie and hotel rooms. I'm talking about a life together, honey."

Her back stiffened as she froze. "You're not going to propose, are you?"

"I'm just talking here," he qualified. "Thinking out loud. Lots of couples get married while one or the other is going to graduate school."

She smiled slightly and looked down at the sheets. "Lots of couples get divorced that way, too. Oh, baby, don't get me wrong. I hear what you're saying, and I appreciate your sincerity, but you've got four years of medical school that are going to need your full attention, then years more of residency. We're talking hundreds of thousands of dollars in costs and a mountain of studying. And let's not forget, I've been teaching kindergarten for only three months. I don't know what I'm doing yet. I don't know if teaching is right for me. I don't want to weigh you down, be a responsibility you have to worry about."

"But…but you were just asking about the big pic—"

"I know," she interrupted. "But, now that we know there's a picture, we've got to look at things clearly before we act. You just got the letter today. It's an emotional time of year. Don't decide anything hastily. Let things digest for a little while. Meantime, I'll do the same."

Julia's family was originally from Maine. So, there was a streak of Yankee common sense and conservatism in her that he liked. It was traits like these that would make her a good wife and mother, he figured. But he also had to admit, he liked that she liked trashy lingerie, too.

He smiled and nodded at her wisdom. "You're right. We've got time."

"Mmm," she smiled.

He leaned over and kissed her believing the future lay before them. But it didn't. Because in ten hours and eighteen minutes, Julia Orton would be dead. The following morning, after leaving the hotel and driving home in her white Honda Accord, she ran a red light and was broadsided by a semi-trailer truck. She was momentarily distracted when she glanced down to look at a picture in her open wallet that was sitting on the passenger's seat. She didn't die instantly, but painfully some two hours after the crash in a hospital ICU. Although Doc had no way of knowing it, one of Julia's last conscious thoughts was that of the little Christmas tree sitting on the desk in their room at the Hyatt.

ANNIVERSARY

It was an older car. A 1969 two-tone Mercury Cougar two-door that was in mint condition, except for the accident it had just been in. It sat at a thirty-degree angle at the bottom of a snowy hill; a trail of tire tracks, tufts of ripped-up grass, and a couple of flattened pine saplings led the way down to it. The inside of the car was quiet and still except for a filtered female voice that was calm yet had a sense of immediacy. The voice said, "Simon, try to stay awake. The police and an ambulance are on their way. Simon? Can you hear me? Simon?"

The front windshield was a spider web of cracked glass. Because of the car's downward angle, all that could be seen through the splintered windshield was snow. The driver was a small-framed slender young man who wasn't sitting behind the steering wheel so much as turned parallel to it; the result of a loose-fitting seat belt, no shoulder harness, and the repeated bouncing the Cougar did as it went down the hill. His knees were tucked up near his face, and his legs were jammed against the driver's side door. The right side of his body seemed wedged in between the steering wheel and center console separating the black leather bucket seats. His right hand lay limp on the floor, while his left hand held the cell phone where the 911 operator kept trying to get a response.

"Simon? Are you still with me?"

The driver moaned painfully and seemed to be only semi-conscious. Suddenly, someone appeared outside the driver's side window. It was a concerned-looking Doc Reynolds. He was thirty-two years old now, his face was fuller and his hair shorter, but he was still a noticeably attractive man. He wore a deep blue nylon coat that went down to his mid-thigh. It had a round paramedic patch on one arm and a shield-shaped patch on the other that read, "City of Charlevoix." The blue coat only intensified the blue of his eyes. Like the car, he stood on an angle with one foot higher on the snowy hillside and one foot lower. He slowly pulled the handle and opened the door. When he did, the driver's legs unfolded like an accordion and fell halfway out of the car. Doc maneuvered around them, then bent down inside.

"Someone order a pizza?" he joked, trying to see how alert the victim was. The driver was a male Caucasian, five-foot-six, approximately one hundred and forty pounds, between sixteen and eighteen years old. No visible lacerations, but there was a little trickle of blood from the left-hand corner of his mouth. When the driver didn't respond, Doc immediately changed his tact.

"Hey, can you hear me, buddy? I'm a paramedic. You've had an accident, but I'm here to help. Okay? Just let me find out the story here."

He gently took the cell phone out of the driver's hand. "Margie, it's Doc. We're on scene now. Do we know anything new?"

"Negative, Doc," the police operator answered. "He hit some black ice, skidded off the road, and went down the hill. His name is Simon Jackson, and he's driving his father's car. That's all I got. After that, he started mumbling about how his dad was going to kill him because it's a restored car. I *did* learn his father's name is Phillip. We're trying to track him down now."

"How far out are your guys?"

"Four minutes."

"Okay. Thanks, Margie." He ended the call, then turned his attention to the driver. Although the young man was in street clothes, he had a "high and tight" military-style haircut.

Doc took the victim's pulse while looking at his wristwatch. Then he glanced around at the topography. A lot of Charlevoix County was flat as a pancake. It was just this kid's bad luck that he skidded off the road and down one of the area's few deep ravines. After ten more seconds to verify the steadiness of the pulse, he asked, "Simon, can you tell me where you hurt? Can you feel your toes? Can you wiggle them?"

The young man responded and one of his Merrells moved around a little.

"Good," Doc said. He pulled a small flashlight out of a tube-like pocket on the arm of his coat and checked the young man's pupil response and dilation.

"Nothing to worry about," he reassured, as he shone the light into one eye, then the other. "I just have to check something...actually, I have no idea why medical people do this. But it always looks cool on *Grey's Anatomy*, huh?"

The young male smiled slightly, then he suddenly winced in pain. "My side," he moaned.

Doc put two of his fingers on the driver's lower right side, the side that was turned toward the dashboard. "Here?"

"No, more toward my back."

The paramedic slid his fingers under the victim to the kidney area. "Here?"

"Yeah," Simon jerked, uncomfortably.

"You ever have problems with kidney stones, Simon?"

"No."

"Are you currently on any prescription medications?"

"No," he said, weakly.

"Are you allergic to any medications?"

The young man barely shook his head, apparently slipping into an unconscious state.

Doc smiled again and nodded. "Okay. You just hold tight. We're going to get you out of here."

He pulled a stethoscope out of his coat pocket, put the earpieces in his ears, slid a hand inside his victim's open jacket, and unbuttoned just one middle button of Simon's shirt, being cognizant of the cold. Doc listened intently to his breathing while sliding the silver head of the scope over one lung, then the other. After nearly a minute, he buttoned the young man's shirt, closed up his coat, and climbed out of the car just as a light, metal sled bed with a brown backboard on it slowly slid down the hill and came to rest next to the Cougar. Attached to the head of the sled was a cable. Up the hill, at the other end of the cable, was a winch attached to the front bumper of an ambulance that was angled across the road so the winch faced the hillside.

There were lit, hissing red flares on the road, about a thirty-yard distance on either side of the ambulance, to warn traffic that both lanes were closed. But there was no traffic in sight in either direction. The ambulance was white with a wide blood-red stripe wrapped around its entire middle. It had a General Motors van cab, but a taller box-like back end for transporting patients. Gold letters that spelled out "Charlevoix" were fanned out in a half-circle on both sides of the boxy back half of the vehicle, with the words "Life Support Unit" underneath. Red and white lights sitting flush in the back half of the ambulance, as well as lights on top of the cab, pulsed rhythmically while an EMT stood in front of the bumper operating the winch with one hand and holding a foam-rubber neck brace in the other. He stopped the winch, and then locked it.

Doc bent down and poked his head back into the Mercury. "Simon, do you think you can put your arms around me and hang on so I can help you out of the car?"

"I, I don't ..." his voice faded before completing the sentence.

"Okay. Never mind."

Sticking his head out of the car again, Doc gestured for his partner to come down the hill. His partner was about the same height, chubby, and had caramel-colored hair as thick as a Brillo Pad. But once summoned, he trotted down the hill in the ankle-deep snow quickly and efficiently for a person his size.

"Sweet ride," he said, referring to the vintage car.

Doc leaned back into the Cougar. "Simon, my partner and I are going to lift you out of the car and onto the sled here. We're going to do it *very* slowly. If anything else hurts besides the pain in your back, you've got to let us know. Okay?"

The young man didn't respond.

"Think we should wait for help with the lifting? Get some more vitals?" his partner asked, handing him the neck brace.

Doc shook his head a little. His partner knew what that small gesture meant. It meant time was critical. Without saying another word, the EMT rounded the car, opened the passenger-side door, then crawled inside to lift and push the driver toward Doc so he could be maneuvered out of the car and placed onto the sled. Within sixty seconds, the neck brace was on the patient, and the move had been accomplished. While the chubby EMT used the locked winch cable to pull himself back up the hill, an approaching siren could be heard in the distance.

"What, what's that?" Simon suddenly asked, his eyes now wide open.

"The cops," Doc answered on his knees next to the sled. "I think they purposely time it so us ambulance guys do all the work."

"No," he groaned. "What's—I mean, who's that?" He weakly lifted a finger and pointed toward the trees. "Did I hit somebody?"

Doc turned and looked into a snowy stand of oak and white birch trees about twenty feet away. No one was there.

He turned back and looked at his partner who was almost up the hill and out of earshot of the young man's query, then calmly began to strap

Simon into the sled. "Is it a thin guy in a long black overcoat? Thin white hair down to his shoulders and kinda slicked back? Yellow eyes? Butt ugly? Looks like he washed his face with a cheese grater?"

"Yeah."

The paramedic nodded knowingly. "It's just the tow truck driver to get your car up the hill. But, you're right. He's one scary lookin' cuss, ain't he?"

Simon closed his eyes and slipped into an unconscious state again. Finished with the straps, Doc rose and gave a thumbs-up to his partner who turned on the winch. "See you at the top, Simon," he said, as the winch motor whined, and the sled was slowly pulled up the hill. When it was about halfway up, Doc stuck his hands in his pockets and turned back to the empty woods.

"Not today, you son of a bitch," he muttered under his breath.

He stood there, stubbornly, for a moment as if actually expecting to see someone. But then, remembering the urgency of the situation, he turned and started to trudge up the hill.

Nearly two hours later, Doc sat in the small emergency room waiting area of Charlevoix Area Hospital on the corner of Park and Lakeshore Drive. He sat on one of the two upholstered benches in a room that could hold no more than a dozen people and was mostly light beige with a light blue accent wall. He had an open *People* magazine on his lap and was looking down at it but he wasn't really reading. He was thinking about Simon. His blue nylon coat sat next to him revealing an eggshell white long-sleeved uniform shirt and black cargo-style pants with large, square Velcro pockets on the sides of the legs. The extra weight he'd put on since college had been distributed to the right places due mainly to rock climbing he used to do when he lived in another state. The confident air of his youth had been subdued by the years and a job that regularly reminded him how life could turn on a dime, or in today's case, a patch of black ice. He looked outwardly calm, but was inwardly anxious.

No one else was in the waiting area except his partner. He was dressed exactly the same, except he was wearing his blue coat that was unzipped and open. He was forty pounds heavier than Doc, but the weight was evenly proportioned over his body so he looked soft and cuddly as opposed to having a ballooning beer gut. His steel wool-like hair was usually well kept, but at the moment, looked a little wild. A full, round baby face and friendly green eyes made him look younger than he was. His name was Lance Vale, he was thirty years old and from a long-time and well-established Charlevoix family. A lot of people knew the Vales, but that wasn't hard to do in a town of less than three thousand people.

"Who played Blofeld in *On His Majesty's Secret Service*?" Lance asked, sipping a coffee he had gotten from a nearby vending machine. He was standing by the emergency room registration desk and keeping an eye on it for the nurse who was in the restroom.

"Telly Savalis," Doc answered, not looking up from his magazine.

"Who sang, not one, but three James Bond theme songs?"

"Shirley Bassey—*Goldfinger*, *Diamonds Are Forever*, and *Moonraker*," his partner answered calmly.

"You know," Lance observed, "I think it's sad that a thirty-two-year-old man has nothing better to do with his life than know this kind of meaningless trivia."

"Not as sad as the guy who thinks up the questions," Doc retorted.

Lance took another sip of his coffee, then switched subjects. "Do you know what today is? You don't, do you?"

Doc looked up, puzzled. "It's not your birthday, is it?"

"No. It's December 1."

"Okay," Doc agreed, tentatively.

"It's your nine-month anniversary. Nine months ago today, you and me started riding together."

"Really? Nine months? Feels like we've been joined at the hip since birth."

Lance squinted at his partner.

"No," Doc corrected, more sincerely, "it's been good. I'm very grateful to you and all the guys at the station for making me feel so welcome." He was referring to the city's Fire Hall on State Street that not only housed the fire department, but also the city's ambulance and police departments.

Lance took another sip of coffee. "We should go out tonight. Celebrate."

"You buyin'?" Doc asked.

"No, you are," Lance corrected, "it's *your* anniversary."

Their banter was interrupted by a doctor in surgical scrubs rounding the registration desk and coming into the waiting room. He was lean and fit and only a few years older than Doc. He was also the only physician on duty in the forty-four-bed hospital. His name was Bob Lancaster.

"Hey, Doc," Doc greeted, putting the magazine down and rising.

"Doc," Lancaster nodded, sliding off his hospital green skullcap that revealed a high hairline and sandy-colored hair.

"Hey, Bob," Lance said. "How's Simon?"

"Resting comfortably now. I'm going to see his folks. A nurse told me they're having coffee in the dining room. There was a lot of internal bleeding, but I'd say he's got better than a fifty-fifty chance."

"Good," Doc said, relieved.

"That's great," Lance agreed.

"Let me ask you something," Lancaster said, directing the question to Doc.

"On the way in, you radioed that the kid had a possible ruptured spleen. How'd you reach that conclusion?"

"Sorry," Doc said, raising an apologetic hand, "making a diagnosis isn't my job, I know."

"No," the physician pressed, genuinely interested, "how'd you figure it?"

"Low blood pressure, an elevated heart rate, he complained of pain in the flank, no history of kidney stones, his seat belt was really loose, and the angle of his body suggested he might've jammed his side into the steering wheel. Basically," he shrugged, "I guessed."

"You guessed right," the surgeon smiled. "He *did* have a ruptured spleen. Your heads-up saved us time and maybe even the kid's life. Seconds counted on this one. Good call, Doc."

"Thanks, Doc," the paramedic smiled, gratefully.

"That's my partner," Lance said, toasting Doc with his coffee.

"This isn't the first time you've nailed a diagnosis since you've been on the job," Lancaster recalled. "Did you ever go to medical school?"

"I read a lot," Doc replied.

"Medical books?"

"Yeah, actually. I don't watch much TV or rent a lot of movies."

"Except for James Bond, apparently," Lance interjected.

"Well, I'm glad you take the job seriously." He glanced over his shoulder. "I'd better go." Lancaster gave Doc a friendly slap on the arm. "Thanks, guys. Good job!"

"Praise from Caesar," Lance said, under his breath, as the surgeon left.

Doc closed his eyes and rubbed his forehead with the tips of his fingers relieving his anxiousness. Then, lightening his mood, he looked at his wristwatch and grabbed his coat, just as the nurse returned from the bathroom.

"6:15. Shift's over, and I'm buyin'."

Charlevoix, Michigan, in Charlevoix County was about two hundred and sixty miles, or a four-hour drive, from Doc's parents in Ann Arbor. It was a small village-like community in the fall, winter, and spring, but its population swelled dramatically to more than thirty thousand in the summer, due to tourism—the town's main industry. As every school kid in the state was taught, Michigan is divided into two peninsulas, the upper and lower. The Lower Peninsula is shaped like a left-handed mitten, and Charlevoix was located on the edge of the mitten, third finger from the thumb.

The town sat on a narrow strip of land, picturesquely nestled between three bodies of water. To the east was Round Lake, aptly named for its small, near-perfect circular shape and often described as the best natural harbor in the Great Lakes region. One end of Round Lake butted up against town, while the opposite end fed into Lake Charlevoix, the state's third-largest inland lake that had fifty-six miles of coastline and was more or less shaped like an upside-down Y. To the west, on the other side of town was Lake Michigan, third largest of the five Great Lakes and the only one located entirely in the United States. Cutting through the center of downtown was a short river, about an eighth-mile long, called the Pine River. It connected Lake Michigan to Round Lake and the sprawling Lake Charlevoix beyond. Although built by nature, the river had been deepened and widened by man to accommodate large vessels, so it resembled a well-engineered channel more than it did a river.

As far back as the 1880s, Charlevoix had been known as a resort town, particularly by Chicago-area businessmen who romanticized about sitting in taverns by the water and hearing the rough-and-tumble stories of sailors who were working on the cargo ships of Lake Michigan. But, the town was never really a hangout for that kind of journeyman sailor. It was the captains of industry, the ones who could afford to captain yachts on the weekends, who built the quaintness and old-money smell of the town. In the summer, watercraft of all shapes and sizes glided up and down the Pine River, going from either Lake Michigan into Round Lake and Lake Charlevoix, or vice versa. Crossing the river was a drawbridge called the Memorial Bridge that was the centerpiece of downtown. It was raised at every hour and half-hour during the tourist season for waiting boats.

Because the town was so ideally sandwiched in between waterways, Charlevoix had a lot more tourist lodging than permanent residences. Throughout town, dotting Round Lake, lining the shore of Lake Michigan and even lining the Pine River, was a charming but eclectic collection of condominium complexes, motels, bed & breakfast choices, and formidable turn-of-the-century summer homes with long, breezy porches and shuttered windows, 90 percent of which were now closed up for the season. Decades earlier, Ernest Hemingway was a summer resident and set many of his Nick Adams stories in Horton Bay on Lake Charlevoix, a mere ten miles away.

Bridge Street—called so because of the Memorial Bridge—was the main thoroughfare of downtown. The heart of town was a straight strip of shops a little less than a half-mile from end to end, and most of the stores were housed in buildings constructed in the 1930s, then renovated in the '50s. Both sides of the street housed shop after shop designed to cater to tourists and impulse buying; an art gallery was next to a fudge store, which was next to a T-shirt shop, that was next to a bookstore, which was next to a restaurant, and so on. During the summer, the street was lined with huge baskets that hung from streetlamps and overflowed with colorful petunias, while tourists walked underneath drinking lattes and toting cameras. It also wasn't unusual for the town's more ambitious college-age residents to work both a day and a night job or for shop owners to put in fifteen-hour days. But, now it was December, the flowers were gone, the drawbridge was inactive, a thin but walkable layer of ice sat on Round Lake, and a third of the stores on Bridge Street had closed up until May.

Fortunately, the Crow's Nest Bar & Grill wasn't one of them. It had an eleven-foot-high embossed tin ceiling and perpetually smelled of beer and peanuts. It was narrow and rectangular-shaped with a twelve-stool bar toward the back on the left-hand side. There were some pictures of one, two, and even three-mast sailing vessels on the walls. There were also some old nautical signal flags hanging in glass frames behind the bar. But ironically, there wasn't a picture of a ship with an actual crow's nest in the entire place.

Doc and Lance sat toward the back in an old wooden booth across from the bar, huddled over plastic baskets holding cheeseburgers and fries. It had just started to snow outside, and the place wasn't busy. George Strait sang on the jukebox while a waitress swept up peanut shells from the worn, wooden floor.

"A good day," Lance declared. "We helped Mary Thomas get to the hospital so she could have her baby, saved Simon Jackson, and got that kid's tongue off the flagpole."

"You can always tell when the cable channels run *A Christmas Story*," Doc observed, referring to the flagpole call of earlier in the day.

"You going home for Christmas?" Lance asked.

"I don't know. My sister and her husband are coming in from out of town and staying with my folks. Then my aunt's family is going there on

Christmas Day. So my parents' place will be pretty crowded."

"You didn't go home for Thanksgiving, did you?"

"To Ann Arbor? No, I worked, remember?"

"Don't you think your parents might want to see you sometime?" Lance asked. "I mean, I don't want to pry or anything."

Doc smiled a little and reached for his Budweiser, knowing that, of course, Lance wanted to pry. That's what he did. Besides being an excellent EMT, and doing the books at his parents' wine store on the weekends, he was a busybody; the kind of guy who liked to know everything about people, then would dole out advice as if it was an endless wad of dollar bills.

"My folks went to visit my sister and brother-in-law in North Carolina for Thanksgiving."

Lance nodded. "That's why you volunteered to work Thanksgiving weekend. Well, if you're going to be around for Christmas, you're welcome to come over to mom and dad's place with Charlene and me for dinner. It's gonna be extra special this year."

"That's nice, man, thank you. I may take you up on that."

"Charlene also wants to know what you're doin' Saturday night?"

"Why?" Doc asked, munching on a French fry and suddenly suspicious.

Charlene was Lance's girlfriend and was just as bad as he was when it came to being nosy. She and Lance were always ready to fix people's problems, whether they had any or not.

"She's got a friend she wants you to meet," Lance answered, nonchalantly biting into his burger.

Doc exhaled a heavy breath. "I love Charlene. You know that. She has many talents. But hosting *The Bachelor* isn't one of them. Remember that last one she fixed me up with?"

"Carol?"

"Caribou is more like it. The woman had thirty pounds on me."

"You got something against full-figured women?"

"Only when they're into Rob Zombie, monster trucks, and challenge me to a chug-a-lug contest within ten minutes of being introduced."

"Okay. So her tastes were a little pedestrian. But you're in God's country, son. There aren't that many eligible females to choose from." Lance put his burger temporarily back in the basket. "I've spent five days a week with you for nine months now. I've seen you do amazing things: start people's hearts, stick your fingers into arteries to stop bleeding, but ..."

"But?" Doc asked, encouraging him to continue.

"But, I still don't feel like I know you. I mean, you play poker with me and some of the guys from the fire hall every couple of weeks, but you don't hunt, follow sports, go out on my boat, have a girlfriend, or meet people. What do you *like?* What do you *think?*"

"I think you've got a cute butt," Doc answered, dryly.

"Really?" Lance asked, wondering if his partner was about to announce he was gay.

"No," Doc deadpanned. He took a swig of beer then decided something. "I'm sorry if you think I've been coy or something. You're a good guy and I really appreciate your friendship. I'll tell you anything you want to know. Ask."

"Okay," Lance said, picking up his burger again. "Why don't you ever go see your parents?" He took a bite while waiting for Doc's answer.

"It's a delicate relationship. We had a falling out years ago over some of the life choices I made, and no, I'm not talking about your butt again. They thought I'd become something more than a paramedic. That's why I moved from Wyoming back to Michigan, to be closer to them and try to heal old wounds."

"If you wanted to be closer to them in Ann Arbor, what are you doing hours away up in Charlevoix?"

"It's closer than Wyoming," Doc rationalized.

"But, you never go see them."

"I've seen 'em a couple of times. Day trips down and back. You just don't know about them."

"Okay," Lance said, putting his burger down again and switching subjects. "What church do you go to?"

"Saint Sealy of the Posturepedic," Doc answered, picking up a small French fry and popping it in his mouth.

"Why aren't you married?" Lance asked, changing subjects again.

"Why aren't you? You've got a great lady you've been dating for years."

"Well, I'm gonna be. One of these days."

"Me, too."

Doc picked up his burger and shrugged. "See? You think you don't know me, but the truth is, you already know all the interesting stuff. I mean, except for that whole money-laundering thing."

Lance arched an eyebrow while Doc took a bite knowing how he liked to say things just to get a rise out of people. He smiled, shook his head, then raised his beer. "Happy anniversary, man."

Doc set his burger down and picked up his beer. "Happy anniversary," he smiled.

They clinked glasses, took a drink, then Lance switched subjects yet again. "Okay. At the beginning of *For Your Eyes Only,* James Bond is visiting his wife's grave. What's the inscription on her tombstone?"

"Are you kidding me? That's, like, incredibly random."

"Do you know it or not?"

Doc thought for a long moment. "'We have all the time in the world,'" he correctly answered. But there was a hint of melancholy in his voice.

THE DEER

Doc lived in a rented cabin on the shore of Lake Charlevoix, a few miles outside of town. A Senior VP at Ford who was a man's man and wanted a weekend getaway built it in the late 1980s. But the executive had a penchant for getting married to progressively younger women. Wife number three didn't like hunting, snowmobiling, sailing, fishing, or basically anything that involved an outdoor lifestyle, so the cabin sat neglected for a year, until Doc rented it.

The cabin itself was a simple but comfortable affair. It was a single-story cedar log structure that, in its day, would have been considered luxurious, but that was twenty-some odd years ago. The back door that led into the kitchen was, for all intents and purposes, the front door since it was the only one used in winter. Off the kitchen was a small laundry room and half-bath. Walking from the kitchen, and changing floors from linoleum to wood, was the living room. Off the living room were two small bedrooms connected by a Jack-and-Jill bath, and a door that led out to a screened-in front porch that overlooked the lake. The cabin sat back thirty yards from the water on a flat piece of land with nothing in front of it but low-lying shrubs and sea grass that looked like the ground was sprouting frozen whiskers. Cutting through this winter beard was a path that led to a surprisingly sandy but small beach where an aluminum dock was erected in summer. Newer, more prestigious, and larger lake homes in the million to two-million-dollar price range sat on either side of the cabin, but about fifty yards away in either direction, so the location had a feeling of privacy.

Back on the other side—the kitchen door-side—people got to the cabin by going down Boyne City Road, then turning onto a gravel lane that bent and wove over potholes for nearly a quarter-mile through a thick forest of mature white pines. They were the kind of pine trees that lost their lower branches as they grew so both sides of the lane that wound to Doc's cabin was filled with tall tree trunks that stretched up to scruffy branches of long-needled greenery some thirty to fifty feet above. As the lane neared its end, it split into three shorter lanes. The middle lane led to Doc's, and the other two led to his neighbors, but neither place was occupied this time of year. To say that the cabin was isolated and easily swallowed-up by the dark canopy of the wooded night was an understatement. But the locale suited Doc. Over the years, he'd learned the valuable difference between being lonely and enjoying his solitude.

Driving down Boyne City Road, just a mile or so from his turn off, Doc was listening to Tony Bennett on the radio. He drove a red Jeep Wrangler with a black canvas top. The snow was still coming down in pronounced fat flakes. Tony was singing the moody, romantic song "Once Upon A Time" from the early 1960s Broadway musical *All American*. When he sang about a girl he once knew with moonlight in her eyes, Doc couldn't help but think of Julia. Sad songs about lost love, particularly older ones, could affect him deeply. He listened to the tune for about a minute with a faraway longing, then told himself to snap out of it and clicked off the radio. Wallowing in the past was unavoidable, he supposed, but wallowing too much was dangerous—particularly at this time of year, so close to the anniversary of her passing.

As he turned onto the secluded lane that led down to his cabin, he busied himself by thinking of several things in rapid succession. If the snow continued, he'd probably have to call Michael. He was a cop, and one of his poker-playing buddies who had a plow attached to the front of his pickup. He had to start thinking about Christmas presents for family. He had to check the woodpile on the side of the cabin to make sure he had enough firewood. He'd probably have to go grocery shopping at Oleson's tomorrow after work.

While his thoughts bounced from one thing to another as the Jeep bounced over the potholes, he didn't notice his increasing speed or see the deer that suddenly darted out of the woods in front of him until it was too late. It was only a brownish blur in the glare of the headlights, then *BAM!* The deer banged off the hood to the left while Doc slammed on the brakes, turned the wheel and the Jeep skidded right. Everything was over in a matter of seconds.

Putting the vehicle in park, Doc just sat there for a few moments letting his adrenaline slow down while looking himself over to make sure he wasn't injured. Being a paramedic, he knew the statistics. Each year, more than fifty-five thousand deer were involved in Michigan traffic accidents and, considering the isolated area where he lived, he always figured it was only a matter of time before he had a deer encounter. Still, he always hoped the time wouldn't come.

Taking a deep, determined breath, he zipped up his blue coat, made sure his gloves were in his pockets, then climbed out of the Jeep. He stepped silently through the snow and looked at the front of the Wrangler with its headlights still on. The hood was dented, a section of the front grill was broken and the driver's side rectangular yellow fog light was hanging out of its socket. Eight to twelve hundred dollars in bodywork, he guessed. His front tires were angled off the lane, but not so much where he needed a tow truck assuming everything under the hood was intact. Shaking his head in frustration, he next saw the trail of dark blotches in the snow going off to the left into the woods. He took the small flashlight out of the narrow pocket on the arm of his coat, clicked it on, and aimed it at one of the blotches. Once in the light, he could see that the blotch was deep red.

"Dammit," he sighed, heavily.

He went back to the driver's side door and climbed into the Wrangler. A few seconds later, he emerged again, carrying a Smith & Wesson snub-nose thirty-eight caliber revolver. When he worked in Wyoming, a cop who was a friend had urged him to buy a weapon and get a concealed handgun permit. "When you're dealing with the occasional drunk or crackhead, most of whom have guns in their pickups, it's just the smart thing to do," the cop had said. "You should keep it in the ambulance." Doc took the advice, but only partially. He had gotten the weapon and permit, but never carried them in the ambulance. It seemed too much of an oxymoron—a gun-toting paramedic.

He had heard from hunters that an injured deer could travel for miles before dropping, depending upon the severity of the injury. He wasn't prepared to follow the animal all night, but he didn't want it to suffer, either. He looked at his wristwatch. It was a little after 8:00 p.m. He decided to give himself twenty minutes to find the deer.

The branches in the pines above him waved leisurely in the wind and were sprinkled with white. The ground was mostly flat, but had a few slight inclines and mounds here and there. Walking amidst the telephone pole-like trees was like being in a black-and-white movie. Colors were drained from the landscape until Doc shone his flashlight here or there. The stains of blood were about four feet apart, and the accompanying trail of hoof prints were unmistakable. Even though he couldn't see the injured animal, he had two things going for him: One was the area where he was walking wasn't thick with undergrowth because white pines traditionally blocked out the sun and their fallen needles keep foliage from growing on the forest floor. The other advantage was the snow. Although it was night, the snow that had made it through the treetops provided a certain luminous quality on the ground. As he followed the blood and the small rounded prints, he began to talk to himself.

"I hope it's not a buck," he said, visible puffs of breath coming from his mouth, while the falling snow began to turn his dark brown hair white. "Bucks have antlers and can charge. Antlers can hurt. On the other hand," he continued, "I don't want it to be a doe, either. I don't want to shoot Bambi's mom." The sounds of a snort and a pained, wheezy breath interrupted his monologue. It came from a slight ravine just beyond his line of sight. The sound made him pause.

"Oh, God," he sighed, already regretting what he was about to find.

He stepped more cautiously forward, raised the barrel of the revolver, came to the ravine, aimed his light down, and was dumbfounded by what he saw. It wasn't a deer. It was a young woman, about twenty-five years old, badly injured, and completely naked.

"What?" he said to himself, quickly lowering his weapon. *"What?"*

He pointed his flashlight down at the ground near his feet, then turned and aimed the light behind him. There were deer tracks all along the way he had just come, but no human footprints other than his.

"What the—"

He slid his gun into the side pocket of his coat and hurried down the gentle incline of the ravine. The woman was lying on her left side, nearly, but not quite, in a fetal position.

"Ma'am? Ma'am, can you hear me?" he said, dropping to his knees and huddled over her. The woman didn't respond. He quickly ran his flashlight up and down her body. Her blood soaked right eyelid was closed and swollen shut. It was the size of a large cotton ball. Down on her side, two ribs had apparently broken off from her rib cage and were protruding menacingly through her torn flesh. He could tell from the angle of her waist that her right hip had either been broken or was dislocated. He could also see she had a compound fracture on her left wrist. All this, combined with very probable internal bleeding, meant the woman was critically injured—maybe mortally. He'd seen victims that had been struck by vehicles before, but this looked unusually bad, especially considering his speed was less than thirty miles per hour at the time of impact.

He looked around, hoping there might be some explanation for such a bizarre discovery; discarded clothing, a snowmobile that was abandoned in the woods, footprints coming from another direction, *something*. He put his flashlight on the snowy ground, took the Smith & Wesson out of his coat, made sure the safety was still on, then put it into one of the large Velcro pockets of his pant legs. Next, he unzipped and took off his coat, then covered as much of her body with it as he could.

"Everything's going to be fine, ma'am," he lied. "I'm a paramedic."

He picked up the flashlight with one hand then put two fingers on her jugular vein with his other. Getting a pulse but an erratic one, he reached for the cell phone on his belt, intending to call 911.

"No," he heard the woman barely whisper. "You, you can't call anyone."

He was stunned that the woman was able speak, stunned that she was even conscious. He bent down closer to her.

"Ma'am?" he said gently. "Can you hear me? Can you tell me your name?"

"You can't call anyone," she repeated. "I…I'm an angel."

"Not if I have anything to do with it," he said.

She suddenly reached up and grabbed his shirt with her right hand. The quick movement surprised him. "You have to take me home … put, put me to bed … let me regenerate."

"Oh, we're on all *sorts* of drugs, aren't we?" Doc assumed. It was the only way she could be moving and having a conversation with him in her present condition. He'd seen accident victims on heroin or mescaline speak very calmly and coherently, even though their injuries were so severe that they were mere seconds away from death. He assumed the same was happening here.

The woman paused for a moment with a strained face, clearly trying to rally her strength and overcome her pain. "W-w-what's your name?"

"Everybody calls me Doc. What's yours? What did you take tonight?"

She raised her head slightly. Trickles of blood ran down her cheek and dripped into the snow. "How do you explain it, Doc? You hit a deer, but found a woman. Where are my footprints? Where are my clothes? If…if

I'm not an angel, then how do you explain it?"

"Look, lady," he responded earnestly. "You don't have time for chitchat."

"You're right. Take me home. Put me to bed. Don't ... don't call ..." her voice trailed off as she slipped into a state of unconsciousness. Her grip loosened from his shirt and her hand plopped silently into the snow.

Doc closed his eyes and rubbed his forehead with his fingertips for a couple seconds, considering her logic. Without his coat, the cold was starting to get to him and he began to shake a little. He moved the light up toward her swollen eye, then paused and leaned in closer, not quite believing what he saw. The right eye that was so badly swollen just moments before now didn't seem to be swollen at all. There was still a nasty gash on the woman's eyebrow that was bleeding, but the puffiness on her eyelid was completely gone.

He looked at her open mouthed, then aimed the flashlight down at her ribs and gently lifted his coat. The two ribs sticking through her side slowly started to retract. They disappeared back *into* her body then apparently reset themselves in her rib cage.

Upon seeing this, a shocked Doc Reynolds yelled, "Whoa!" recoiled back on his butt in the snow, and dropped his flashlight.

CLAIR

There wasn't a lot of space in Doc's bedroom; just enough room for a queen-sized bed with a headboard of wrought-iron bars, a nightstand to the right of the bed with a small Tiffany lamp, a white wicker rocking chair in the corner to the left, and next to the chair was a door that led to a small closet. A dresser across from the foot of the bed sat next to another door that led out into the living room. The furnishings straddled the line between cozy and cramped. There was also a third door next to the closet that led into a full bath with two sinks and a tiled tub with a shower. It connected the cabin's two bedrooms together. Doc could've put the woman in the other bedroom, but the bed in that room wasn't made and he wanted to get his injured guest settled as quickly as possible. A little sliver of light pierced the darkened bedroom. The bathroom light had been purposely left on, and its door was slightly ajar.

The woman lay in bed on her back. She was still naked, but for several hours, she'd been under a sheet and a clean, but old patchwork quilt that the cabin owner's second wife purchased at an antique store. Doc sat motionless in the wicker rocking chair watching his strange visitor. His left elbow sat on the chair's armrest, and his chin was sunk deep in his hand. It had now been six hours since he had first found the woman, but he still didn't know what to think. Who *was* this person? How did she wind up naked in the woods? Why were there deer prints in the snow leading up to where she lay, but no human footprints? More importantly, why wasn't she dead? How could her wounds seem to miraculously self-heal?

He'd been trying to rationalize things to himself for hours. He had read something a couple of years earlier in a medical journal about people who had remarkable powers of recuperation. The cases were rare, but he figured this woman must be one of them. He also told himself that there *had* to be footprints back in the woods, but he just didn't see them because he was so focused on the woman and her injuries. As for her being naked, well, he did have neighbors on either side. There were other houses down other lanes in the vicinity. Maybe one of his neighbors had returned to their lake home for the holidays. Maybe she had hopped out of bed and was running away from an abusive boyfriend or husband. He was sure there was a logical explanation.

But, for all of his rationalizing, there was something else he kept returning to; the possibility that something extraordinary was happening. That's why he had decided not to call anyone yet. That's why he had put the woman to bed as she requested but didn't attempt to dress her wounds. In his business, he had to trust his observations, and he would have staked his life on the belief that he hit a deer. In fact, she had even *acknowledged* that he had. Maybe his guest did have unusual healing powers, but that didn't explain apparent shape shifting, nor did it explain ribs retracting and resetting themselves. What he had witnessed was nothing short of fantastic, and he somehow just knew that the usual medical procedures would have proven ineffectual. Perhaps she was some sort of government experiment with self-calibrating titanium implants. He recalled there was a military base over in Grayling. Perhaps she was an alien. He could embrace either possibility more easily than accept her being from heaven.

As for the way she looked, he really hadn't taken the time to take stock of her earlier—other than the fact that she was attractive—but he did so now. She was about five-feet-four, in her early to mid-twenties and curvaceous like Kate Winslet was in *Titanic*. She had a high forehead, prominent cheekbones, full lips, and long blonde hair that was parted in the middle and was in large, naturally curly ringlets. With her long, closed eyelashes and her eyebrows darker than her hair, she looked like a Norse goddess, but at the moment, a Norse goddess that had gone twelve rounds with Mike Tyson. As for the other details of her body—arms, legs, toes, birthmarks, scars, areolas—he frankly couldn't remember. He had been too focused on her wounds and the sheer shock of finding her in the snow to note such particulars. But he did remember her fingers, they were long, slender, and seemed gentle.

He slowly rose from the chair, opened the bathroom door a little to widen the sliver of light into a stream, then walked over to the bed. The cut above her right eye was now scabbed over and looked a day or two old. Amazing, he thought. He stooped down and carefully lifted the side of the quilt and blood-spotted sheet underneath to check her ribs.

"Enjoying the view?" she suddenly asked. He dropped the covers and jerked back in surprise. She opened her eyes and turned to him. They were bright green. Not unnaturally so, but still, the greenest eyes he'd ever seen.

"I...I was checking your wounds," he stammered innocently. "I'm a paramedic."

She turned her gaze to the inactive ceiling fan, then to the light tan knotty pine-paneled walls around her. "Where am I?" she asked, clearly but weakly.

"In my house. In my bed," he answered, drawing near again but still stooped down.

She brought her eyes back to his, blinked as if to focus, and studied his face.

"You're Doc. I remember."

"Very good," he acknowledged. "And you are?"

She thought for a moment, the smooth skin on her face was pale, but had more color than an hour earlier. "I'm Clair."

"Clair who?"

She thought for another moment. "Just Clair."

"Okay, just Clair," he said, softly. "Can you please tell me something? Can you tell me why your injuries are healing so fast?" He gestured to her left wrist. "Can you tell me how broken bones are going back into your body and apparently resetting themselves?"

"I told you," she said plainly, "I'm an angel."

"My mom once told me the Easter Bunny lived in my dad's greenhouse—didn't make it so."

"Nevertheless, I *am* an angel," she insisted.

He took her conviction in stride. "So, your boss's name is Charlie?"

"He's been known by many names over the centuries," she replied, apparently not getting the joke.

"Uh-huh."

She looked at him quizzically, then smiled faintly. "I guess I can't blame you. I was told many wouldn't believe if I had to reveal myself."

"What? You mean, like, in angel school or something? Can we please cut the crap here, Clair? If you die, I'm guilty of vehicular manslaughter, at best, and maybe even something worse because I didn't notify anyone about hitting you."

"Why did you do that? Why didn't you call anyone, Doc?"

"Because you asked me not to. Because there are things here I don't understand. You shouldn't even be alive, let alone talking. The outside of your body was a mess, but it's healing without any treatment. Who knows what's going on with your insides? You're probably bleeding internally in a half-dozen different places"

"Eight, to be exact," she confirmed.

"See, *that's* what I mean. How could you know that? Who *are* you, really? Are we dealing with national security issues here? I've done what you've asked, against all my better judgment, and I think I deserve the truth."

She nodded, agreeing but losing strength.

"The truth is, I'm an angel sent to Earth from God Almighty. When angels arrive, the first thing we usually do is take the physical form of a bird or animal, so we can travel anonymously. Doves are very popular. So are cats. But, I thought being a deer would be neat."

"Neat?"

"It's very appropriate for northern Michigan, don't you think? But then, your vehicle came out of nowhere and—"

"Wait a minute," he interrupted. "My vehicle didn't come out of nowhere. I was going down a well-established right of way with the headlights on. And I was going under thirty. How could you not have seen me?"

Her green eyes looked downward with embarrassment.

"I ... I could've been distracted," she admitted.

"Distracted?"

"Daydreaming."

"Daydreaming? Angels daydream?"

"Look, this wasn't what I planned. I'm sorry, okay? But you can't call anyone and, deep down inside, you know what I'm saying is true."

He looked at her suspiciously. "How do you figure that?"

"Because even though most won't believe in me, deep down inside, you *do*."

"Boy, have *you* got a wrong number," he responded, seriously.

"I know it. I feel it."

"What you're feeling is probably blood filling your lungs." Just at that moment, she started to cough. "See?" he said.

Her breathing became heavier. "I've got to rest now, Doc. Go on with your life, as if nothing's happened. Just let me be and I'll regenerate. Oh, but I've got to warn you, I won't be able to maintain human form. It takes too much energy while my body is healing. Just so you know."

"What? What does *that* mean?"

Clair's long eyelashes flickered with exhaustion. Her head drifted to one side, and she fell back asleep.

Doc looked at her thoroughly confused, then slowly rose and walked into the bathroom that connected the two bedrooms. Closing the door, he rubbed the back of his neck, utterly exhausted. He wondered how he was ever going to get through his workday that was quickly approaching. Although red-eyed and tired, at least he, now, believed that, whoever or whatever Clair was, she wasn't going to die on him. This fact alone caused him tremendous relief.

"Go on with my life as if nothing's happened?" he finally asked himself quietly in the mirror. "She didn't see me because she was daydreaming? What do angels daydream about? Saint Peter in a Speedo?" He shook his head and looked at his red, baggy eyes.

"This is wrong. An angel can't be hurt. If someone's an angel, how can an *angel* be hurt?"

The more he thought about it, the more ridiculous the notion seemed. With new determination, he opened the door and marched back into his bedroom, but then yelled and jumped back.

There, under the covers, was a twelve-hundred-pound polar bear lying on its back and snoring loudly. Its wide paws and long claws rested peacefully outside the quilt. Suddenly, the entire framework of the bed gave way from the weight, and the mattress collapsed to the wood floor, causing Doc to jump back and yell again. Undisturbed by the breakage, the polar bear merely moaned and shifted its body slightly, ripping the sheets. Its white furry hind legs stuck out several feet beyond the ends of the quilt and mattress.

ADJUSTMENT

The next day, which was a Friday, was a strange one in Wyatt "Doc" Reynolds's life. After very little sleep in the guest bedroom on its unmade bed, he went to work in the same clothes he had worn the day before. He left the cabin that morning without showering or checking in on his houseguest, partly because he didn't want to disturb her and partly because he was afraid of what he might find if he did.

Down at the fire hall he went through his paces, but he was dog-tired, and everything seemed to be in slow motion. There was the constant temptation to say something about what had happened the night before, and no matter who he was talking to—Lance, a cop acquaintance, or a patient—he found it hard, even surreal, to be engaged in normal conversation. Then there was his Jeep. It was drivable, but had to be dropped off at a body shop. On top of everything else, there was the weather. It had gotten a little warmer, and, throughout the day, there was a fine mist in the air from the brooding low-lying clouds that hung over the Charlevoix area and only added to the surrealistic feel of everything. It made things look eerie and out of step with the cheery Christmas decorations on the streetlamps and in the shop windows on Bridge Street.

Even the one-and-only ambulance call of the day was strange. It was a hunting accident just outside of town where a bow hunter had mistaken another bow hunter for a deer and shot him in the gluteus maximus. It was odd to see a guy out in the woods wearing a camouflage snowsuit and a bright orange cap with pull-down earflaps limping around and sipping on a Moosehead beer while an arrow was sticking out of his rear. Lance, on the other hand, found the whole scene hysterical. He labeled the setting,

"When Things Go Wrong In Sherwood," as if it were a *The Far Side* cartoon. He'd also gone to high school with the victim and couldn't resist saying, "Hey, Joe, I always thought you had something stuck up your ass. Now I'm *sure* of it."

After work, Lance took Doc to Oleson's Food Store in their ambulance, then began to drive him to his cabin since his Jeep would be in the shop for the next several days. Lance lived just a half block from the fire hall and would return the ambulance, then walk home. Throughout this hazy Friday, Doc had resisted spilling the details of his amazing experience to his partner. But once they were through town and turning onto Boyne City Road, he couldn't help but ask a couple of leading questions.

"Do you believe in God?"

"Sure, I do," Lance answered, without hesitation.

"You ever have any doubts about it? God? Heaven? Hell? The whole afterlife thing?"

"Lots of people have doubts. That's pretty normal."

"I guess," Doc agreed. He looked through the windshield at the dark, thick silhouettes of the trees on either side of the road, intermixed with the occasional house outlined with Christmas lights. The lights seemed inviting against the lonely, woodsy landscape. "What about angels? Do you believe in them?"

"What? You mean, like, Guardian Angels?"

"Yeah."

Lance thought for a second. "I don't know. To tell you the truth, I don't think about 'em much. Hey, what James Bond film won an Oscar for Best Sound Effects?"

"Well *think* about it," Doc said, a little annoyed his partner wanted to change subjects. "If God exists, do you think angels exist? Do you think they could be here on Earth? In Michigan? In Charlevoix?"

"Why? Do you think you saw an angel?" Lance snickered.

A crop of goose bumps sprouted on Doc's arms, but he ignored them.

"I'm just trying to talk about something that has more meaning than a trivia question about Sean Connery's chest hair. You were saying last night that we've worked together for months, but you feel like you don't know me. So, I'm trying to talk to you here. Do you think there could be angels on Earth and in Charlevoix?"

Lance scratched his thick, stiff hair and gave the matter more serious consideration.

"Absolutely," he finally concluded. "If God wants angels here, then angels are probably here."

"And God wouldn't let anything happen to his angels, would he? I mean, he wouldn't let 'em get hurt, or anything, right? Matter of fact, if someone's an angel, they *couldn't* get hurt, right?"

"Is there a point to this?" Lance asked, clicking the turn indicator as they approached the lane leading to Doc's cabin.

"I'm just wondering about whether or not angels exist, and if they do, could one get hurt somehow, someway, that's all."

The driver looked at his partner and frowned. "Uh, if these are the kind of conversations we're going to have for me to get to know you better, never mind."

As the boxy ambulance slowly made its way down the lane over the crunchy, half-frozen gravel and snow, the high beams of the headlights illuminated the silvery tire tracks where Doc had turned sharply and gone off the road.

"That where you hit the deer?" Lance asked.

"Yeah."

"What was it? A buck or a doe?"

"Pretty sure it was a doe."

"And you never found it? You searched around thoroughly?"

"I never saw the deer again," Doc answered, honestly.

"Poor thing," Lance said, shaking his head. "That's tough, but it happens to a lot of 'em. They get hit, then stagger off somewhere to die."

"Yeah."

As they approached the cabin, Lance couldn't help but notice that a light was on in the kitchen window.

"Hey, you left a light on."

"The sun goes down so early this time of year, I don't like coming home to a dark house," Doc fibbed, knowing that he had left no lights on.

As the white ambulance with the dark red stripe bounced over the last pothole in the lane and rolled into a turnaround just outside the back kitchen door, the light in the kitchen suddenly went off. Both men couldn't help but see it.

"Bad bulb," Doc explained, quickly turning to gather up his three paper bags of groceries.

"Are you entertaining someone?" Lance grinned, becoming both curious and suspicious.

Doc took a moment to remain composed and control his pounding heart. "Yes," he deadpanned, "the mayor's wife. I'm cooking for her tonight."

"Really?"

"No, Lance. *Not* really. My kitchen light blew out, I'm not entertaining anyone, and I will see you at 8:00 a.m. Monday morning. Thanks for the ride, and please thank Charlene for the invitation to hang with y'all on Saturday night. But, to tell you the truth, I'm just real tired and want to chill this weekend."

"Okay," Lance said, understanding. "You gonna be alright out here without wheels?"

"Someone from Enterprise is bringing me out a Kia tomorrow morning."

As Doc unbuckled his shoulder harness, something caught Lance's attention out of the corner of his eye. He turned to the darkened kitchen window, then his jaw went slack.

"W... what was *that*?" he asked.

"What was what?" Doc replied, turning to the window and now visibly nervous.

"In your kitchen window, I thought I saw a... a..."

Doc flinched slightly, waiting to hear the words: *Polar Bear*.

"Horse," Lance uttered.

"What?"

"I thought I saw a...nah...that's crazy. You don't have animals in your house, do ya?"

Doc froze momentarily, not knowing what to say.

"Just the mayor's wife," he replied, trying to make light of what Lance thought he saw. "She gets pretty wild."

The chubby driver looked at Doc for a moment, then grinned and pointed a finger at him, getting the joke and deciding the evening shadows were playing tricks on him.

"Yeah. I think *I* need to chill this weekend, too. I'll see ya, Monday, man."

"You got it," Doc shot back, with a corresponding finger. "Oh, by the way, *Goldfinger*." He smiled and got out of the vehicle, closed the door, then waited in the turnaround with his groceries in hand until the red taillights of the ambulance were well down the lane before taking his house keys out of his blue nylon coat.

As soon as he opened the door to the kitchen, even before he clicked on the overhead lights, he noticed the offensive odor. It smelled like the inside of a portable toilet—the kind put out at a county fair or placed on a construction site.

"Clair?" he called, cautiously coming into the house. He clicked on the lights, closed the door, and set his groceries down on the counter by the sink. His nose was still wrinkled by the offensive smell, when, suddenly, he saw it. There, on the linoleum floor, just in the front of the wood floor where the kitchen ended and living room began, sat a large pile of fresh horse dung.

"Eeeww," he said, repulsed by the sight. "You're kidding me, right? I mean, *you're kidding!*"

The kitchen was small, only twelve by fourteen feet. But it housed all the necessities of a stove, oven, refrigerator, microwave, and breakfast table with four chairs. The Ford executive who built the place back in the 1980s liked to experiment, making hunter's soup, so the room had a dated, but efficient, look to it. Although the outside of the cabin had traditional log walls, the interior walls were planed to accommodate cabinetry and counters. The cabinets were pine and had four panes of glass in each door so one could see the dishes and glasses contained on the shelves within. Above were four lights on a black track lighting fixture with a separately controlled "pot light" that sat flush in the ceiling above the sink and kitchen window. This was the light Doc and Lance had seen on, then go off, as they came down the lane.

Slipping off his coat, Doc placed it on the back of one of the kitchen chairs and walked gingerly toward the connecting living room. As he did, he noticed that not only was there a pile of horse dung on the floor, there were other types of feces in the living room, as well. At least a half-dozen of them; seeing this, his already open mouth dropped open even more.

"I can explain," Clair said. She stood barefoot in his bedroom doorway and was wearing a dark green plaid bathrobe his parents had given him years ago. The cut over her right eye was still visible but the scab was gone and only a thin cut line remained. Although she was an undeniably attractive woman, she was also visibly tired, pale and worried. Doc ignored these facts—not to mention the remarkable feat that she was even out of bed and standing—and glared at her indignantly.

"What is this?" he said, pointing to the floor and a particular pile.

"It...it's horse do-do," she replied, timidly.

"And *this?*" he asked, pointing to another mound, his anger rising.

"Polar bear excrement," she said, with downcast eyes.

"And *this?*" he said, pointing to a small blob of feces on the back of a well-worn leather sofa.

"Canadian Goose."

"Isn't anybody in heaven housebroken?"

"I can't help it, Doc. Changing forms and losing control of bodily functions while I regenerate is no different for me than a twitching nerve is for you."

"*I don't care!*" he barked. *"This is insane!* Look, Mrs. Noah, take your animals, your problems, and your crap and get out of my house!"

"There's nowhere else I can go right now," she explained.

"You said it yourself, this wasn't part of your plan. So, go do whatever it is you *do* and leave me alone!"

"I told you, I can't help it," she said, becoming emotional. "I…I—" she suddenly put her hand on her stomach, then turned and made a quick beeline through his bedroom and into the Jack-and-Jill bath that connected the two bedrooms.

Doc took a frustrated breath, closed his eyes, rubbed his forehead, and subdued his anger. No matter what he might have been feeling about Clair or how confusing things were, as a paramedic, he knew that none of that mattered. The professional thing to do was focus on his patient. So that's what he did. He followed her into the bathroom where he found her on her knees, hunched over the toilet, and vomiting what looked like a combination of phlegm and blood. He stood behind her and held her forehead. It was a reassuring gesture his mother used to do for him when he was a boy.

"It's okay, Clair," he said, with an empathetic tone. "Just get it out of your system, kiddo. We'll figure everything out. I promise."

Suddenly, right before his eyes, Clair's body began to shift into another shape. Her forehead became larger and more prominent. Each shoulder expanded another foot within two seconds ripping the seams of his green plaid robe. Her curly golden hair quickly shrunk back into her now enlarged skull and was immediately replaced with an outcropping of short, black wiry hair. In fact, wiry black hair sprung out on her arms, legs and chest. Her human breasts shrunk and her stomach became more rounded and protruded. Her hands with the long slender fingers that were clutching the rim of the toilet became twice their size and turned black and leathery. In less than five seconds time, Doc had gone from holding the forehead of a sick human being to holding the forehead of a two-hundred-and-twenty-pound female gorilla. Upon experiencing this, he yelled and jumped backward, fell into the bathtub, and grabbed the shower curtain as he fell, ripping it off its rings. The curtain featured the silhouettes of some antlered moose, and they fell on top of him. Meantime, the gorilla seemed surprised by Doc's recoil. It snorted and scrambled into his bedroom on all four paws.

Struggling for a moment to get the curtain off him, and totally ignoring the pain from smacking the back of his head against the tiled wall, Doc quickly climbed out of the bathtub then shut and locked the connecting door between the bathroom and his bedroom. Breathing heavily and his adrenalin pumping, it took a full twenty seconds of holding the door knob to convince himself the jungle beast on the other side wasn't going to try to reopen it.

"Clair?" he finally called, once the initial shock of her transformation had begun to wear off. He grimaced slightly, now realizing there was a painful lump growing on the back of his head. "Miss Kong?" he called, trying to make light of the scary situation.

He thought he heard something by way of a response, but he wasn't sure. After waiting another ten seconds, he slowly unlocked the door, cracked it open, and peeked inside his bedroom. The unmade bed still lay on the floor collapsed out of its frame, and the little table on the right hand side of the bed with the Tiffany lamp was turned over. The lamp's bulb was broken. There was a renewed pungent odor of feces in the air, but he couldn't tell from where, or what kind it was because of the darkened room. There was an overhead fan with a light fixture on it, but it, too, was off.

The gorilla sat on the floor hunched up in the corner just beyond the upturned Tiffany lamp; a large hairy black blob in a tiny room. It still wore the green plaid robe but the garment was now badly ripped at the arms and shoulders and hung open at the waist. The animal's large head slowly turned away from Doc and faced the knotty pine-paneled wall. The creature also seemed to whine slightly; perhaps out of pain, or maybe out of embarrassment over its primate form and lack of bodily control. Either way, Clair was a piteous sight that made him forget about his throbbing head and earlier anger. Making a decision, he bravely walked over to her without hesitation, then sat down beside her in the corner.

"We'll get through this," he said, softly, putting an arm around her hairy, muscular shoulder. "I'm really sorry I yelled at you. We'll get through this together. Hey, c'mon—don't feel bad," he encouraged. "I've got Chiquitas in the kitchen."

Her large black head slowly turned away from the wall and came to rest on his shoulder.

A LITTLE HELP

Even before Clair's bright, jade-colored eyes opened, a warm, comforting aroma slowly brought her out of a long and much needed sleep. At first, her subconscious thought that a turkey was roasting in the oven out in the kitchen. But then, as her eyes focused in on the room from a small stream of light coming from the bathroom door being ajar, she realized it was chicken. Chicken and carrots. She smiled and nestled down in her pillow savoring the smell. She hadn't smelled chicken—or anything else for that matter—in a long time.

A few seconds later, she noticed the T-shirt and sweatpants she was wearing. They were a man's, obviously Doc's. Then, she noticed the fresh sheets she was lying on. The box springs and mattress still lay on the floor with the bed frame collapsed around it, and the wrought-iron headboard tilted on a twenty-degree angle leaning over her, but the ripped and soiled sheets from the polar bear were gone. As she became more alert, she did have a vague recollection of lying on the bathroom floor anticipating vomiting again while her host was in the bedroom cleaning up after her.

She looked at her hands, then ran her right hand over her black-and-blue left wrist, checking the compound fracture from two nights earlier. Satisfied that regeneration was going the way it should, she slowly swung back the covers, put her feet on the floor, and slowly stood up. She spied the digital alarm clock on top of the dresser. Pointing a slender finger at its red numerals she said, "You're a clock," as if to verify the object. "11:02... two minutes after eleven," she realized.

Stopping briefly to enjoy another deep inhale of the chicken, she walked over to the bathroom and gently pushed the door open. Inside was the lingering smell of factory plastic coming from a new white shower curtain that had been hung. But that wasn't all. In between the sinks on the counter was a new toothbrush, a tube of toothpaste, a bar of soap, three pairs of white panties and bras, all different sizes and folded up, three pairs of women's jeans, likewise slightly different sizes and folded, and two different sizes of women's sweatshirts. The designs of the sweatshirts were identical. They were white with blue lettering on the chest that read "Charlevoix Yacht Club." There was also a hairbrush and a new pair of black one-size-fits-all women's stretch slippers. Looking gratefully at the objects, Clair slowly picked up the hairbrush then turned her eyes to the mirror. The cut over her right eye was fainter, but she was still paler than a normal human. She also had no makeup and was fighting sharp stabbing pains in her abdomen. She started to brush her hair, but then stopped and looked at herself as if to say, "What's the point?"

Eighteen minutes later, she opened her bedroom door, which was really Doc's room, and stepped into the living room. Directly ahead of her, across the room on the opposite wall, was a good-sized fieldstone fireplace where maple logs burned and hissed. There was a tightly woven black mesh screen with three folding panels that sat in front of the fire and kept the sparks from popping and landing on the wooden floor. In front of the fireplace, facing each other and about six feet apart, were two worn brown leather sofas. In between the sofas was a large wood plank coffee table that could hold drinks, magazines, bowls of popcorn, games of Scrabble, and propped-up feet. A ten-by-seven area rug with a red and blue Native American design sat under the coffee table and disappeared under the front of each sofa.

To the right of the fireplace was a writing desk with a laptop computer on it. Above the desk were shelves of books and a Bose radio and CD player. There were also three medium-sized U-Haul cardboard boxes of books stacked up next to the desk. She could tell this because the boxes were marked "Books," in Magic Marker.

The far right wall of the living room featured two waist-high windows with opened dark red curtains that looked out onto the screened-in porch. Next to them was a door that led out to the same. On the porch was some folded lawn furniture and stacked sections of aluminum dock that promised warmer, lazier days. In between the two waist-high windows was a little table standing against the wall. On the table with a white pillowcase wrapped around its base was the decorated Christmas tree Doc had gotten a decade earlier at Walmart. Four of its thirty multi-colored miniature lights had burned out over the years, but it still cheered up an already comfortable room.

Across the room, opposite the tree and against the far left wall, was a locked gun cabinet with a glass door, and, next to it, was the entranceway to the kitchen with its linoleum floor, small laundry room, and half-bath going off of it. In between the two bedroom doors next to where Clair stood was a flat-screen TV and DVD player sitting on a stand, so those seated on the leather sofas could view either the fireplace one way, or the TV the other way. Although the interior walls were planed unlike the log exterior, the living room wasn't paneled knotty pine like Doc's bedroom. The walls were a smooth off-white with a hint of dusky gold. Keeping constant vigil over the living room with black marble eyes was an Elk's head that sat above the fireplace. It was a trophy taken years earlier when the Ford executive was on a hunting trip in Montana with wife number one.

Noticing the clean smell of Murphy's Oil Soap on the recently washed wooden floor, Clair followed the stronger aroma of chicken through the living room, past the gun cabinet, and around the left into the kitchen. She wore her new slippers, underwear, a pair of jeans that fit perfectly, and the smaller of the two Charlevoix Yacht Club sweatshirts.

Once in the kitchen, she discovered that the smell of chicken and carrots wasn't coming from the oven, but from a stainless-steel pot sitting on the stove. Inside the pot, homemade chicken soup was simmering. Doc was just putting a mop away in a corner closet when he turned to see her. Since he wasn't working, he was dressed in a pair of jeans, Timberland boots, a black T-shirt, and an olive green pullover sweater.

"Good morning," he greeted.

"Hi," she said, somewhat sheepish.

"How are you feeling?"

"More human," she replied. She self-consciously pulled the left sleeve of her sweatshirt down so the bruise from the compound fracture wouldn't be so noticeable.

Doc chuckled at the "more human" response, but didn't know if she was trying to be funny or just sincere with her answer. "I, uh, the rental car company brought me out a car first thing this morning," he explained, gesturing toward the kitchen window where small gray Kia Spectrum sat out in the turnaround. "So, I went to Kmart. But I didn't know what size you wore so I bought a few things in different sizes."

"Kmart?" she asked, apparently not understanding him.

"It's a store. They've got everything you need. It's like heaven, only with Blue Light Specials."

Her face flickered with a smile. She didn't know what he meant, but she knew he was making a joke.

"Are you hungry?" he asked. "Do you think you could keep down a little soup?"

She leaned toward the pot and took another deep smell. "Yes, please. It smells absolutely wonderful!"

"My mom's recipe," he said, moving to a cabinet to get a bowl. "The noodles aren't homemade, but it'll still do you good."

She walked over to the kitchen table, pulled back a chair, and sat down. As she did, she glanced around with a half-smile admiring the pine and glass cabinets, the dishes, the Formica counters, and the track lighting above, as if she'd never seen such surroundings before.

"Everything okay?" he asked.

"It's different when you're here."

"Excuse me?"

"It's different—being told what to expect and then actually being here."

He nodded slightly, not exactly sure how to respond.

"Thanks for everything you've done, Doc," she said. "Your discretion, cleaning up the house, the fresh sheets, the clothes…" her voice trailed off as she realized something. "You… you put me in pajamas last night, too. Didn't you?"

"Well, not while you were playing *Gorillas in the Mist*," he replied, ladling out a small helping of soup for her. "And they weren't really pajamas. Just a T-shirt and some sweatpants, but they were clean."

He brought the soup over and set it down on the table in front of her. Then got her a napkin and spoon, then went over to the fridge and got out a thirty-two-ounce bottle of Vernors Ginger Ale.

"Then, then that would mean," she observed, somewhat nervously, "you… you saw me in the buff."

"A *lot*," he confirmed, grinning. "I checked your side where those ribs were sticking out, the alignment of your hip, your wrist, pretty much every nip and tuck. I even checked out your birthmark shaped like a maple leaf on your—"

"I know where it is," she interrupted, stirring her soup, obviously embarrassed.

"Don't worry," he said, pouring her drink and bringing it over. "It was strictly professional. Besides, you're not my type."

"And what type is that?"

"Celestial."

"So, you believe me, then?" she asked.

"Let's just say, unless this is a flashback from my experimental drug days, I haven't got a better explanation right now. Let me ask you something—do angels get hurt like this a lot?"

"I honestly don't know."

"What's up with all the 'changing into' stuff?"

"Think of it this way: you just got me a bowl of soup, a spoon, and a napkin. You didn't even think about your actions, but it took several things happening at once: depth perception, hand-eye coordination, muscle use, thousands of nerve endings firing at once. But if you were injured, any one of those abilities could be lost. Well, under normal circumstances, maintaining a human form would be as easy for me as getting the soup was for you. But, these aren't normal circumstances."

"Why animals?"

"Probably because I was in animal form when I—when we met." She smiled slightly, took a sip of her drink, then looked at the glass. "Is this Vernors?"

"A Michigan original," he confirmed. "Although I'm not sure they even make it here anymore."

"What do you know," she smiled with a faraway look in her eye. "First brewed by a Detroit pharmacist named James Vernor in 1866."

She shook off her nostalgia, set the glass down and tried the soup.

"Mmm, fabulous!" she said, sincerely. "To have the gift of taste again. Smell. To feel warm. Cold."

"You don't have senses in heaven?" he asked.

"Don't get me wrong," she said, "they don't call it 'Paradise' for nothing. But it's not physical."

"But, it seems like you were," he concluded. "You know Vernors. You said, 'To have the gift of taste *again*.'"

"Yes, I've been here before," she admitted. "But not in a while."

While she sipped and enjoyed her soup, Doc went back to doing what he was doing before she came into the room. He returned to the kitchen closet, opened the door and lifted a nearly full white plastic garbage bag out of its metal container. There were many questions he was anxious to ask his houseguest but he knew that being impatient wasn't going to get answers any sooner. So, he excused himself, took the garbage outside through the kitchen door, put it in a garbage bin that was locked to keep the wildlife out, and when he came back inside, Clair was nearly finished with her meal.

"Would you like some more?" he offered, stomping the snow off his feet on a mat just inside the kitchen door. "I also picked up bags of Purina Dog Chow, Cat Chow, Horse Chow, you know—just in case."

She looked at him not understanding.

"I'm kidding," he explained.

"Oh," she said, taking another sip of her Vernors. "No, I don't think I should put too much into my system right now. But this really hit the spot. Thank you."

"You're welcome. Are you through, uh, changing into things?"

"No. But as I get stronger, it'll happen less."

He crossed over to the table and sat down opposite her, not being able to resist interrogation anymore. "See, that's something I don't understand. If you're an angel, how can an angel get hurt in the first place?"

"But I wasn't an angel when your vehicle struck me," she reminded. "I was a deer. I was physical. I don't know how often angels get hurt, but I do know that there can be consequences when you work in the physical world."

"But, why?" he persisted. "I mean, why isn't—" he hesitated, apparently not wanting to say the word God out loud, "your boss helping you?"

"Aren't I alive when I should be dead? Aren't I healing much faster than a normal human would?"

"That's just a little help."

"How much help am I supposed to get?"

"I... I just don't see why you would be allowed to get hurt in the first place."

"A lot of humans don't understand why God allows certain things to happen," she replied. "Even us angels wonder sometimes. That's a natural occurrence from the gift of being able to reason. But, in the end, Doc, our reason, our logic, isn't his. It's as simple as that."

"Yeah, but—"

"What's your given name?" she asked, interrupting him.

"Huh?"

"Your name isn't really 'Doc,' is it?"

"No, it's Wyatt. Wyatt Reynolds."

"Do you have a baptism name?"

"Yeah, but I never liked—"

"What is it?" she insisted.

He looked at her, pausing for a moment, then answered, "Gabriel. Okay? Happy now? It's Gabriel."

"Interesting," she said, thoughtfully, rising from the table and taking her dishes over to the sink. "As I'm sure you know, Gabriel is the name of an archangel. He's mentioned in ancient Greek texts, Jewish texts, Muslim, Christian, even in the writings of the Bahai faith. Several times he's been described as a protector, other times as the angel of death."

"So?" Doc said, also rising. "Don't worry about the dishes. I don't want you to be in the middle of washing them and then turn into something without opposable thumbs."

"Good point," she agreed, putting the dishes down. She paused, looked out the window admiring the snow-covered pines on the other side of the turnaround, then turned and headed back toward the living room. "So, nothing," she said, as she went. "I'm just saying Gabriel's an old, respected name; a being that's been mentioned in the writings of many faiths throughout the centuries. Angel of death, protector… perhaps a protector *from* death."

Forgetting about the dishes temporarily, he followed her into the living room. "You lost me," he said.

She wandered over to the fire, stooped down in front it, then put her hands out to warm them. "I can't tell you how nice that feels," she mused. Then she turned her attention back to more immediate things. "You haven't asked what I'm doing here, Doc. You haven't asked why I'm here on Earth."

"Believe me, I was getting to that," he said, sticking his hands in his pockets.

"I've come to stop something," she said, looking at the fire.

"Stop what?"

She turned to him seriously. "A murder. The killing of a young woman named Farren Malone."

"What? You serious?"

"But I can't do it alone," she continued. "Not now. Not in my current condition. I hate to ask, but I could sure use a little help."

"What? You mean *me*?"

She nodded.

His face flushed a little. "No," he said, definitely. "I'm not your guy. I'm not—I don't—" Before Doc could finish his sentence, Clair suddenly gasped, struck a wide-eyed expression, then quickly shrank, disappearing inside of her clothing. A few seconds later, a rat scurried out of one of her pant legs.

MRS. HUFFMAN

The red numbers of the digital alarm clock on the dresser in Doc's bedroom read 5:18 p.m. Even though it wasn't officially evening yet, it was already dark outside, the result of Daylight Saving Time and the fewer hours of sunlight in the winter months. Doc lay on one of the leather sofas in the living room. The back of his head was pointed toward the TV that sat in between the bedroom doors while his feet were pointed toward the fieldstone fireplace. The fire had fizzled out hours earlier, but there was light in the room from an end table lamp, the kitchen track lighting off to the left, and the lights from the small Christmas tree to the right of the room on the little table next to the screened-in porch. The room was noticeably cooler than earlier in the day. A breeze blew down the open chimney flue and caused everything in the room to have a slightly ashy smell.

Sitting on Doc's chest was a Timberland boot box; no doubt it originally housed the boots on his feet. Although the box had its lid on, a few air holes had been poked into the top. He held the box with his left hand and wore a Band-Aid on the fleshy part of it in between his forefinger and thumb. Although his eyes were closed, he wasn't really sleeping so much as cat napping. He was thinking of a Christmas season a long time ago when he and his sister were quite young. He was maybe eight; she was around ten. He was remembering how this time of year used to be filled with magic. It was a time when anything seemed possible, a time brimming over with the happiness of anticipation.

His thoughts were interrupted by the box on his chest suddenly rattling violently. His eyes flew open, he muttered, "Oh, no," then he tried to quickly lift it off his chest. But he didn't have time. Within a couple seconds, a brown rodent the size of a Labrador Retriever burst through the cardboard with large closed eyes and wiry whiskers—a second after that, it morphed into blonde-haired, green-eyed Clair, who was now lying on top of him sleeping and naked.

Grunting from the additional sudden weight, he moaned, "She's not going to like this."

He tried to maneuver a foot onto the floor. As he did, one of her arms fell off the sofa and dangled over its side.

"Uh, Clair?" he said softly to wake her. "Clair?"

After several seconds of no response, he decided to shake her shoulder. Her body was soft and warm, but in this particular position, he was very uncomfortable.

"Clair," he said, blowing some of her long curly locks off his lips. "C'mon, you've got to wake up. *Hey!*"

She moaned a little and her eyelids sleepily opened. She raised her head, then looked down at the blue eyes staring up at her mere centimeters away.

"This isn't what it looks like," he offered, wanting to explain the situation before she even knew there was one.

She looked around, realized she was lying on top of him without any clothing, then instinctively sprang up.

"W… what am I doing on top of you?" she asked, surprised and aggravated. She placed a hand over her crotch and pressed an arm across her chest. "Where are my clothes?"

"I put them in my bedroom."

She turned and dashed into the bedroom. Doc was actually too stiff from the sudden weight on top of him to get up quickly, so he didn't see her rounded attractive derriere bounce up and down as she darted away.

"Why was I lying on you?" she demanded, clicking on the overhead fan light in the bedroom then shutting the door behind her.

"You turned into a rat, remember?" he called, slowly sitting up. "I had you in a box resting on my chest. I'd just laid down a couple of minutes earlier."

"You had me in a *box?*" she called back, clearly not pleased with the thought.

"Well I'd just spent all morning cleaning up after you, then made you soup. I didn't want the place messed up again. Besides, you bit me."

"I bit you?"

"*Hard,*" he answered looking at the Band-Aid on his hand. "There aren't going to be any side effects, are there? Am I gonna have an overwhelming desire to listen to Christian rock?"

"Now I remember," she called, "you grabbed my tail."

"You were running around and pooping all over the place. How else was I going to get you in the box?"

"Serves you right," she said, defensively.

"Serves me right?"

"Yes. It would be nice to get through one day, *one* twenty-four-hour period without you seeing me naked."

"Oh, like I *planned* all this?" he called, rising off the sofa and becoming agitated. "If you're typical of what angels are like, no wonder Jesus's first miracle was turning water into wine. He probably needed the drink!"

The bedroom door opened again and Clair emerged wearing the same clothes she had worn that morning. She appeared more calm and reasonable.

"You're right," she agreed, taking a deep breath. "You didn't plan any of this. I imagine this whole thing has shaken you up pretty badly. I'll pray for you to have no memory of me after I'm gone. It'll be like I was never here."

"You do what you've got to do," he replied, unconcerned. "But for whatever it's worth, whenever I've seen you naked, all I've ever thought about were your injuries and what was going on inside of you with this, 'regeneration,' or whatever you call it. You're very pretty, but thinking about you in an amorous way is—well—sort of like kissing my sister."

She smiled a little, accepting and appreciating his answer. He looked around the room, noticing the cold. "I'd better re-stoke the fire."

While Doc rebuilt the fire, Clair took a shower. Afterwards, she happily chirped about the water splashing on her face and the feel of soap on her skin. Then both of them dined on chicken noodle soup with dark pumpernickel bread. During dinner, Clair didn't talk about her mission on Earth or the woman she had mentioned earlier named Farren Malone. She confined her conversation to lighter topics: how wonderful it was to have senses again; she asked Doc why he liked living out of town and in the woods; she talked about additional clothing, her shoe size, and other necessities she might need. Although grateful for his shopping trip, she admitted she wasn't much of a "dungaree girl." The only thing of a supernatural nature that Doc did mention during dinner was that he hoped he wouldn't be made to forget about her. He said he didn't understand a lot of things about his guest, but that didn't mean he wanted to live the rest of his life without the benefit of what he had witnessed and learned. Clair didn't answer him one way or another on the subject. All she said was that she'd think about it.

After the dishes were done, Doc put on a CD of soft, instrumental Celtic music, then he and his guest settled down on the leather sofas in the living room. He sat on the sofa nearest the kitchen, and she sat down on the one across from the wooden plank coffee table nearest the porch. She kept gazing at the fire, admiringly. The glow of the flames reflected in her long blonde hair and gave her head a slight golden aura. He even noticed that the cut above her right eye was now completely healed.

"We're going to have to talk about how I need your help sooner or later," she finally said.

He pursed his lips with hesitation. "Clair, with all due respect, I've done my bit. I've taken you in, I've kept quiet, I've let you use my home as your own personal outhouse, this is all just a little too—"

"Isn't saving lives what you do?" she reminded.

"Yeah, but—"

"Just hear the facts. That's all I ask."

He took a deep, resigned breath. "Fine... tell me about Fallon before you change into Flipper, or something."

"Farren," she corrected, not getting the Flipper reference. "Farren Malone, although her married name is Farren Malone Huffman. She's twenty-nine, born and raised in Charlevoix, and was married two months ago. Her parents, Jackie and Paul Malone, drowned in Lake Michigan when she was seventeen. Their sailboat got caught in a sudden squall. After that, her grandfather, on her mother's side, raised her. The two of them run the Portside Marina in town. Do you know it?"

"I know where it is, but I've never been there. I don't own a boat, although my partner does."

"Partner?"

"The Emergency Medical Technician I work with."

"What's the difference between a 'paramedic' and an 'Emergency Medical Technician?'"

"You don't know?"

"You think I'm supposed to know everything because I'm an angel?"

He shrugged. "I don't know what I'm supposed to think. Forty-eight hours ago, my biggest question in life was, 'What happens to socks when you put two in the dryer but only get back one?' *Now...*" he opened his hands quizzically. "A paramedic has about two years more training than an EMT. There are more procedures we can do for a patient—administer drugs, that kind of thing."

She nodded. "Do you know Farren or the Malone family?"

"Like I said at dinner, I've been in town less than a year."

"That's right," she remembered. "Anyway, Farren's an Intended One."

"Intended One?"

"An exceptionally kind and compassionate soul; the way man was always intended to be, but frequently chooses not to be. Saint Nicholas was an Intended One. So was Gandhi, Mother Teresa, several others."

"You mean, this woman is going to be famous? Change history or something?" he asked.

"No. Not all Intended Ones wind up in the public eye. In fact, most of them don't."

He rubbed his forehead with his fingertips, pausing for a moment. "So, who's going to murder her? Does somebody break into her house, or—"

"Her husband."

"Her *husband?* The guy she just married?"

"He didn't marry her for love—although he probably enjoys being intimate with her—he married her for her property."

"She's rich?"

"No," Clair said, tucking her legs up and under her. "Let me explain: Farren's husband, Charlie Huffman, is a thief and a professional con man, although she doesn't know it. He's originally from Flint and has swindled people out of hundreds of thousands of dollars over the years. He's also addicted to gambling and has gotten himself into trouble with a very dangerous loan shark named Bartholomew. Charlie's into him for seventy large ones." She paused. "Did I say that right? Seventy large ones?"

"If you meant seventy thousand dollars," he replied.

"Good. That's what I meant," she confirmed. "Rather than kill Charlie, Bartholomew has decided to use him and have him do what he does best—run a con. Bartholomew likes the Charlevoix area and knows that Farren owns the land that the Portside Marina sits on. It's prime real estate on the edge of Round Lake just before it feeds into Lake Charlevoix. He also knows it's her family's legacy, and she'd never sell it. He made inquiries about it anonymously through a local realtor about a year ago. But if he got a hold of the land, he could knock down the marina, keep the docks and boat slips and build a several-story condominium complex there. With views of Round Lake and downtown one way, and Lake Charlevoix the other, he could make a fortune. So, about seven months ago, Charlie met Farren and began to woo her. Like you, he's very good looking and can be quite charming."

Doc sat up a little. "'Woo?' You use interesting words. So you think I'm good-looking and charming, huh?"

She suddenly put her hand on her stomach as if a case of nausea was threatening.

"No, please. Not now," she said, glancing up toward the ceiling.

"Do you need to go to the bathroom?" he said, still seated, but cocking his arms on the sofa cushions to push himself up.

She waited a couple of moments before answering, trying to determine what was going on inside of her. "Not yet. But I'd better finish my story."

"I think I get it," Doc said. "Charlie pursued Farren, swept her off her feet, and she married him. Now, he's going to kill her, or have her killed, and make it look like an accident. As her husband, he'll inherit the marina and land, which he'll then sign over to Bartholomew to clear the slate with him. That it?"

"That's it," she said, rubbing her stomach tentatively.

"Fine," he said, standing up. "I'll warn her. Now, let's get you to the bathroom."

"Wait a minute," Clair said. "You can't just walk up to a total stranger and say, 'Excuse me, your husband is planning to kill you.' There's no evidence, no proof. It's the word of a stranger versus the man she fell in love with."

"But, the guy's got to have a criminal record, right? I know a lot of cops here. I can do a background check."

"There are no charges against him or any of his aliases in Charlevoix County. And although he's been arrested and charged in Flint, he's never been convicted. Look, Doc, this is going to take some finesse. If you handle this the wrong way, Bartholomew could kill Charlie, Farren, maybe even her grandfather, then buy the marina at public auction through a dummy corporation. Believe me, you *don't* want that on your conscience. This has got to be handled in such a way where Charlie is exposed, and Bartholomew figures trying to get the marina after the fact isn't worth the heat."

"So, what am I supposed to do?"

"Meet Farren, befriend her, gain a level of trust with her and have her find out about Charlie and Bartholomew for herself by planting certain thoughts in her head. Thoughts I can help you with."

She also rose to her feet, although more slowly than he did. "I admit, it would be easier making friends with her if you were a woman, but, we'll just have to do the best we can."

She started moving toward the bathroom that connected the two bedrooms together. Doc followed behind her.

"How much time do I have?" he asked.

"To tell you the truth, I'm not sure. But this con has already gone on for months, and I know Bartholomew is getting impatient."

"How do you know that?"

"Last week, a couple of his thugs had a motivational talk with Charlie. They cut off one of his little toes."

FIRST IMPRESSIONS

It was another pale, frigid, nickel-colored morning, as Father Ken Pistole threw the last of the salt on the sidewalk leading from the rectory, past a row of small rose bushes covered with white Styrofoam boxes for protection from the cold, to the back of Saint Ignatius Catholic Church. Unlocking then opening the thick wooden back door that was rounded at the top, he stepped inside the vestibule.

Built in 1932, mostly from the contributions of a parishioner who owned a large shipping company, it was a crucifix-shaped building that could hold three hundred of the faithful. It had a high, arching thirty-foot ceiling, stained glass windows with mosaics of red, gold, blue, and pink to the right and left of the center aisle, and original dark-stained wooden pews that creaked when the parishioners sat. The venerable old church also had a newly carpeted floor within the last year and hidden hallways on either side of the "cross beam" of its shape. The hallways were behind the confessionals that were also on either side. The hallway to the right had a staircase at its end that led down to the basement, bathrooms and a meeting room. The one on the left had a door at its end that hid a staircase leading up to the tall organ pipes that sat in the wall behind the altar fronted by a latticework of white-painted wood and plaster. A twelve-foot crucifix hung in front of the latticework.

Hanging down from a dark chain twenty-two feet in the air in between the two steps that led up to the altar and the first row of pews was an old, ornate chandelier that originally came from Hungary. Like the windows, it featured glass multicolored panels in front of its light bulbs. The large, hanging fixture had kept many a child momentarily fascinated during the long rituals of the mass.

The echo of Father Ken stomping his feet in the vestibule disturbed the chilly candlelit serenity inside. It was just after 9:00 a.m. Monday morning. Coming onto the altar from the right-hand-side entranceway, he immediately noticed the church lights were on and the extended scissors lift, with its crisscrossing metallic braces, stretched all the way up to the chandelier. It was a smaller model as scissor lifts went. He also saw the back of someone in the railed cage above changing the bulbs.

"Good morning, Russell," he called up to the ceiling in his burly voice. He was a portly man in his early sixties and had mostly white hair and a trimmed white beard; it hid some shrapnel scars on his chin, leftover from his days as a Chaplin in Vietnam.

"Morning, Father," a distinctly female voice called back.

Surprised, the priest looked more closely up at the cage. "Farren?"

"Hi," Farren Malone Huffman called back in her usual cheery tone. "Russell wasn't feeling well, but he knew this was the only day the window company was going to lend you the scissors lift. So he called me. You don't want the congregation praying in the dark, do you?"

"I don't like the idea of you being up there alone. Why didn't you call me? How'd you get into the church?"

The lift made an electronic humming sound and started to descend slowly. As it did, Farren came more clearly into view. She was a well-toned woman, but lean, standing at five-foot-five. She had thick black hair that was cut short in a pixie style with exposed small ears and nonchalant bangs. She had prominent cheekbones like Clair, although more rounded, large, round M&M brown eyes, and a pair of dimples on her fresh-looking face that deepened considerably when she smiled. She also had a few freckles on her nose that gave her a distinct tomboy look. Her hands were delicate looking but strong, and her fingernails were just as likely to have grease under them as having nail polish on them. Most of the men in town considered her more cute than pretty, but her full lips and wide smile could turn a head or two when she dressed up. She didn't resemble the kind of girl one would find in the pages of *Cosmo*, but maybe in an *Orvis* or *Coldwater Creek* catalog. She wore practical K-Swiss boots with deep treading, faded jeans, a long-sleeved green turtleneck and a red down vest.

"I called Russell last night because I needed to get some large cooking pots out of the Social Center. He told me he wasn't feeling well and asked if I'd change the bulbs for him. So I just picked up his keys on the way over."

"He asked *you* to man the lift?"

"Why not? After all, I schlep cabin cruisers around with the marina's forklift. Besides, it's done. Easy-peasy."

"Well, thank you very much," the priest said, impressed. "You're a handy lady to have around."

The cage came to rest. She raised a section of guardrail and hopped out.

"So, why did you need the pots?" Father Ken asked.

"Barnard United Methodist wants to borrow them for their turn of Room at the Inn."

"Ah," the clergyman nodded. Room at the Inn was a national nondenominational program that fed and housed the homeless. The area churches would take turns—Catholic, Methodist, Presbyterian and so on. There weren't a lot of homeless people in the Charlevoix area, but there were some.

"So, how's Charlie? How do you like married life?" Even though the priest didn't perform her marriage, he had met her new spouse a couple of times before.

"About the same as single life," she smiled. "He's on the road all the time."

"What does he do again?"

"He's a project manager for a large construction company that's licensed in several states. He troubleshoots from one job site to another. In fact, a little more than a week ago, he had an accident with his foot at one of the sites."

"Nothing serious I hope."

"Actually, it kind of was. But, I guess it could have been worse. Taught him to wear steel-toed boots, that's for sure."

Father Ken thought for a moment, recalling something.

"Then, it *was* Charlie I saw a couple of days ago."

"You saw him?" Farren asked, surprised.

"Well, at least I *think* it was him. It was at a distance. He came out of a pawnshop, then rounded a corner. I called out to him, but he didn't answer. It sure looked like Charlie, though. It was a guy who was definitely limping. In fact, he had a cane."

"Where was this, Father?"

"Traverse City, this past Friday."

Farren furrowed her brow, not quite understanding. "Well, he *has* been using a cane, and when he works out of state, he *does* fly in and out of Traverse City. But, Friday he was working in Milwaukee. He worked all weekend there. He doesn't even land until this afternoon."

The priest was nearly positive the man he had seen in Traverse City, some fifty-two miles away, was Charlie Huffman, but he didn't press the issue. "I must've been mistaken," he smiled. "After all, I did call out to the fellow and he didn't respond. Anyway, thanks for changing the bulbs. With all the help you and Russell are around here, I'd be lost without you guys."

"Anytime, Father," she smiled, reaching for her cell phone. "I'll call the window company and tell 'em they can pick up the lift whenever. Let me put the spare bulbs away, then I'll drive it out front."

"Thanks, Farren. And tell that grandfather of yours I want to see him in church more often. Showing up for only the biggies like Christmas and Easter doesn't cut it."

"I'll tell him," she smiled again.

What Father Ken had said about Farren being a big help was certainly true. Russell, the church's handyman, was supposed to be helpful. That was his job. But Farren gave from her heart. St. Ignatius had a dozen or so parishioners who were always willing to pitch in, and Farren was one of the dozen. Besides Room at the Inn, she was also on the church's Cleaning Committee, Annual Picnic Committee, Blood Drive Committee, Christmas Dance and Auction Committee, and she read weekly to an elderly woman who was nearly blind. In fact, an hour later, she was perusing the shelves of a small bookstore downtown on Bridge Street, intending to pick up some new reading material. As she did, she was unaware that Doc was standing on a sidewalk across the street and watching her through the store's large front window.

"She'll be the prettiest girl in the bookstore," Clair had told him, knowing Farren's routine of checking out new titles every Monday.

"Just bump into her, say, 'Excuse me,' then introduce yourself," he mumbled. "Or, ask her something. Ask if her name is Lorraine. When she says, 'No,' you could say you were supposed to meet a beautiful girl there by that name, and you just assumed she was her."

He rethought the strategy and shook his head. "Really lame... 'Course, I could always say I hit a deer that turned into an angel who told me about her. That's always a nice icebreaker," he said sarcastically. "Then, I can show her my snapshots of Bigfoot."

He stood with his hands sunk deep in his jacket pockets not knowing how to proceed and shivering. The sun was climbing higher, but it was still obscured by gray clouds that threatened snow, and the temperature was only about twenty degrees. The wind whipping up behind him from Round Lake and unobstructed by a city park just off shore, called East Park, didn't help matters. He'd also left his stocking cap in his blue paramedic coat at home. He was wearing street clothes and a leather WWII-style bomber jacket with a wool collar. He had called in sick at work and was concerned that someone he knew might see him since the fire hall was a mere one block inland from Bridge Street.

"This is stupid," he muttered to himself. "No recently married woman is going to have idle chitchat with a total stranger."

He saw she had selected a book and was heading toward the cash register.

"How do I *do* this?" he wondered out loud. Being blessed with good looks and an endearing smile, he never had any trouble meeting girls when he was younger. Even now, the occasional phone number still found its way into his pocket. But this was different. This wasn't about romance or even friendship. This was a secret mission to share critical information, but only after a rapport had been established. He felt like a spy; a spy working in Siberia who had forgotten his stocking cap. Checking the traffic, he slowly started to cross the street. He could see the cashier ringing up Farren's purchase and decided that physically bumping into her was probably the best way to introduce himself. He crossed the street and was on the sidewalk, almost to the door, when a voice called out to his right.

"Hey, Doc. Merry Christmas!"

He turned to see George Pratt on the same side of the street several storefronts away. George was in his early seventies and owned the ACE Hardware in town. Back in April, he'd had a heart attack, and Doc and Lance had stabilized him and gotten him to the hospital. It was another one of those cases where seconds counted.

"Hi, George," the paramedic called, taking a step or two toward him. "How are you doing?"

"Not bad, not bad."

"I heard from Doctor Lancaster that you had some problems with your eyes after your episode."

"Depth perception. But it's getting better," George called back. "My optometrist gave me some eye exercises and a new prescription."

"Good." Doc said, walking backward toward the bookstore and waving. "Keep at it. Happy Holidays."

As Doc turned forward again, his face ran smack into the metal edge of the just-opened bookstore door, as Farren Malone Huffman was coming out. The whack of the door was so forceful against his forehead, he fell backwards onto his rear and lay spread-eagle on the cold sidewalk, unconscious.

"Oh, my God!" Farren yelled, surprised. "*Oh, my God!*"

Having seen the whole thing, George Pratt's jaw dropped open, but then he shook his head, smacked his lips, and sighed.

"At least my depth perception is better than *his*."

Less than an hour later, Doc slowly opened his eyes. From the rounded surgical light fixture staring down at him and the thin beige curtains surrounding him—a color purposely chosen to illicit a calming feeling—he knew exactly where he was: the emergency room at Charlevoix Area Hospital. Bob Lancaster appeared through an opening in the curtains wearing his usual surgical scrubs sans the skullcap and smiled reassuringly.

"Good. You're awake. Hey, Doc."

"Doc," the patient acknowledged, still groggy.

"How do you feel?'

"Am I supposed to feel like a sledge hammer hit me between the eyes?"

Lancaster smiled again. "Yeah, pretty much."

"Then I'd say I feel about normal," Doc responded.

"You gave yourself a concussion and got knocked out cold," Lancaster explained. "I'm not sure if it was from the door on your forehead or the sidewalk on the back of your skull when you fell. Either way, it's gonna feel like a tequila hangover for the rest of the day." He pointed to the patient's hand. "And did you get bit by a rodent, or something?"

Doc looked down to see that somewhere in between following Farren and being knocked unconscious, the Band-Aid on his hand had fallen off. "It's nothing," he said. He gently put a finger to his forehead feeling the gauze that had been taped over a small cut and a large lump. "How did I get here?"

"How do you think?" Lancaster asked. "The Life Support Unit."

"I came in my own ambulance? Oh, this is embarrassing."

"Oh, it gets better. You were brought in by your own partner and Harry Stanton."

Harry was Doc's boss. He started to rub his forehead in frustration but then suddenly stopped because of the lump there. He raised his head a little and felt the corresponding lump on the back of his head. By coincidence, it was almost exactly where he had smacked his head when he fell backward into the tub. He couldn't help but think that knowing Clair was, so far, mostly a painful experience.

"Perfect," he moaned. "I feel like hell, I didn't accomplish what I set out to do, and now my partner and my boss know I lied about being sick today."

"Yeah, but you feel sick *now*," the sandy-haired physician smiled, "so it was only a half-lie. I wouldn't worry about it. Everybody takes a sick day this time of year. How else are we going to get our Christmas shopping done, right? Hey, you up to seeing somebody?"

"Harry and Lance?"

"No. They went to get your car and bring it back here. Lance remembered you had a rental, and the license plate number was on your key chain. They figured it couldn't be far from where you were. I'm talking about the lady who was on the other side of the door you walked into."

Guessing it must be Farren out in the waiting area, Doc's mood immediately improved.

"Uh, yeah. I guess."

"When Harry and Lance come back, have Lance drive you home, and Harry can follow. Take it easy the rest of the day and take tomorrow off, if you need to. No strenuous physical activity. Don't do anything that requires thinking."

"Okay. I'll just watch reality TV then."

"I'll give you a prescription for the pain. But it'll make you drowsy, so *stay* home today." With that, Lancaster disappeared between the opening in the beige curtains. After a few moments, Doc slowly sat up and swung his feet over the side of the treatment table. As he closed his eyes and felt the back of his head again, Farren peaked her head in between the curtains, smiling timidly.

"Hi," she said softly. "I'm Farren. I was coming out of the bookstore when—I am so, *so* sorry about what happened."

Seeing her up close, he noticed that she was more attractive than from what he had observed across the street. But being Doc, he hid his approval and squinted at her instead.

"Not as sorry as you're going to be when my attorney has finished with you."

Unfazed, her dimpled smile widened as she stepped through the curtains.

"Yeah, Lance said you like to do that."

"Do what?"

"Say things just to mess with people."

He cracked a little smile, realizing she had his number and extended his hand. "I'm Wyatt Reynolds."

"Doc. Yes, I know," she acknowledged, shaking hands with him.

"You know Lance?" he asked, a little surprised.

"Small town. We went to high school together. He was a senior when I was a junior. I used to hang out with his girlfriend, Charlene. He used to drive us crazy asking trivia questions about *Star Trek*. He doesn't still do that, does he?"

"No, he's outgrown that," Doc replied, not telling her the rest of the story; that Lance had merely replaced Captain Kirk with 007. "So, he's been dating Charlene since high school?"

"I know," she nodded. "It's crazy. They've been dating forever. We don't hang out that much anymore, but Lance has a boat he keeps at my marina so I see them pretty often in the summer. And back in high school, Charlene and I were on the Junior Varsity cheerleading squad. So, we've got some history."

His eyes widened as a realization struck him.

"Shortly after I moved here, about nine months ago, Charlene tried to fix me up with an old cheerleading buddy of hers, but—"

"But you said no," she interrupted, knowingly. "Yeah, that was me. The excuse I got was you were too busy settling in to meet anyone. Really good for the ol' ego," she recalled. "A few months later, she asked me about hooking up with you again. But by then, I was involved with someone."

He looked at her totally surprised with his mouth slightly open. "Charlene never gave me a name or pointed you out."

"Why should she? You said no."

"It's just—she's fixed me up on a blind date since," he explained, "but she didn't look—I mean—she wasn't anything like—" he stopped himself, not wanting to say anything negative about someone she probably knew. "I'm sorry," he finally said. "*Si tantum EGO had notus.*"

"What?"

"Latin. 'If I had only known.'"

She smiled. "*Vous etes pardonne.*"

"What?"

"French. 'You are forgiven.'"

He nodded appreciatively and noticed the white plastic shopping bag she held. "So, what did you get?"

"What?"

"You were coming out of a bookstore—what book did you buy?"

"Oh. *Pride and Prejudice*," she said, dipping one of her small hands into the bag. "I read to an elderly lady who doesn't see very well anymore, and she's never read the novel. I used to have another copy of it, a 1922 edition that was supposedly a valuable collector's item. But I misplaced it somewhere along the way."

"If your elderly friend wants to know Jane Austen, why not start with her first published novel, *Sense and Sensibility*?"

Farren arched her dark eyebrows, impressed.

"You know Jane Austen?"

"Well, yeah. Doesn't everyone?"

"Not in this town. We're more of a *Great Lakes Angler* kind of crowd." She looked at him for a moment, then decided to test him. "If you know Jane Austen, then what was the original title of *Pride and Prejudice*?"

"What do I win if I answer correctly?"

"What do you want?" she replied.

"The date we never had."

She smiled apologetically and held up her left hand. "Sorry. I just got married eight weeks ago."

"Congratulations."

"Thanks."

"Then, how about a platonic lunch between friends. I mean, since you know Lance and Charlene, we're practically family, anyway."

She smiled, awkwardly looking for a gracious way to turn him down. He noticed it immediately.

"When I say platonic, I *do* mean platonic," he reiterated. "Lance was just complaining the other day that I've been in town for nearly a year but I never do anything or meet new people. Ask him yourself. So let me do something about it. Bring your husband, if you like. I'm turning over a new leaf. I want to know everybody in town and all their business."

"That's not necessarily a good thing," she chuckled. "Besides, you haven't answered my question."

He slid off the examination table and stood up. His knees buckled a little, and she quickly reached over to steady him.

"*First Impressions*," he answered, smiling his million-watt smile.

SECRET INGREDIENT

The sun was directly overhead as Lance drove the gray Kia Spectrum past the Norman Rockwell-like storefronts on Bridge Street, over the drawbridge and the Pine River, past the Pointes North Inn, heading toward Boyne City Road and the turnoff to Doc's cabin. They had just come from Walgreens where Doc got his prescription filled. Although the temperature was still below freezing, the clouds had parted and the sun was now out, causing everything to be so bright—one had to either wear sunglasses or squint. The snow, about four to five inches deep in most places, glittered off rooftops and lawns like diamonds strewn everywhere. Icicles hung from power lines and tree branches like crystalline tent stakes holding winter firmly in place.

Riding in the passenger-side seat, Doc noticed that a lot more Christmas decorations had sprung up around town over the weekend. He held an icepack Bob Lancaster had given him and alternated it every half minute or so from his forehead to the back of his skull. His lumps were too sensitive for the icepack to sit directly on them, but the plastic pack applied in their vicinity helped to deaden the pain. Following behind the Kia was a city ambulance with its dark red stripe and gold lettering. Harry Stanton, the town's senior paramedic and Lance and Doc's boss, was behind the wheel. He was forty-six years old and dressed exactly like Lance from the black cargo pants with the square Velcro pockets to the blue nylon coat with the patches on the arms. He was tall, wiry, had deep creases in his face, dark Ray Bans on his nose, and his hair was cut so closely to his head it appeared nearly shaved. When Lance and Harry stood side by side, they slightly resembled Laurel & Hardy. From the drugstore and all through town, Doc remained mostly quiet. His lumps were throbbing, and he didn't feel much like talking until they were well down Boyne City Road, and he knew that home was only a couple of minutes away.

"I'm really sorry I wasn't straight-up with you and Harry about being sick today," he said. It was the second time he had apologized since they had left the hospital.

"No worries," Lance replied, sincerely. "You haven't had a sick day since you started, and I think you've already got like a week's vacation time built up. Harry didn't seem upset about it. I think you're entitled."

"Still, I shouldn't have lied. I should've just asked him for the day off."

Lance shrugged, unoffended.

"So, you and Charlene were going to fix me up with Farren Malone, huh?"

"She's a cutie, ain't she? But, I don't know. It's probably a good thing you two never got together."

"Why do you say that?" Doc asked, moving the icepack from the front of his head to the back.

"You've always struck me as a man of the world," Lance observed. "You've lived in Wyoming, Arizona before that. With your depressing good looks, I assume you've had your share of relationships."

Doc looked at him a little puzzled, for he had never talked about any of his previous relationships with Lance except in the broadest of terms.

"Well, you *have,* haven't you?" his partner reiterated, expecting a response.

"Yeah, I guess," he conceded.

"Well, there ya go. I don't know about Farren's experiences. She's always been a goody two-shoes; a unicorn and flowers kind of girl."

"Unicorn and flowers?"

"There were girls in high school that were into heavy metal, other girls that were into sports, and other girls who were boy crazy. Then, there were one or two that, y'know, drew unicorns and flowers on their notebooks—the good girls, the chaste."

"That was Farren?"

Lance nodded. "And after her folks died, all she ever did was work. I'd be goin' fishin' with the guys, and Farren would be workin' at the marina. Or, me, Charlene and some friends would go out waterskiing, and Farren would be workin' at the marina. Then, a lot of us left town to go off to college—"

"And Farren was working at the marina," Doc finished.

"Yeah. So like I say, it probably wouldn't have gone anywhere. You two don't have a lot in common."

"Not like me and Caribou, who was into Rob Zombie," Doc reminded.

The Kia slowed down as Lance approached the turnoff that led through the white pine woods back to the cabin.

"What about this guy she just married?" Doc asked, switching the icepack from the back of his head to the front again. "Know anything about him?"

"Not much," Lance admitted. "He keeps a boat at the marina. That's how they met. But, he hasn't been in town that long. You've been in town longer than he has. I know Shelly Dreyfuss, who owns the FDT store, loves him. When he and Farren were dating, he sent her roses, like, every week."

"Of course he did," Doc mumbled.

"What?" Lance asked.

"Nothing." He was quiet for a minute while the car hopped up and down over the potholes. The tall pines and sparkling snow around them was like a picture-postcard advertisement for cross-country skiers to come to northern Michigan.

"How about her wedding? Were you and Charlene invited?"

"Nobody was. They eloped at this little touristy wedding chapel outside Petoskey. Not even her grandfather, Gus, who basically had changed his whole life to raise her after her folks passed, was invited. Word I heard was he was pretty pissed off about the marriage."

The Kia bounced over the last pothole in the lane, which wreaked havoc with Doc's head—and made a U-turn in the turnaround. The ambulance was another thirty seconds behind. As Lance made the turn extra wide so the ambulance would also have room to maneuver, he couldn't help but notice that someone had made two snow angels in the snow to the right of the kitchen door, just under the kitchen window.

"Snow angels?" he asked, looking at Doc puzzled with a half-smile.

Doc stared at the outlines in the snow and knew instantly Clair had to have made them. But he didn't have an immediate explanation for his partner. So, he just looked at Lance straight-faced and said, "So?"

"You made snow angels early this morning?" Lance repeated, wanting confirmation.

"Yes," Doc answered, swallowing hard.

"A thirty-two-year-old man?"

"I *like* snow angels," Doc replied, with a hint of challenge in his tone.

Lance put the car in park and paused. "Oooo-kay... you're a strange guy. No wonder you called in sick."

"This from a man who actually researched online what shoe size Daniel Craig wears."

Clutching his ice pack with one hand, Doc unbuckled his shoulder harness and opened the door with the other. "Thanks for driving me home. I'll be in tomorrow."

"Only if you feel up to it," Lance said, turning off the engine and handing Doc the keys. "Don't rush it."

While Lance walked over to the arriving ambulance, Doc did the same to thank and, once again, apologize to Harry. Then he stayed outside to watch the vehicle turn around and bounce its way back the way it came. After the ambulance was a safe distance down the lane, he turned back to the snow angels and noticed that there were boot prints going around the right side of the cabin toward Lake Charlevoix. He recognized the treads of the boots were his and realized Clair must've found and put on his spare pair of boots and winter coat to venture outside and explore the day.

"Clair?" he called, walking around to the right. "You out here?"

Rounding the side of the cabin with its cedar-colored log exterior, he spotted one of his boots standing unoccupied in the snow near the back wall of his bedroom. Then, two feet beyond that, was his other boot. Then, another foot beyond that was Clair's new jeans. Sticking out of the waist of the jeans was her panties, followed by her white sweatshirt with the blue lettering that read, "Charlevoix Yacht Club." Beyond that, was Doc's blue nylon paramedic coat.

"Ugh" he sighed, "*Animal Planet* again."

He looked around half expecting to see anything from a rat to a rhinoceros, when a skunk poked its small snout out from under some snow-covered scrub. He knew it was Clair immediately because of the bra strap hanging around its furry black neck.

"I'm telling you now," he said, no longer surprised by the morphing phenomena, "you spray me, and I'll beat you with a stick. I don't care if I go to hell. Understand? I don't care."

He walked over to the black-eyed rodent still carrying his ice pack and took the hanging bra off the animal. Then he started to gather up the discarded clothing. "Don't tell me, you just *had* to go outside and enjoy the majesty of winter? Right? The gift of cold?" He stopped his sarcastic commentary and sighed again. "I suppose there *is* a bright side. I'd rather have you doo-doo out here than in the house."

He turned to the skunk. "Hey, Pepe Le Pew, are you done doo-dooing?"

The creature clucked something in response that sounded similar to the squirrel.

"Good," Doc said, pretending to understand. "C'mon, let's go inside."

With his bundle of gathered-up clothing, as well as the icepack, Doc trudged his way back through the snow toward the kitchen door. The furry black creature with the single white stripe down its back waddled behind. As it did, it clucked again.

"Yes, you can have Vernors," Doc replied, pretending to understand.

Clair stayed in animal form until a little after 4:00 p.m. She spent most of the afternoon roaming around the living room and Doc's bedroom, while the claws on her paws clickity-clacked on the wooden floors where there weren't any area rugs. Meanwhile, Doc lay down on one of the leather sofas in the living room and napped until he was awakened by quickly moving human footsteps followed by the sound of his houseguest vomiting in the bathroom. Her distress only served to remind him that, even after four days of her remarkable self-healing powers, she was still quite sickly and fragile. Once the nausea subsided, Clair took a shower, then felt up to eating something. A routine was actually starting to develop from her weird recuperative process. After a dinner of a salad and hamburger for him, and chicken broth over white rice for her, Doc also wanted a shower. It wasn't until 6:40 that evening that the two of them were finally ready to settle down and have a serious discussion about the day's events. By then, Doc had built a fire and a light snow was falling outside.

"Do you have any Christmas music?" Clair asked, appearing from the kitchen with a dishtowel in her hands and wearing her white Charlevoix Yacht Club sweatshirt, jeans and black slippers. The black and blue bruise on her left wrist leftover from the compound fracture was now gone.

"I think we can do something about that," he replied, stooped in front of the fireplace with a poker. He was wearing a change of clothing from that morning, but was still casually dressed in jeans, a white T-shirt, and a lightweight maroon V-neck sweater. The gauze and tape on his forehead were gone revealing a small cut and a growing bruise, though it was hard to see. A sprig of wavy brown hair drooped down from his forehead covering most of the discoloration. He set the poker in its stand and went over to the Bose radio and CD player sitting on one of the bookshelves above the writing desk. Clicking it to FM, he searched the airwaves until he recognized the familiar musical introduction to "White Christmas."

Having disappeared back into the kitchen to put the dishtowel away and turn off the overhead track lighting, Clair re-emerged in the living room entranceway carrying two mugs with a warm, nostalgic smile on her face. Having recently showered, her long, naturally curly blonde hair was especially curly.

"They still play Bing Crosby," she said, very pleased.

"Absolutely," he agreed. "It wouldn't be Christmas without him. When exactly *was* the last time you were on Earth?"

"Let's just say, 'White Christmas' was newer," she answered.

"What have you got there?" he asked, nodding to the mugs.

"Hot chocolate. I found some mix in the cabinet, and I even added a secret ingredient from the spice rack."

"What secret ingredient?"

"If I told you, it wouldn't be a secret."

"Thanks," he said. He moved from the bookshelves over to the fireplace and set the three-panel black mesh wire screen up in front of it. Then he sat down on the leather sofa to the right of the room, on the same side as the writing desk and bookshelves. She set both mugs on the wooden-plank coffee table between them.

"How's your head?" she asked. "Would you like me to fill up your icepack?"

"No. The nap and prescription helped a lot, thanks."

She sat down on the sofa opposite him, nearest the kitchen, and tucked her legs up and under her.

"So, you met Farren today, although not exactly the way you intended," she began. "And, you're going to see her again?"

"She agreed to have lunch with me later this week," he confirmed.

"Excellent. What did you think of her? What did you learn?"

"She's prettier than I expected."

"Something more relevant," Clair suggested, looking for a way to help her charge.

"Well," he said, thinking while reaching for his mug, "she's a romantic."

"What makes you say that?" she asked, likewise reaching for hers.

"She reads Jane Austen, speaks French, is a sucker for flowers, and used to draw unicorns on her notebook in high school."

"That's good," she noted, taking a sip from her mug. "That could be very helpful."

"How do you figure?" he asked, blowing on his hot chocolate.

"If she's a romantic that gives me insight on how she sees her relationship with her husband. The better I understand that, the quicker I can dismantle it."

Doc took a drink of hot chocolate, nodded his approval, and then considered the larger picture. "This is so weird. I'm sitting here having hot chocolate with an angel, listening to Bing Crosby and plotting to break up a marriage."

"Plotting to separate a killer from his victim," she corrected.

"Why her?" he asked. "Why specifically help Farren? Why not help the starving child? Or, the terminal cancer patient? Or, the person who's been out of work for two years? Or, the victims of some madman's genocide?"

"How do you know that others *aren't* being helped?"

"Oh, c'mon," he scoffed. "You know perfectly well what I'm talking about. There's a lot of suffering and injustice in the world."

She smiled subtly, as if she'd heard the comment dozens of times before.

"There will always be suffering and injustice in the world. That doesn't minimize the danger that Farren is in."

"Yeah, but why?" he persisted. "Why does there *have* to be suffering and injustice in the world?"

"You want me to answer a question men have asked for centuries?"

"Well—*yeah*. I mean, when am I ever going to have another chance to talk to an angel?"

Clair took a long sip of her drink before answering. Her green eyes were still kind, but her tone was resolute. "Okay. First of all, I'm not God. Don't assume that because I'm in his service, I can speak for him. Second, I don't honestly know the answer to your question. But, I suspect it has something to do with this: If man doesn't have problems to solve, he never grows as a species. Third, even if I *did* know the absolute answer, I wouldn't tell you. That would only lessen the faith of billions of souls who've lived and died before you who didn't have the opportunity to talk with a celestial being. I won't dishonor them that way. Fourth, answering your question has nothing to do with the task at hand, which is to save Farren. Fifth—"

"Okay, okay!" he said, cutting her off. "I get it! You're not going to reveal any 'Great Mysteries' to me."

"No," she confirmed. "Not even the secret ingredient of my hot chocolate."

They were both quiet for several moments, perhaps as long as a minute, listening to the music, watching the fire, and drinking their drinks. With the lights from the small Christmas tree to the far right, next to the screened-in porch glowing warmly, the scene was downright cozy, and they both seemed to realize and relish it until Doc, in his quirky, irreverent way, broke the mood.

"So, Jesus and Mary Magdalene; did they ever—y' know?"

"*Doc!*" Clair protested.

"Sorry," he shrugged. "Just curious."

TWO DAYS EARLIER

Two days earlier in Southfield, Michigan, a suburb of Detroit, people hurried in and out of a Kroger grocery store that was in a strip mall off Telegraph Road, tending to their Saturday shopping. It was late afternoon, starting to get dark, and a typically gray Michigan winter's day, only more so because of the city setting and carbon monoxide in the air from the busy traffic on Telegraph.

The man in the dark blue Ford F150 pickup truck had been sitting in the parking lot looking things over and chain-smoking Winstons for a half-hour. He sized up the elderly African American man ringing a bell and standing next to a red Salvation Army collection pot chained to a tripod. He calculated the walking distance from the store's entrance on one side of the building to the exit, twenty-five yards away on the other side. The bell ringer was approximately in the middle of the two doors in front of thirty or so standing Christmas Trees lined up for sale. The man in the pickup truck checked the temperature. He watched to see if the strip mall had any private security force patrolling its parking lot. He monitored the traffic flow and timed the streetlights on Telegraph Road behind him. He noted that no Kroger employee was standing outside selling Christmas trees near the bell ringer. He listened to the rock 'n' roll station WRIF on his FM radio, and when the Rolling Stones' "Sympathy For The Devil" started to play, he smiled at the ironic timing.

Charlie Huffman was thirty years old and every bit as good-looking as Wyatt Reynolds. But, where Doc had darker features, Charlie was blond and Arian. Both had blue eyes and were fit, but Charlie was a little taller, had two-days' growth of beard on his square jaw, and his hair was shorter than Doc's. Although good-looking, he also had deep crow's feet at the corner of his eyes for a man his age—no doubt the result of too many cigarettes, Jack and Cokes, and long nights at the craps tables. He had a flinty squint to warn off strangers he didn't want to talk to, and although his hair was blond, it had also been black, brown and even prematurely white depending on the city and con he was running. Charlie Huffman thought about things like that: how he could change his appearance, where the nearest exits were in restaurants, and having an alternate license plate for his truck.

Taking a thirty-ounce soda fountain cup filled with water and ice he had gotten at a 7-Eleven, he climbed out of the truck into the biting air, leaving his cane in the front seat. His tan fabric coat that hit at mid-thigh and had a corduroy collar looked exactly like the coats of a half-dozen other men he had seen going into Kroger. It was anonymous. Charlie liked anonymous. To make himself even more so, he put on a Detroit Lions baseball cap and pulled the cap down low on his forehead.

He took one last deep drag from his smoke, dropped the butt on the gray concrete parking lot, then strolled toward the grocery store's exit. He tried his best to hide his limp—the result of having a little toe amputated by a loan shark's goon the week before—but it was still more noticeable than he would have liked. No matter, he told himself. It couldn't be helped. Having made his exterior observations about the store and surrounding area, he now focused in on a customer he could see through Kroger's large front windows. It was a heavyset Middle Eastern woman at register five who was nearly finished checking out. She was wearing a black pashmina hijab, a long scarf-like garment that covered her hair and framed her face under the chin. The cashier was ringing up the last of her purchases just as Charlie stepped onto the sidewalk by the exit.

Taking a quick glance at the Salvation Army bell ringer, who was wishing an entering customer a Merry Christmas at the other side of the store, he quickly poured the water and ice onto the sidewalk, then walked over and maneuvered around one of the standing Christmas trees as if he were looking it over. As he did, a young mother with a child wheeled her grocery cart full of bagged groceries through the sliding doors of the exit. The front wheels of the cart slid a little from the just-spilled water, but the mother quickly reacted and maneuvered the cart around the spill. It was another forty-eight seconds before the heavyset Arab woman came out. By then, the temperature in the teens had turned the water into a slick patch of ice. Unlike the nimbler, younger mother, the Arab woman had no grocery cart but instead carried heavy plastic bags of mostly canned goods in each hand. When her black tennis shoes stepped onto the ice, she slipped, went down quickly, and Charlie could hear one of her elbows crack into the concrete. A second later, she wailed like a scalded dog. When she did, the elderly African American bell ringer hurried over to assist. People in the parking lot hurried over, too. Everybody's attention was on the crying woman and her canned goods rolling this way and that. Nobody watched the man who emerged from behind the Christmas trees.

Moving with confident fluidity, Charlie stuck his empty cup into one of the trees, pulled a pair of heavy-duty wire cutters from his coat pocket, and clipped the chain securing the donation pot to its tripod. Looking neither right or left, he lifted the pot and carried it back across the parking lot to his truck, climbed in, started the engine, pulled out to Telegraph Road, waited another ten seconds to catch the green traffic lights in the direction he was going, then turned onto Telegraph and disappeared into the stream of flowing traffic.

Pulling into an alley behind another strip mall about three miles away, Charlie put his truck in park, used the wire cutters to cut the small padlock on the pot's lid, then opened it and looked inside. The season had brought out the generous side of shoppers. A large green pile of presidents—Washingtons, Lincolns, and even a couple of Hamiltons—stared up at him.

"Ho-ho-ho," he grinned snidely, pleased with the take.

There were also lots of coins, but he ignored that for now and grabbed the paper money. When the last bill had been stuffed into the pockets of his fabric coat, he unbuckled his shoulder harness, took the pot, and climbed out of the truck. Then he opened the aluminum toolbox in the bed of the pickup directly behind the cab and put the pot inside it, next to the four other Salvation Army collection pots he had stolen that week. Charlie Huffman worked for a living, but it wasn't as a project manager for a large contracting company. His livelihood was hustling, conning and stealing. Father Ken Pistole *had* seen him in Traverse City the day before, which was a six-and-a-half-hour drive north. But Charlie would have never acknowledged him. Besides not wanting to be caught in a lie about spending the week in Milwaukee, there was a woman who lived just outside Traverse City that he usually saw for a day or two every week, and he wanted to keep her and his play in Charlevoix separate.

Glancing up over the flat roof and air conditioning units of the strip mall, a billboard for a downtown casino in Greek Town caught his eye.

Timothy Best

He smiled to himself, deciding in an instant where his next stop would be.

THE MUSHROOM HOUSE

    Besides being situated between three beautiful waterways—Round Lake, Lake Charlevoix, and Lake Michigan—another distinguishing feature about the city of Charlevoix was the architecture of a deceased local man named Earl Young. From 1921 through the early 1970s, the diminutive Young built thirty elf-like homes in and around the town. These homes looked like they could have been plucked from a J.R. Tolkien Hobbit shire. The houses were small, sometimes rounded in shape although not in perfect circles, and the exterior walls were made from the abundant glacier-hewn boulders in the area. The more rounded homes had roofs that resembled mushroom caps. Most of these roofs consisted of thick wooden shingles, but resembled being thatched. Many had tall chimneys that were fat and wide at the bottom but narrowed as they reached for the snow-flaked sky. There was even a restaurant in town called The Weathervane that Young had been commissioned to build. The locals referred to these dwellings as "mushroom houses," for indeed, they looked like they had sprung up from some mutant spore.
    Farren Malone Huffman and her husband, Charlie, lived in one of these Earl Young-built houses. It was a cozy two-bedroom single-story that barely spread out to a thousand feet. From an overhead perspective, it was teardrop shaped. A wall ran nearly straight down the middle of the tear vertically from top to bottom separating the front of the house from the back. One entered through a door that was near the top of the tear, and this led into a living room that ran the entire length of the front half of the house. At the end of the living room was a concave fireplace with a

rounded wood mantel over it that curved in a slight "U" to match the shape of the wall. To the right of the fireplace, and, after a few feet of wall, was a doorway that led into a small master bedroom on the backside of the house. Next to that was another doorway that led into a bathroom, and next to that was yet another doorway that led into a spare bedroom. Then, there was a stretch of living room wall that had a sofa backed-up against it, and, opposite the front door, there was an open archway that led into a kitchen behind the wall with the sofa. Off the kitchen was a small laundry room. Instead of the standard eight-foot high ceilings, the mushroom house had ten-foot-high-ceilings, giving the rooms a more spacious look.

Farren had purchased the place when she turned twenty-five, leaving her grandfather, Gus, to occupy her parent's house on West Upright Street. She loved her grandfather, but as she became an adult, she also wanted the opportunity to live independently and escape the ghosts of the house where she was raised. Her grandfather understood this desire perfectly. He had lost his wife years earlier and had also felt the need to leave their home and the haunting memories behind.

At 6:30 p.m. on Monday night, just about the time that Doc and Clair were settling down in the front of the fire with Bing Crosby and hot chocolate, Charlie pulled his F150 pickup to the side of the road in front of his and Farren's mushroom house. It was unusual for him to be coming home on a Monday night. Normally, he was gone Monday through Friday, but the pickings for making money had been slim until the week's end, causing him to work into the weekend. Each week, Charlie had to come home with pay from a fictional job. His loan shark backer for the con, Bartholomew, had originally set him up with a bank account to act as take-home pay, but Charlie had already foolishly burned through that, and, considering what had just happened to his toe, he was afraid to ask for more.

Wearing the same green turtleneck and jeans she had on earlier in the day, Farren waved from the living room window where she was putting lights on a five-foot Scotch pine Christmas tree. There was a newly purchased wreathe with a large red bow on the front door, a Manheim Steamroller CD playing on the stereo, and Cornish hens roasting in the oven with their warm, seasoned aroma thick in the air. Although there was no fire burning in the fireplace, there were lit candles on the curved fireplace mantel next to some nicely framed old family photos. With the snow falling and the cold air making everything crisp and clear, Charlie was about to walk into a cottage-like home that seemed to come straight out of a Thomas Kinkade painting.

He waved back from the truck, putting on his game face. Truth be told, he liked certain things about his new wife: her consistently upbeat attitude, the way she embraced the marriage, and how hard she tried to please. He also enjoyed making love to her because, after all, she was attractive in a girl-next-door sort of way. But, the very things that appealed to Charlie in one way turned him off in another. Depending on his mood, Farren's consistently upbeat attitude could strike him as seeing the world through naïve rose-colored glasses. Her willingness to please could also be interpreted for weakness and a need to be led. And although she was sincere in bed, she didn't seem to enjoy his particular taste for rougher sex. But Charlie didn't analyze such things too much. He wasn't going to put his life on the line with Bartholomew for Farren or anyone else. He likened his wife to a three-dollar Blackjack table. He didn't mind playing, but the real action was over at the Caribbean Stud Poker table.

"Hey, baby," he greeted, coming into the house with a slight limp and setting down his cane and duffle bag.

"Hi," she said, going over to the front door. They embraced in a long kiss, then a tight hug. "God, I missed you this week," she sighed, the dimples on her face deep in a satisfied smile.

"I missed you, too," he said, softly. "It's great to be home." He looked around. "Everything's amazing; awesome tree, pretty girl, nice music, and something smells good in the oven."

"Cornish hens," she answered, releasing him from her arms. She picked up his duffle bag and took it into their bedroom. "How's your foot? How was your flight?"

"I'm using the cane only about half the time, and the flight was fine." He walked over to the tree and looked it over. "But I'm not around for long, so don't unpack my stuff. They want me at the home office in Flint tomorrow afternoon for a meeting, then I'll be gone the rest of the week."

"Oh, no," she moaned from the bedroom, disappointed.

"Yeah, I know. But everybody's scramblin' to get things done before the end of the year. We got any beer?"

"Of course. I'll get you one," she said, coming out of the bedroom. "Guess you already ripped off your tag, huh?"

"What?"

"The baggage claim on your duffle," she answered, passing the living room sofa and heading into the kitchen. "Guess you already took it off, huh?"

"Yeah, actually," he lied. "I did."

Being the professional con man he was Charlie knew how to change subjects quickly.

"Hey, got somethin' for you." He followed her into their small kitchen that was decorated mostly in Mackenzie-Childs-like black-and-white checks and produced a stuffed white envelope from his fabric coat pocket. He put it on the counter next to the refrigerator while Farren got out a bottle of Sam Adams and a pilsner glass from the fridge.

"See? Chilled," she said, referring to the glass and knowing it would please her husband.

"You're beautiful," he smiled, tossing his jacket on a nearby chair.

She poured the beer for Charlie, handed him the glass, and then picked up the envelope. "What is it?"

"Open it," he said, bringing the glass to his lips.

She opened the envelope and saw that it was stuffed full of twenty and fifty dollar bills.

"What's this?" she smiled.

"Fourteen-hundred bucks. Christmas bonus from Leo. Use it any way your heart desires."

Leo was a name Charlie had mentioned several times before. He was his fictional boss at the construction company, although she didn't know he was fictional.

"Wow," she smiled, impressed. "Honey, that's fabulous! He paid you in cash?"

"Tell you the truth, I think ol' Leo wanted the bonuses kept under the table from the government. We got any nuts?"

"Uh, sure," she said, stepping over to a cabinet and retrieving a can of Planters. "Well, the money is sure welcome. Especially since Leo's been irregular about paying you."

The truth was that the money Charlie scrounged up each week was the result of any number of events. Sometimes it was a card game where he cheated. Other times, it was a money-changing con where he would confuse a young cashier while they were breaking a twenty-dollar bill for him. In the middle of getting his change, he'd also produce a dollar and ask for quarters, then he'd quickly hand the cashier back a five from the twenty and ask for singles, *then* insist he had just given them a ten. He'd get the cashier so turned around, he always made money on the change he got back. Still other times, he'd just steal things outright like the Salvation

Army pots. Other things that he could get his hands on like smart devices, laptops, iPods, and watches he cashed in at pawnshops. Then, there were bets on the ponies, visits to casinos, and a half-dozen other dubious things he did.

The money he brought home varied from week to week, and going to casinos was, by far, the toughest thing for Charlie to do because it was so difficult to stop gambling and walk away when he was ahead. But then he'd remember the trouble he was in with Bartholomew and his recently separated little toe. Reminders like that helped to control his urges. An example was the fourteen-hundred dollars he managed to bring home. Although, at one point, his winnings in the Detroit casino two days earlier had been more than six grand.

"You know how the economy is," he shrugged. "Things are tough all over right now. Leo makes it up to me when he can."

She got a glass bowl for the nuts then poured some in.

"I guess so. But it would be nice to have a more predictable income and have you home more often. You know, I was talking to Larry Melzick over at Melzick Construction, and they're doing that big new hotel—"

"Baby," Charlie interrupted, grabbing a handful of nuts. "We've been through this before. Leo's been good to me and the economy *will* get better."

"Don't you want to get off the road and be in one place?" she asked.

"Would it hurt your feelings if I answered honestly and said, 'I don't know?'" he answered in between chews. "I've been doin' this for so long I don't rightly know if working in one place all the time would make me happy. Besides, aren't the homecomings worth the wait?"

Farren smiled, slipped on some oven mitts, then took the hens out of the oven.

"We've got to let these cool for a bit," she said, putting the tray of hens on top of the stove. "Dinner will be ready in about ten minutes if you'd like to wash up."

"Tell you what I'd like," he said, setting his beer down on a counter, wiping his salty hand on his jeans, then coming up behind her and wrapping his arms around her waist. "How 'bout a little snack before we have dinner?"

She knew what he was implying and smiled at the thought, but wanted to steer him in another direction. She also wanted him to brush his teeth. He smelled like peanuts, beer, and cigarettes.

"I've got a better idea," she said, slipping off her mitts, then turning to him and wrapping her arms tenderly around his neck. "How about a nice dinner, then let's finish putting the lights on our first Christmas tree, snuggle on the sofa, watch the snow and go to bed early."

"Sounds great," he agreed, smiling at her. "But a little snack to kick things off would make the evening twice as good."

He slowly but firmly took her arms from around his neck and started to pull them down toward the ground—meaning, he wanted her on the floor.

"Charlie, please, honey," she said, still smiling but uncomfortable. "Not now. Not in the kitchen."

"Been drivin' through the snow to get to you, baby," he said, softly. "Been missin' you all week, gave you every dime of my bonus, and I'm goin' back out tomorrow to hit it hard for you. Now, what're you going to do for me?"

Actually, she *had* done a lot for him. She bought the Christmas tree, went grocery shopping, made dinner, bought Charlie his favorite beer, chilled a glass, and put on music. Farren always had a tendency to do more. She didn't want to disappoint people. She was a caregiver. That was why she did so many things at the church. She gave so much because she wanted someone to treat her like she treated others, and except for her grandfather, Charlie came the closest to that ideal, although she knew he had his rough spots. She told herself, patience and giving was what married people did. She remembered those qualities in her parents. So, even though she really didn't want to, she forced a smile and allowed herself to be pulled down to the floor.

LUNCH

The Portside Marina was located off East Dixon Street and down a mostly dirt lane lined with closely planted rows of ten-foot-high Leyland Cypress trees on either side. Considered more of a shrub than a tree, the rows of sturdy cypress looked like scruffy frosted missiles standing upright. More than once, they had caused headaches for boat owners who were trying to haul a particularly wide boat down the lane to the marina.

The lane emptied out into a large square gravel parking lot that could hold as many as thirty cars. But on this particular day, there were only three. Lining the west side of the lot looking toward downtown Charlevoix and Bridge Street, were several empty boat trailers lined up side by side. To the east, toward Lake Charlevoix, were two buildings, a large red aluminum storage facility and the marina store. The store had a tan sandstone veneer and a slight A-frame to it that suggested it was built for a more upscale business. Two large ceiling-to-floor windows overlooked the iced-over Round Lake to the south. At the edge of the frozen shore were three long five-foot-wide concrete docks about twenty to twenty-five feet apart with several empty boat slips to the right and left of each. The middle dock had two Shell Gasoline gas pumps at its end, but they'd been turned off and covered for the winter.

Straight across from the docks, on the other side of the lake, a young mother was teaching her preschooler how to ice skate, and their giggling echoes carried all the way back to the marina. The entire complex sat on a point of land where the smaller, circular Round Lake fed into the much larger Lake Charlevoix. Back in the 1960s and early '70s, the sandstone veneer building had been a bar and twenty-two table restaurant called the

Portside Bar & Grill. Farren's parents bought the property, wisely kept the established "Portside" name, and turned it into a marina the same year she was born. Seventeen years later, after her folks died, her grandfather, Gus, came to live with her, was appointed her guardian, and helped her run the business.

The inside of the store no longer resembled a restaurant, although the counter and cash register were exactly where the bar had once stood. Now, it was a combination of a convenience and general store of nautical necessities. New Mercury outboards with shiny black cowlings sat authoritatively in stands next to glass coolers with sliding doors that sold soda, milk, and beer in season. There were five evenly spaced aisles of shelves that held personal floatation devices, ski ropes, water skis, wet suits, anchors, flare guns, lake charts, potato chips, toilet paper, cookies, and more. The outboards looked out of place and unusually large in their stands because most people saw them only in the water and rigged to the backs of boats with the shafts and propellers submerged. Although the store had a lot of different merchandise, everything shared one thing in common: It was a place where the promise of summer and good times out on the water lived. The smell of engine lubricant, neoprene wetsuits, and brass ship lanterns recently polished with Brasso came together in a symphony of aromas that appealed to even a land lover like Doc as he opened the front door and entered from the parking lot.

It was now Wednesday, two days after meeting Farren. By being here on a workday, he was breaking with his usual routine. Instead of going to lunch with Lance at Sadie & Jake's Gallery & Cafe on Bridge Street and being inundated with questions about James Bond films, he drove his gray Kia Spectrum over to the marina to have lunch with the woman he was supposed to protect who had accidentally put him in the hospital.

Besides the pleasant cacophony of smells in the store, he also heard a CD of the Ray Conniff Singers harmonizing about walking in a winter wonderland. As he looked around, he saw there were two other men in the store, both in their seventies. One was wearing a yellow golf shirt with a navy blue pullover sweater, black jeans and Sperry Docksider shoes that were out of season, considering the five inches of snow outside, yet they made perfect sense in a marina environment. The man was fit and trim, and Doc guessed this was Farren's grandfather. He had medium thick salt-and-pepper hair, stood about five-feet-ten and had a day or two of white stubble on his distinguished face that accentuated eyes as chocolate brown as his granddaughter's. There was no denying that he was a senior citizen, but he still looked ruggedly handsome. Just from a glance, it was obvious that every wrinkle, every white hair, every callous on this man was well earned. Doc figured he was a guy who had stories to tell. The other man was about the same height and age but much heavier and flabby. He wore a rust-colored stocking cap, a brown down-filled coat that was unzipped, and black rubber galoshes that were unbuckled and fanned out above his shins like he was wearing a shiny turkey on each foot. When Doc came into the store, the salesman and customer were in mid-conversation.

"I'm tellin' you, man," the fitter one said, "a four-stroke is going to give you better gas mileage, slower trawling speeds, and easier maintenance. You want the Honda."

"Four-strokes are too heavy, Gus," the other man complained. "They slow down the boat."

"They're not that heavy anymore," Gus argued. "If you wanna go faster and are concerned about weight, lose fifty pounds." He turned to Doc. "Be with you in a second."

He turned back to the man with the galoshes. "C'mon, Harley. It'll be the last outboard you'll ever need."

"You're probably only pushin' the Honda 'cause they're imported and you can charge more for parts and maintenance."

Gus looked at his customer unemotionally and blinked his brown eyes.

"Amazing, Harley, you figured out my plot to pay for the Porsche I ordered for Christmas."

"You got a Porsche?" the larger man asked earnestly, not realizing that Gus was being facetious.

The thinner one looked at his customer while biting his tongue and raised a finger.

"I'll be right back." He turned and walked passed a display of sunglasses toward Doc.

"Yes, sir?"

"Hi. I'm here to see Farren."

The older man noticed the paramedic patch on Doc's blue coat and the flesh-colored Band-Aid on his head peeking out in between the overhanging hair on his forehead.

"You're the guy she put in the hospital, right?"

"Yes," he nodded, with a small, embarrassed smile. "Doc Reynolds."

"Man, we are *so* sorry." He extended his hand. "I'm Gus Cooper. Farren's grandfather."

"Nice to meet you, sir. And, don't worry about it. Stuff happens."

Gus nodded toward his customer. "That over there is Harley Kimblemire." He raised his voice. "Who is about to make a serious mistake if he buys the Mercury instead of the Honda."

"I think Mercurys are better," Harley called back.

"You also think you saw an alien spacecraft in Bubba Martin's corn field."

"I *did*," Harley insisted. "It was silver and had these coil things and hissed!"

"It was Bubba's still," Gus answered, then he turned to Doc. "See what I'm dealing with? Farren's in the storage barn—the big red thing you passed on your way here. You've got to go back outside to get there."

"Thanks."

"Hey," Harley called, as Doc turned to leave, "ain't you the one who saved George Pratt's life with that mouth-to-mouth stuff?"

"Yes, sir," Doc said, turning back. "Mr. Pratt required mouth-to-mouth resuscitation when we arrived on the scene."

"Geez," Harley gawked, screwing up his pudgy face, "that didn't involve the tongue or anything, did it?"

Doc looked at Gus. "I see what you mean. Good luck."

The storage barn wasn't really a barn but a cavernous one-hundred-foot-long, forty-foot-wide, and thirty-foot-high red-aluminum pole building where some of the Portside Marina customers stored their boats in winter. It had two airplane hangar-like sliding doors on tracks that were twenty-five feet high, twelve feet wide, and electronically controlled. There was also a regular doorway next to the bigger ones, where people could enter and exit without having to open the hangar-like doors. Inside, on the concrete floor, was a snugly parked collection of boats. Some were on trailers while others sat in large steel-framed storage cages. The cages were twelve feet long by eight feet high and had two tracks of soft rubber wheels on the bottoms on opposite sides where boats were slid into place by a forklift with long rubber-sheathed arms. They were stacked in rows of two, and the cages were on the backside of the barn, the side farthest from the parking lot. In all, there were twelve cages, and ten out of the twelve were occupied with watercraft. Although Doc didn't know much about boats, he could see that boats of all types filled the barn. Some were inboards, and some were outboards. Some were cabin cruisers, and some were cigarette boats. Some were center-console fishing boats, and one, in a designated detailing area, was an old-fashioned teakwood pleasure boat that had just been refinished because large heaters were positioned around it, and the air was thick with an aroma of varnish. They had all been packed away like expensive sardines. So many boats tucked into one building was a testament to Gus and Farren's ability to maximize storage space.

Near the walk-in door where Doc entered was a workbench with a stool where motors could be serviced. It sat near a metal shelving unit filled with spare engine parts collected over the years. Hanging down from the ceiling on short chains was a series of ten fluorescent-tube lighting fixtures with two tubes in each. But these weren't enough to adequately illuminate the place, so the storage barn had some dark, shadowy places, except for the workbench area that had its own clamp-on light. One boat was, by far, the largest in the barn and, no doubt, was the last craft towed into place after the other boats had been secured. It sat almost in the center of the barn, but a little to the left, near one of the two empty storage racks and was on the largest boat trailer Doc had ever seen. Bigger than a weekend cabin cruiser, it was a small yacht, thirty-six feet long, and taller than two stories high from keel to bridge. Just above the hand-painted name on the stern that read, *Joyride*, Doc spotted Farren on the deck. She was wearing her red down vest with an old Central Michigan University sweatshirt underneath and blue jeans. She was also wearing a pair of white earmuffs and the tip of her nose was a little red as if she'd been working in the barn for a while.

"Ahoy," he called up to her. "Nice dinghy you've got there."

"Hey," she called with a deep dimpled smile. "How're you doing? How's your head?"

"A lot better, thanks. You ready for lunch?"

"It's nearly ready. Come aboard."

He looked at her not understanding. "Come aboard?"

"Yeah." She pointed to the starboard side. "There's a wooden ladder leaning up against the hull. You're not afraid of heights, are you?"

He walked around the stern to the side of the boat nearest the storage barn's giant sliding doors and saw an old extension ladder with pieces of carpeting duct taped to the ends leaning against the hull. Being a rock climber, he scrambled up the ladder effortlessly, swung a leg over the silver railing and stepped onto the stern deck.

"I thought we'd have lunch here instead of going out to some restaurant," she said. "I've got to run the batteries in this monster anyway. Hope you like lasagna." She walked over to the cabin and slid open a sliding glass door.

"C'mon. Galley's this way."

He followed her through the glass door and down three steps into a central cabin that was a combination living room, galley, and dining room. To the left was a comfortable cushioned sitting bench attached to the side of the hull with storage shelves beneath it. The bench could also extend out and, with an additional cushion, be made into a bed. To the right, was a half-circle booth-style eating area that could easily accommodate five people who could slide around behind the table. Beyond the table, separated by a partial wall, was the galley itself. It had a microwave, small stainless-steel refrigerator, sink, granite counters and built-in wooden cutting board. Mounted high in the partial wall separating the booth from the galley was a flat-screen TV/DVD player where diners could watch a movie if they wanted. Across from the galley was a head with a shower, and past the galley and head, going into the bow, was a stateroom with a queen-sized bed. The entire interior was tastefully done in Minnesota maple and complementary earth tones. Small overhead halogen lights provided the finishing touch and gave everything an art-gallery glisten. The cabin was considerably warmer than the barn, and the lasagna smelled inviting.

"Whoa," an impressed Doc said, looking around. "This yours?"

"If it were, I wouldn't be running a marina," Farren replied. "No, this belongs to the CEO of a bank over in Petoskey."

"What's something like this go for?"

"A Carver Mariner? Thirty-six feet, twenty thousand pounds, two-hundred-and-fifty gallon fuel capacity—between three and five hundred grand, depending on the age and features."

"You know your boats."

"That's my business." She took her earmuffs off, just as the microwave beeped, then slipped on a pair of oven mitts. "To tell you the truth, it's unusual for us to have a boat this size. Most of the bigger watercraft gets stored at other places. Still, we've got Pro Lines, Danzis, Boston Whalers, Lunds—you a boater?"

He shook his head. "Rock climber."

"It's just as well," she said, putting the lasagna on the counter. She took off the mitts, then opened a drawer to get some placemats. "What they say is true: A boat is an endless hole into which one pours money."

"Here, let me help," he offered. He took off his blue nylon coat, laid it on the sitting bench, then took the placemats from her and set them on the table.

"For me, it's books. I spend too much money on them, then never want to get rid of them. Oh, that reminds me—" he peeled open one of the Velcro sleeves on his pants pockets and pulled out a small book no larger than his palm.

"Here," he said, offering it to her.

She set two plates down on the counter she had just gotten out of a cabinet and looked at the book, intrigued. "What is it?"

"A collection of Jane Austen's favorite quotations. Either said by her in real life or by one of her characters in print."

She thumbed through the pages and smiled broadly. "This is very cool. Thank you!"

"It's not a gift. It's a loaner," he said. "I don't give gifts to married women who put me in the hospital. I'm funny that way."

She smiled again, then set the book down, opened a drawer and got out some forks and knives. Spotting napkins in a holder on the counter, he plucked up a couple.

"So, you're an EMT, like Lance?"

"Paramedic."

"That's right. Charlene told me. I'd forgotten. So why isn't an attractive paramedic like you, who collects books and reads Jane Austen, married?"

"Probably because I spend too much time reading books," he answered, liking the fact that she thought of him as attractive.

She handed him the silverware, then turned her attention back to the lasagna checking its steaming, cheesy top. "Did you ever come close?"

"To marriage?"

She nodded.

He paused before setting the table. "Once," he smiled, faintly.

She noticed the momentary faraway look in his blue eyes.

"Sorry," she offered. "It's really none of my business."

"No. It's fine. How about you? How do you like married life?"

"It's great," she said, a little too quickly and insincerely.

He chuckled. "You say, 'It's great,' like I say, 'It's fine.'"

She glanced up at him not sure whether or not she liked the observation. He saw it instantly.

"Sorry," he offered. "Never jump to conclusions," he reminded himself.

"No," she replied, cutting into then dishing out the lasagna, "it *is* great.

It's just—well—he travels during the week, and even though I knew that before we married, knowing it and living it are two different things. In a way, it feels like I'm still single, except now I buy beer on the weekends and spend a lot of time sweeping cigarette butts off my front step."

"'Happiness in a marriage is entirely a matter of chance.' It's a quote," he explained, gesturing to the book he had just loaned her.

"Charlotte Lucas said it in *Pride and Prejudice*, yes, I know. What would you like to drink?"

"What've you got?" he asked, smiling at her literary astuteness.

She opened up the stainless-steel fridge and peeked inside. "Coke or Mellow Yellow."

"Whatever you don't want. Either one is fine. So, what's the lucky guy's name? What does he do?"

"His name is Charlie Huffman," she said, closing the fridge, then getting some glasses. "He's a project manager for a large construction company."

"Cool," Doc acknowledged, carrying the plates over to the table. "What exactly does a project manager do?"

Farren popped open the soda cans and poured while answering. "Well, his construction company, Miller Construction, headquartered in Flint, has projects in several states. If one has trouble or falls behind schedule, Charlie goes in and works with the foreman, architects, engineer—whomever—to straighten things out. This week, he's in Toledo. Last week, it was Milwaukee. He flies in and out of Traverse City a lot."

"I see," he said.

She brought the glasses over to the table. "Smells great," he observed. "And you get an A for originality. After all, when am I ever going to eat on a boat like this again?"

"And all without seasickness," she added. She gestured to the half-circle table, and Doc slid into the booth-style bench. Before eating, Farren closed her eyes and said grace. Doc didn't close his eyes and pray with her, but he politely bowed his head until she said, "Amen."

"So, how did you two meet?" he asked, putting his napkin on his lap and picking up his fork.

"He came to town in early May looking for a place to keep his boat for weekend getaways. It's a nice little twenty-foot Stingray. Used, but in decent shape."

He took a bite of his food, said it was delicious, then continued his questions.

"So, Charlie brought his boat to town, and you got to know each other on the weekends?"

"Actually, when he first came to town with the boat, things were pretty slow at his company. He didn't have to travel anywhere for something like two whole months."

"He just hung out here, in Charlevoix?"

"Yep, stayed on his boat right here at the marina, although I think he froze his butt off. May can still be a pretty chilly month around here."

"That's how you guys got to know one another?"

"Uh-huh," she answered with her mouth half-full. "Then, when things got serious, he just moved here. I mean, he doesn't have to be based in Flint if he's travelling all the time."

"Hmm. Very convenient."

She arched a dark eyebrow, sensing a disapproving tone.

"What does *that* mean?"

He paused and looked at her innocently. "It means, 'Hmm. Very convenient.'"

"Sorry. I get a little defensive sometimes. My grandfather thinks everything happened too fast."

"Well, from 'How you doing' to 'I do' in five months *does* seem to be a little on the quick side. Unless, of course, you're Britney Spears or Kim Kardashian."

She smiled, fondly recalling. "It was crazy. I'd never done something so impetuous. I just jumped in."

"Jumping in is good," he concurred. "So long as you know where you're landing."

They fell silent for a few moments while they ate, except for Doc complimenting her again on the lasagna.

"So, what's your story?" she finally asked. "I remember Charlene telling me that you're originally from Michigan, but you've been living out west?"

"Jackson Hole, Wyoming, for three years," he nodded. "Although the locals only called it 'Jackson.' Before that, Sedona, Arizona, for three more."

"You were a paramedic in both places?"

"After I got recertified, yes."

"Interesting," she noted.

"What?"

"That you would choose to work in towns that were like Charlevoix, small, but get a lot of tourists."

"Why would that be interesting?" he queried, taking another bite of lasagna.

"Statistically, you'd treat more people who were visiting; people you were never going to see again or know." She stopped her analysis and smiled. "Of course, I'm not sure that's a valid observation, either."

"I never thought of it that way," he said. "I thought it was about me wanting to live in scenic places."

"And why only a few years in each place? She asked, popping another forkful of food in her mouth. "Are you one of those guys afraid of commitment? A gypsy soul?"

He raised his thick brown eyebrows, mysteriously. "Maybe I'm the kind of guy who can't hold a job. Maybe I've got a checkered past."

She paused from eating and looked him over.

"No," she smiled, instinctively knowing better.

"Maybe Charlie has," he threw in, nonchalantly.

Just then, his cell phone beeped loudly.

"Excuse me," he said. "That's my emergency ring tone." He connected the call. "Lance, what's up?"

"Where are you?" Lance asked. He had Doc on speakerphone in the ambulance and was driving through traffic on the other side of town with the siren screaming.

"Portside Marina. Why?"

"Portside Marina? You're about a quarter-mile away from a 911 we just got. A nine-year-old boy fell off a two-story roof on Nettleton."

"What?"

"One of the neighborhood kids said that Santa makes test runs before Christmas, and the kid went up on his roof to see if there were any sled and reindeer tracks up there. He got into the attic and climbed through a window while his mom was on the phone."

"What's the address?"

"Twenty-three. Family's name is Redman."

He looked at Farren. "Twenty-three Nettleton, do you know where that is?"

"Sure," she said.

"How far out are you?" he asked into the phone.

"Seven minutes, I was across town near Castle Farms."

"I'll meet you there." He ended the call, then rose and grabbed his jacket. "I don't know the town as well as Lance. There's a GPS in my Jeep, but it's in the shop."

"C'mon," she said, hurriedly rising. "Nettleton's only a minute away. I'll show you. What's going on?"

"A nine-year-old boy fell off a roof."

"Oh my God."

Two minutes later, they were off the boat, out of the storage barn, and in Doc's Kia. As they were leaving, Doc told Farren about what the neighborhood kids had said about Santa and test runs.

"My folks used to tell me the same thing," she remembered. "We used to wake up Christmas day at my grandfather's."

"Gus?"

She nodded. "He lived in Mount Pleasant, three hours away. We used to open my presents a day or so early, so my folks didn't have to lug them all over the state. Meaning, Santa came to our house during one of his test runs." She pointed. "Turn right, up here."

"Do you know these people? A family named Redman?"

"I can't connect any faces with the name. But I might once I see 'em. It's a small town."

"Is that the real reason we were eating on the boat?" he asked. "You were afraid of the gossip out in public? A married woman having lunch with a single man?"

She looked at him momentarily, but then was distracted by someone running across the street up ahead.

"That's got to be it over there," she said, pointing to two women kneeling in the snowy front yard of a house and a third quickly arriving carrying a blanket. They were all huddled around someone in the front yard of an old white Victorian two-story with a turret, large porch and black shutters.

"Steep pitch," Doc said to himself, eyeing the roof and slowing down. "Look," he said, turning to Farren, "does the sight of blood bother you?"

"I... I don't think so."

"All right," he said, coming to a stop in front of the house and putting the car in park. "If I ask you to do something, you do it without hesitation. Okay?"

"Okay," she promised.

He unbuckled his shoulder harness and she did the same. "Let's go," he said.

Hurrying over to the women, Doc introduced himself. "Hello, ladies,

I'm Wyatt Reynolds, a paramedic with the city. Everyone calls me Doc. The ambulance is on its way. I was having lunch with my friend, Farren, here when I got the call. Who's Mrs. Redman?"

"I am," a woman in her early thirties answered. She was attractive and petite with light brown hair in a bob, and her eyes were red and wet. Her nose was likewise red, and her hands and arms were shaking, the result of emotional stress, as well as being outside without a coat. "I was on the phone with my mother—just distracted for a minute—when Austin went upstairs to the attic. He *knows* he's not supposed to go up there without permission, but we'd been talking about Santa. Some of the neighborhood kids who go out of town for Christmas mentioned this thing about Santa making test runs and..." as the woman talked on, Doc was only half-listening. He saw the snowy scrape marks where the child had slid off the roof, and calculated the height from the gutter to the shrubbery below with its broken branches. Then he looked at the boy lying in the snow on his left side, wrapped in a blanket about seven feet away from where he figured he should have landed.

"Was he moved?" Doc asked, interrupting the mother who was still telling her story.

"He was impaled on some of the branches in the bushes where he landed," the mother explained. "A couple of branches are still sticking out of his back. I didn't know what to *do*," she said, fighting back a crying jag. "I know his spine could've been injured when he fell, and moving him is bad, but I couldn't leave him in the bushes with branches stuck in him like a pincushion."

"Of course not," Doc said, reassuringly.

"I brought a blanket," said one of the other two women. She was a redhead, the other woman was a blonde. Doc and Farren correctly assumed these were neighbors.

"The boy's in shock," the redhead continued. "So we wrapped him in a blanket. You're supposed to wrap accident victims in blankets." She looked at Farren. "My sister-in-law's a nurse," she said, with authority.

"You all did the right things," Doc confirmed. He stepped over to the boy who was apparently unconscious and knelt down beside him. He was petite like his mother and had medium brown hair.

"Hi, Austin. My name's Doc. Can you hear me?" The boy rolled his barely open eyes, but didn't verbally respond.

"I kept him home from school today because he complained of a sore throat," his mother explained.

"I'm going to look at your back for a second, okay, buddy?" Doc continued. "I'm just going to lift the blanket."

He raised the blanket. The boy was wearing a Transformers sweatshirt and had two branches, each about the size of a golf scoring pencil, protruding straight out from the right side of his back near the spine. He also had three other blood-soaked holes in the sweatshirt where branches jabbed into him when he landed. Seeing the sight of her child's blood in the snow and foreign objects sticking out of him, the mother started to cry. Doc lowered the blanket and cut her off with a business-like tone.

"Mrs. Redman, listen to me. If Austin's gone into shock, the blood flow in his body has slowed down, which is a *good* thing. Right now, I need information. I know you're upset. I know you're scared. But I need you to talk to me. Okay?"

The woman nodded while attempting to control her emotions. The blonde-haired neighbor put an arm around her shoulder for support. Doc reached under the blanket, then felt the victim's wrist while looking at his wristwatch.

"Is Austin allergic to any medicine that you know of?" he asked.

"No."

"Is he taking any type of medication now?"

"He... he had hot tea and Children's Tylenol this morning."

"That's all? He's not on any other type of regular medication?"

"No."

"Is there a history of diabetes or anemia in your family?"

"My mother's diabetic."

"Has Austin had any other serious injuries or surgeries?"

"No."

"Tonsils, appendix, broken bones, anything like that?"

"No."

"How about his blood type. Do you know it?"

"I think it's O-positive."

"Most people have O-positive," the redheaded neighbor said.

"That's right," the blonde-haired neighbor concurred.

Doc removed his hand from the boy's wrist. Then got out his small flashlight and opened one of the child's eyes to check pupil dilation.

"Let's be sure," he said. "Do you have his immunization records?"

"I...I think so."

"Good. It might be listed there, if not..." he turned to the two neighbors. "While Mrs. Redman is looking for those records, would one of you ladies call Austin's doctor? Once you've got the office on the line, hand the phone to Mrs. Redman, and she'll authorize for his medical records to be e-mailed to the emergency room. Also, if one of you has a cell phone, Austin's father should be notified and told to meet us at the hospital."

"I don't want to leave my baby," the mother said.

"This is what Austin needs right now," Doc replied. He looked at all three women, none of whom had bothered to put on coats. "And, please, ladies, put some coats on, too. Austin will need the adults around him strong and healthy."

"C'mon, Jessie," the blonde-haired neighbor said to the mother.

As the three women went inside, Doc turned to Farren. "Come here and hold his shoulder." While she moved in front of the child, Doc maneuvered around to his back and pulled the boy's blanket back. Reaching for the Buck Tool on his belt, he opened it to needle-nose pliers. "I've got to snap off those branches, so we can lay him flatter."

"Can't you just pull them out?"

"I could, but they've gone straight into his back like arrows and I don't know how deep they go in. By trying to pull them out in the field, I could actually do more harm than good. This might hurt the boy, so if he wakes up, make sure he sees a reassuring face and hold him firm.

"Understood," she said, placing a hand on the victim's shoulder.

Using one hand to steady the protruding branch, Doc broke off as much of the wood as he could with the pliers. The boy reacted with a sharp breath and moaned.

"You're doing fine, honey," Farren said to the youngster, soothingly. "Everything's going to be okay."

The paramedic quickly did the same with the other branch, then addressed Farren.

"I don't have my stethoscope and need to check his lungs. Come around by his head and slowly angle him back, but not so much where the branches in him are touching the ground."

"Right," she said nervously.

While she repositioned herself then gently turned Austin, Doc put his ear on one side of the boy's chest to monitor one lung, then the other. As this was happening, the victim slowly opened his eyes.

"M...mommy," he called weakly.

"Mommy's coming right back, sweetie," Farren said, looking down at him and smiling; although from his perspective, she was upside down.

The youngster's eyes drifted from Farren, down to Doc still with an ear on his chest, then to his left.

"Who's that?" he asked.

"That's Doc," Farren answered. "He's going to get you to the hospital. Right now, he's listening to your breathing, so let's be quiet for just a moment."

"No, *him*; the scary man out there."

Farren looked across the Redman's front yard. No one was there.

"Is it a man in a long dark overcoat?" Doc said, raising his head. "Thin, long white hair? Kinda looks like Mr. Filch from the Harry Potter films only with a lot of cuts on his face?"

The boy nodded, concerned.

"Ah, it's nobody," Doc shrugged. "Just the garbage man." He turned around and spoke to the empty lawn as if someone were there. "There's nothing to see here. Austin's going to the hospital and he'll be fine. You understand me? He'll be *fine*."

Farren looked at Doc, then in the direction of where he was talking, but wisely decided not to say anything.

"Austin, can you tell me where you hurt?" Doc asked.

"I want my mommy," the child whined.

"She's coming right back," he reassured. "I promise. Can you tell me where you hurt?" He turned his back to the boy and pointed to his kidney region. "Here?"

"No. M...more in the middle?"

"High middle, or lower middle?" Doc asked.

The boy thought for a moment. "J...just the middle."

"Okay." He turned back around and looked at Farren. "Let's get him on his side again."

Just then, they heard a siren approaching in the distance.

"Hear that?" Doc asked. "That's your ride to take you to the hospital where you're going to feel a *lot* better."

"The man is still there. I want my mommy!"

"Didn't I tell you? She's going to come, too. Ride with you in the ambulance," Doc said, ignoring Austin's previous comment.

"The scary man is still over there!" the child cried, tears welling in his eyes.

"Austin, listen to me," Doc reassured, with a little urgency. "I'll take care of the scary man. He's not going to come any closer. He's not going to hurt you! I promise!"

"It's O-negative," Mrs. Redman called, coming out the front door and now wearing a coat. The neighbors behind her were also wearing coats.

"You're *sure* it's negative?" Doc asked, covering the boy again.

"Yes, I just got off the phone with his doctor."

He frowned, not liking the news.

"What?" Farren asked.

"A lot of people have O-positive. But O-negative is more rare, and Austin's going to need a transfusion. He's lost some blood."

"Then we're in luck," she replied. "He's just my type."

"You're O-negative?"

She nodded.

"You positive?"

"No. Negative," she smiled.

He smiled back as Lance pulled up in front of the house. "Okay," he said, getting to his feet. "Be right back. Mom, talk to Austin. He's awake." He turned and started to jog across the lawn toward the ambulance. As he went, he looked in the direction of the scary man the boy had seen in the long dark overcoat.

"Not today, you son of a bitch," he muttered under his breath.

PROGRESS

It was a little after 4:00 p.m. when Doc's Kia pulled into the lane that led to the Portside Marina's parking lot. The sun was already sinking low over Lake Michigan and during the short drive back, Doc and Farren had been mostly silent. Oddly enough, however, neither one was bothered by this or felt the need to fill in the quiet with frivolous chatter. They seemed to be naturally comfortable with each other without talking, and this was something both of them noticed.

Pulling up to the smaller doorway of the storage barn and next to Farren's frost-covered mustard-colored VW Beetle, Doc put the Spectrum in park, looked at his companion, and smiled.

"You did good today."

She gestured to the paramedic patch on his blue nylon coat. "You do good every day."

He shrugged. "It's a job."

"It's a calling," she corrected. "It makes a difference in people's lives. Let me ask you something. Who did Austin think he saw out there on the lawn?"

"The bogey man, angel of death, the ferryman that takes us to the other side," he answered, nonchalantly. "Some people see a bright light, some have out-of-body experiences, others see a scary man in a dark overcoat."

"Do you ever think he's really there?"

"I didn't used to. I thought it was a common delusion with trauma patients. But, these days, I'm not so sure."

She looked at him for a moment, weighing whether or not she wanted

99

to ask about something else, then decided she did.

"What did you mean about Charlie having a checkered past?"

"What?"

"Just before you got the call about Austin, you said that maybe you had a checkered past. I said, no you didn't, and you said maybe Charlie did. Why did you say that?"

"I ... I was just making conversation," he said, deflecting an intentional slight aimed at her spouse, but a slight that was still the truth.

She nodded, was quiet for a moment, then looked around at the fading pink light of the day. "The thing is, you could be right. Charlie seems to be a man of secrets. Don't misunderstand me, I love my husband, and I'd never do anything to dishonor our vows. But—" she stopped and shook her head. "God, why am I even telling you this? Never mind." She put her hand on the door handle, intending to leave.

"Wait," he said. "I think you want to tell me something because you saw today how fragile life is. Besides, sometimes it's easier to talk to a stranger. I mean, we're not strangers, but we did just recently meet. So, if you want to share something, I'm under Hippocratic Oath to keep it confidential."

"Paramedics take a Hippocratic Oath?"

"I will for you."

She smiled faintly, then took a moment to organize her thoughts. "Charlie might not go where he says he does."

"I don't understand."

"There's never any tag on his luggage, and his bag is too big for carry on. You know how, when you check your bag at the airport, they put a destination tag on it?"

He nodded.

"There's never any tag on his luggage. He says he tears it off right away when he gets his bag, but I never see any boarding passes or itineraries, either. A few days ago, my pastor thought he saw him in Traverse City on a day he was supposed to be in Milwaukee. Then, there's his pay. It varies wildly from week to week. I know things are up and down in the economy right now, but ..." She shook her head. "I don't want to be one of those suspicious wives who are always asking their husband to prove things. I don't want to comb through cell phone bills or pilfer his pockets looking for reasons to be hurt. Then, there's my Grandfather. He really doesn't like Charlie. We eloped and it really hurt him. I had no idea how much it would."

"I see," Doc said, taking everything in and not believing his good fortune. Farren had just shown him the proverbial cracks in the floor. She was revealing doubts, even if they were small, about her husband. Clair had never mentioned that she might have concerns like this, and he figured it made his job a *lot* easier. Still, he told himself to play things cool.

"Seems to me there's a simple way to calm your fears."

"What's that?" she asked.

"Besides just talking with Charlie, you say he flies in and out of Traverse City Airport. Just drive there one day, when he's gone, and see if his car is in the long-term parking lot. TC is only an hour away. Better yet, check the mileage in his car from week to week. It's easy to calculate the distance from Charlevoix to TC and back."

"He drives a pickup" she corrected, "and those are exactly the kind of suspicious antics I *don't* want to do."

"They aren't antics," he reassured. "You're newly married, and you've known your husband for less than six months. This is just a little self-assurance about your life partner that you can probably laugh off and forget about in the future. Just because someone gets married, that doesn't mean perfect trust is built in. We're human. Trust is built over time, day by day, conversation by conversation. But it's harder to build when a couple is constantly apart. It's not impossible, just harder."

She brushed her dark pixie-like bangs off her forehead. "I'm sorry. I guess I'm just a little tired after giving blood. Forget I even said anything."

"It's okay, Farren. That's what friends do. They talk about stuff. Hey, I've got an idea. I haven't done any Christmas shopping yet for my mom, dad, sister, or brother-in-law—why don't we both take a day off, drive over to Traverse City, and if we happen to go by the airport, we happen to go by the airport."

She smiled politely, then clicked open the door. "Let me think about it."

"It would be nice to spend some time together where we didn't wind up in the emergency room," he added.

"I'll think about it," she said, climbing out.

"Thank you for lunch."

She leaned down while the door was still open. "By the way, I wasn't afraid of gossip or being seen with you in public. I just thought eating on *Joyride* would be a nice and different type of lunch."

"It *was* very nice and very different. Thank you," he smiled.

She smiled back at him, shut the door, then walked toward the marina store, instead of the storage barn.

Four hours later, just after 8:00 p.m., Doc and Clair were doing dishes back at Doc's cabin, she was washing, and he was drying. This had been Clair's best recuperation day yet. She had gone almost seven hours without changing into anything, and when she did—today it had been a llama—she was only in animal form for a half-hour. Even better, the transformation occurred just as she was about to step into the shower, so none of her clothes were torn up by the change. Meanwhile, all of her cuts and bruises were gone, and she'd vomited only twice while her host had been at work.

Her appetite was steadily improving, too. Doc made a London broil with mashed potatoes and green beans for dinner. It was her heaviest meal since the accident, but she seemed to digest it fine. Earlier that day, she had even bundled up and taken a short walk along the shoreline of Lake Charlevoix. She spoke enthusiastically during dinner about how wonderful the uneven and frozen sand felt on the soles of Doc's borrowed boots, the taste of the sharp air in her lungs, and the comforting sight of the ice-fishing shanties dotting the edges of the lake. He rolled his eyes over her love for the ordinary. She also spoke of how nicely and quickly things seemed to be evolving with Farren. "Fantastic progress," she called it. But, the more positively she spoke about things, the more moody and reticent he seemed to become.

Realizing his attitude was worsening, he excused himself after the dishes were done, put on his WWII bomber's jacket and heaviest boots, and went for a walk. As his houseguest had done earlier, he wound up down at the shoreline, staring at the motionless, marble-glazed water. He heard snowmobiles off in the distance, buzzing through the night like large winter insects, but couldn't tell if the vehicles were on land or out on the lake. He looked up at the sky and was grateful for the partial break in the cloud cover. The previous year, Charlevoix had gotten more than a hundred and ten inches of snow, and he wondered what the accumulation would be this year. He saw a shooting star quickly dart from east to west. Whenever he saw one, he thought of Julia and how she loved to make wishes on them. But thinking of her made his melancholy worse. He intended to keep walking until his mood improved, but within twenty minutes, the cold had forced him to return to the cabin.

Stomping his boots on the mat in the kitchen, he saw that Clair had made a fire for him. During the past few nights, they had developed an evening routine of conversation, Christmas music, fires, and hot chocolate. One night, they talked about the books in the unpacked boxes Doc kept over by the writing desk. Clair had poked through them one day and wanted to know about everything from a used textbook called, *Anatomy & Physiology*, to another called, *Medicine In The Field*. Another evening, they talked about Christmas music and singers, where she had said one of her favorites was Rosemary Clooney. The evening conversations were also sprinkled with talk of Farren, Clair's health, and how wonderful creation was in general. On still another night, Doc had even asked about reincarnation, but all Clair had said was, "Yes, interesting notion," giving him no further insight one way or another. Their conversations were a verbal dance of sorts. Doc was always trying to subtly extrapolate information about the different plane of existence that Clair came from, while she seemed to want him to demonstrate a certain reverence toward God that he was never willing to give.

"An excellent day, today," she began, after Doc had slipped off his jacket and walked into the living room. She was sitting on the leather sofa near the writing desk with, as usual, her feet tucked up under her ready for their verbal dance to begin. But Doc was in no humor for it tonight.

"You think?" he asked quietly.

"The two of you worked together to save that little boy's life, Farren revealed that she has doubts about her husband, and we now know her grandfather—obviously a perceptive guy—has issues with Charlie. This is all very, very good progress."

He walked over to the fireplace, glanced briefly at the Elk's head hanging on the fieldstone, then looked at the healing rat bite on his hand. Next, he looked at the fire. He sunk his hands deep into his pockets but didn't sit down.

"Yeah," he finally said, "let's leapfrog over Austin Redman's two cracked vertebrae, probable nerve damage, five serious puncture wounds, nicked lung, and congratulate ourselves on making progress with Farren today."

She looked at him quizzically, her long golden ringlets shining in the firelight. "You think that little boy was *made* to fall, so you could spend time with Farren?"

"I think your boss sucks," he said, flatly. "You're watching over Farren, but who was watching over that kid? All he wanted to do was see if there were sled and reindeer tracks on his roof. He was just being a kid. And *now*, because of it, he'll spend weeks in the hospital, need back surgery, need weeks of physical therapy—"

"But he'll make a full recovery," she interrupted. "You said so, yourself."

"I said his doctor was 'cautiously optimistic' for a full recovery. That's not the same. And why did he have to be scared half to death by some vision? Who is that guy, anyway?"

Clair looked at him for a moment before answering, trying to gauge his attitude. "What do you want me say, Doc? Bad things happen. Scary things are out there. Free will gets exercised, yes, even in nine-year-old boys, and there are consequences. That's one reason why it's called Earth and not heaven."

"Your boss sucks!" he repeated, more emphatically. "And you can tell him I said so."

"I don't have to. He can hear you."

"Good!"

She looked at him for a moment, but he ignored the gaze of her green eyes and stared at the dancing flames of the fire. Then, she slowly closed her eyes, brought her open palms to her face, lowered her head, and placed her face in her hands. A few moments later, he noticed.

"What's wrong? You feel ill? You need to throw up?"

She stayed motionless with her face in her hands for another ten seconds, then slowly raised her head and looked at him.

"Several thousand years ago, a star exploded on the far side of your galaxy. The light from this explosion won't even be visible on this planet for another sixteen years, and even then, only through the most powerful of telescopes. But, this discovery will be another piece in the puzzle of man understanding his universe. It will be a discovery that, along with hundreds of others, will expand man's knowledge and, eventually, this knowledge will greatly benefit deep space explorers and colonists. The man who will discover this exploding star will be a twenty-five-year-old graduate student named Austin Redman. It'll be the first of several important discoveries he'll make. And, all because, when he was nine years old, he fell off a roof, and while he was recuperating, his uncle bought him a telescope."

Doc took his hands out of his pockets and sat down on the leather sofa across from her, intrigued.

"Is all that for real? Did … did you just pray about it and get an answer?"

"No," she replied with a little smile. "I made it up. But the point is, there are bigger things in play here than you can possibly imagine. Just because you have the ability to question God doesn't mean you're entitled to know his intentions, or would even understand them if you did."

"Why not?"

"Because you're not him. Because man uses only one-third of his brain, because God requires faith, and because faith is *work*."

He stood up again, not liking being fooled, jammed his hands back in his pants pockets and turned to the fire.

"'God is a concept by which we measure our pain.' John Lennon," he quoted.

"'We walk by faith, not by sight.' Second Corinthians," she answered back.

"'Prayin' to a God that I don't believe in,' the Script," he said.

"'Seek and you will find.' Matthew, chapter seven," she retorted.

"'That's me in the spotlight, losing my religion.' R.E.M.," he shot back.

"'Trust in the Lord with all your heart and lean *not* on your own understanding.' Proverbs, chapter three."

"'I send up my prayers wondering who's there to hear?' Joni Mitchell."

"'God does not listen to sinners. He listens to the Godly man that does His will.' John, chapter nine."

He thought for a frustrated moment, then, not being able to think of anything relatable, quoted the first thing that popped into his mind.

"'It's ... it's fun to stay at the YMCA!' Village People."

She stood up, exasperated. "I'm sorry you're not getting the answers you want, Doc. But, it's not my job."

"Just what *is* your job, Clair? Oh, I forgot, *I'm* doing your job!"

She looked at him angrily, then headed toward the bedroom. "I think we'd better call it a night. I'll pray very hard for Austin Redman, as hard as I possibly can."

When she got to the bedroom doorway, she turned back to him. "But Doc, make no mistake about this: Don't you *ever* say what you said about my Lord—*your* Lord—again. 'Blasphemy against the Holy Spirit will *not* be forgiven.' Luke, chapter twelve. Matthew, chapter twelve."

He opened his mouth to speak, but then thought better of it.

They looked at each other for another moment, and then Clair shut the bedroom door.

INVITATIONS

Thursday, December 8, had been a full week since Doc Reynolds, from Ann Arbor, and Clair, from heaven, had run into one another. By all outward appearances, the curvaceous golden-haired houseguest with the vibrant green eyes and Nordic cheekbones seemed to be healed. Inside her, however, regeneration, as she called it, was still taking place.

It was another busy day for Lance and Doc as they worked amidst the ivory-painted landscape of northern Michigan. It began with transporting a deceased body from the hospital to the Winchester Funeral Home. It was an eighty-two-year-old woman who had suffered a stroke in the hospital, and the city was helping out with transportation, since the funeral home's hearse was in the shop. Next, there was a snowmobiling accident off M66. Then, in the afternoon, a man in his early twenties had to be taken to the hospital for exposure to the cold. He was in the middle of an argument with his wife when she threw his favorite bowling trophy out of their mobile home. When he foolishly went outside to retrieve it, wearing only a bathrobe and slippers, his wife locked him out. Too proud to make a scene, and living out in the country, the man walked for almost three miles to his brother's house.

The longer the day went on, the more depressed Doc seemed to become. He worked himself into one of those "What's-the-point-to-it-all?" kind of moods. He had wondered for years about whether or not God even existed—and had just about made up his mind that he didn't—prior to meeting Clair. He wondered about all the random and bad things that God allowed to happen in the world. There was no rhyme or reason to it, at least none that he could see. He also wasn't normally conflicted about his job, but he was today. Every time a seasonal song, Christmas tree in a window, or even a plastic front-yard Santa reminded him that this was the happiest time of the year, he also remembered that, as a paramedic, he was constantly fighting unhappiness—unhappiness and pain. The battles went on regardless of the holidays, and even if he won a couple, he was enlisted in a war without end.

Having had harsh words with Clair the night before, he decided to give himself some distance and have dinner in town. Since he always used his cell, he never had the landline connected at the cabin, so there was no way of letting her know that he was going to be late. The idea of her waiting there, maybe staring out the window and expecting him like some sort of otherworldly pet, bothered him. But in another way, he liked the idea of exercising his free will and independence. He didn't feel like he had been able to do so since they met. Still, by the time the workday was done, he was feeling guilty about not going home when she would normally expect him, so he split the difference. He decided to go home late, but also pick up a few new things for her.

Declining yet another dinner invitation from Lance and Charlene, he went shopping down on Bridge Street after work and bought two more women's tops, two pair of slacks, some casual brown shoes, a pair of dressier black shoes with slight heels, and a make-up sampler tray with base, eye shadow, brushes, and lipstick. He also bought a sleep shirt that, ironically, had chubby winged cherubs on it. He didn't want to buy too much more because he didn't know when Charlie intended to make his move against Farren, and consequently, how long Clair would be around. He also didn't want to buy anything more because he couldn't afford to. He lived on a city employee budget and wondered if maybe heaven had some sort of expense department to which he could submit receipts. But then, he figured, probably not.

About 7:10 p.m., as he was passing Van Pelt Alley, he noticed all the people doing Christmas shopping downtown. During summer and fall, the downtown area buzzed with tourist activity right up until 10:00 p.m. But things died down dramatically in winter. So to see people bustling here and there, and all apparently in good cheer like a scene from a Dickens novel, lightened his heart—until, that is, he noticed everyone around him seemed to be either a couple or a family. He watched one couple walk by holding hands. Then saw another arm in arm. He spotted small children either hanging onto a mom's mitten-covered hand or riding on a dad's shoulder. All of this togetherness made him feel isolated and apart. His thoughts wandered, as they always inevitably did, back to Julia. He wondered about the children they might have had. How many? What gender? How old would they now be? The lost possibilities were tortuous for him.

It wasn't any better when he went into the Crow's Nest Bar & Grill. The place seemed to be packed with couples or families. Alan Jackson sang about his daughters on the jukebox, and the usual smell of beer and peanuts was occasionally interrupted by the whiff of some kid's baby shampoo or Watermelon Bubble gum. Spotting an empty booth with a table that was still beading water from having just been wiped down, he cast his eyes toward the wooden floor and moved anonymously through the bar, his boots crunching the discarded peanut shells as he went.

He sat down, ordered a beer, and had his face buried in a menu when he heard a voice ask, "How's that little boy who fell off the roof?"

He looked up to see Farren's grandfather, Gus, standing at the booth. He held a nearly empty beer bottle in one hand while a couple of fingers on his other hand were hooked to the collar of his suede winter coat slung over his shoulder.

"Gus. Hey, how are you?" Doc greeted. "Sit down. You had dinner?"

The older man slid into the booth seat opposite him. Except for a different color golf shirt, he looked exactly as he had the day before, right down to his two-day growth of white stubble and Sperry Docksiders.

"Thanks, but I've eaten. Now I'm workin' on dessert," he said, taking the last swig from his longneck. "So, how's the kid?"

"I spoke to his doctor today. He's concerned about nerve damage. He was going to confer later with a specialist at the University of Michigan. My guess is he'll be flown down there in the next couple days."

"That's tough," Gus noted, empathetically. "But, it's a good thing Farren happened to be with you when you got the call so she could give blood."

"Very true."

The waitress came and took Doc's dinner order while Gus ordered another beer. By the time she left, the Alan Jackson song had finished, and Burl Ives had replaced him singing, "Holly Jolly Christmas."

"Odd time of the year for us single men, huh?" Gus observed, looking around the place at all the families and couples.

"But a great time for kids," Doc noted.

"How's your head?" Gus asked, gesturing to the Band-Aid still on Doc's forehead.

"Fine. Which reminds me, where's Farren? She told me her husband works out of town during the weekdays, so I just figured you two probably had dinner together a lot."

"Our relationship has changed since she got married."

"Mind if I ask why?"

"Let me ask you something, first," Gus said, scratching the label off his empty beer bottle with a thumbnail. "What's your interest in my granddaughter? I mean, we both know she's pretty as a picture. But she's also married."

"Fair question, I guess," Doc admitted. "My interest is, I'd never met your granddaughter until she whacked me with that door. When I woke up in the hospital, she was there, and an invitation to lunch was extended. Actually, that's not entirely true. She asked me a question, we bet a lunch on my answer, and I won. That's it. End of story."

"What was the question?"

"What was the original title of Jane Austen's book, *Pride and Prejudice?*"

"And you *knew* that?"

"I did."

"Yeah," Gus figured, "she *would* be impressed with somethin' like that."

The waitress brought the beers, a Budweiser for Doc and a Moosehead for Gus. As she walked away, Gus picked up his beer in a toast. "To bachelors surviving the holidays."

"And, any grandmas run over by reindeers," Doc noted, referencing the silly seasonal song.

They clinked bottles and drank. Then Gus answered Doc's previous question.

"You ever meet someone where you knew something wasn't kosher? Even though you couldn't put your finger on it?"

"A bad feeling, sure."

"That's how I feel about Charlie. Maybe I'm just an old, overprotective fart, but he's always made my antenna go up. And then, when he and Farren ran off and eloped after only knowing each other for less than six months, frankly, it teed me off. It was so out of character for her."

"She's a grown girl," Doc reminded him. "Well past twenty-one."

"True. But I'm the only immediate family she's got," Gus said, taking a quick swig from his bottle. "I changed my life for that girl; raised her since she was seventeen. I'm not one to be calling the kettle black about eloping. I mean, hell, I did it myself. But I deserve better than being told about it after the fact. It's not like I had these visions of her being married in a church, but I *did* think things would go down differently."

"Did you talk to her about it?"

"Sure. And she's apologized a bunch. But she still married the guy too quickly and, even if they had dated longer, I just can't warm up to him."

"So, there are really two things we're talking about here," Doc clarified. "You don't like Charlie, and, even though Farren's apologized repeatedly, you don't like that she eloped even though *you* did."

"Yeah? So?" Gus said, a little defensive. "I can be contradictory and have more than one thing buggin' me if I want. I can have a hundred things bug me if I want. People in their twenties who call everything 'amazing,' or sixty-year-old men that marry thirty-year-old girls, or women that put on makeup while they're driving."

"You certainly can, Gus," the younger man smiled, taking a drink of Bud. "You say you changed your whole life for Farren. If you don't mind me asking, what do you mean?"

"I used to live in Mount Pleasant. Farren's parents, my daughter Jackie and her husband, Paul, drowned when their sailboat capsized in a sudden storm on Lake Michigan. I quit my job and came back here to take care of Farren and help run the marina. She'd already lost her parents, so I wasn't going to uproot her from her home, school and friends. She really knew her stuff at the marina. But, who was going to do business with a kid? I've always been good with engines, so I learned about boats and put a more mature face on the business to help her out until she came into her own."

"I'm sorry," Doc said, sincerely. "Losing your daughter and son-in-law, moving into their house, having to clear out their stuff, changing your life; it must have been tough."

"*Damn tough*," Gus agreed. "Damn tough," he repeated, more quietly. "But it wasn't my first roundup with loss. Besides, Jackie and Paul loved the water, loved sailing. At least they died doing what they loved. Every sailor knows there's risk out there. Did you know storms on the Great Lakes can be more treacherous than storms on the ocean?"

Doc nodded. "The lakes are smaller and not as deep. So dangerous waves can rise up faster and catch boaters off-guard with little or no warning."

"You a boater?"

"I read. What did you do in Mount Pleasant?"

"I was a teacher at Central Michigan University. I was qualified to teach sociology. So naturally, they had me teach Theology of Western Religions."

Doc's eyes widened with interest. "Theology? Then, you would know about Christian icons and symbols. Like, like angels."

"Yeah, I guess. You interested in angels?"

Just then, the waitress brought Doc his dinner. He'd ordered a basket of fish and chips. But after she had delivered the food, he showed only marginal interest in his dinner in lieu of what Gus might know.

"How long have angels been around? Been part of recorded history?"

Gus took a drink from his beer, thinking. "The word 'Angel' comes from the ancient Greeks. It means, 'Messenger of God.' Angels were written about in the Old Testament, and they've also been mentioned in different texts upon which both Christian and non-Christian faiths base their principles. In Islam, for example, an angel is supposed to have brought the Koran to Mohammad. So, they've been around for many, many centuries."

"Do you think they're real?" Doc asked, picking up a French fry and munching on it.

"Well, if they're not, a lot of people have been wrong for a lot of years."

"That's not what I asked. Do *you* think they're real?"

The older man thought for a moment, stroking the short hairs on his chin.

"Teaching about stuff and believing in stuff are two different things ... Hell, I don't know. Depends on what day it is and how much I've had to drink."

"How many types of angels are there?"

"Wait a minute," Gus said. He raised his head, glancing around the bar. Finally, he spotted who he was looking for. "Hey, Ken. Ken! C'mere."

Father Ken Pistole rose from a booth across the bar where he was eating pizza with a family and came over. His white beard was neatly trimmed and much thicker than Gus' stubble. He was ten years younger than Gus but, being much more rotund, was in poorer physical shape. Instead of his clergyman's collar, he was wearing a casual shirt with a double extra-large Notre Dame sweatshirt over it.

"You two know each other?" Gus asked.

The priest looked Doc over, noting his uniform and the patches on his coat.

"Well, obviously, you're with the city. But no, we haven't formally met."

"Ken, this is Doc. Doc, this is Ken. He's the head papal pusher over at Saint Ignatius and can tell you anything you want to know about angels."

"You're a priest?" Doc asked, surprised because of the casual dress.

"Yeah. But he's still an alright guy," Gus offered.

"Scoot over, Cooper," Father Ken said. Gus slid over and the larger man sat down. "What's all this business about angels?"

Both men looked at Doc inquisitively. After a few silent seconds, he cleared his throat and took a swallow of Budweiser, feeling self-conscious.

"Uh, well, as a paramedic, I deal with badly injured people all the time. And, sometimes, people say they, y' know, see things ... like, like angels. Which got me to thinking: How many different types of angels are there? See?"

The two men sitting across from Doc glanced at one another, then Father Ken apparently decided to accept the rationale.

"In the sixth century, a theologian named Dionysius gave angels their rankings."

"Historians have argued for centuries whether or not these rankings were divinely inspired," Gus added, "or, was ol' Dionysius just anal and needed to organize things."

"Dionysius divided angels into three classifications," the priest continued, "or, 'choirs.' The First Choir attends to God, the Second Choir attends to the natural world—the sky, the sea, the stars—and the Third Choir attends to man. In each choir, there are three classifications, from Seraphim and Cherubim in the First Choir, all the way down to Archangels and plain ol' Angels in the Third. So, according to Dionysius, that would make nine different types."

"Meaning, if people you treat are saying they see angels, those would be from the Third Choir. The choir that attends to man," Gus concluded.

Doc nodded, thinking.

"Aren't you going to eat your fries?" Father Ken asked.

"Help yourself," Doc answered, still thinking.

"Do you mind if I ask what religion you are, son?" the priest queried, plucking up a couple of fries.

"I was baptized Catholic, but I haven't been to church in a long time."

"Well, you're in good company," the clergyman said. "Neither has

Gus. But, there's hope for you boys yet if you're talking about angels instead of the figure of some waitress. Here's an idea: We're having our annual Christmas dance Saturday night—music, drinks, food, and an auction for charity. Your granddaughter's working the dance," he reminded Gus. "Why don't you two come? After all, it's not like I'm saying you're both backsliding lazy Christians who are putting your souls at risk and have an obligation to attend mass or anything." He looked over his shoulder. "I've got to get back to the Johnsons. It was nice meeting you, Doc. Hope I helped." Father Ken picked up another French fry from Doc's food basket before he rose and walked away.

"Beautiful, isn't he?" Gus observed. "He can make you feel welcome and spank your ass all at the same time."

An hour later, Doc was back at his cabin, sitting at the writing desk in the living room next to the fireplace. As usual, a fire was hissing and crackling while he checked the weather on his laptop and Amy Grant sang on the radio. Clair was in his bedroom with the door closed, but the two were in mid-conversation.

"You know, I was going to be mad at you for coming home so late," she called through the closed door. "I mean, you're my only link to the outside world. But, when you showed up with clothes *and* makeup *and* shoes, plus you had a conversation with Farren's grandfather who we now know for sure does not approve of Charlie—well—things are going better and faster than I could've hoped."

"More snow's on the way, although the temperature is actually going up," he called back, closing the computer. "Listen," he said, turning in his chair toward the door across the room, "how do we know we've got time for me to gain Farren's trust? How do we know that Charlie hasn't already made plans to kill her tonight? Tomorrow?"

"We don't," she answered back. "Not for sure. But I think if something were imminent, he'd let me know."

"You mean, Big Daddy?"

"Yes. Besides Gus not liking Charlie, did you two talk about anything else?"

"Not really. Farren's pastor came over and invited us to that Christmas dance I told you about."

Just then, the bedroom door opened and Clair stepped out into the living room. She was wearing a long-sleeved red silk blouse, pleated black slacks, black leather shoes with slight heels and a shiny wide black belt. Doc had always known she was attractive, but now that she was dressed up and had lipstick and makeup on, the blonde-haired, green-eyed visitor looked positively devastating.

"What do you think?" she asked, a little unsure.

Doc slowly rose from his chair with an open mouth. "Whoa," he uttered.

"Pants like this on women are okay?" she queried.

"More than okay. You're the kind of woman poems are written for, countries go to war for, and men turn into babbling idiots for."

"Thank you, Doc," she beamed. "That's one of the nicest things anybody has ever said to me. I'm grateful for the first set of clothes you bought, but dressier clothes are more my style than a sweatshirt and dungarees. Thank you so much!"

"You're welcome."

Pleased with herself, she couldn't resist the urge to spin around like a fashion model, and then she giggled. "I know I'm not supposed to care about things like clothing and makeup, Vernors, and snow and the warmth of a fire, but there are so *many* wonderful things about this life, and it surprises me how much I've missed them."

"How long did you say it had been since you were last here?"

"I didn't," she answered, seeing his ploy to get information out of her that wasn't pertinent to her assignment. "But, believe me, you should stop and smell the roses every day."

She walked over to the fire and extended her arms with open palms to feel its heat. Doc stepped over to her peeling off the Band-Aid on his forehead.

"How's my head look?"

She glanced at his forehead. "Much better. How's your hand where I bit you?"

"As long as I don't break out speaking in tongues, fine. Look, why don't you come to the parish dance with me Saturday night?"

"What? Are you crazy? I can't do that!"

"Why not? Did you change into anything today?"

"No, but the day's not over."

"Did you throw up?"

"Once. Right after you left this morning. But the nausea soon passed."

"There ya go. If you can go thirteen hours or so without shapeshifting, you've *got* to be pretty much healed. Surely, you can go to a dance for a couple hours. We'll introduce you as my sister from North Carolina who came for a visit."

"You and I don't look anything alike," she said, dismissively. She brushed passed him and headed into the kitchen to make some hot chocolate.

"It doesn't matter," he reasoned. "Everybody's going to be looking at you and thinking about how pretty you are to notice that." He followed her into the kitchen where she was getting some mugs out of the pine cabinets with the glass pane doors. "C'mon, Clair. Don't you want to get out of this dinky cabin? Be out among people? Dance? You could talk to Farren yourself. Meet your very reason for being here. Get some first-hand insight."

She seemed tempted for a moment, then shook it off. "Yes, right up until I turned into a camel or something. Then what would you do with me?"

"Put you in the nativity scene on the church's front lawn," he deadpanned. "C'mon, if you talk to your Boss about it, I'm sure he'll help out. Have faith."

"Is this why you bought me new clothes?" she asked.

"No. I swear. The idea came to me just now."

She looked at him not sure whether or not to believe him while pouring some milk into a pan. Noticing this, he stopped his line of conversation. "You know, there *is* a microwave right over there. You don't have to use the stove."

"I like using the stove," she said.

"You mean, every night that you've made hot chocolate, you've done it on the stove?"

"Is that a problem? Don't you like my hot chocolate?"

"I love your hot chocolate. I'm just trying to save you time."

"I'm an angel. I have an eternity of time."

"Whatever. What about Saturday?"

She looked at him with body language and pursed lips that said "no." But Doc knew better. Or, at least he hoped for better.

THE DANCE

Snow lightly fell in front of the headlights of the Kia as Doc and Clair headed down Boyne City Road toward town and the St. Ignatius Social Center. The snow wasn't threatening on this particular night, but instead gently swirled over the two-lane blacktop and around the pines, oaks, and birch trees as though the entire county was encased in a gigantic snow globe that someone had just shaken. Both driver and passenger looked very handsome. Clair was wearing the same red silk blouse, black belt and pants she had modeled two nights before, and she was also wearing brand new purchases of a dark green overcoat, gold earrings and an elegant-looking, yet inexpensive, gold necklace. Doc was wearing a black trench coat, white shirt, dark red tie, and what he called his "new suit." It was a charcoal-colored two-piece that he purchased at an outlet store three years earlier in Wyoming, but this was only the fourth time he had worn it, so to him, it was still new.

"I don't know about this," Clair said, quietly. She seemed glad to finally be out in the world again, but was apprehensive about the evening to come.

"It's going to be fine," Doc reassured, sitting behind the wheel and watching the road. "You haven't turned into anything all day, you haven't been sick, and Farren is the reason you're here. It's time to get in the trenches and help me. Besides, if there was going to be a problem with regeneration tonight, your boss would've warned you."

"Not necessarily," she said. "And why do you always do that?"

"What?"

"Call him 'my boss.' He's God Almighty, and he's your boss, too."

"You're just nervous about tonight," he concluded. "Look, we'll hang near an exit, keep our coats close by, and if anything happens, we'll be out of there in two shakes." He turned to her and smiled. "It would be a sin not to take you out. You look fabulous."

She shook her head a little embarrassed while her glistening red lips pulled back into a smile. "Ooohhh, I should have never let you talk me into this. But you *are* persuasive. I just hope you're equally persuasive with Farren."

She spotted a lit and inflatable green-skinned Grinch wearing a Santa suit on a front lawn. Her eyes followed it with curiosity as they passed by. Doc noticed her intrigue.

"I guess a lot's changed since you were last here, huh?"

"The decorations have, but, Christmas is still Christmas," she replied.

"Let me ask you something. I know you said you weren't going to, y'know, reveal any 'Great Mysteries' to me, but I've got to ask—was Jesus really God's son?"

She looked out the window as they drove by more seasonal lights. After a moment, she responded. "Jesus of Nazareth had no manager, no media coverage, or formal education, yet everyone knows him. He was just a guy from an obscure little village who preached about loving one another and loving God. He wasn't the first to do that, but he *was* the first who claimed to be God's actual son. Elijah, Moses, Mohammad, Buddha—no one else ever claimed to be God's son. He preached for only three years, but here we are twenty centuries later, and he's the central figure of the human race. All the kings that ever ruled, all the empires that ever stood, all the armies that ever marched have not had the effect on the world that this one, poor, uneducated carpenter did. So, what do *you* think?"

Doc took a moment before answering. "I think there's a lot of people in the world who would say Jesus was a good man, but not God's divine son. What about them?"

"What *about* them?"

"Do they all get one-way tickets to hell because they don't believe?"

She smiled again. "It's true, Jesus said, 'I am the way.' But good, compassionate people who give of themselves are still good, compassionate people, aren't they? People should be judged by individual actions, not by what groups they belong to."

"So, what you're saying, then, is that all those Bible-bangers who claim you're going to hell if you don't accept Jesus as your personal savior are wrong?"

"I didn't say anything of the kind, Doc. But ultimately, God, being God, can decide for himself who he wants by his side. Wouldn't you agree?"

"Yeah," he half-smiled, "I would."

Six minutes later, they were pulling into the freshly snowplowed parking lot of the Saint Ignatius Social Center across the street from the church. Large mounds of snow stood in all four corners of the crowded lot and looked like mini-mountains, while the lot's tall halogen pole lights gave everything a slightly copper tint. All through town, Doc noticed that the closer they got to their destination, the quieter Clair had become.

Pulling into a space in front of one of the snow mounds and as close to the center's front doors as he could get, he put the Spectrum in park and turned off the engine.

"Ready?"

She looked across the street at the old brick crucifix-shaped church and gently put her long, slender fingers on the passenger-side window as if to touch it. It was uncharacteristic for her to be filled with such introspection.

"I can't go with you, Doc," she finally said. "I have to do something else."

He looked at her not understanding. "You...you have to do something else? What? You've got a date?"

"Actually, I do," she said, examining her seatbelt then figuring out how it unlocked. "You go to the dance without me. We'll rendezvous back here in two hours."

Assuming she wanted to go to church and pray, based upon the longing way she was looking at it, he protested. "Wait a minute. In the first place, you can't just stroll into church because it's locked. In the second place, you don't have a wristwatch. How are you going to know when two hours are up? In the third place, you're supposed to be my visiting sister, remember?"

"Did you tell anybody your sister from North Carolina was visiting?"

"Well, no, but—"

She clicked open the car door and stepped out. "I've got to do something. I'll meet you back here in two hours."

"Yeah, but—"

She smiled at him, as if to say, "Don't worry about it," then shut the door and walked through the lightly falling snow toward the church.

He watched her go for a few seconds, then undid his seatbelt, and muttered to himself, "No. This is dumb. What about Farren?" Once out of the car, he closed his door and looked in her direction again. His eyes were off her for only a few seconds. But, when he looked toward the church, she was gone.

"Clair?" he called. His blue eyes scanned the subtle orange glow of the parking lot. Since the lot had been freshly plowed, there were no footsteps for him to follow. But he knew she couldn't have gone all the way across the street and into the church in the few seconds it took for him to climb out of the Kia—at least, not if she were a normal human.

His first assumption was that she had morphed into an animal. But that didn't quite jive because he saw no discarded clothing or an animal roaming around. He looked up at the sky half-expecting to see a winged figure. After a couple more moments of fruitlessly looking around, he decided to stick to the plan, go the dance, and return to the car in two hours.

The Saint Ignatius Social Center was built in 1963. Ground was broken in the fall, exactly five months to the day before the Beatles first appeared on *The Ed Sullivan Show*. Inside, it had tan cinderblock walls, and one wall, nearest the parking lot, had large rectangular windows that could be rolled opened in the summer like Venetian blinds. It had a worn, gray linoleum floor and a fully equipped, but older, kitchen tucked away behind two large swinging doors with a small circular window in each door. The center was used for everything from wedding receptions, to parish bingo, to Room At The Inn. The twenty-foot-high drop ceiling was an original fixture and consisted of hundreds of off-white twelve-by-twelve-inch pressed paperboard panels. Some of the panels were stained by water while a few others were missing from the ceiling altogether. Several brushed nickel metallic bowls hung down on silver poles from the ceiling with four light bulbs inside each bowl. The lights were on rheostats and turned down low. A large four-foot-wide Christmas wreath, tastefully decorated with plastic grapes, apples, pears, nesting birds, and white twinkle lights, hung on one cinderblock wall, a "Della Robbia Wreath," Doc had learned from working at his dad's nursery. There were also two seven-foot-high decorated Christmas trees strung with multicolored lights that stood on either side of a portable stage made up of choir risers. On the stage, a DJ stood behind a table and spun records.

In front of the stage there was a large square of cleared-away floor where people were slow dancing to Dean Martin. Outlining the dance area were linen-draped tables with a lit votive candle in a glass holder on each table. In opposite corners of the center were two cash bars, as well as free snack tables with wheels of cheese, crackers, vegetable trays, and cookies. There was another long, linen-covered table under the rectangular windows, where many items were displayed for an auction to be held later in the evening. The items ranged from quilts to paintings to a weekend getaway at the Grand Traverse Bay Spa & Resort, with all the proceeds going to the parish. The center was pretty crowded. People milled about, ranging from ages twenty-five to eighty, and all of them were quite dressed up, which was something of a relief to Doc since he was wearing a suit and tie. The large wreath on the wall was made of real tree boughs, so the main room had a pleasant evergreen scent. All in all, the Saint Ignatius Social Center looked very festive and inviting in a retro Andy Williams sort of way. The scene didn't really bear any resemblance to places or events in Doc's past, yet it still felt familiar to him, as though maybe he'd seen a similar setting in a movie or had once dreamed of a place like this.

Just outside the main room was an entranceway and vestibule with a large closet. Normally, the closet held stacked folding chairs and janitorial supplies, but tonight it was a coat check. After checking his coat, Doc started to slowly move through the crowd—past a woman wearing a snowman sweater and older gentleman wearing a Santa hat—trying to spot Farren. His search was interrupted by a female voice calling out to him.

"Doc?"

He turned to see Charlene Rogers, Lance's exuberant girlfriend approaching. She was twenty-nine, same age as Farren, but shorter with a cookie dough body in a white dress that was a little too tight. Her highlighted brown hair was teased and puffed-up to make her pudgy frame look slimmer and, like her boyfriend, she had a youthful pleasant-looking face. Lance followed behind her, looking dapper in dark slacks, a green turtleneck, and a sports coat.

"I don't believe it," she gasped. "Doc Reynolds actually out in public? Doing something else besides playing poker with Lance's loser fire hall buddies? Amazing!"

"How are you, Charlene?" he said, leaning over to give her a kiss on the cheek. "You look wonderful."

"Hey, man," Lance greeted.

"I didn't know you two were Catholic."

"We're not," Charlene said. "But this is one of the nicest dances of the year, and they have an auction with lots of cool things." She turned to her boyfriend. "Which reminds me, I saw a basket full of bath stuff I *really* want."

"So, what're you doin' here?" Lance asked.

"The pastor invited me. I met him the other night when I was doing some Christmas shopping. And then, I guess, Farren's working around here, too."

"Lance told me about how you two met," Charlene said. "I think it's hysterical."

"My head didn't think it was so funny," he answered, touching the still visible but healing cut on his forehead.

"Oooo, I'm sorry," Charlene cooed. She kissed the red tips of her fingers then touched his forehead to make it all better. "So isn't Farren adorable? I'm tellin' ya, you should've jumped on it when you had the chance. Oh, I mean, not *literally* have jumped on it, but, you know what I mean."

"I know," Doc smiled. "C'est la vie."

"Hey," Farren called, making her way through the crowd. She was wearing a sleeveless green-spangled dress with a high turned-down collar. The dress wasn't a mini-skirt, but it broke several inches above the knee and nicely accentuated her shapely legs. Christmas tree earrings dangled from her ears giving her neck an elegant appearance. Her bare slender arms revealed longish swimmer's muscles, as well as three thin golden bangles on her left arm that made a pleasant chiming sound when she walked. Like the Social Center, she looked retro, but warm and inviting.

"I thought that was you across the room," she said to Doc. "Hey, guys," she greeted Lance and Charlene.

They both said hello back.

"Wow. You look beautiful," Doc said.

"Thank you," she smiled.

"He was referring to me," Lance quipped.

"Honey, aren't you cold without sleeves?" Charlene asked.

"No. Charlie and I were in the kitchen earlier making up platters for the snack tables. It's like an oven in there."

"Oh, Charlie's here?" Doc asked. "I'd like to meet him."

"Last I saw he was working the coat check room with Luanne."

"I just came from there. I didn't see a guy," Doc said.

"Let me see if I can wrangle him up," Farren answered. She pointed a finger at Lance, reminding. "It's Christmas, y' know. Perfect opportunity to give a long suffering and deserving woman an engagement ring."

"Geez, I'm thirsty," Lance said, looking around and suddenly disinterested. "C'mon, sweetie. Let's go to the bar."

"Thanks for tryin', hon," Charlene smiled, as Lance took her by the hand and led her away.

Farren leaned into Doc and spoke quietly. "I probably shouldn't have said that. But what the hey? He's been stringing her along for years."

"So, is this your party?" he asked, glancing around.

"Oh, no. Lots of people worked on the dance. I just bought the food, made up the snack trays, hung the wreath, and decorated the trees."

"Only that, huh?"

"Other people set up tables, made flyers, set up the bars, donated or made things for the auction—"

"Okay," he cut in. "But you did your share. The more I get to know you, the more it seems like you're always doing your share, and then some."

"What a nice thing to say," she smiled, her dimples deepening. "Let me see if I can find Charlie."

She gracefully weaved through the crowd heading toward the coat check, her bracelets clinking together as she went. Smiling, Doc turned and surveyed the room. Couples slowly moved to and fro on the dance floor while the Eagles sang "Come Home For Christmas." Another couple held hands as they stood in front of one of Farren's Christmas trees near the DJ's table, admiring the decorations. Still another couple laughed as they stood at a snack table and threatened to throw cheese cubes at one another, but didn't. The longer he watched these activities, the more the smile on his face faded, until his expression was one of envy and self-consciousness. He was standing in a room full of people, but he felt totally alone. As his eyes slowly sank from the dancing couples holding each other tightly to the floor in front of him, he was unaware that twenty feet away, Farren had turned back to look at him before leaving the main room to go to the coat check. Seeing him in profile, she recognized his expression instantly. It was the silent desire to be with someone, but it was also something more: an expression of great loss. She knew this expression well. She used to come to these dances and watch couples with the same quiet sadness. Now she was married and things were different, but she still watched Doc empathetically for several seconds before walking away.

Meanwhile, in the makeshift coatroom, Charlie Huffman was in the back of the room hidden from view behind four full portable coat racks on wheels and was rummaging through people's pockets. He was supposed to be hanging up coats from the check-in table while Luanne Peters handed out coat-check tickets and chatted with arriving guests in the front. He was looking for loose change, a pocketbook, an iPod, or anything of value he might be able to pawn later.

"Charlie?" he heard Farren's voice call.

"Be right there, babe," he calmly responded, taking a forgotten five-dollar bill out of somebody's pocket and slipping it into his own.

He emerged from behind the racks with a smile. He wore khaki slacks, a red polo golf shirt, and a blue blazer. His limp was hardly noticeable, and he hadn't used his cane in days.

"What do you need, sweetie?"

"Can you take a moment and meet somebody?"

"If the beautiful Luanne can spare me."

Luanne Peters was about sixty and plump, but she giggled like a schoolgirl at Charlie's compliment. "Oh, go on with you," she blushed.

He rounded the coat-check table.

"Who am I meeting? An old boyfriend?" he asked, playfully.

"No," she smiled, as they began to walk.

"Your ninth-grade math teacher that you had a terrible crush on?" he guessed again.

"No, I never had a crush on Mrs. Aberdine," she explained.

"Okay, I give."

"It's Doc Reynolds."

Charlie looked at her blankly.

"You know, the paramedic I told you about?"

Now, he remembered. "The guy who threatened to sue us?"

"He was kidding, honey. Actually, I'm surprised he's here tonight. I know he doesn't get out much."

"Maybe he's sweet on you."

"Well, I'm taken and he knows it. But, he's kind of new in town and I *do* think he wants to meet some people. With you being new in town, too, maybe you guys will hit it off."

"That's why I love you—Saint Farren," he whispered sexily in her ear.

A few seconds later, they caught up with Doc who was chatting with

Father Ken.

"Hey, Father," she greeted. She gestured to Doc. "Have you two met?"

"We have," the priest replied.

"Then Doc, I'd like you to meet my husband, Charlie."

The men smiled and shook hands. Doc couldn't help but notice Charlie's firm grip, blue eyes, square jaw, rugged good looks, even the fact that he might be more fit than himself. He disliked him instantly.

"Nice to meet you, partner," Charlie said. "I'm really sorry about what Farren did to your head."

"It's okay," Doc replied, politely.

"She's a wildcat," the blonde-haired man grinned. "Bangs your head and scratches my back." He chuckled while Farren gave him a wide-eyed look of disapproval, then he turned to the priest.

"Oh, sorry, Padre. I'm kidding, of course."

Father Ken smiled. "No worries, Charlie. I'm just glad you came tonight and could help us out. It gives me the chance to get to know you better."

Charlie turned to Farren. "Sorry, sweetie. Poor joke. My bad."

She looked at him sternly, but forgave him.

"Doc was just asking me about Gus, but I haven't seen him," the clergyman noted. "Is he here tonight, Farren?"

"Sorry, Father. You know Grandpa."

"I used to," the priest nodded. "I'd like to again. It's been too long since I kicked his butt in Parcheesi."

Just then, the DJ started playing Nat King Cole's version of "The Christmas Song." Farren turned to Charlie.

"Oh, that's my favorite. C'mon, honey, dance with me."

"I don't think my foot's quite ready for dancing yet." He looked at the men to explain. "Job site accident. But maybe Doc here will stand in for me."

"Uh, sure. If that's okay?"

"Of course it's okay," Charlie smiled. "It was my idea. C'mon, Father. I'll buy you a beer. Then, I've got to get back to the coat check."

Charlie and Father Ken started moving away through the crowd while Doc and Farren walked over to the dance floor. As Doc took her right hand, then slipped the fingers of his left around her shapely waist, he was cognizant of how nice she smelled and how good she felt, but he kept these observations to himself.

Substitute Angel

"He seems nice," he offered, as they started to dance.

"He's a diamond in the rough," she explained, referencing his inappropriate comment.

"What did Father Ken mean when he said, he 'used' to know Gus?"

"For a while, he and Grandpa were pretty tight. But, you know how friendships go. They ebb and flow."

"Sure."

"Besides, Grandpa's got a lot on his mind right now."

He nodded and glanced off in Charlie's direction. As he did, she, too, was secretly taking note of how nice Doc felt, which frankly surprised her and made her feel a little guilty, although they were doing nothing wrong. After several silent seconds and a slow synchronized turn, she spoke:

"Do you mind if I ask you something personal?"

"Not at all."

"Who was she?"

"Who was who?"

"The girl you came close to marrying but lost?"

Her question caught him off guard. "I ... I don't—"

"You mentioned her at lunch," she reminded. "No doubt Lance, or Charlene, or both told you about my parents. I know about loss. I was watching you before I got Charlie. You were watching couples on the dance floor the same way I used to. You want to be with someone, but the memory of a loss holds you back. Am I right?"

He cast his eyes away from her to the floor. He could feel himself blushing.

"I'm sorry," Farren said, softly. "I crossed a line I shouldn't have."

"No. It's okay. Friends tell friends stuff."

They danced silently for a few more moments, each enjoying and absorbing the Nat King Cole recording like never before. As they slowly turned again on the linoleum floor amidst the twinkling lights from the wreath and the reflections cast by the nearby Christmas trees, Charlie observed them while he stood in a short line at the bar with Father Ken. The priest was tempted to ask him about whether or not he had been in Traverse City that one day, but politically decided not to and instead spoke pleasantly about other things. Charlie pretended to listen, but he was really focused on the body language between Doc and his wife. They were holding each other a little too close, and he squinted in disapproval.

"Her name was Julia," Doc finally volunteered. "We met late in our senior year at Eastern Michigan."

"You loved her?"

"Yes."

"What happened?"

"After about six months, I brought up the subject of marriage one night. It wasn't a formal proposal, it was more like a feeler to see if we were thinking in the same direction."

"And she turned you down?"

"No. She said we shouldn't decide things too hastily. There were a lot of new career directions going on with both of us at the time. But, the next morning, her car was broadsided by a semi-truck."

"Oh my God."

"I found out later it took more than an hour to cut her free from the twisted metal. It's also possible some of her injuries were misdiagnosed. She died in the Intensive Care Unit. That was ten years ago this month."

Farren kept dancing, but her large brown eyes began to fill with tears. She blinked and a tear suddenly slipped over an eyelash.

"I'm so sorry, Doc."

"It was a long time ago," he said. "But sometimes, things come to the surface a little more than I'd like this time of year."

They danced quietly for a few more moments.

"That's why you became a paramedic, isn't it? That's why you don't stay too long in one place. You don't want anyone else to get too close."

"I don't know about *that*," he questioned.

"No, it makes perfect sense."

His eyes drifted away again. There was more truth to her observations than he wanted to admit.

They danced for another moment, then Farren wiped her eyes and shook her head. "I lost my parents when I was a teenager, but, at least I knew they were my parents and would've done anything for me. But, you, you don't know where you stood with Julia, do you? Was she just a girlfriend? Fiancé? Did she have the same depth of feeling for you that you felt for her? The accident left a lot of unanswered questions, didn't it?"

Her observations surprised him a little.

"No. I know she loved me."

The song came to its familiar conclusion with the guitarist strumming a few measures of "Jingle Bells." When they stopped dancing, Farren went to the nearest unoccupied table and took a paper napkin off it to dab her eyes and blow her freckled nose. "Sorry," she said. "Things get to me sometimes more than they should, too."

"Actually, I'm glad you asked," he replied. "I haven't spoken out loud about Julia in years. I've kept her tucked away. Just like you've kept concerns about Charlie tucked away."

Now it was her turn to blush. She smiled nervously. "See? We have to be friends now. We know too much. I ... I'd better go see how the snacks are holding out. Thanks for the dance, Doc—and for telling me. Your secret is safe."

"Thank *you*," he smiled.

She turned and moved away through the crowd. As she did, he noticed that some of the brighter lights coming from the vestibule caught the green spangles of her dress and made them sparkle like fireflies. He cracked a small smile at the notion of fireflies in December.

THE AUCTION

"It's time for the auction, everyone," Father Ken announced, standing next to the DJ on the choir risers with a microphone in his hand. The rheostats in the Social Center were turned up, and the room gradually filled with light. "Now, I'm sure you've all had the opportunity to peruse the magnificent things we have here to bid on tonight. Quilts, pottery, paintings, gift certificates, and the big-ticket item this year is a romantic weekend getaway for two at the Grand Traverse Bay Spa & Resort over in Traverse City.

"Joy, what's first?"

A handsome woman in a blue dress picked up a six-bottle case of wine from the linen-draped auction table and carried it up to the priest. The wine had been donated by the store owned by Lance's parents. "You know, our Lord had a high respect for wine," Father said. "It was his first miracle at Cana. But I'm not sure if he made Rose, Chablis, or Muscato." The crowd chuckled as the clergyman took a little card off the case that was taped to its side. On the card was the suggested starting bid price.

As Doc watched the proceedings from a corner near one of the cash bars, Lance came up to him.

"Got a second?"

"Sure. But, don't you want to watch the bidding on your folks' wine?"

"This is more important," Lance said, walking him a few feet away from the crowd.

"What's up?"

"Charlene is driving me crazy. There's this basket of soap, bath beads, and junk that she's decided she's just *got* to have. She wants me to get it for her for Christmas."

"What's the starting price?"

"Fifty bucks."

"So get it for her," Doc shrugged. "Get the girl what she wants."

"That's just it," his partner said. "I *did* get what she wants. I got her an engagement ring. I'm going to give it to her Christmas Eve."

"That's great!" Doc smiled. "Congratulations. She'll be ecstatic."

"Don't look so happy," Lance said, looking around nervously. "She'll figure it out. I want it to be a total surprise. The thing is, the ring really tapped me. I've got about twenty bucks in my pocket and no checkbook. So, if I bid on this basket, do you have the cash to cover me?"

"Where'd you run off to?" Charlene asked, interrupting and approaching the men. "They're bidding on your parents' wine."

"Uh, Lance, here, was just telling me you've got your eye on a basket of bath goodies," Doc said.

"Did you see it on the table?" she said, enthusiastically. "It's got sponges, herbal shampoo, exfoliating cream—I was just saying to myself yesterday that I needed some more."

"Me, too," Doc agreed. "There's just not enough exfoliating being done in Charlevoix. Listen, Charlene, if you'll permit me, you've been so kind since I've moved here, so generous with dinner invitations and blind dates and your friendship, could I bid on the basket for you as a way of saying thanks? I don't care about ol' what's-his-face here, but I really *do* want to express my appreciation to *you*. May I have your permission to bid on it?"

She looked at him with big puppy eyes that were becoming moist. "Oh my God, that is the sweetest thing anybody's ever said to me. You can bid on the basket for me, dance with me, and if you give me time to ditch Lance, you can take me home, and we'll try out those jasmine bath beads in the basket."

"I've said *plenty* of nice things to you," Lance defended.

"What a chivalrous gentleman," Charlene cooed. "You could learn from this guy."

"*Sold*," Father Ken announced holding the microphone and pointing to a man in a leather sports jacket, "to Josh Dalton for one hundred fifty-five dollars."

"Hmm, not bad for seventy bucks worth of vino," Lance observed.

As the auction progressed, first with the case of wine, then a homemade quilt, then a fine watercolor painting of the lighthouse that sat at the end of a breakwater where Lake Michigan entered the Pine River that cut through downtown, Doc slowly meandered through the bidding crowd to get a look at the basket that would soon be the featured item. It was light colored and about twice the size of an Easter basket with a big red bow on its handle. It was neither the best-looking item on the display table or the worst. As Doc approached, he saw that Farren and Charlie were also standing at the table surveying the goodies.

"You guys going for that weekend getaway at the Grand Traverse Bay Resort?" he asked.

"That'd be nice, since we never had a honeymoon," Farren said, "but no. Actually, I was eyeing that basket there. It'd be nice to pamper myself a little after a day of buffing hulls and cleaning out fuel lines."

"Sorry ma'am," Doc replied. "I'm going to get that for Charlene; my way of saying thanks for her and Lance taking me under their wing since I came to town."

"You're going to get ripped off, partner," Charlie observed, eyeing the basket's contents. "Everything in there comes to about thirty bucks, but they're starting the bidding at fifty. So, right from the get-go, it's a losing proposition."

"But it's all for programs the church supports," Farren reminded. "Room At The Inn, our sister parish in the Philippines, lots of good causes."

"Oh, I don't mind being conned if it's for a good cause," Doc said, looking at the basket, then raising his eyes to Charlie. "It's the bad cons people have to look out for."

Charlie's eyes shot to Doc just as he looked at Farren. "So anyway, don't get your heart set on it, kiddo."

Just then, the lady in the blue dress came up next to them and picked up the basket. As she did, Charlie and Doc's eyes met. The blonde-haired man gave the paramedic a calculating look, not sure if Doc knew something about his true intentions, or if he had merely made an ironic and coincidental statement. Either way, the gambler in him had been aroused.

"You know, honey," he grinned, "Doc's right. It's overpriced, but it *is* for the parish. So if you want that basket, darlin', you shall have it." He looked at Doc. "Sorry, man. You're gonna have to fight for it."

"That's okay, honey," she said. "I think what Doc wants to do for Charlene is sweet."

Doc looked at Charlie, smiled confidently, then turned to face Father

Ken, who was examining the basket at the DJ's table.

"Next, we have this lovely gift basket brimming with bath items: sea sponges, two washcloths, some sort of cream, bath beads—I don't know what all this stuff does exactly—but I *do* know this boudoir booty would make a great gift."

He took the card off the handle with the suggested starting bid price. "Let's begin the bidding at fifty dollars."

"Fifty dollars," Doc called out, raising his hand.

"Fifty dollars from Doc Reynolds, thank you, sir," Father said, holding the microphone in one hand and pointing to him with the other.

"Fifty-five dollars," Charlie called out.

"Fifty-five dollars," the clergyman responded with another point. "Thank you, Charlie Huffman."

"Sixty-five dollars," Doc responded.

"Seventy-five," Charlie countered before Father Ken had time to acknowledge the previous bid.

"Eighty!" an elderly man called out from the back.

"Forget it, honey," Farren whispered, leaning into her husband.

"We have a bid of eighty dollars from Ed Hilicker," Father Ken said.

"Eighty-five," Charlie called out with a raised finger, ignoring his spouse's advice.

"One hundred dollars," Doc replied.

The elderly man in the back shook his head. People in the crowd looked at Charlie to see what he would do.

"Wow!" the priest beamed with a smile. "You guys must know something about those bath beads that I don't. The bid now stands at one hundred dollars."

"One hundred and ten," Charlie said with a raised finger. This time, a couple of people actually gasped because everyone knew the bids were well beyond the basket's true worth.

"A hundred and fifty," Doc quickly answered.

"What is he *doing*?" Lance said under his breath to Charlene.

She looked at Doc with a glazed-over stare of admiration. Standing at only five-feet-one, and her high school cheerleading figure as long gone as her Duran Duran cassettes, this was the first time in years men had ever competed over something she was involved in; and two good-looking men at that.

"Quiet, Lance," she said, relishing the moment.

"Two hundred," Charlie called, which caused more gasps.

Farren shot her husband a wide-eyed stare of disbelief.

"Two fifty," Doc announced, businesslike.

George Pratt, owner of the ACE Hardware who was watching the bidding, leaned over to his wife. "Smacked his head the other day. It ain't right yet."

"Two seventy-five," Charlie retorted.

"I don't know what *his* story is though," George added. "Maybe just an idiot."

Doc simply held up three fingers in silent response.

"Uh, this, this is unbelievable," Father Ken gawked. "Eh, the bid for the basket of bath items now stands at—"

"Three fifty!" Charlie interrupted.

The crowd drew a simultaneous breath. All eyes fell to Doc. He slowly turned toward his competitor and smiled. "Too rich for *my* blood."

There was a brief shimmer of victory on Charlie's face, but it quickly changed when he realized three things: He had to cough up three hundred and fifty bucks. He was paying over ten times what the basket was worth. And his competitive nature had gotten the better of him. It also didn't escape his notice that maybe the con man had been conned. Maybe Doc had planned all along to raise the bidding only to withdraw.

"We've got a bid from Charlie Huffman for three hundred fifty dollars," Father Ken said into the microphone. "Going once, twice," he shot a finalizing finger at Charlie, "sold for three hundred and fifty dollars! Now *that's* the spirit of giving, ladies and gentlemen!"

The crowd burst into loud applause. Charlie tried to mask his anger by cracking small smiles at this person and that. Farren's stare of disbelief smoldered into a glare. Father Ken laughed, shrugged, pointed at Farren and Charlie and explained, "Newlyweds!" Doc likewise shrugged and moved through the crowd over to Charlene.

"I'm sorry, Charlene," he said, sincerely, "I tried."

When he got to her, she reached up, put an open chubby but small hand on each side of his face, and planted a large kiss on his mouth in gratitude for the effort. Lance, standing next to her, just rolled his eyes knowing how emotional she could get about things, while Doc looked at her wide-eyed. Simultaneously, Farren took Charlie aside after a couple of people congratulated him on his generous nature. Her bracelets were still clinking together as she moved.

"Three hundred and fifty dollars? Are you *crazy?*"

"Hey, my little girl wanted it," he smiled, slipping an arm around her and trying to put the best spin on it.

"Three hundred and fifty dollars is a new dishwasher, toilet and vanity, and bedding, all of which we need right now. From week to week, I don't know if you're bringing home two hundred dollars or two thousand. And now, you waste hundreds of dollars on, on nothing?"

"Good thing I got that bonus, huh?" he reminded. Then, he put on an air of contriteness. "I suppose you're right, it *was* pretty irresponsible. It's just, you said you wanted it, I wanted to please you, it *is* for programs the church supports, and I guess ol' Doc over there just threw down a gauntlet I couldn't refuse. I'm sorry, babe." He glanced around the room. "But look at the bright side."

"There's a bright side?"

"Right now, every woman here is saying to her man, 'Why can't *you* do something like that for me?'"

He batted his blue eyes at her. She was just about to say something when Patty Simpson, a fellow member of the Blood Drive Committee, came up to her. "I wish my Jim would be that impulsive for me sometime." She smiled at Charlie and moved through the crowd. He turned and grinned at Farren like a Cheshire cat. "C'mon, Girl," he urged. "Show me some dimple."

She smiled, sighed, and shook her head, exasperated. "Bonus or not, I wish you hadn't done this."

"I've only got five bucks on me," he confessed. "You got the checkbook?"

She looked at him, not approving of his presumptuousness.

"I could cut cards with Padre Ken," he offered. "Double or nothin'?"

"Excuse me, boys," Charlene said across the room and on the verge of happy tears again. "I've got to go powder my nose." As soon as she was out of earshot, Lance spoke quietly to Doc.

"I thought you'd lost your marbles there for a second, bidding so high on that thing."

"Never fear," Doc reassured.

"Hey, name me the Bond girl who, in real life, married an actor that would go on to have a starring role in a series of comedies that would heavily parody James Bond?"

"Jill St. John," his partner answered, without thinking. "*Diamonds Are Forever*. She married Robert Wagner who played Number Two in the Austin Powers movies. Let's get a drink." He turned and headed toward the nearest bar.

"Amazing," Lance mumbled, as he followed.

A half-hour later, the auction was nearing its end. Although there was still another hour or so of dancing afterward, Doc's two hours were up. He retrieved his coat from the coat check and looked around to say goodbye to folks, but couldn't find anyone. Father Ken was still auctioneering on the choir risers, Farren and Charlie were back in the kitchen making more snack plates, Gus never showed, and Charlene and Lance had disappeared somewhere. When he walked outside, he noticed it was still lightly snowing and another quarter to half-inch of fresh powder covered everything in sight.

As he walked across the lot, he could hear the amplified voice of Father Ken saying, "Sixty, I have sixty dollars. Do I hear seventy?" becoming more distant. At nearly the same time, something caught his eye in the coppery glow of the parking lot lights. Lying on the pavement was Clair's new dark green overcoat. A few feet beyond that was one of her black leather shoes. A few feet beyond that, her black slacks.

"Oh, no," he sighed, knowing a transformation had taken place.

He looked around, then quickly started to pick up the abandoned clothing while urgently calling her name in a loud whisper.

"Clair? ... Clair? ... Here, Girl. Whatever you are, you're still a female, right?"

Following the trail of clothes, he rounded the front of a car parked two spaces away from the Kia and discovered a plump sheep wearing the same gold earrings and necklace Clair had been wearing earlier.

"Aw, geez," Doc moaned. He held the clothing in one hand while rubbing his forehead with the tips of his fingers in the other. "I thought we were past this."

The sheep bleated at him.

"I'd ask, 'What's new?'" he said, "but that would be redundant. Let me put the clothes in the car. Don't go away."

He dug into his coat pocket for his keys, clicked and unlocked the door, threw Clair's coat, shoes, and clothes into the back seat, then hurriedly returned to the animal. He was so focused on keeping Clair from being seen in her present condition that he was totally unaware that someone already *had* seen. The reason why Doc couldn't find Lance and Charlene to say goodbye was because they, too, had decided to leave. Charlene had gone to the powder room one final time while Lance had gone outside to warm up his Chevy pickup that was parked five spaces away from Doc's. Lance had just brushed the snow off his windshield and had raised an arm to greet his preoccupied partner when he suddenly stopped, stunned to see a sheep in the parking lot and Doc addressing it. He crouched down behind his Chevy in curious fascination as Doc hurried back to his wooly companion.

"I want you to know the jewelry still works," he quipped.

Overhearing this, Lance's jaw dropped open.

The sheep bleated at him again. Doc bent down and picked up the animal.

"Keep it down, will ya," he said, struggling with the creature's weight and legs. "People are starting to leave."

He walked toward his car awkwardly carrying the sheep. "Just be patient, and I'll have you home and in bed in no time."

Lance's jaw dropped even lower. He couldn't believe what he was hearing. It was shocking. Stunning. But, in a weird sort of way, the assumptions his racing mind was now making did explain a few things. Like, why Doc wanted to live out of town and in the woods, why he never showed any interest in hunting, why he was so reluctant about blind dates, maybe even that horse he thought he saw in the kitchen window the week before. As the seconds passed, Lance's assumptions pole-vaulted further and further away from the truth and landed on conclusions of the sexually bizarre.

"There we go," Doc said, setting the sheep down on the passenger-side seat. "Don't eat the seatbelt. Remember, it's a rental."

The sheep bleated at him again.

"We'll be home soon. Hot chocolate for me and a bottle of Woolite for you."

He quickly shut the door, rounded the driver's side, got in the car, then started the engine. Lance crouched even lower behind his vehicle, making like his favorite secret agent while Doc backed up and his windshield wipers wiped off the fresh snow. Once the Kia had passed by Lance's Chevy and was pulling out into the street, he slowly rose.

"Poor bastard," he said, shaking his head and watching the red taillights of his friend's rental car disappear into the night. "Poor sick, twisted bastard."

STEPS BACK

Doc was dozing on the sofa when he heard the sound of human footsteps running across the living room. He cracked open his eyes, sat up and caught a glimpse of Clair's pale, naked bottom as it bounced through the doorway into his bedroom, then darted left into the Jack-and-Jill bath like a white-tailed deer disappearing into the woods. Taking the nudity in stride, he looked at his wristwatch. It was 2:22 in the morning. Clair had been in animal form for about four and a half hours. This was clearly a setback in her regeneration process—at least, to the best of his understanding.

Hearing her vomiting in the bathroom, he sat up and looked at the comforter that was folded in half on the floor and the bowl of water that had been put out for his guest while she was a sheep. Surrounding the comforter were newspapers that had been spread out. He'd learned a lot in the last several days about how to deal with the incontinence of an injured angel. He rose from the sofa, scratched the top of his head, and sleepily headed into the darkened kitchen. He opened the fridge and retrieved a can of Vernors.

Getting a glass while looking out the window and seeing it was still snowing, he opened the can, poured some ginger ale into the glass, then shuffled silently in his stocking feet out of the kitchen and back through the living room. He was still wearing his suit pants and white dress shirt, but his shirt was untucked and his jacket and tie had been hung over a chair in the kitchen hours earlier. Arriving at the closed bathroom door in his bedroom—which, for more than a week had been Clair's bedroom— he waited outside until the sounds of vomiting ended, then knocked gently. It opened a crack, then he slid his hand with the glass through the opening. Hearing a weak, "Thank you," he withdrew his hand, shuffled through the bedroom back into the living room, and shut the bedroom door behind him so Clair could have some privacy while she dressed. She didn't always get sick to her stomach when she transformed back into a human, but the chances of it were greater than fifty-fifty.

At 2:47 a.m., she emerged from the bedroom and walked softly into the living room carrying her glass that still had a swallow of ginger ale left in it. She wandered over to the sofa nearest the writing desk and wilted into it wearing the sleep shirt with the winged cherubs that he had bought her. It was long sleeve and pink with the figures drawn in white. It came down over her thighs to break about six inches above the knee. Her legs were bare, but she was wearing her black slippers. She had taken off her jewelry, washed all the makeup off her face and looked pale and drained. It was too late in the evening to build a fire, but the little Christmas tree next to the porch was on, and Doc had lit, and moved, a fat, three-wick candle from the kitchen to the wood plank table in between the two sofas.

"What happened tonight?" he yawned, sitting on the opposite sofa. "You were doing so well. Why the relapse into animal form?"

"I told you I wasn't sure about going out tonight," she reminded. "Guess I'm not as regenerated as I thought."

"I thought you were coming to the dance with me. Why the sudden change of plan?"

"It's not important right now. How did things go with Farren?"

"Oh, *now* you're interested in Farren?" he asked, a little irritated.

"C'mon, Doc," she said wearily. "I don't want to fight. I'm too wiped out."

He pointed to her glass. "You want some more Vernors?"

"Yes, please, a little." She drank the last swallow then handed him the glass. "So, tell me about tonight?"

"I think I might have blown it with Farren," he said, rising. "Like your regeneration, taken a step back."

"What do you mean?"

"Her husband and I got into a measuring contest tonight."

"Measuring contest? What were you two measuring?"

He stopped halfway toward the kitchen, turned and looked at her. After a moment, "Oh, 'that' kind of measuring contest," she said, understanding.

He turned and started walking again. "There was an auction for charity, and we both wound up bidding on the same thing. The bidding got stupid high, and then I pulled out causing him to pay an awful lot of money for an awful lot of nothing. So, Farren's probably not too happy with me right now."

"Hmm," she said, thinking. "What prompted you to do anything to aggravate Charlie?"

"I don't know," he answered, pouring more Vernors from the kitchen. "She's a really good person, y' know? Sensitive, giving, intuitive—and he's just ... he's just sort of slimy. *Well-packaged* slimy, but still slimy."

She thought for a moment while he returned from the kitchen and handed her the glass.

"Thanks. Maybe what happened tonight isn't as much a step back as you think?"

"What do you mean?" he asked, sitting back down.

"Maybe getting into a bidding war showed Farren a glimpse of her husband's gambling problem."

He grimaced, rubbing his forehead. "Maybe. I wish you would've been there, though."

"Pray about it tomorrow when you go to church."

"What?"

"Tomorrow—I mean, today—is Sunday. Pray about what happened with Farren and Charlie when you go to church."

He leaned back on the sofa and smiled slightly. "I'm not a member of Saint Ignatius."

"Well, whatever church you go to," she said, taking a drink.

"Clair, you were here last Sunday. I don't know if you noticed, but I don't do church."

"Oh," she said, genuinely surprised. "I thought you missed worship last week because I was still so ill."

He shook his head. "No."

"Why don't you go to church? God's given you so many blessings. Surely, you can give him one hour."

"Let's not go there," he suggested. "Until you showed up, I wasn't even sure God existed. And now that I know he does ..." his voice trailed off, not sure he wanted to complete the thought.

"Without faith, it is impossible to please Him," she quoted. "Hebrews, chapter eleven."

"I wish you wouldn't do that," he said, rising. He stuck a hand in his pocket and nervously started to jingle his change.

"What?"

"Quote the Bible like it was scripture."

"Excuse me?"

"Look, scripture isn't even scripture. How many versions of the Bible are there? They can't all be right. And what's the most popular? The King James Version, right? It was commissioned sixteen hundred years after the death of Jesus. With all the editing and intervening centuries, how can anybody know what's true?"

She was just about to respond, but turned and noticed his closed laptop on the writing desk. "That thin little case of yours over there—your 'computer'—you can research things on it, yes? Like an encyclopedia?"

"In a way."

"Why don't you ask it your questions?"

He stopped fiddling with his change, shrugged, walked over to the writing desk, sat down, and opened the laptop. His Yahoo home page was already up.

"Versions ... of ... the ... Bible," he spoke, as he typed. He punched "search" and waited.

"Well?" she asked.

"There isn't just one response," he explained. "There's a bunch—pages of articles, opinions, links to other sites."

"Pick one," she said.

"Any one?"

"Any one."

He clicked on a site, waited a moment for the connection, then read.

"What's it say?" she asked.

He read for a couple more moments. "It says, there are more than fifty variations of the Bible in the English language, alone. But, they aren't different versions so much as translations. It says, there is only one Bible, but scholars and theologians interpret the words, phrases, and meanings of things differently."

"So, there aren't different versions," she concluded. "Just translations. Now, ask if the Bible is historically true."

He did as she suggested.

"How many responses are there?" she asked.

He read for a moment. "Over forty-five million."

"Do you think all forty-five million responses say the Bible is *not* historically true?"

"What's your point?" he said, impatiently.

"The stories in the Bible may be translated differently, but they're all essentially the same. You asked how anyone could accept the Bible as truth, why don't you read some of those forty-five million responses? You might discover that the more archeologists uncover history, the more the old and new testaments are verified."

"Yeah, but why does everything have to be so hidden in parables and open to interpretation? Why are there so many outright contradictions in the Bible?"

"The Bible was written by several men over the course of many centuries. Ancient Greek texts, letters from the apostles, the author of one document not necessarily knowing what another author had written. Of course there would be contradictions. But then, man has always been a walking contradiction, hasn't he. People teach their children not to lie, but then we tell them little lies to protect them. People know that smoking is bad for them, yet tens of millions still do it. Countries want peace, but they also want a huge stockpile of weapons to ensure it."

"I thought the writers of the Bible were supposed to be different," he reminded, "divinely inspired."

"Doc, prior to my arrival, I was told there were seven billion people living on Earth. Each person has his or her own powers of reasoning and relates to things differently. Maybe the Bible is *supposed* to be the way it is to reach the greatest number of souls. You think things are hidden in parables, but the next man might *need* a parable to illustrate a point. What you see as 'contradictions,' others won't, given their particular life and circumstances. I hear you asking a lot of questions, but I don't see you seeking a lot of answers."

"Maybe Jesus should just do a return engagement," he suggested, closing the laptop. "Put everyone on the same page. After all, it *has* been over two thousand years."

"He raised the dead, fed multitudes, caused the blind to see, and that *still* didn't put people on the same page the *first* time he was here," she reminded. "I suggest you go to church regularly and learn about the benefits of faith."

He rose from the computer, exasperated. "Oh, well, if you're going to throw faith at me when I'm trying to have an intelligent discussion about God ..." He looked at his wristwatch. "It's late. I really need to get some sleep. I'm sorry if I did something tonight that weakened my relationship with Farren. Again, why do things have to be so convoluted? Why can't you just speak to Farren in a dream or something? After all, *you're* the angel."

"But, you're the one who agreed to help. Forget about whether or not you go to church and believe there's one version of the Bible or a thousand. Forget about whether or not you even believe in God. Are you a man of your word, or not?"

He took a deep breath and jammed both hands into his pants pockets. He liked to think that he was.

SNOWBOUND

Sunday—the tenth day on Earth for Clair—was a quiet one for Doc and his otherworldly guest. The snow continued throughout the night until nearly 9:00 a.m., covering the Charlevoix area with an eight-inch winter blanket. It was one of those snowfalls that had started so slowly and descended so gracefully, the accumulation had snuck up on the community.

The lane from Boyne City Road leading down to Doc's cabin could no longer be navigated, so Doc made a call to his poker-playing buddy, Michael, the cop, who said he could clear the lane later in the afternoon. Like Doc, Michael didn't work on Sundays, but being the good civil servant he was, there were a number of other people he felt obligated to plow out first. Nurses who needed to get to the hospital for their shifts and cops that had to get to their cruisers at the fire hall. The snow hadn't caused any deaths or serious injuries, but it was still giving people headaches. Power lines were down on Elm Street, the roof of an old barn off M66 had partially collapsed, and several vehicles had slid off the road and needed assistance, especially in the Ironton Ferry area.

Doc told Michael he wasn't in any particular hurry for plowing, so he and Clair went for a walk down the lane, since there was absolutely no chance of her being seen by anyone. Despite the fresh powder, the sun shone brightly and the temperature was rising. He wanted to take his Olympus camera and shoot some pictures of the tall pines on either side of the lane that had been reinvented by the snow, but his guest asked him to leave it behind for fear she might show up in a photo. "There can't be any physical evidence of me after I'm gone," she explained. Doc expressed surprise that her image would even show up in a picture, to which she replied, "I'm an angel. Not a vampire." He was tempted to snap of picture of her with his phone when she wasn't looking, but didn't.

For most of the day, Clair and Doc did domestic things. He kept a fire going, she made the beds. He did the laundry, she cleaned the bathrooms. He read, she prepared pork chops for dinner. Although it was never far from his mind that he was sharing his house with a celestial being, not every moment could be focused on her mission, God, or theological bantering. Indeed, he found the bantering frustrating and ultimately tiring. So the two of them just occupied space politely and harmoniously like any other young couple might do on a snowbound Sunday afternoon. As the day went on, though, there was one thing he noted: as attractive as Clair was, and for as many times as he had seen her naked, he hadn't lied to her about his amorous feelings. He honestly didn't have any for her and he wondered about that.

He also wondered why Farren kept creeping into his mind. As the hours passed, he realized it wasn't just because she was in danger. He kept thinking about how helpful she'd been with Austin Redman and how he liked that she liked literature. He admired how she accompanied him to the emergency room after he banged his head. He liked that she read to an elderly woman, had made him lunch and served it on a yacht, and he liked how she decorated the Social Center for the dance. He also couldn't forget how great she looked in that green spangled dress or how good she felt in his arms when they danced. Technically, Clair was the more attractive of the two, a real voluptuous head-turner. Farren, with her freckles, tousled bangs, pixie haircut and lean arms, was more like somebody's tomboy kid sister. Still, his thoughts kept returning to her, and this concerned him. It seemed the more he told himself that it was wrong to be attracted to her, the more he thought of yet another thing to like about her. It reminded him of Julia and the bad timing of their relationship—they shouldn't have gotten involved, therefore they did. He feared such feelings might interfere with him doing his job and keeping her safe from Charlie. He was even a little concerned that such thoughts might not meet with the Almighty's approval. He figured he was already on thin ice for his years of doubts and simmering resentment about losing Julia, and he didn't want to make his standing any worse. Then again, there was a rebellious side to him that didn't much care what his Creator thought. Doc and the Lord were disconnected and had been for a long time.

Michael showed up to plow the lane out about dinnertime. Doc put on a coat and went outside to invite him in, and Clair was prepared to hide out in the bedroom if he did, but it had been a long day for the off-duty cop, so he passed. When Doc went back inside, he discovered a trail of discarded clothing and a gray wolf sitting on his still-broken bed. Taking the metamorphosis in stride, he led the animal outside so it could do its business. Twenty minutes later, Clair had turned back into human form and was huddled over the toilet in anticipation of nausea, but this was one of those transformations where no nausea occurred, and her stomach felt pretty good. So, they had dinner, although the pork chops were a little tough because of the delays and reheating.

After the dishes were done, they watched *Christmas In Connecticut* on DVD. Clair marveled how it was wonderfully clever that a Hollywood movie could be contained on a little silver plate that could be viewed anytime. She also said she had always thought that Barbara Stanwyck was beautiful. Meanwhile, Doc tried to calculate the last time she had been to Earth based upon tidbits of information she'd revealed. She knew Vernors Ginger Ale, Bing Crosby, and the classic 1945 Warner Brothers film, but she didn't know about Kmart, how to use the microwave, and she showed little interest in things like his laptop, TV, or DVD player until they came into use. Then again, she did understand the basic principle of his computer and the Internet, and she did know the world population. So it was hard for him to pinpoint what she might know from her last visit, versus what she might have been briefed on in preparation for this visit.

After the movie, it was time for comfortable clothes and hot chocolate. Clair went to the bedroom to put on her pink sleep shirt with the cherubs, black slippers, and a pair of Doc's sweat pants while he went outside to collect a few more logs from the woodpile.

As Clair was warming up the milk on the stove in the kitchen and Doc re-stoked the fire, he made an observation about her shirt.

"You know, I thought you would've said something by now about that shirt I got you."

"I did thank you for it," she remembered, calling from the kitchen.

"I was talking about what's on it. The cherubs?"

"Oh ... very cute, very appropriate."

"I thought it might remind you of home."

"As I've said before, Doc, my plane of existence is spiritual, not physical. The way angels really are and how man perceives us are slightly different."

"You mean, angels don't have wings?"

"The Old Testament speaks of angels having wings in Isaiah. But I think a Roman Emperor named Constantine had as much to do with it as anyone."

"Really?" he called, putting the black screen in front of the fireplace. "How's that."

"In the fourth century, Constantine converted to Christianity," she continued, pouring the milk into mugs. "When he did, the whole Roman empire converted, meaning, dozens of pagan gods were displaced. Pagan gods with wings like Cupid, Hermes, and Mercury. So, artists started to depict angels with wings as a familiar way for the early Roman Christians to embrace the one true God."

She stirred the hot chocolate mix into the mugs while he sat down on the leather sofa nearest the kitchen, thinking. "You said a mouthful when you said, 'The one true God.' What about all the people who lived and died and worshiped pagan gods prior to Jesus' arrival?"

"What about them?" Clair said, slowly walking into the living room with their mugs. "God has always loved the righteous and compassionate." She put the mugs down on the wood plank table, then sat down opposite him on the leather sofa closet to the desk. "Think of all mankind as a growing child, the whole species is on a path of learning and development that will eventually mature and lead to the Father. Paul even wrote about it in a letter to the Ephesians. Of course, other things could happen along the way, too. You could blow yourself up in a nuclear war, drain the Earth of its resources, a huge meteorite might strike the planet; it's stuff like that that keeps things interesting."

He picked up his mug and looked at her straight-faced. "You've got a lousy bedside manner."

She smiled, leaned forward, and picked up her mug. "You're missing the point. The Earth, mankind, *you*—it's all a journey. Along the way, there's good and bad. Some things are easy; other things are hard. What's important is to look for answers every day. Do the best you can. Keep your faith strong. Treat others as you would want to be treated. That's really all God wants."

"I thought you weren't going to reveal any 'Great Mysteries?'" he said, taking a sip of his drink.

"I haven't. But, you tend to think things are all smoky and mysterious with God, and they're not. Yes, he's a big concept, and there may be some things we'll never understand. But, other answers come if we strive for them. In the meantime, it doesn't take much to please him. Remember, he gave Moses only ten commandments."

They fell silent, sipped on their hot chocolate, and watched the crackling fire. Doc liked Clair. But, frankly, he didn't want to hear any more about God. Being with his houseguest was sometimes like being in an endless religion class—a class he didn't sign up for.

The following day, Doc's Wrangler was ready for pickup. He went to the body shop at noon and left the Kia that Enterprise Car Rental would retrieve later, then swung by the hospital to drop off some paperwork for his boss, Harry Stanton. He had noticed that morning that Lance had been more quiet than usual, but didn't think much of it. He dismissed his silence as pre-engagement jitters now that he was finally going to commit to Charlene. Lance also passed on lunch, saying he wanted to do some Christmas shopping for his parents. But, again, Doc didn't think anything of it.

At the hospital, he rounded a corner near a wall displaying several different artists' renderings of the automated lighthouse on the breakwater at the beginning of the Pine River from Lake Michigan and ran nearly head-on into Farren's granddad. He wasn't wearing his usual crewneck sweater and golf shirt. Today, it was a long-sleeved red plaid shirt with jeans, but as always, he looked fit and chipper with his two-day growth of white stubble.

"Gus?" he said, surprised. "Fancy meeting you here. How're you doing?"

"I'm doing great, my boy. Fantastic!" the older man smiled more animated than he had ever seen. "How're you?"

"Good. I looked for you Saturday night. Thought maybe you might show up at the church dance."

"It's not my scene. But I hear it was nice."

"What're you doing here?"

"My doctor wanted me to take a couple of tests. You know, just standard checkup stuff, and Farren blew off her usual Monday visit to the bookstore to come with me and give another pint of blood for that Redman boy. So, we closed the marina for a couple hours."

"Farren's here?"

"I'm going to meet her in the cafeteria for lunch. Want to join us?"

"Thanks, but I think I'll pass. Hey, do you ever play poker?"

"Occasionally," the old man answered. "But I'm not very good." He said it in such a way that Doc didn't really believe him. "Why?"

"I play poker every couple of weeks with some guys from the fire hall. Just nickel-and-dime stuff. We're not very good, either. But we have beer, pizza, a few laughs. I think we're putting the game on hold until after the holidays. But, once we resurrect it, care to join us sometime?"

"Sounds like fun. We can all be not very good together," Gus winked. "I'll give you a call."

"Just don't invite my grandson-in-law," the older man requested.

"Not a problem. See you later, Gus."

"Take care, Doc."

After Gus had rounded the corner and was gone, Doc thought for a moment about whether or not he wanted to go to the lab where blood was usually drawn. At first, he decided not to, but then changed his mind since he had no other immediate plans or reasons to see the woman he was supposed to protect.

In the small lab area, Farren was just sitting up from a table and a young blonde female med tech was just picking up the clear plastic bag of red blood lying under it when Doc walked into the room.

"Hi, Doc," the blonde technician smiled, clearly pleased to see him.

"Hey, Susie. Miss Farren, I heard you were here."

A little disappointed that the paramedic had dropped in to see Farren and not her, the med tech said she had to label the blood, excused herself, and left the lab. But her obvious eyes for Doc didn't escape Farren's notice.

"I think you've got a fan, there," she observed, struggling to roll down the right sleeve of her cowboy-cut denim shirt over the cotton ball and Band-Aid at the bend of her arm.

"Yeah. All twenty years of her," he answered, uninterested. "But she's a nice girl. I ran into Gus in the corridor. He said you were down here."

"How did his tests go? Did he say?"

"No, but he was in a great mood."

She nodded. "Good. So what brings you here?"

"Paperwork. Gus said you came in to give more blood for Austin?"

"I did, but it looks like he's not going to need it. I went up to his room to say hi, and his mom told me that after a second battery of X-rays and additional tests of his reflexes, his doctors have decided spinal surgery won't be necessary."

"Really?" he said, surprised. "Wow, that's, that's *great!*"

"His mom said it'll cut his recuperation time in half."

He smiled and nodded at the good news, then changed subjects.

"I'm glad I ran into you. I feel like I owe you an apology for that silly bidding war Charlie and I got into Saturday night. It was—I don't know—testosterone run amok or something."

She snapped the cuff of her shirt and looked at him, her clear brown eyes weighing his words. He knew instantly she wanted more of an explanation.

"Look, don't take this the wrong way. I'm not trying to hit on you or anything. But, since I've gotten to know you a little, I've been kicking myself for not taking Charlene up on that blind date way back when. I mean, I *did* want to buy that basket for her. But, I also think I got into it with Charlie because I was a little envious. He ended up with you, and I never got to bat. Matter of fact, I never even got my butt off the bench. And, I *know* that's a stupid thing to say to a married woman, and I apologize for even saying it, but, anyway ..." He paused, "I'm going to stop now before I put my *other* foot in my mouth." He opened one of the Velcro flaps of his black pants and pulled out his wallet. "Let me give you something to help defray the ridiculous cost of that basket?"

"No," she said, brushing her bangs aside. She continued to look at him as if she were trying to decide something. He assumed she was deciding whether or not to be put off by what he had just revealed.

After an anxious couple of moments, she hopped off the table. "I was thinking of going Christmas shopping tomorrow in Traverse City. Any chance you might be able to come? Strictly as friends, you understand?"

"Sure," he said, rather surprised. "I'll trade shifts with one of the weekend paramedics. Or threaten to release the picture of my boss wearing that pink tutu he likes so much."

She smiled. "You've got my cell number. Call me later."

They walked out of the lab and into the hall. When they did, a man about Doc's age spotted Farren and called, "Nice to meet you."

"Nice meeting you, too," she called back. Then, the man went on his way.

"Friend of yours?" he asked.

"Austin's uncle. I met him upstairs."

"Oh?"

He came all the way from Marquette. He brought the kid a gift that really made him happy."

"Oh, yeah? What was that?"

"A telescope."

The hairs on the back of Doc's neck stood on end. He paused, half-smiled, and rubbed his forehead with the tips of his fingers.

SECRETS REVEALED

On the side of Highway 31 heading toward Traverse City, there was a snow-smattered green sign with white lettering that told travelers they were precisely halfway between the North Pole and the Equator. Doc's newly repaired red Wrangler sped by this pinpoint of longitude and latitude kicking up clouds of vagrant snow on the two-lane interstate. He and Farren were enjoying pleasant, but nothing-in-particular, conversation as they embarked on a day trip to do Christmas shopping.

They'd gotten a late start, not leaving Charlevoix until nearly 11. A boat owner had called Farren unexpectedly and wanted to meet with her about re-rigging his outboards. The sky was overcast with billowy clouds although it was supposed to be clear by evening. She was wearing a heavy off-white woolen sweater, a white knit hat with long earflaps hanging down, jeans, and her K-Swiss boots. She also had a heavier coat, but it was lying on the back seat. The hat made her look slightly like a Basset Hound, but with her dimples and freckles, a really cute one. He was also wearing jeans, his Timberlands, a black turtleneck, and his brown leather bomber jacket.

During the one-hour drive, Doc never asked if Farren wanted to go to the airport to check and see if Charlie's truck was really there. In fact, the only thing that was said about Charlie was when he casually asked where he was working this particular week, and she answered he was back in Milwaukee. He sensed that, even though they were going to Traverse City, she hadn't quite decided whether or not to check up on him. So he didn't push it. He figured the mere fact that she had suggested they go was progress enough.

"Your Jeep's warmer than I would've thought," she noticed, eyeing the black canvas roof and holding a Danish he had just bought her a couple of miles back.

"Yeah. It's not bad. Except I have to continually brush the roof off in a heavy snow so the fabric doesn't get damaged."

"So, who do you have to shop for?" she asked, taking a bite of her Danish.

"My mom, dad, sister, and brother-in-law, Lance and Charlene, and there's a used bookstore on Front Street I like to check out whenever I'm in town."

"Do you get over to TC a lot?"

"No, not much. But I remember going there with my family and camping at the state park across from the public beach on the bay when we were kids."

"Are you close to your parents?" she asked, taking another bite of her pastry.

"Not as close as I'd like to be. That's why I moved back to Michigan. Ten years ago, I had a falling out with them. I was accepted to Wayne State University Medical School but didn't go. Needless to say, they were—" he searched for just the right but not overly dramatic word, "disappointed."

"What happened?"

"Julia died."

She stopped in mid-chew as he continued.

"Things are better now. I've still got some fences to mend. But, overall, better."

She started chewing again while thinking.

"So, Julia died, you became a paramedic instead of a doctor, then you left the state?"

"Not right away. There were some sad Sara McLachlan and James Taylor songs, some drinking, a belligerent attitude, even the broken heart of a young lady or two who were innocent bystanders in the train wreck of my life. *Then* I left."

She nodded. "I understand the anger. I had a lot myself after my folks died."

"How did you finally get a handle on it?"

"It was a combination of things: my grandfather, my faith, Father Ken, time, just growing up, I suppose. My mom used to say, 'You can make the world better, or you can make it worse.' You can't make things better with a chip on your shoulder."

He thought about what she said while she finished her Danish.

"I'd appreciate it if you kept what I just told you about me private. I don't really share stuff like that with other people, although with you, I seem to want to."

She smiled and dabbed her full, rounded lips with a napkin. "That's because you know I'm safe. I'm an old married woman who won't take the information and make judgments against you."

They were quiet for a few moments while flat, white cornfields followed by rows of dormant cherry trees rolled by.

"How about you?" he asked, keeping his eyes on the blacktop. "Who do you have to shop for?"

"Everybody. Charlie, Grandpa, my banker—"

"You get a Christmas gift for your banker?"

"If you saw the marina's books, you'd understand."

He smiled while she looked him over, curiously. "So, you kinda wish we'd have gone on that blind date, eh?"

"Well, I don't know," he drawled, with false hesitation. "Blind dates—in fact—the first several dates of a relationship are all BS, anyway."

"Why's that?"

"Cause everybody's on their best behavior. Nobody reveals anything. Everybody wants to be as neutral as possible until the relationship is further down the road. Then, the *real* secrets about a person come out."

"Oh, yeah?" she said, her curiosity piqued. "Tell me something you wouldn't reveal about yourself until you were several dates into a relationship."

"Naaaa."

"C'mon," she said, playfully. "You chicken?"

He thought for a second.

"Uh ... well, I probably like chick flicks more than the average guy would admit."

"You read Jane Austen. No surprise there. Besides, no girl would think that's a negative. Try again."

"Eh ... I don't go to church."

"Good."

"Good?"

"No, not that that's good. But, that's something that might change a girl's perception about you."

"How 'bout you?"

"What?"

"Tell me something about yourself you wouldn't reveal until you were several dates down the road?"

She thought momentarily. "I don't have—I *didn't* have a lot of sexual experience with men until I, y' know, got married."

He smiled slightly. "Like you said, many wouldn't perceive that as a negative. Try again."

"I think if men fish for sport, they ought to practice catch and release."

"Good," he nodded. "A lot of guys wouldn't agree with that. I think women who purposely arrive somewhere late just to be fashionable, are rude."

"I don't like men who watch sports all the time."

"I don't like a woman who's messy."

"I don't like horror movies."

"I've never watched an episode of American Idol."

"I sometimes drool in my sleep."

"I sometimes fart in my sleep. So loud I wake myself up."

She looked at him and giggled. Then continued. "I've got a scar on my back from falling on a broken cleat."

"I don't have a gall bladder, which can sometimes give me pretty bad cramps after I eat."

"I can sustain a belch longer than any man I know."

"Really?" he asked.

"Really," she said, confidently.

"Prove it."

For a couple of moments, it seemed like she wasn't going to demonstrate her prowess; but then she swallowed some air, opened her mouth, and out came a deep guttural belch. Considering the tone of her pleasant speaking voice, it was as if somebody else were inside of her because of its low, rumbling resonance. Like a large chainsaw, the belch roared on and on, causing Doc to actually look at his wristwatch.

After nearly ten seconds, the vibrating of Farren's upper esophageal sphincter settled down leaving an amazed Doc Reynolds in its wake.

"Good God, woman!" he gawked. "That's not a belch. That's … that's a foghorn on the Queen Mary. That's an Early Warning System for small towns."

"Now you think me unladylike," she pouted.

"Never," he assured. "But, I don't think you could ever get lost in the woods."

She looked at him smiling, her brown eyes sparkling. She found this conversation not only fun, but liberating.

"I've been known to use other people's toothbrushes," she continued.

He gestured to the top of his head.

"I might be getting a bald spot."

"There was a time, after my parents died, that I had four cats."

"I'm allergic to cats."

"Me too," she laughed. "I found that one out the hard way. I've got a doll that I slept with 'til I was eighteen."

"I had a mole that had to be removed from my testicles."

She pointed toward her mouth. "I have to wax my upper lip or I'll get a mustache."

"I think long letters are better than short texts."

"A raccoon once got into the storage barn at the marina and I thought it spoke to me."

"I've got an angel living in my house that changes into animals."

She looked at him. He looked at her. Then, they both burst into laughter.

Lansing was the capitol of Michigan, but once past Grayling heading north, Traverse City, or "TC" as some called it, was the unofficial capitol of the upper part of the Lower Peninsula. Nestled against Grand Traverse Bay, Traverse City called itself The Cherry Capitol Of The World, and indeed, along with tourism, cherries were a huge part of the economy. In summer, there was even a weeklong Cherry Festival where one could sample everything from cherry preserves to cherry pancakes to cherry pies. In winter, there was a healthy ski industry. With a permanent population of fourteen thousand five hundred, it offered the best selection of shopping in the twenty-one-county northern-Michigan region.

They started their excursion at the Grand Traverse Mall. Ironically, it was just down the road from the Cherry Capitol Airport, but Farren never said a word about wanting to go there. At JC Penney, she bought a picture frame for Father Ken. He picked up a set of king-size sheets that his sister had hinted at the last time they spoke on the phone. At Target, she bought Charlie a pair of jeans and a sweater that Doc reluctantly had to model for her. As they passed Victoria's Secret, he kidded that he was fairly certain Charlie would rather see her in something from there as opposed to having new jeans and a sweater. She responded that Charlie had gotten her some intimate apparel—and that she was happy to wear it—but the allure was kind of shattered when she would come out of the bathroom wearing her new lingerie with thick, white athletic socks. She explained how she inherited poor circulation on her father's side and that her feet were always cold, particularly in her small house in winter.

Having someone to go shopping with really put the two of them in the Christmas mood. They knew it was all in their imagination, but the decorations seemed a little prettier, salespeople seemed a little nicer, and small kids standing in line to see Santa seemed a little cuter. A couple of salespeople even assumed Doc and Farren were married. When they did, she just smiled and looked at him, and he appreciated the fact that she didn't feel it necessary to correct strangers.

As Doc browsed through Home Furnishings in Macy's, trying to find some inspiration about what to get his parents, he finally broached the subject of his companion's spouse.

"I suppose it's a little late now, but is Charlie cool with us hanging out together like this?"

"Why wouldn't he be?"

"Gee, let me think: Newly married attractive woman going out of town with an incredibly handsome single guy."

"Everybody comes to TC to Christmas shop," she waved off. "Three or four years ago, I did my shopping here with Lance. Charlene couldn't get off work and she didn't go crazy. Besides, I didn't want to make the drive by myself. It could be hazardous for a woman alone in all this snow. Highway 31 has long stretches of nothing."

"Hmm," he nodded, not having considered that.

"As for the incredibly handsome guy stuff, I gotta tell you, the whole loud-farts-in-your-sleep thing kinda killed it for me."

"Great. Thank you," he smiled. "So glad I'm scoring points here."

She giggled girlishly as something caught her eye. "How about a small table lamp for your folks?" She pointed to one in particular that she liked. "It could go on a desk, a nightstand, a little corner table?"

He looked it over. "I don't know if they'd like the style. But *I* do."

They strolled on from Home Furnishings into Men's Wear. She smiled at another couple going in the opposite direction arm in arm, while the store's music system played "Carol Of The Bells" by the Trans Siberian Orchestra.

"What *is* it about Christmas?" she asked. "Sure, there's the religious aspect and the joy of children, but it's something more."

"Highest suicide rate of the year," he deadpanned.

She gently nudged him sideways with her hip, then continued her thought. "It's like, this is the way it's *supposed* to be. People being kinder, more generous, families coming together, even wars in non-Christian countries have ceasefires this time of year."

"That are never kept," he reminded.

"But they try," she said, admiringly. "Man's capable of so many good things. I think we love Christmas because once a year, for a little while, we get a glimpse of what we *could* be."

He smiled at her warmly. "You remind me of someone."

"Julia?"

"No. But, she lives in heaven, too."

She looked at him curiously, but he didn't offer an explanation.

They shopped at the mall until 3:30, then loaded up the Jeep with their gifts and went downtown. They had a late lunch at a pub on Union Street, and Farren picked up the tab to pay Doc back for the gas. Then, they walked over to Front Street so he could visit the used bookstore he'd mentioned earlier. They saw a sign outside of a bank that said the temperature was only twenty-two degrees, but neither seemed to be bothered by the cold. They were enjoying doing something different than their normal routines, enjoying the season, and genuinely enjoying each other's company.

The bookstore was in an office building built in the 1940s that had been remodeled to accommodate several shops on its first floor. There was a 1960s style T-shirt and poster shop, an art gallery, a store that specialized in things from Ireland, a pottery place, and the bookstore. It wasn't particularly big, but it was jammed with thousands of previously owned books, both hardcover and paperback. The smell of old paper and ink filled the air as if one could simply breathe deep and absorb a classic story.

Farren had mentioned that she had always wanted to learn about astronomy, and Doc helped her find a book about the constellations and the myths behind them. As she was thumbing through this book, and he had wandered over to a stack of history books and was perusing a paperback about Thomas Jefferson, she happened to look up and see something. At first, the expression on her face was restrained disbelief. But, as she slowly walked across the room to the other side of the store, the disbelief turned into a more stunned expression etched with winces of confusion. Sitting on a table, under a small, lift-away Plexiglas case, was a book on a stand. It was a copy of Jane Austen's *Pride & Prejudice*; a

1922 edition, just like the one she told Doc she had misplaced.

He looked up to see her standing motionless—not even breathing—before the glass case and knew that something was wrong. When he walked over, stood next to her, and looked at the book, he figured it out instantly. Her losing her rare copy, or at least her *believing* she had lost it, was how they met in the first place.

"It's a 1922 edition," she said, under her breath. She stared at it blankly. All the color had drained from her face. "It's mine. The binding's cracked in exactly the same place ... my ... my mom gave me that book when I turned thirteen. She inherited it from her mom."

Doc motioned for the store manager to come over. He had white hair, thick glasses, and was in his sixties. He had a protruding belly that spilled over a smaller waist and tight, hugging black and yellow suspenders that seemed to hold him all together.

"Could you tell us a little something about this book, please?"

"You have good taste," the manager said with an accent that suggested Boston. "A 1922 *Pride and Prejudice*, published by Hobson of London. Halfway through a printing of five thousand copies, the printing house burned down and only a few hundred editions survived. We almost never get anything in here this rare."

"How long have you had it?" Doc asked.

"About two weeks."

"How—" Farren stopped herself, not wanting to complete her question, but after a moment, found the composure to, with glistening eyes, "how did you get this copy? Could someone tell me?"

"I bought it," the manager said. "Got it from a man who was from out of town."

"How do you know he was from out of town?" she asked.

"He wanted cash. Wouldn't take a check. He also asked me if there was a pawnshop in the area."

Farren's moist eyes became even fuller. She remembered what Father Ken had said: He thought he saw a man who looked like Charlie coming out of a pawnshop.

"Anything else you remember about him?" Doc asked.

"Yes. Good-looking blond-haired chap, but walked with a cane. Normally, I wouldn't remember. We get so many people in here. But a 1922 *Pride and Prejudice* doesn't come through the door every day."

"Could I see it, please?" she asked.

She handed her book about constellations to Doc while the manager slowly lifted up the Plexiglas case. Then, he noticed somebody waiting at the cash register.

"Please be very careful with it," he said, setting the case aside. "I'll be right back." He headed toward the cash register, while Farren looked at the book still on its stand. Doc watched her staring at it with her large, wet, brown eyes as if it were a portal through time.

"The night my mom gave it to me, I left it face down on a table out on the back patio of our house on West Upright. It started to rain. I ran out and got it right away, but a few drops splashed on the back cover and stained it."

She slowly reached out, picked up the book, and turned it over. As a tear rolled down her cheek, she gently ran her finger over the water stains both of them knew were there even before she looked.

"Why?" she said softly, closing her eyes. "Why would Charlie take this out of our home? Why would he sell it?"

Doc knew the answer—Charlie didn't work for a construction company and had taken and sold the book to put cash in his pocket—but didn't respond. She wiped her cheek with her palm as the store manager came back over.

"What do we think?" he said.

"How much are you asking for it?" Doc queried.

The manager rubbed his chin, considering. "The cover's not in pristine condition, and it's been read a lot … I'll let it go for three hundred."

"We'll take it," Doc answered without hesitation. He reached for his wallet.

"Doc, no!" she gasped.

"An excellent Christmas gift," the manager smiled. "You'll want this in a box."

As the manager turned and headed back toward the cash register, Doc looked at Farren.

"How it wound up here is between you and Charlie. But it should be with its rightful owner."

"I don't have that kind of money right now," she whispered.

"We'll worry about that later," he said in a low tone, pulling out his Visa.

He went over to the cash register and paid for the book. She lingered for a moment by the empty stand and Plexiglas case and, once again, closed her eyes with sorrow. But a few seconds later, they reopened with resolve.

The manager put the book in a box and put the box in a bag. After he thanked Doc, and had moved on to another customer, Farren walked over.

"Do me a favor?" she asked.

"You bet."

"Take me to the airport."

ASTRONOMY LESSON

It was only 5:40 p.m., but already dark as Doc finished his third slow patrol of the long-term parking lot at the Cherry Capitol Airport. After driving up then down lane after lane of parked cars not once, but three times, it was obvious that Charlie's dark blue Ford F150 wasn't on the property.

"Want me to go around again?" he asked.

Farren didn't verbally respond. She merely shook her head and wiped away another tear that had streaked her face. Her white knit cap with the long earflaps only framed her sadness all the more, and it tore at Doc's heart. He reached behind her seat, and his hand fumbled around on the floor until it found a small packet of Kleenex that he offered her. She thanked him in a voice little more than a whisper, then they pulled out of the parking lot onto South Airport Road and started heading north toward Highway 31 and back home to Charlevoix. All of the day's fun and Christmas cheer had now evaporated like a snowflake in the desert.

They drove for several minutes in silence except for Farren blowing her nose. Once they were out of town and passing the several-story dark-glass silhouette of the Grand Traverse Bay Spa & Resort that loomed out of place against the snowy landscape, he felt he had to speak.

"Do you mind if I ask you something?"

"You mean, like, why I'm so stupid?" she spat out, self-deprecatingly.

"You're not stupid," he reassured. "When you call Charlie during the week, does he have an office phone?"

"No," she said, in between sniffles. "Because he travels from site to site, his cell is the best way to reach him. But if it's off, I can leave a voice mail or get a message to him through the receptionist at the home office."

"In Flint?"

"Yes."

"So, you've called the home office?" he asked, wanting verification.

"Yes, a couple of times."

"Do you happen to know the number?"

"It's an 800-number programmed into my cell."

"Good. Let's call it now."

"What? Why?"

"Just indulge me."

"No, Doc," she said, dabbing her eyes. "I don't know what's going on exactly, but I don't want to do a knee-jerk reaction. This is my marriage we're talking about. Besides, it's after five. The office is closed."

"Fine. Then see if he's got a voice mailbox in the company directory. Or, maybe you'll reach somebody who's working late."

"Why?"

"Because—it's possible he doesn't work there anymore. Maybe he never did."

"Of *course* he works there," she protested. "I've called the receptionist and left messages."

"But his truck isn't at the airport, Farren. So he's *not* in Milwaukee. And he sold a family heirloom and let you believe *you* lost it. That means he needs money. These are some pretty serious deceits we're talking about. Call the home office."

"I don't want to!" she said, defensively. "Not until I've had time to think things out."

"But—"

"Please, Doc," she interrupted.

After thirty more seconds of silence, she quietly asked, "Do you think there's a logical reason—some explainable rationale for Charlie's behavior? Like drugs, or something?"

"No. I don't think it's drugs," he answered, knowing better. "But, even if it were, I'd never lie to my wife. I ... wouldn't."

There were several things he figured he was supposed to say at this juncture. Maybe he should've pushed Farren harder about calling the home office of Miller Construction to see if Charlie really worked there, which he knew he didn't. If someone in the past had been answering the phone and was covering for Charlie, maybe he should suggest that they compare that number with the phone number listed on the Miller

Construction website. Maybe—probably—Charlie had given her a bogus number. But then, how could he suggest such a thing to her? How could he encourage her to uncover lies about her husband without sounding like he was trying to assassinate his character or was a jealous boyfriend? The truth was, he *was* trying to expose Charlie's character, and he *was* jealous. But, he didn't want to alienate himself with Farren by doing so. She was already feeling confused and betrayed, maybe that was enough. Maybe the best thing to do was simply support her in silence and be available if she wanted to talk. He looked at the frost growing on the corners of his windows. The sky had cleared up, but the temperature had dropped.

They rode for another twenty minutes in silence. The only thing he asked was if she'd like to hear some music. She said yes, but no Christmas music. So he found a public radio station playing Bach chamber music, which she approved of. The somberness of the harpsichord, flute, and cello seemed to suit her sadness.

"Can we ... would you mind finding a place to pull over for a minute?" she finally requested, breaking the long silence.

There was a roadside picnic area that was closed for the winter but, for some reason, the county road crew had plowed it out. Probably so snowplows would have a place to turn around on the two-lane Highway 31. Doc pulled in, turned off the lights and radio, but kept the engine and heater going. The late afternoon seemed to get very quiet except for the occasional semi-truck roaring by and leaving a swirling flurry of white powder behind it.

Farren slipped off her cap and ran her fingers through her matted hair, struggling to express what was in her heart.

"Don't ask me why I'm asking this ... when Julia was alive ... when you were with her ... were you ..." she paused, looking for just the right word.

"Was I what?"

She wanted to ask if he was gentle with Julia when they made love because that wasn't her experience with Charlie. But she shook her head deciding not to pursue the thought. Instead, she took a heavy breath and pursued another.

"You see your peers going off to college, starting careers, starting families, while you're doing the same thing you've been doing since you were fifteen—taking care of rich people's toys. You tell yourself, 'That's okay. Hang in there. Be a good person. You may not get rich, but someday you'll meet someone to share your life with.'

"But the years pass. You get scared. You're alone. And then, one day, you meet someone. He's new ... not like the guys you've known since grade school. He pays attention to you, sends you lots of flowers, and you think, 'Yes, *finally*, I'm special to someone.' You get starry-eyed. Impulsive. You move fast because you know what loss feels like, and you don't want to lose out again. And, even though everything isn't perfect afterward, you rationalize by saying, 'What is? ... Be patient ... it'll work out.'"

She leaned sadly against the passenger-side door, not knowing what else to say. He looked at her, then through the front windshield and up at the sky. It was now nearly totally clear except for a couple of small lingering clouds and some stars were already out. Getting an idea, he unbuckled his shoulder harness.

"C'mon," he said, turning off the engine.

"What?"

"Put your hat on. I want to show you something."

"It's gotta be, like, ten degrees outside."

"Sturdy northern Michigan girl like you? That's a heat wave. C'mon," he insisted, opening his door.

She wasn't enthusiastic about getting out, but she slipped on her hat, put on her coat that had spent most of the day in the back seat, and then slipped on her gloves. While she was doing this, Doc walked away from the road twenty yards or so and broke a small branch, about the size of a pencil, off an older snow-covered oak tree.

Zipping up her coat and following behind, using his footprints as a path in the seven inches of snow, she approached him impatiently. "Okay. What?"

"Up there," he said, pointing to the sky with the stick. "See those three stars all in a line?"

"Orion's belt," she recognized.

"Right. But, do you know the other stars that make up the constellation?"

"I ... I think so," she said, becoming interested.

"Let's be sure." He moved around behind her shoulders and leaned in close. He started to point out the additional stars that made up the figure of The Hunter, although they weren't all visible yet.

"There are different explanations about how Orion became a constellation," he began, "you'll find him in Arabian, Indian, Egyptian, and Greek mythology. One of the most popular stories is that Orion was a great hunter who liked to boast about all the animals he had killed. Then, one night while he slept, a giant scorpion named Scorpio killed him by stinging off his leg. After this happened, the gods put both of them in the sky, but put Scorpio in the summer sky and Orion in the winter sky, so the two would never have to meet again. If you look carefully, you'll see that Orion even has two dogs with him, Canis Major and Minor."

"You know all this from reading?" she asked.

"No. At Eastern Michigan I took an astronomy elective and really got into stargazing. One of these days, I'm going to buy a nice telescope. The kind where you can just program a star's coordinates and the scope goes automatically to the location."

For the next several seconds, they were silent. She continued to look at the sky and hear his steady breathing behind her. From her peripheral vision, she could see his breath coming over her shoulder then disappearing onto her chest. He kept his eyes on the sky as well, but what he was really doing was absorbing the traces of perfume he could detect from her, even in the nearly sub-zero temperature.

After twenty motionless seconds of this nearly erotic nothingness, she took a small step forward and turned to him, but they were still standing close.

"Why are we out here? Why are you doing this?" she asked, looking up at him.

"It's important to me that you know who I am," he said. "It's important that you know I grew up in Ann Arbor, that my dad owns a lawn-and-garden nursery, and my mom's an accountant. It's important you know I have a married sister in North Carolina. I like to read. I'm good at understanding how the human body works like other people might be good at crossword puzzles. I want you to know about Julia, and that I think you've handled your losses more graciously than I've handled mine. You've bravely stayed put while I ran away. I want you to know I understand why you jumped into a relationship with Charlie. It's important you know all these things because I don't think you know the man you married very well, and if we're going to be friends, I, at least, want you to know *me*."

Another wave of tears began to swim in Farren's eyes. But they weren't because of Charlie's actions. They were partly out of gratitude for what Doc had said, and partly out of guilt because, ever since they had danced together Saturday night, he had likewise been stealing into her subconscious, and she didn't know what to do about it. In fact, she had actually prayed that any thoughts other than friendship for Wyatt "Doc"

Reynolds be purged from her mind. She felt guilty about such thoughts, about inviting him to come to Traverse City, even though she had framed it with, 'Strictly as friends.' She even felt guilty about having suspicions about how Charlie spent his weeks before she ever met Doc. But in the blink of an eye and now standing before him, all that guilt melted into resigned sadness. Standing before her was a good man. But a man who could only play a limited role in her life, and she was sorry for that.

"Thank you for the astronomy lesson," she said. "We'd better go." She folded her arms, stepped around him, and walked away through the snow.

As they were pulling out of the picnic area and picking up speed back on the highway, Doc tried to do what Clair would want.

"Do me a favor," he asked. "Don't keep what happened today hidden away. Talk to people you trust about it; Gus, Father Ken."

"I don't have all the facts, Doc," she protested. "I don't know Charlie's side of the story."

"That's true. But, you don't need Charlie's side of the story to know you've been lied to. Sometimes the counsel of others can really help."

"It's easy for people to be armchair quarterbacks," she observed.

She didn't say anything more, and, from the way she turned her head and looked out the passenger-side window, it was clear she didn't want to hear anything more about today's events. He wanted her to talk about it with others because it would put doubts in people's minds about Charlie. And if, God forbid, anything should happen to Farren, then people would at least know something wasn't right between them.

He wondered if he should talk to his cop-buddy, Michael, about Charlie. After all, now he had a tangible reason to. He had just decided to do so when Farren asked for his confidence.

"I need some time to think about all this," she finally announced.

"Understandable," he replied.

"I don't want to air my dirty laundry," she explained. "So I'm going to ask that you not discuss this with anyone. This is important to me, Doc. I want your word on this."

Reluctantly, he promised he wouldn't say anything to any other human being.

LATER THAT NIGHT

At 7:26 later that night, Charlie Huffman was just walking out of the Soaring Eagle Casino, a three-hour drive south from Charlevoix in Mt. Pleasant, Michigan. It was bone chilling cold. The fact that he was farther south didn't make a difference in the temperature. In fact, considering the wind-chill factor, Mt. Pleasant was actually colder than either Traverse City or Charlevoix. He was carrying a small, simulation leather club bag with handles in one hand and dialing a number on his cell phone with the other when a white Cadillac Escalade with tinted windows pulled up to the curb in front of him. Looking up and recognizing the vehicle, he kept his reaction hidden although his shoulders visibly slumped.

"Hello, Charlie," he heard a deep voice say behind him. He turned around to see Stanley, one of Bartholomew's enforcers and the man who had clipped off his little toe with a pair of pruning shears, approaching from behind. It only took a second for Charlie to realize Bartholomew, who was based in Flint, was making the rounds at casinos with his crew. As a loan shark, Bartholomew had people he was paying under the table throughout the state, as well as clients to check up on.

"Stanley," Charlie said, flashing a convincing, but insincere, smile, "I was just calling you."

"Really?" Stanley asked, disbelievingly.

"Really," the blond-haired man replied, showing him his cell phone and the number displayed on its screen, but not yet engaged.

Stanley glanced at the phone and nodded approvingly. He was about the same age as Charlie but built like a linebacker. In fact, Charlie had heard something about Stanley trying out for the Detroit Lions years earlier. He had a broad chest, thick, stubby neck, wore his brown hair short, and had a flat, wide nose that had been broken more than once by people who, no doubt, got more than their noses broken in return. Stanley wore khaki slacks, Johnston & Murphy loafers with leather tassels, a long-sleeved dress shirt with a sweater vest and, despite the cold, a lighter-weight North Face jacket. He didn't have any visible tattoos or piercings. He looked more like a collegiate football player than he did an enforcer for a loan shark with rumored mob connections. Then again, this was Michigan. It was corn-and-cherry country. It was a state full of farmers, laid-off autoworkers, and people who liked to hunt and fish. Wise guys in leather jackets named Vinnie or Bruno were in New York or maybe Chicago, not in Mt. Pleasant.

"Mr. Bartholomew would like a word with you." Stanley said, in a business-like tone. He gestured to the waiting Escalade.

"A word? Sure it's not a body part?" Charlie quipped.

"One never knows, does one?" Stanley responded, mysteriously.

"Damn, and I just stopped limping, too," Charlie mused. He was plenty scared, but if he was going to be worked over or separated from another appendage, he figured it was going to happen anyway, and he wasn't going to give Stanley the satisfaction of appearing intimidated. He took a deep breath then walked over to the Cadillac.

Climbing into the back seat, he didn't see Bartholomew, but he did see another one of his muscular employees behind the wheel. This one's name was George. He and Charlie had actually hung out a little back in Flint. They both had something in common having spent time in a number of foster homes. George liked Charlie and vice versa. But business was business with George, and Charlie knew it. He was dressed in a heavier jacket than Stanley, and, with his horn-rimmed Buddy Holly-like glasses, he also didn't look like what one might expect, except for his bench-press build.

"Hey, Charlie. Merry Christmas," George greeted, as Stanley shut Charlie's door, then rounded the SUV to the passenger-side door.

"Merry Christmas, George," Charlie reciprocated. He waited until Stanley had opened his door, and then asked, "We goin' to Mr. B's hotel, or something?"

"Or something," Stanley answered, settling into the front seat and being mysterious again.

The three men rode for about twenty minutes, past flat, snowy fields and an occasional oil well. To fill in the silence, George mentioned that it was a little-known fact that Michigan was one of the top twelve oil-producing states, and the Mt. Pleasant area had one of the richest deposits. They eventually came to a newly developed trailer park called Chippewa Valley. There were only four mobile homes on the property. One of them was a sales office, and the other three were models. All of them were lit up. The property could hold nearly one hundred homes and had an automated gate that George opened with a garage door opener. They drove past the sales office, past a few flat lots that had cardboard signs on stakes in front of them indicating the lot number, and pulled into the shoveled drive of the first model home. It was a doublewide with a bay window but the tan curtains inside were drawn. The half snow-covered sign out front identified this particular model as "The Presidential."

Once out of the Cadillac, Charlie glanced around as he walked up the sidewalk that was cleared enough to make a narrow path. There weren't any trees within a half-mile radius. There weren't any barns or houses, either. For a guy who always checked where the nearest exits were in restaurants, this isolated setting made him uncomfortable. The only sound was the wind blowing slightly and the crunch of his feet on patches of brittle snow not cleared off the sidewalk.

"Stomp your feet before you go in," Stanley told Charlie.

Coming to two concrete steps, he stomped any excess snow off his feet, then climbed the steps and opened the front door.

He walked into the living room of The Presidential, but there wasn't much in it. There was a linoleum floor that looked convincingly like wood, a large square maroon area rug, a floor lamp that was turned on, a few signs that were leaning up against a white wall opposite the front door that said, "Financing Available" and "No Money Down," and two upholstered office chairs with the arms facing each other about six feet apart on the area rug. They were the kind of chairs that one might see in a waiting room or opposite an executive's desk. Behind and adjoining the living room was an L-shaped counter for the kitchen beyond. No doubt when furnished, barstools went in front of this counter for eating. The overhead lights in the kitchen were also on. Sitting in one of the chairs in profile to Charlie as he came in was a young man about twenty-five. He had blond hair and was good-looking like Charlie, although in a different way. Charlie's hair was shorter, and his face was more chiseled and masculine. The younger man's hair was longer, thicker, and his features were more baby-faced. He wore a nice Pendleton sweater and blue jeans. His heavier winter coat and stocking cap were lying on the maroon area rug next to him.

"I'm not intimidated by the waiting game, guys," the stranger announced unconvincingly as Charlie walked in, followed by Stanley then George. It was at this point that Charlie noticed the young man was strapped into the chair. Plastic cable ties connected his wrists to the arms of the chair while his ankles were fastened to the front legs.

"Good for you, Daniel," Stanley said. "Over here, Charlie." He gestured to the chair opposite the young man. "Take your coat off and have a seat."

The con man knew the setting and circumstances were bad news. *Very* bad news. But he kept his cool, mustered a cocky smile and did as he was told.

"Who's *this?*" the younger man asked, incredulously.

"Daniel, Charlie. Charlie, Daniel," George said, making the introductions.

"How ya doin', partner?" Charlie greeted, trying to act unconcerned. He set his club bag down and took off his anonymous tan cloth coat with the corduroy collar. He dropped the coat next to the club bag he carried inside, sat down, then Stanley put one of his arms on the arm of the chair and started to secure him like the other guest.

"Is this really necessary, George?" Charlie asked, looking to his buddy.

"Stupid question," George replied.

"You boys kill me, and there's going to be coal in your stockings," Charlie joked.

George smiled and Stanley huffed as he finished with Charlie's wrists, then squatted down to secure his ankles.

"So, what's your story?" Daniel asked his fellow captive.

"For someone who's not intimidated, you sure look it," Charlie observed.

"I know what's happening here," Daniel said. "You're like a plant, aren't ya? You're pretending to be in trouble with Bartholomew, too, right? You're here to, to, scare me, or get some information out of me, or somethin' like that, right?"

Charlie looked over at George again. "Is he for real?"

George just rolled his eyes, amused. When Stanley was finished with the cable ties, he patted Charlie on the cheek and the two large men left the trailer. Now alone with only their bindings, Charlie and Daniel looked at one another for several seconds in silence.

"So, what's going to happen here?" Daniel finally asked.

"Well, partner, if I were a bettin' man, and I *am*, I'd say, one of us is going to die."

"W ... what?"

"Old Barbary pirate tactic; bring two men together who owe the leader a debt, kill the prisoner who owes the lesser amount, and it motivates the other prisoner to pay back the higher debt not only quickly, but with interest."

"This ... this is bull," Daniel said, nervously. "It's not good business to kill me. My father is, like, *really* rich. I mean, he's got a couple of guys he keeps around for security for himself. Know what I'm sayin'?"

"You're assumin' you're the one who's in trouble here, kid. Maybe it's me."

Daniel looked around the room nervously, and then tested the strength of the plastic ties holding his arms, which ended in a fruitless grunt.

"What do you do, kid?"

"Student. I'm a student at the college."

Charlie looked him over. "Little old for that, aren't ya?"

"I changed majors," he explained, defensively. "Lots of people do."

"Yeah? So, what did you change from?"

"Photography to Art History."

"Oh, of course," Charlie said, smirking. "Much more lucrative."

They were interrupted by the sound of feet stomping outside, then the front door opened. With a gust of bitter wind, Bartholomew walked in alone. He was a short, stocky man, Farren's height of five-feet-five, and in his mid-fifties. He had a brush cut haircut, slightly sagging jowls and wore an expensive camel hair overcoat. He had black rubbers on his Berluti leather shoes to protect them from the snow and wore black dress slacks. Some said he was of German heritage. Others said Russian. In either case, he was a man who liked to sprinkle conversations with big or unusual words. Charlie had known Bartholomew for years but still didn't know his first name. He came in carrying a portfolio case, as if he were going to try to sell his prisoners lots in Chippewa Village.

"I swear," he observed, in his sandpaper voice, closing the door behind him. "They say there are colder places. But I can't think of any."

"I heard Anchorage got down to twenty below a few days ago," the younger man blurted out.

Bartholomew turned his hazel eyes to the smooth-skinned college student.

"I was speaking rhetorically, Daniel. I wasn't actually soliciting a response."

"Right ... sorry, Mr. B."

"Charlie, how're you doing?" Bartholomew asked. He walked past the two men over to the L-shaped counter, put the black portfolio case down on top of it, then unbuttoned his overcoat. "How's the foot?"

"I'll live. At least, I'm *hoping* I will."

Bartholomew eyed the club bag on the floor next to Charlie's discarded coat.

"Stanley tells me you had a good night at the casino."

"A *very* good night. Did Stanley also tell you I was right in the middle of calling him when he came up behind me?"

"He did," the loan shark said. He slipped off his coat and laid it on the counter. He wore a nice crew neck sweater and dress shirt underneath. "So, did you two boys meet?"

"Yeah," the younger man answered. His torso was twisted around so he could see Bartholomew behind him at the counter.

The short man looked around the trailer and extended his arms a bit.

"What do you think of The Presidential? Of Chippewa Village?"

"You own this trailer park?" Daniel asked.

"Just one of several businesses I own," Bartholomew nodded. He turned back to his overcoat, dug through one of the pockets, and produced a Beretta PX4 Storm 9-millimeter pistol. Its black stainless-steel barrel was short and stubby. The entire weapon wasn't much bigger than the owner's open, thick hand. But Charlie knew what a 9-millimeter could do, particularly at close range. "In just a couple of years or maybe less," Bartholomew continued, "all my business dealings will be one-hundred percent legitimate. "So," he repeated, "what do we think of Chippewa Village?"

"It's beautiful, Mr. Bartholomew," Daniel said, starting to lose his nerve at the sight of the weapon. "*Really, really* nice."

Charlie took longer to answer. "A model called 'The Presidential' in a park called 'Chippewa Village' doesn't make much sense to me."

"You know, I told my project manager the identical thing," the older man agreed. "But, there *is* a sales strategy to it. The Indian name obviously appeals to the Native American market in the area and, 'The Presidential' gives what's essentially cheap housing a more upscale packaging. It's all packaging these days."

"I do understand packaging," Charlie admitted. "After all, that's what I am, ain't I?"

Bartholomew's jowls slid back into a smile. "That's right, Charlie. You're packaging."

He started to pace and look around at the white walls and drawn tan curtains, like he might be one of Daniel's professors in a lecture hall. "Let's see what we've got here... Daniel loves the ephemeral rush of gambling. He's not as addicted as you, Charlie, but he shows promise. He's into me for ten grand. That was three weeks ago. Now, with interest, he's into me for twenty."

"But, but you *know* I'm good for it, Mr. B," Daniel reminded.

"Well, I know your father's rich. He's got three car dealerships and fancies himself a tough guy. But you've missed two payment deadlines already, and my encouragements to pay promptly have thus far proven feckless. Because of your youth, your potential as a future customer, at least, while I'm still in this business, I've cut you some slack."

The loan shark put a hand on Charlie's shoulder as he strolled behind him.

"And, then, there's Charlie. Usually, Charlie's ability to pay me back is axiomatic. Five grand here, ten grand there, but right now, he's behind the eight ball. You're into me for seventy grand, Charlie. Plus the cost of your boat, plus money put into a checking account for your imaginary job. You've taken this money, which, by the way, you were only supposed to withdraw in weekly supplements, and blown it—blown it on the ponies, blackjack, and now you're reduced to doing things like stealing from the Salvation Army just to have take-home pay. Your little shenanigans have put a several-months-long operation at considerable risk."

"You know about the Salvation Army pots?" Charlie asked, surprised.

Bartholomew stopped pacing. "You're a big investment, Charlie. You can't take a leak without me knowing about it. You lost your toe for being stupid as much as anything else." He started pacing again. "Now, through all of this, I've been patient. Unwavering. A virtual Rock of Gibraltar. I haven't mentioned anything about the cost to watch your back, nor have I said anything about that woman who lives outside Traverse City that you like to go visit every week for carnal gymnastics. You know, the one who has the second phone line with the hijacked 800 number and pretends to be the operator at Miller Construction when your wife calls?"

"We always knew this was going to take time," Charlie reminded him. "Look, even if you don't build anything on Farren's land, the lakefront property, alone, is worth a half-million. That's over six times what I owe you plus any out-of-pocket costs. Look in the bag on the floor.

There's twenty-seven grand there. I was calling Stanley to let you know I'd made a big score tonight and was going to offer it to you to help cover some of the set-up costs. You *know* that."

The short, stout man shrugged and made his way over the counter and the Beretta.

"*Maybe* I know that, Charlie. Maybe you spotted Stanley in the casino. Maybe you conveniently placing a call to him at just the exact moment he came up behind you was you simply being your melliloquent self."

"Can, can I say something?" a confused Daniel asked.

"Certainly," Bartholomew replied, picking up the Beretta. He turned back to the bound men and folded his hands behind him with the pistol in one of them. "Contribute to my analysis of the situation, Daniel. By all means."

"You don't have to do this," he implored. "Please don't kill me, Mr. Bartholomew. I'll get your money. I'll get it in two days. I swear to God I will!"

The older man looked at him curiously for a few seconds, and then turned to Charlie.

"What did you do? Tell him the Barbary pirate thing?"

Charlie pursed his lips and shrugged slightly.

Bartholomew smiled and shook his head.

"No, Daniel. I'm not going to kill you …"

The young man breathed a sigh of relief. But then loan shark finished his thought. "Charlie is."

He stepped over to Charlie. Tucked the Beretta in his belt behind him, then produced a pocketknife from one of his pants pockets and opened it.

"All this time, Charlie, you've been working under the assumption that either I, or Stanley, or George was going to dispatch little wifey-poo. But I think you've got to do it. That's the only way you can be fully vested. Especially after being so capricious with the bank account. If I, or one of my associates, killed Daniel, you'd be an accessory, but you'd have something to leverage against us. I can't allow that."

"Wait, wait a minute here," the young man said, now clearly panic-stricken.

Bartholomew cut Charlie's right wrist free of the plastic cable tie, then closed the knife and slipped it back into his pants.

"Now, let me show you something," he continued.

"Mr. Bartholomew, *please!*" Daniel begged, starting to cry. "I'll *get* the money!"

The jowl-faced man pulled out his gun, extracted the clip, and showed it to a somber-faced Charlie. "See? Full clip. Ten rounds. I suppose you could put a couple into me, get my knife, cut yourself free, then walk out of here."

Charlie looked at him knowing better. "Yeah, with Stanley and George waiting around somewhere outside."

"Well, there is *that* conundrum," the loan shark agreed, scratching under his chin. "But, *I'd* be pretty screwed. I'm talking about trust here, Charlie. I've got to trust you to know the job that you began is going to be finished."

"*Pleeeeease*," Daniel whined, feeling partially dead already since the other two men were ignoring him.

"Daniel, I can see you're in the dark," Bartholomew said, slapping the clip back into its handle and tucking it behind him again. He walked over to the counter and picked up the black portfolio. "When I was a boy, my father used to take me fishing in Charlevoix. It's a gorgeous town. In fact, the city fathers call it, 'Charlevoix the beautiful.' I've always said to myself, 'Someday, someday, I'm going to own property there,' and I never forgot that promise."

Tears streamed down the college student's face. He mouthed the word "Please" to Charlie, but no sound came out. Meanwhile, the man with the portfolio and gravelly voice continued, as if he were telling a surreal bedtime story.

"After I did a little research, I determined the coolest piece of property that's already zoned for both business and residential belongs to a certain young lady named Farren Malone. Nearly a year ago, I had a real estate agent approach Miss Malone about selling her land. But it was left to her by her late parents, so she considers it her family's legacy. Undeterred, I switched to Plan B. I arranged for our Lothario here to meet her. Charlie batted his eyes, bought some flowers, a whirlwind courtship ensued, and they got married a couple of months ago. Soon, the new missus Huffman is going to have an accident. Charlie will inherit the property, and then it'll be turned over to me as recompense. And, here's the fun part ..."

He got down on one knee next to Daniel and unzipped the case. The young man's shoulders were quivering and his nose was running as Bartholomew opened the case and showed him an artist's rendering.

"We're talking a six-story, thirty-unit condo complex with views of Round Lake and downtown Charlevoix one way, then Lake Charlevoix the other. See? A guaranteed water view no matter which exposure a buyer picks." He turned one of the plastic pages as a wide-eyed Daniel felt compelled to look at them. "Now, I know what you're thinking: 'Is location enough?' I've been worried about that, too. After all, there's plenty of available real estate in Charlevoix. But look, each unit will have a double-door stainless-steel refrigerator, Italian-tiled foyer, granite counters in the kitchen and trey ceilings in the bedrooms. They'll have Berber carpet that'll hide stains and tracked-in sand. And, we're talking the high-grade Berber, mind you. Plus, heated towel racks in the bathrooms. These units are going to be to die for!" He stopped himself, looked at Charlie and smiled. "Hey, that's pretty funny, isn't it?"

Farren's spouse cracked a faint smile. He'd never seen Bartholomew so animated or enthusiastic about a subject before. He never realized the man who owned his life was also a closet interior designer.

"Mr. B, *please*," Daniel whimpered. "I'll get you the twenty grand. I'll get you *fifty!*"

Bartholomew flipped another page and continued. "At an average of one-point-two million, times thirty, that's thirty-six million dollars. Even in a slack economy, if they go for, say, eight hundred grand, that's still twenty-four million. Plus, there's the dock and boat-slip rentals and maybe even a little bar and restaurant in the lobby. In this economy, it'll take some time to sell the units, but the tenants will be first class all the way."

He closed the portfolio and looked at Daniel as if he'd just finished reading a children's story. "So, you see, son. You're playing a critical role in a big operation. You're the glue that holds the bond between Charlie and me. Besides, your life's pretty inconsequential. Because your father's rich, you think you're entitled to cruise through school, stretch four years of college into six, gamble with money you don't have, and you don't keep your word about paying debts on time. You think flirting with the criminal element is galvanic, but it's nothing you or your daddy's money can't ultimately handle, and the fact of the matter is *you're wrong!*"

Bartholomew bellowed the end of his last sentence. He emotionally went from zero to sixty in a second. "I *hate* little rich kids like you!" he yelled, displaying classic bipolar symptoms. "You've been given every opportunity imaginable, but you've squandered it. You've never had to pay for the consequences of your actions. Well, today Danny boy, you're *paying!*"

"*I'll get you the money!*" Daniel screamed, not knowing what else to say. *"I'll get you the mon-ee-ee-ee-eey!"* his words were now intermixed with uncontrollable sobs.

Bartholomew zipped up the case, pulled out the pistol from behind him, stepped over to Charlie, and put the Beretta in his free hand.

Realizing all the pleading in the world wasn't going to save him, a red-eyed, runny-nosed Daniel did the only thing he could think of.

"Our Father," he began in a quick, shaky voice, "who art in heaven…"

Holding the gun in his hand, there was a second—but only a second—that Charlie felt truly sorry for Daniel. But when all was said and done, he wasn't going to put himself at risk for anyone—not Farren, and certainly not for this whimpering, pleading amateur.

"Sorry, kid," he said, stone-faced. He took aim at the student's forehead and clicked off the safety.

"…Thy kingdom come," the prayer was abruptly interrupted by the loud crack of the Beretta. Daniel gasped, and then fell backward in his chair. The back of the chair landed on the carpet with an echoing thud due to the emptiness of the room, then everything was suddenly still. Still, except for the subtle sound of the blood spurting from Daniel's forehead. It was right at that moment that Charlie realized the true purpose of the maroon rug. It would be rolled up and carried out with Daniel's body inside it.

"So," Bartholomew said, clasping his hands together and jovial again. "Hungry? I know this great Mediterranean place."

Charlie Huffman had never killed anyone before. He looked at the upturned soles of the two shoes facing him, then at Bartholomew. He briefly turned the gun toward the loan shark, but only to convey his displeasure at being manipulated. After a few seconds, he loosened his grip and offered the butt of the weapon to his captor.

WHAT GOD DOES

Clair opened the scissors and carefully ran the edge of an exposed blade along the side of the Christmas ribbon giving it a curl. She set the scissors down on the wood plank coffee table in the living room and looked at the perfectly wrapped Christmas present with satisfaction. On the floor and leather sofa next to where she sat were other brightly colored packages she had volunteered to wrap for Doc. Leather gloves in a box for his dad, perfume for his mom, sheets for his sister and her husband, a glass photo frame montage for his parents that could hold seven photographs of various sizes, and a book for Lance called *The Ultimate James Bond Guide of Interesting Facts*. He had bought it several months earlier and decided to reveal the secret of his 007 expertise by sharing it with his partner.

Past the bits of cut ribbon, Scotch tape and rolls of wrapping paper on the table, Doc stood in front of the small Christmas tree in between the windows overlooking the screened-in porch. It was a humble thing as Christmas trees went; several of the ornaments had lost their luster or had hairline cracks from being carted all over the country, but Doc couldn't part with it.

She watched him watching the tree for a moment and knew he was thinking about Farren and the revelations of the day. He'd only been home from their shopping excursion for a couple of hours and had told her about the Austen book and Charlie's truck not being in the airport parking lot. He figured he was still keeping his promise to Farren since he had said he wouldn't repeat the events of the day to another "human being." Although she was pleased and called the news "a wonderful blessing," Doc clearly didn't share her enthusiasm. The more the evening went on, the more introspective he became. He didn't even ask her about the fresh scent of Pine Sol on the kitchen floor when he came in, which indicated yet another animal transformation and another mess, or messes, that were cleaned up earlier in the day.

"All done," she announced, referring to the gifts he had purchased thus far.

He turned with his hands stuffed in his jeans pockets. "Wow, beautiful," he said, politely. "Just like someone at a department store did them."

"Thanks," she smiled. "I was afraid I'd lost my touch."

"What do you mean?" he asked, curiously.

"You know," she said, changing subjects, "this was always going to happen. In order for Farren to learn about Charlie's true nature, she was always going to get hurt."

"I know."

"And his true nature's only half the story, Doc. The other half is what he intends to do to her."

"I know that, too," he replied. He closed his eyes and rubbed his forehead with the tips of his fingers. "It's just... you should have seen her this afternoon. When we were circling the airport parking lot looking for Charlie's truck, it was like you could literally see the life draining out of her."

"A broken heart isn't the same as being murdered," Clair proclaimed, matter-of-factly. "She'll survive, I guarantee it. Let's just hope Charlie's hold on her isn't so strong he tells her a bunch of lies and she believes him because she wants to."

He didn't respond. He strolled over to the flames in the fieldstone fireplace while the radio played an old rendition of "Good King Wenceslas" by Percy Faith and his orchestra.

"I was thinking about talking to my friend, Michael, on the police force about Charlie. I mean, now that I have something tangible to talk about. But Farren asked for my discretion. What do you think?"

"Let's see what she does," the angel replied. "I think your suggestion that she talk to people like her grandfather or her priest was excellent. If Charlie knows that other people know he's been lying to her, the jig is up."

"You think it's that simple?" he asked, turning from the fire to her. "He's exposed as a liar and everything's over?"

"Why not? If people know Charlie's true colors, then something unexpected happening to Farren looks awfully suspicious. If he's exposed, he's blown his con and can't pay Bartholomew. He'll have no choice but to run. My guess is, Bartholomew will reluctantly abandon his interest in Farren's land and look for another opportunity."

"You mean, another victim," he concluded.

"Maybe. That's Bartholomew's free will to exercise. But if he does—well—the Lord's resources are pretty vast."

"Maybe God should just zap this loan shark with a heart attack," he suggested.

"Maybe. God does what God does. I told you a story about Austin Redman becoming an accomplished astronomer. It was totally made up. But, based on what you told me yesterday about his uncle visiting, there must have been something in my story the Lord liked."

Doc turned back to the fire. "What was wrong with Julia's story?" he muttered.

"What?"

"Nothing," he answered. He looked at the flames and tried to remember the vividness of her blue eyes.

BEING THERE

The light tan brick fire hall on State Street was, like any fire station in any town, essentially a big garage for trucks. But the arrangement was slightly different from larger towns in that the fire trucks also shared space with ambulances and frequently even police cruisers. It was also different in that the fire hall with its five closed roll-up bay doors was connected through a short hallway to Charlevoix's Police Department and City Hall.

Inside the hall, spit-and-polished fire trucks with open, waiting doors occupied the first four bays, and Lance and Doc's ambulance sat in the fifth bay, the one closest to the City Hall side. Its doors were likewise open and an orange extension cord ran from one of the wall sockets through the open back doors to a panel on a sidewall with a gauge that was for the vehicle's electronics. Despite a warm front that had moved in early that morning causing icicles to drip and the streets to be wet from snow runoff, the inside of the hall was dry and the floor gleamed like someone could literally eat off of it.

Doc was in the back of the ambulance and had just finished cleaning the suction unit and restocking the medicine drawers when he decided to check up on Farren. She was working in the marina storage barn and standing at the stern of a twenty-two-foot Danzi runabout. She had taken it out of its storage cage, bow first, with the forklift that had its two long prong-like arms sheathed in thick rubber so as not to scratch the fiberglass hull. The arms held the boat suspended about five feet off the ground. Farren had just removed the propellers on the two built-in propeller shafts that were angled upward when her cell rang. Meanwhile, over at the workbench with metal shelves that housed engine parts, Gus, with his usual two-day growth of white stubble, sat on a stool under a table light futzing with an Evinrude outboard clamped to a sawhorse. A pair of half-frame bifocals sat on the edge of his nose.

"Hello?"

"Hey, good morning, it's Doc."

"Hi."

"What're you doing?"

"I'm over in the storage barn putting new blades on a twin-prop Danzi. How 'bout you?"

"Checking oxygen tanks and restocking gauze."

"That's us," she smiled, bending down and digging through a Fed Ex box to unwrap one of the newly arrived propellers, "Titans of business."

"I just wanted to call and see if you were okay?"

"Yeah, I think so."

He fiddled with the buttons on the overhanging medical radio. "I, I was wondering if you talked to Charlie after you got home last night."

"He called, and we spoke for a minute," she said, slipping a new propeller on one of the shafts, "but I said I wasn't feeling very well, which was true."

"Oh ..." he said, twirling the radio's microphone cord with his finger, "so I guess you didn't confront him about—"

"No," she interrupted. "I didn't. I think a conversation like that ought to be had face to face."

"Sure," he replied, a little disappointed that she hadn't hit the issue head-on with Charlie. "Absolutely. Good call. Well ... I, uh, I just wanted to make sure you were all right. Except for you finding the book, I ... I really enjoyed yesterday."

"You're sweet."

"Okay. I'll, uh, I'll talk to you later. Take care." He pushed the end button on his phone quickly and self-consciously, wishing he hadn't made the call and feeling like he was in high school again.

"You, too," she replied, before she realized the connection was broken. She looked at the phone a little concerned. It was a look that didn't escape her grandfather's eyes.

"Was that Doug Richards, askin' about a bubbler he ordered?"

"No," she said, digging through the Fed Ex box again to get the second of the new propellers. "It was Doc Reynolds."

"Mmm," he responded, pulling out the Evinrude's oil filter.

"What does that mean?"

"What's going on with you two?" he asked, candidly.

"Nothing's going on," she said, slipping the propeller onto the second shaft. She dipped a hand into her pocket and pulled out two cotter pins, then slipped one pin each into the tips of the upturned propeller shafts. "Why?"

"You made him lunch, went shopping with him, I heard you two were dancin' pretty close together Saturday night, and his face lit up like a Christmas tree when I mentioned you were at the hospital Monday."

"It did?" she asked, visibly pleased. But, then she quickly caught herself. She grabbed a pair of pliers and started to bend the tips of the cotter pins to hold the props in place. "Uh, nothing's going on. I made him lunch because I lost a bet. We went shopping because it's hazardous for me to drive to TC alone. And, we danced last Saturday night at my husband's suggestion. Can't two adults who happen to be members of the opposite sex just be friends?"

"At my age, yes. At your age, it's kinda like a fat woman walking into Baskin-Robbins and asking for Double Mocha Chocolate, but only a sample spoonful."

"You think I'd be frivolous with my responsibilities as a married woman?"

"No," he smiled. "I think you're a nice girl from a small town with a trusting nature who hasn't figured out yet that all men are dogs."

"Would that include you?" she teased.

"You bet. Old dogs are the most dangerous. They know more tricks."

She smiled, then looked at him regretfully while his nose was buried in the engine. "I never should have run off and gotten married like I did. My Grandpa should've walked me down the aisle."

She turned her attention back to the propellers, double-checking the fit. Gus looked up from his work at her. She had apologized for eloping before, but she had never admitted that he should have participated in her wedding. To him, it wasn't just a matter of mere semantics. It was an indication that she needed him. He slid the bifocals off his nose, rose from the stool, and walked over to her while wiping his hands with a rag.

"Just for the record, I like Doc. But I don't know how this new pal of yours fits into the scheme of things. Maybe you don't know, either. But, if I can help with anything, if you ever wanna talk, you know I'm here for you."

She smiled, gratefully. But Gus could also see there were traces of sadness in her face. He knew something was going on with his granddaughter, but he also knew her well enough to know she wasn't ready to talk about things yet.

Back at the fire hall, Lance peeked around one of the ambulance's open rear doors holding a shiny black metallic walkie-talkie in each hand. "How're we lookin'?"

"Restocked and ready for battle," Doc answered. "What've you got there?"

"New walkies," Lance said, handing both to Doc. "Longer range and they supposedly have super-sensitive transmitters and receivers that cut through the ambient noise on an accident scene—approaching sirens, wind, rain, that kind of thing."

"Nice," Doc said, taking them and slipping them into a canvas field pack.

Lance looked around the garage behind him. "Did you happen to see that guy Harry was talking to a little while ago?" He was referring to Harry Stanton, their boss.

"No."

"Harry's old partner, Todd Moises. He and Harry used to ride around in this very unit back in the day."

"That so?" Doc said, moving toward the rear door. "Todd still an EMT? Still with the city?"

"Naw, he's out of the business now. He and Harry had a falling out. But, it was for Todd's own good, and they've since patched things up."

"What happened?"

"Todd was a bit of a pill popper. 'Course, EMTs were working a lot more double shifts a few years ago, too."

"Harry called him on it?" Doc asked, checking the electronics gauge. Seeing that everything was charged, he disconnected the power cord, then hopped out of the ambulance.

"Yeah. What do they call it? An intervention? Tough love? But, it was only because Harry cared, y' know?"

"Of course," he agreed, wrapping the orange cord around his elbow and open hand as he walked slowly over to the socket near a phone mounted on the wall. "It was the right thing to do."

"I mean, if *I* were screwing up, but didn't think there was a problem, I'd want you to tell me."

"And vice versa," Doc replied, unplugging the other end of the cord.

"Really? You mean it?"

Doc paused and turned to his partner. "Do you want to tell me something?"

Lance glanced right, then left, then walked over and spoke in a hushed tone. "I want you to know, I haven't said anything to anyone. Not even Charlene."

"Cool. Thanks. About what?"

"About special feelings you've developed that a lot of people wouldn't understand or approve of." He was referring to the sheep he'd seen him with in the parking lot Saturday night, but Doc thought he was referring to Farren.

The paramedic looked at his baby-faced, chubby companion genuinely surprised.

"How ... how could you possibly know?"

"I know, okay? I know. I gotta tell ya, partner, it doesn't change my opinion about your abilities as a professional, but what you're doing is wrong."

"Technically, I haven't done anything," Doc said. "But, you're right, even thinking about these feelings isn't really healthy."

"Gee, you think?"

Lance looked around the garage again. "Well, I'm relieved to hear you haven't done anything yet. But, have you been down this path before? Does this have something to do with why you left Wyoming? You didn't have to, like, leave the state to avoid a scandal or anything, did you?"

"What? No, of course not," Doc said. He likewise looked around the garage deciding to take his friend into confidence. "I don't even know how this happened. I mean, somehow, someway, she's awakened feelings in me I thought I'd never have because she's—you know." Doc meant "married," but Lance thought he meant "a sheep."

The EMT looked at his partner seriously. "Dude, you've got to talk to somebody."

"Not right now. There are bigger issues at stake. Things I can't really talk about. I need to see how things play out this week."

"Play out?"

"Yeah, with her."

"Well, where is she now?"

"Over in the storage barn at the marina."

"Portside Marina?"

"Yeah."

Lance didn't understand, but, before he could say something, they were interrupted by the loud blaring sound of an alarm going off in the hall followed by a dispatcher's voice on the PA system, announcing an emergency call and giving the address. It was a call for both a fire truck and the Life Support Unit.

Lance started heading toward the open driver's side door of the ambulance.

"We'll talk about this later," he said, with an emphasizing point of his finger. He looked around. "Where's my coat?"

"Both of ours are in the unit," Doc responded, dropping the cord to the shiny floor and quickly closing the vehicle's back doors. "There really isn't anything more to talk about," he added, rounding the passenger side then climbing into the cab next to his partner. "But I do appreciate your thoughts, buddy."

As the large bay doors rolled up and open and Lance started the engine, he made one more comment on the subject.

"Hey, I think it's twisted, okay? I'm not going to lie about that. But, I want you to know that I'm here for you."

DINNER

The call that the Fire Department and Life Support Unit responded to was the best kind of call there was—a call where nobody was needed. It was off of Sequanota Road. A small electrical fire started when an eighty-five-year-old woman accidentally dropped a wire hanger behind her dryer in her laundry room, and the curved metal head caught on the prongs of the wall plug that were pulled halfway out of the socket. The plug was halfway out of its socket from the last time someone had moved the dryer to clean behind it. The old woman had a son who happened to be with her at the time, folding towels. As soon as the metal-on-metal contact happened, causing sparks to fly, the son quickly opened a junction box and turned off the circuit breaker. Everything was over in about ten seconds. Although sparks flew and a part of a wall was blackened, there were no flames per se. But blueish smoke filled the laundry room, causing the woman to have breathing problems, so the fire department and paramedics responded.

For the remainder of that day, Lance didn't broach the subject of Doc's "special feelings." For the time being, he figured the mere fact that Doc knew that *he* knew was enough. He figured he'd recommend counseling when the opportunity presented itself. Doc, of course, had no idea about Lance's conclusions, but he wasn't particularly eager to continue talking with his partner about what he thought they'd been discussing that morning, which was Farren. He didn't want to do so, partially because he didn't talk much about himself, anyway, and partially because he wasn't sure how such feelings had developed or where they were going. As a result, the remainder of the day was like being in an

Ingmar Bergman film. Doc and Lance went through the paces of normality, which even included a couple of James Bond trivia questions, but there were volumes of unspoken things going on under the surface.

It was the same with Farren. In fact, she found herself going to confession early Wednesday evening at St. Ignatius to open her heart on such matters. She entered the church through the front doors that arched at the top, walked down the center aisle past the multi-colored stain glass windows on either side, then, three-quarters of the way down the aisle, turned left and sat down in a squeaky pew waiting for her turn in the confessional. There were only three other people in the church, so she knew the wait wouldn't be long.

As she sat there, she glanced up at the large crucifix hanging on the back wall of the altar, in front of where the church organ pipes were hidden, then her eyes turned to the large ornate chandelier hanging above the first row of pews. She wondered if her parents used to sit and imagine her walking under it wearing a wedding gown. She looked over to her right and remembered the pew they usually sat in. It was near the entrance to the hidden hallway that went behind the confessionals and led to a stairway that went down to the bathrooms in the basement. But those confessionals weren't in use today.

Then her mind drifted to Doc. She liked that he made a living helping people. Even if he didn't go to medical school, his profession was one that made a difference. She liked how compassionate and calm he'd been with Austin Redman. She even admired how he seemed to revere the memory of Julia, although she wondered if that would ever get in the way of him falling in love again. She liked his blue eyes. They were bluer than Charlie's. She even liked how he sometimes said things just to get a rise out of people. A little irreverence was a healthy thing, she figured. She thought of other things, too: how he knew the stars, how he liked to read, how he bought her Jane Austen book back for her, how they could be comfortable with each other in silence. Lastly, she thought of how she had known him for just a little more than a week, yet she felt like she knew him better than the man she married. All of these thoughts were the ingredients of an attraction, but an attraction simmering in the broth of a Catholic upbringing. She felt very conflicted.

A few minutes later, it was her turn in the confessional. She silently slipped behind a red velvet curtain and knelt down facing a wall in the darkened small cubicle. After a few moments, Father Ken slid open the window, seated on the other side, and Farren spoke quietly into a dark square of screen.

"Bless me, Father," she began, by making the sign of the cross, "for I have sinned. It's been three months since my last confession.

"I recently got married. It was a spur of the moment decision—an elopement, actually. I was following my heart. But in doing so, I unintentionally hurt a family member who had always planned on being at my wedding. I didn't think of it as a sin at the time, and I've apologized several times since, but I really hurt this person, and I'm sorry."

"Gus is a big boy, Farren," Father Ken responded in a hushed voice. "He'll survive. But it's good that you realize he felt wronged."

That was one of the disadvantages of living in a small town and being part of a small parish. There was no such thing as anonymity in the confessional.

"I've also been pretty mad at God the past several days," she continued. "Grandpa had a physical and some X-rays revealed a couple of shadows on his lungs. I thought he was going to be taken away from me like—well—I thought he might be very sick. But as it turns out, he wasn't. It was just a glitch with the machine. A second set of X-rays and an MRI revealed everything was fine. So, I was angry for nothing."

"I'm very glad to hear he's okay," the priest replied. "It's important to lean on your faith when bad things happen. That's why it should be continually cultivated. Some people say bad things are a test of faith. I don't think that's right. Life is a gift but a fragile one. People get sick, people die, unexpected things happen. When they do, faith can be of great comfort. But it's got to be there and strong in the first place. So don't be angry, Farren. Don't even feel tested. Just be resolute in the deep faith I know you have."

She nodded and knelt quietly for a moment, thinking about Doc's advice to take those she trusted into confidence about Charlie. She was even considering talking to the priest about feelings she was developing for a certain man other than her husband.

"Is there anything else?" the clergyman asked.

She opened her mouth to say something, but then decided against it and shook her head.

"No, Father."

"Okay. Say ten hail Marys and have Gus call me. Maybe we can resurrect our weekly Parcheesi games."

She cracked a smile while the priest gave her an absolution blessing.

For the next couple of days, things were quiet between Farren and

Doc. Clair urged him to find a reason to make contact, but he said the next move was hers. She reminded him that this wasn't a chess game but an effort to save her life. He disagreed saying it was exactly like a chess game, and that as long as her boss granted them the time, Farren needed to mull things over and reach her own conclusions. Clair reminded him again that the Lord was his boss, too, but he politely ignored her. On Thursday, another unseasonably warm day where the temperature shot up to nearly fifty degrees, Doc and Lance responded to a call involving a fifty-five-year-old man who had a heart attack while stacking firewood. The call took them around Lake Charlevoix nearly all the way to the town of East Jordon. Unfortunately, the man was already dead by the time they got there, and resuscitation efforts proved futile. Still, there were bright spots this day. Later in the afternoon, Doc ran into Simon Jackson at the hospital. The young man was in a wheelchair and hadn't been released since the accident with his father's vintage Cougar, but he was well on the road to recovery. Also on Thursday, Clair went a full twenty-four hours without changing into anything. Whatever setback she apparently had Saturday night, she seemed to be over it now.

Friday was another warm day, and instead of snow, it started to rain late in the afternoon. Charlie drove into town listening to "Ramblin' Man" by the Allman Brothers. Bartholomew had left him a thousand dollars from his winnings in Mt. Pleasant, so he had several wrapped Christmas presents in his truck for Farren. He'd called her about an hour outside of town to report his approximate arrival time and was surprised to see her sitting outside on the front step of their small mushroom house waiting for him under an umbrella. She was wearing a navy blue pea-style coat and her white knit cap with the long earflaps. On her lap was a fabric tote purse. As soon as he pulled up, she rose and walked toward the truck. He noticed that inside the house, the lights were off on the Christmas tree.

"Wonder what's up with the ol' ball and chain?" he said, under his breath, but changed his attitude with a wide smile the instant she opened the door.

"Hey, baby. What're you doin' sittin' on your pretty little buns outside in the rain?"

"We're going out for dinner," she announced, matter-of-factly, climbing in.

"We are? Don't I get a kiss hello?"

"Drive, please," she said, closing her umbrella then shutting the door.

Charlie raised his eyebrows, went along by saying, "Yes, ma'am," and put the truck in gear.

The Weathervane was one of the nicer restaurants in town. It sat on the north side of the Pine River that connected Round Lake to Lake Michigan, and, even though there was a layer of ice on Round Lake and along the shoreline of Lake Michigan, the river hadn't yet frozen. There was a wall of windows that overlooked the river and the Memorial Bridge, and Charlie and Farren were led to a candlelit linen-covered table next to this wall. Earl Young of the mushroom-houses fame had designed the restaurant, so the entire place had a gnome-like quality to it, even though it was a larger building than his cozy, compact homes. If this had been July, the Weathervane would've been packed and watercraft of every description would've glided gracefully by in the river, passing diners dressed in Tommy Hilfiger shirts and Vera Wang casuals. But this was December, so the place was half-full, Johnny Mathis sang "Silver Bells" in the background, a gas fire sputtered in the fireplace, and summer fashions had given way to woolen plaid shirts, jeans, and thick socks.

After they were seated and drinks had been ordered, Charlie, who could see that Farren was obviously perturbed, started off the conversation.

"I can tell just by your attitude I'm in the doghouse about somethin'. So, before we even get into it, let me say that I love you, and I'm sorry."

"I want to see your flight itinerary, Charlie," she said, slipping off her hat, "I want to see it right now."

"I never hang onto those things, darlin', you know that."

He was so casual in his response, it angered her. She dipped into her fabric tote and pulled out a box. Opening it, she produced her 1922 edition of *Pride and Prejudice*. When she did, the expression on Charlie's face visibly changed. His smirk fell off his chin like an icicle from an eaves trough. He looked at the book, then at her just as the waitress brought over their drinks. She had ordered hot tea. He had ordered a beer.

"Take this back," he said, handing the server the full pilsner glass. "Bring me a double bourbon."

Sensing the couple didn't want chitchat from her, the waitress simply answered, "Of course," and headed back to the bar.

"Where'd you get that?" he asked, gently scratching the blond stubble on his cheek.

"The same place you got rid of it," she replied, coolly. "How could you do that, Charlie? I have maybe three things that my mother passed along to me from her mother, and that book was one of them. I spent a couple of nights tearing the house apart looking for it to read to Mrs. Mitchell. I even asked you about it one night when you called, and you said you hadn't seen it. And all the time, you knew *exactly* where it was: in Traverse City."

"That's why the short phone conversations this week," he concluded. "Baby, I *can* explain."

"Can you? Then explain where you've been too, 'cause it sure wasn't in Milwaukee."

Even though Farren had caught him in more than one lie, he couldn't help but admire her tactics. She'd not only taken him out to a public place where they couldn't create a scene, she'd taken him to a fine restaurant where, just by virtue of the atmosphere, voices couldn't even be raised. Not bad, he thought, for a gullible small-town girl.

"You're right," he admitted. "I wasn't in Milwaukee this week. Matter of fact, I haven't been to a lot of the places I've told you I was. That's why you haven't seen any itineraries or luggage tags on my duffle. Honey, I got laid off about a week before we got married. That's why we didn't have a honeymoon. That's why I pushed pretty hard to just run away and get hitched. I didn't want to lose you."

She screwed up her face as if the information had been a cold splash of water. "You... you based our whole marriage on a lie because you didn't want to *lose* me?"

The waitress came back with Charlie's bourbon. After they listened to the evening's dinner specials and she had left again, the conversation continued.

"Farren, I know I've been guarded about my past. I told you my mom had me out of wedlock, and I was raised in a foster home. But what I didn't tell you is my mom put me in a dumpster intending to throw me out with the rest of the garbage. Fortunately, I had strong lungs, someone heard me, and that's how I became a foster child. But it wasn't in just one home. I was in four different foster homes before I was fifteen. My last foster dad—well—let's just say he had a good right hook.

"When you're brought up like that, you learn not to trust anyone. You *don't* spill out your problems to people. Especially people you care about. It's a sign of weakness."

He paused and looked down for dramatic effect, then even mustered moist eyes. "I don't know if it was love at first sight, but I *do* know it was like I came to life when I met you. Men are supposed to be the providers, not lay troubles on the doorstep. So, yeah, I've been takin' off every

Monday and comin' back most weekends. What've I been doin'? Looking for full-time work. I've still got some friends in the construction industry and workin' day jobs on sites when I can get 'em. Sometimes it's for a little money, sometimes it's more. And, let's not forget, in a very real way, I've paid for my sins by losin' that toe. As for your book? Hell, Farren, it was old and you never used it. I had to get my truck serviced one week. I needed the cash. I didn't know you were going to want to read it to some old lady."

He wrapped his hands around his drink and looked down at it as if it were a crystal ball, searching for what his wife might say or do next. There was even some truth in what he had said. That was the mark of an expert liar, seamlessly interweaving fact with fiction.

"What about the number I called at work?" she asked.

"The switchboard operator is an old friend of mine who agreed to cover for me until I found a new job. I just didn't think it would take so long. Guess there's a reason why they say, 'Will the last one in Michigan please turn out the light.'"

She expelled a heavy breath not knowing how to respond. It was just as well; the waitress came back and wanted to know if they were ready to order. Farren said they needed some more time.

"I don't know what to say, Charlie. You're trying to justify the fact that for weeks, months, you've perpetuated a lie. And what's worse, you've piled other lies on top of it: How work was going that week, what was going on with Leo back in the home office, even what the weather was like in the cities you were supposed to be in. What were you doing, going online and checking weather conditions in Columbus, or wherever, before you called?"

"I'm so sorry, honey," he said, taking a large gulp of his drink.

"You played me for a fool!"

"Oh, no, Farren. No, you've got it all wrong. I didn't want *you* to think you married one."

He rose from the table. "Hang on for one minute. I'll be right back."

He walked past the waitress, asked her to please be patient, then went over to the coat rack near the door, dipped his hand in the pocket of his tan fabric coat, got his truck keys, and went outside. Meanwhile, Farren poured her tea and looked out at the rain gently falling on the other side of the glass. She briefly thought about the unusual change in temperature the past couple of days and wondered if it was the result of global warming. She wondered if a light winter meant an early spring and how that might impact her business. She wondered why Charlie hadn't shown more interest in her suggestion the previous week that he talk to Larry Melzick over at Melzick Construction, especially since he was unemployed. She wondered if there was a good marriage counselor in town who would be discreet if they decided to go that route. Just as Charlie came back into the restaurant carrying a square gift-wrapped box, she thought of Doc's simple if somewhat ineloquent statement when they were driving home from Traverse City: "I'd never lie to my wife. I ... wouldn't."

"This was obviously going to go under the tree," Charlie said, referring to the box, "but maybe you should open this now." He set down a water-beaded package on his chair, which was about the size of a 12-pack, then started moving the wine glasses and bread plates so he could set it before her.

"Charlie, no," she said, softly but sternly. "You can't buy your way out of lying with a present."

"Of course not," he agreed. "But, please. This will actually help explain something."

She opened her mouth to protest again, but it was too late. He'd already put the nicely wrapped box on the table in front of her. She looked around self-consciously at some other patrons subtly watching while they ate their Caesar salads. Robert Goulet was now singing "The First Noel." The waitress was watching them, too. She brushed her bangs aside nervously and finally decided it would be an even bigger scene if she didn't accept the offering. So she forced a smile as Charlie sat back down.

The wrapping paper was a heavy gold foil, the mark of an expensive store. Underneath the foil was a cardboard box with fancy script that read, "Widmyers of Grand Rapids." She had never heard of Widmyers, but had a few customers from the Grand Rapids area.

"Here," Charlie said, handing her a pocketknife to cut through the clear tape on the box.

She took the knife, opened it, and cut through the tape. Unfolding the cardboard lids, she next saw a thin layer of bubble wrap. Lifting the bubble wrap, she discovered a fine leather-bound version of Jane Austen's *Persuasion*, then *Emma*, then *Mansfield Park*.

"It's Austen's novels," Charlie said. "Her complete works. All in nice leather bound editions. I *did* feel bad about taking your book, sweetie. So, I replaced one book with six. I would've even bought back your *Pride and Prejudice*, 'cause I made pretty good money this week, but when I called the bookstore in Traverse City, the guy said it had already been sold. I never dreamed it was to you, but I'm grateful that it was."

Farren ran her fingers over the leather cover of *Persuasion*. Even though Charlie had done wrong, she had to admit, it was a sweet gesture to try to make amends.

"You gotta believe me," he continued. "When I got laid off, I didn't think, 'Gee, let me run right home and dump this failure on my girlfriend.' Especially since your grandfather doesn't like me. I thought, 'Okay, this sucks. But with some smoke and mirrors and a little luck, I can turn this into a positive. I'll get a new job, make it sound like *I* wanted to change jobs, and maybe it will even turn into a step up for us financially.' I had no idea things would go south. I ... I just wanted you to be proud of me. It was stupid to deceive you, and I deeply, deeply apologize."

She looked into his blue eyes while trying not to become emotional. She thought she saw earnest regret; but what she was really looking at was an expert con man.

"I fell in love with *you*, Charlie. Not your job or how much money you make. To me, lying is as bad as being unfaithful."

As he nodded sincerely, she had no idea her husband already *had* been unfaithful—every week, like clockwork.

"Men don't see it that way," he said. "So much of who we are is connected to our job. When that's taken away, you feel less of a man."

"Deceiving your life partner doesn't make things better."

"I know. And again, I'm sorry. I guess, coming from so many dysfunctional homes, I'm just not used to having a loving, understanding partner."

Mentioning his troubled upbringing again cracked the armor of her anger. He noticed the small sympathetic slant in her eyebrows and applied some reverse psychology.

"Look, I don't think either one of us really wants to have dinner at the Weathervane tonight. So let's get the check, I'll take you home, drop you off, then I'll go get a hotel room for the weekend to give you some space. I think they've got a few thousand vacant ones around here."

She smiled faintly and shook her head. "That won't be necessary. I ... I've been stringing popcorn every night for over a week and I've finally got enough for the tree. We could go home and put it on if you want?"

"Put on that Harry Connick Jr. Christmas CD?" he asked.

"Sure," she said, her smile widening.

He smiled and nodded, knowing that it was time, *really* time, to dispose of his wife.

INTO THE MIST

Ten minutes after they had finished having sex, Farren looked over at Charlie in bed. He was lying on his side with his back to her, so she assumed he was asleep. She quietly slipped out of bed and into her teal terrycloth bathrobe, then looked around on the floor of their small bedroom for her white athletic socks. The robe was worn, a gift from Gus when she turned twenty-one. As she spotted one sock and slipped it on, then the other, the old garment hung off her athletic frame nicely. With her pixie-style haircut slightly mussed and the few freckles on her nose, she looked downright sexy in a Doris Day kind of way.

"Wow. We ought to fight more often," Charlie joked, turning over and stretching. "That was incredible."

She smiled slightly and didn't say anything. In her view, he'd missed the point of their going to bed. Her passion was to emphasize her love for him, regardless of whether or not he was working, and also to remind him that he could confide in her. It saddened her that he didn't get that.

"We got anything to eat?" he asked.

"Are you hungry?"

"Well, yeah. We never did have dinner."

"I think there's some eggs and sausage in the fridge."

"Perfect," he yawned. Without his shirt on, his fit physical shape was obvious. Besides his round biceps and firm pecs, he also had a smattering of golden hair on his chest, just enough to add to his overall Arian look.

"I'm dyin' for a smoke," he said.

"Not in the house, please," she called, stepping into the house's only bathroom, which was a small separate room next door.

He leaned over the side of the bed, spotted his boxer shorts, and slipped them on while still lying down.

"So I guess you went to Traverse City this week, huh?"

"Tuesday," she answered through the wall. Keeping the bathroom door open, she raised her robe and sat down on the toilet. "I went Christmas shopping."

"With Gus?"

"No."

"One of your church committee buddies?"

"No, with Doc Reynolds."

"Wait a minute," he said, rising out of bed. "The guy that cost us three hundred and fifty bucks last week?"

"He didn't cost us three hundred and fifty bucks, *you* did," she answered, reaching for the toilet paper. "Which reminds me, we owe him three hundred dollars."

"*What?* For what?"

"He bought my Jane Austen book back for me."

He grabbed his jeans off the end of the bed, now suddenly annoyed. "Well, that's just *great!* First, he dupes me into spending money we can't afford. Then, he takes my wife shopping. Now, we wind up owing him hundreds of dollars. But, hey, at least he knows I'm a thief! I assume you told him you thought you'd lost the book."

"Since he doesn't know a lot of people in town, I wouldn't worry about it."

There was a break in the conversation while the toilet flushed, then Farren washed her hands. "He didn't dupe you out of anything, Charlie," she continued, coming back into the bedroom. She looked around the floor, then spotted and picked up a pair of white panties. "Nobody asked you to bid against him. In fact, I specifically said, 'Forget it,' as I recall." She stepped into her panties and pulled them up under her robe. "And he didn't take me shopping, either. I asked him. Before this warm spell, it's been snowing a lot, and I wanted someone to go with me as a safety precaution."

"Well I don't like it; my wife cavorting around with a single guy."

"Cavorting?" she asked, amused. "That sounds like we were skipping rope or something. C'mon," she smiled, making light of the subject, "do you really want to spend the night talking about Doc Reynolds?"

"I don't want you leaving town with him again."

"Promise," she said, raising her right hand.

"Or having lunch. Or doing *anything* with him."

She looked at him impishly. "Guess you're just going to have to find a job in town so you can keep me from cavorting, huh?"

He smirked, his annoyance subsiding. "I just might, girlie."

"Go have your smoke," she said, passing him on the way to the kitchen. "I'll make some breakfast."

He swatted her on the butt as she passed. It was supposed to be a playful thing, but it stung even through her terrycloth robe and panties. She jumped and gasped. Charlie seemed to have a thing about being aggressive to the point of inflicting pain, especially when they were intimate. He hadn't been like that when they were dating, but after they got married, it was as if some true hidden nature of his was coming out. She had so far mostly tolerated it in the name of love, but she knew a confrontation about it was coming. However, that wouldn't be tonight, she thought. She didn't want to reprimand him figuring he'd been reprimanded enough this Friday night.

A few minutes later, Charlie was dressed and wandered out of their bedroom. He passed the bathroom and spare bedroom, walked through the living room with its slightly concave fireplace and mantel that held some old family photos, passed the Christmas tree, now lit, and saw Farren whipping up eggs in her white socks and teal robe in their black-and-white check kitchen. She was humming "God Rest Ye Merry Gentlemen." It took less than ten seconds to walk from the back bedroom of their small house to the front door. Slipping on his tan fabric coat with the corduroy collar, he checked the pockets to make sure he had his cigarettes, lighter and cell phone, then went outside where the rain had turned into a fine, cloudy mist. Even though it was still early—about 9:30—the night was quiet and the streets were empty. His square jaw was momentarily illuminated by the orange glow of his lighter as he fired up a Winston, then he surveyed the night. The Christmas lights on the shrubbery of the neighbors now seemed eerie because of the weather. The air was thick and damp, but weirdly warm for the norm of December. He stepped away from the living room window so Farren couldn't see him, got on his cell phone, and dialed a Flint exchange.

"Stanley? Hey, it's Charlie Huffman. Got a second? Good. Tell Mr. B I'm going to take care of business in the next day or two. But right now, I need a little favor from you and George. My wife's made a new friend who might be a fly in the ointment. A male friend … no, she's too dumb to be unfaithful, but I don't want him askin' any questions. I want to make sure he's not around when plans are set in motion."

A few miles away at Doc's, Clair was in the kitchen and had just finished ironing Doc's eggshell white paramedic uniform shirt. While she put it on a hanger and hung it up in the small laundry room off the kitchen, Doc came wandering out of the spare bedroom, where he'd been sleeping the past sixteen nights. He wore a long-sleeved black pullover shirt with jeans, and his hair was still damp and spiky from having just gotten out of the shower. Clair was wearing some olive green khaki slacks and a plum long-sleeved blouse with her black slippers.

"You didn't have to do that," he said, coming into the kitchen and seeing his shirt was ready for work the next day.

"Yes, I did," she said. "For more than two weeks you've fed me, clothed me, nursed me, kept quiet about me, and most importantly, helped me with my mission. You've been a good substitute angel." Then, as an afterthought, she added, "Except for not calling Farren these past few days."

He maneuvered himself around the ironing board and went over to the refrigerator.

"She's a married woman, Clair," he reminded, opening the door. "I can't talk to her and hang out with her every single day. There has to be a natural evolution, an appropriateness to this type of thing." He got himself a beer, then turned back to her.

"Want one?"

"No thanks. I understand what you're saying. I really do. But I think things are reaching a crescendo, and time is getting short."

"You get a heads-up from your boss or something?"

"No, it's just a feeling. And, I wish you wouldn't say that. He's your—"

"I know, I know," he cut in, twisting off the cap of his Bud Light. "He's my boss, too. God, I wish you wouldn't keep saying that."

"I wish you wouldn't say 'God' like that all the time," she responded, setting the iron on the counter to cool, then taking down the board.

"Why? Is the Maker Of All Creation sensitive to little ol' me using his name? And not even in vain?"

"It's a matter of respect."

He shrugged unconcerned and took a swig from his bottle.

"The gentleman who died yesterday," she queried, changing subjects. "You didn't say much about him last night other than he died."

"Yeah, so?"

"Can you tell me anything about him? I'd like to pray for his soul."

"Not much," he said, going over to the kitchen table and sitting down. "His name was Jacob McConnell. Male, Caucasian, fifty-five, six-one, two hundred and thirty pounds, or thereabouts. His daughter, who came to the hospital, said he lived alone. He had a wife, his second, who left years ago because he hit her once too often, and the daughter hadn't spoken to him in nearly a year because of his drinking."

"Sounds like a charming guy," she said, putting the ironing board away in a narrow closet.

"My job isn't to judge 'em, just save 'em. Or, try to, anyway."

"I'll pray for him."

"Would've been nice if your boss—sorry—if 'we' could've gotten there five minutes earlier. It would've made a difference."

"Perhaps," she said, sitting down at the small table across from him. "But if God says, 'It's time,' it's time."

He nodded, but she could see he wasn't in agreement. It was because he didn't want to continue the line of conversation.

"Okay," she said, suddenly slapping her hand down on the table, exasperated, "what *is* it with you?"

"What?"

"The longer I stay in this house, the bigger that chip gets on your shoulder about God. Right now, it's about the size of a Redwood."

"Why do you always have to bring up God? Haven't we had some other very nice conversations? About music? Literature?"

"Why do I always …? Doc! I'm an *angel!*"

"Whatever," he said, rising from the table. "Would you like to go for a walk? Have you been outside today?"

"Don't change the subject," she said. "Why are you so angry with the Lord?"

"Who says I'm angry?"

"I do."

He looked around at nothing in particular, becoming impatient. "If he sees and knows all, he knows."

"Well, *I* don't."

"Why should I talk to you about my life?" he snapped. "You've been in this house for over two weeks, and I don't know *anything* about you. Plus, you don't keep your word. You said you'd go with me to the dance, but then you didn't." He opened his mouth to say more, but then changed his mind and walked into the living room dismissively. She rose from the table and followed. "You might feel better if you unburdened yourself?" she suggested.

He spun around to her. "Am I a good person?"

"What?"

"Have I done everything you've asked?"

"Yes, you have."

"Damn right! I've saved dozens of lives all over the country. I'm helping to save Farren's life. I even moved back to Michigan to make peace with my parents. But what about my life, Clair? Where's *my* life?"

"I... I don't understand."

"Doesn't matter," he said, taking another drink of beer and turning to the flames in the fireplace. "Tomorrow's December 17. I'm always weird that day. Just ... just ignore me. You want some Christmas music?" He set his beer down on the wood plank table and started to head to the Bose radio and CD player on the bookshelf above the desk.

"She was never going to marry you, Doc," his houseguest suddenly announced.

He stopped in his tracks, and then slowly turned to her.

"What did you say?"

"Julia. She was never going to marry you."

His mouth slowly fell open. It seemed as if he stood there speechless for a long time, but in reality, it was only a few seconds.

"I never told you about Julia," he said. "There isn't even a picture of her in this house. Not unpacked, anyway."

"Did you really think after I came to be here I wouldn't find out something about my host?"

She stepped around to the leather sofa nearest the kitchen and sat down. She gestured to the other sofa opposite her. "Sit down, Doc."

"I don't want to sit down," he said, still frozen in place. "What did you mean?"

"It would've been better if you had voluntarily talked about her," she noted. "It would have—"

"Never mind the psychobabble," he interrupted impatiently. "What did you mean she was never going to marry me?"

"Love isn't always a two-way street. Certainly you've seen that with Charlie and—"

"She loved me," he cut in.

"No, Doc, she didn't."

"That's *bullshit!* What do you know about it, anyway?"

"She was going to end it with you the night before she died. That night at the Hyatt hotel."

He paused, momentarily stunned that she would know where they stayed and the intimate details of his life. But, he was even more stunned by her news of Julia's intentions.

"Th… that's ridiculous!"

"She didn't tell you that night because you'd just been accepted into medical school, and she didn't want to spoil your big news."

"That's not true!" he said, his volume rising. "We loved each other! We even exchanged presents."

"*You* gave her presents. She gave you a token pen and pencil set that a relative gave her that she didn't want."

"No," he refused, still louder. "We were planning a future! A future your loving, benevolent God crushed when he crushed half her organs! I was going to save lives as a doctor. Why did he have to kill my future with her?"

"There wasn't any future! *She didn't love you!*" Clair insisted, leaning forward and now speaking as loudly as him. "It was an affair to her, Doc! It was sex! Men sometimes see a woman and think, 'I'd take her to bed, but I wouldn't take her home to meet Mom.' You don't think women rank men the same way? And, for the record, you *chose* not to be a doctor!"

He stared at her, disbelievingly. She calmed down, rose, walked over to him, and extended her arm. "Take my hand."

"Why?"

"Because people tend to romanticize the past. They remember what they want, not necessarily what's true. If you take my hand, you'll remember the night before she died accurately."

"I remember everything about that night *perfectly*," he defended. "What are you? The Ghost of Christmas Past?"

"Memory and imagination are housed in the same areas of the brain. If you don't believe me, look it up in your medical books. I've no doubt you believe you remember every detail as it happened. Just take my hand for one second and be sure." She looked at him and smiled kindly. "C'mon, Doc. Do you honestly believe I'd show you anything other than the truth?"

He looked at her, rolled his eyes, breathed a heavy breath, and briefly touched her long, slender fingers. It was actually more of a slap than a touch.

"Okay. *There*," he said. "Happy?"

"Think back," she said, softly, like a psychiatrist inducing hypnosis.

He paused, trying to recall the events of nearly ten years ago at the Hyatt. After they had made love, Julia went into the bathroom. Although he never witnessed this, she sighed while looking at herself in the mirror. The sigh could've been because she was disappointed with what she saw, or it could've meant something else. It could've been because she was about to do something hard, like put the brakes on their relationship. After she came out of the bathroom wearing a black turtleneck, she climbed into bed and spoke about the Christmas tree. He turned around and looked at it on the table over by the porch. Slowly, the fog of the years started to lift and he began to remember bits and pieces.

He remembered Julia asking, "You ever wonder where we're going?"

Then he remembered her saying, "You spent too much on presents. You ought to take my stuff back."

He took a couple of slow steps over toward the tree, as if being near it would help put the past more clearly into focus.

"I'm very happy for you, Doctor Doc," she had said, patronizingly patting his hand after he presented her with his acceptance letter from Wayne State.

"Happy for *us*," he had corrected.

Next, he recalled her stiffening her back and asking, "You're not going to propose, are you?"

"I'm just talking, here," he had said. "Thinking out loud. Lots of couples get married while one or the other is going to graduate school." And she responded, "Lots of couples get divorced that way, too." Quickly followed by, "You've got four years of medical school that's going to need your full attention."

Then, he remembered something else she had said, "Let's not forget, I've only been teaching kindergarten for three months. I don't know what I'm doing yet. I don't know if teaching is right for me. I don't want to weigh you down. Be a responsibility you have to worry about."

The clues were subtle, but he was beginning to realize, the clues were there. He had always been surprised that Julia had said yes to his suggestion that they get a hotel room "to rehearse" that first time, and had always assumed that her feelings had grown and flourished like his. Yes, it may have been about sex initially, but he truly fell in love. Perhaps because of his good looks, prior experience and getting his way with women, or simple arrogance, it never dawned on him that she didn't feel the same way and that he was just hearing what he wanted to hear.

He recalled how she said they should "digest" the news about his being accepted into medical school instead of making plans and running headlong into things. He remembered saying to her, "You're right. We've got time," and her response was, "Mmm." It was neither positive nor negative. It was just a response. It was just something to say.

"Oh, Christ," he said, under his breath. "She was. She *was* planning to end it. I didn't realize."

"You already know the day she died, she ran a red light," Clair continued, soberly. "But nobody knows *why* she ran the light. She was looking at a picture in her wallet—a picture of her new boyfriend."

He closed his eyes and rubbed his forehead as a tear fell from his lash and splashed down his cheek. He looked at the Christmas tree for a moment, then turned back to her.

"Was it really necessary to tell me about the picture?"

"Yes, Doc, I think so. For ten years, you've been carrying a torch for someone who was never going to be here for very long. She was someone who liked having sex with you, but didn't love you. It's wrong for you to spend your life being angry at God. But, if you're going to be, you should at least know all of the facts. That's my thank you for helping me."

He looked around the living room visibly dazed trying to find his leather WWII-style bomber jacket.

"I, uh… I need…" Those were the only words that came out. He walked out of the living room, went into the spare bedroom, and returned a few moments later wearing his jacket and holding a pair of brown leather gloves. Then, without looking at Clair, he walked through the living room, went into the kitchen, and out the kitchen door. Her green eyes followed him with empathy, but also with the wisdom that she had done the right thing by telling him.

The mist was still heavy in the air outside. He started to walk down toward the lake, but, hearing the distant buzzing of either a chainsaw or snowmobile, turned and walked back past the cottage and down the lane that eventually led to Boyne City Road. Within a minute, he had wandered off the lane and was out among the tall white pines. He heard the wet, melting snow crunch under his shoes and realized he was wearing casual shoes that weren't really conducive for snow, but he kept walking, anyway. In another minute, he was regretting that he hadn't brought a hat for his damp hair. It was noticeably warmer, but his head was still chilly. Within another minute after that, he realized his nose was running and he had nothing to wipe it with. Even in despair, it seemed as if God was mocking him. All those years, all that pining over Julia, had been for nothing.

After a few more minutes, he came to a fallen tree, brushed the snow off some of its trunk, and sat down. He wiped his nose on one of his gloves, looked at the thick mist all around him, then stared up at the sky. He couldn't see anything. It seemed as if everything, including him, was leaking moisture. He imagined this was what the character Marianne Dashwood felt like in Jane Austen's *Sense and Sensibility* when she discovered that John Willoughby had abandoned his affections for her because he had found someone else with money. But then, he decided, this was worse. Marianne's deception had only lasted a couple of months. His deception had gone on for ten years. Julia's death had triggered several key decisions in his life: not pursuing medical school, the falling out he'd had with his parents, leaving the state, being with other women but not falling in love with them, his doubts about, and resentment toward, God, and since Clair's arrival, a rekindling of that resentment. In an instant, it all came crashing down on his shoulders, and they began to shudder.

"Stupid man," he uttered, not being able to hold back the tears. "You're a stupid, *stupid* man!"

He buried his face in his gloved hands and began to sob heavily. It was hard to distinguish because of his grief, but he actually uttered a prayer. It was the first prayer he'd said in years. It was very brief and consisted of only two shaky and barely audible words that escaped from the depths of his despair:

"I'm sorry."

RESCUER

Doc stayed in the woods for another twenty minutes. When his tears finally subsided, he rose from the tree trunk with a thoroughly soaked rear and headed back to the cabin. It had started to rain again by the time he arrived at the kitchen door, and he had no idea of what he was going to say to Clair. Had she done him a favor by revealing the truth? At the moment, he couldn't say.

Fortunately, he didn't have to face her. Knowing that he would return an emotional wreck, she left the recessed pot light on over the sink in the kitchen, the fire going in the living room, the small Christmas tree on, and had sequestered herself in her bedroom. Her bed was still broken, but at least the box springs and mattress had been separated from the frame and the wrought-iron headboard. The made bed, with its patchwork quilt, sat neatly on the floor like a remnant from a hippie commune while Clair sat quietly in the white wicker chair in the corner to the left of the bed. She knew Doc needed both space and privacy, so she folded her fingers together and prayed for him.

In the interim, he shook off the wet night by sitting on the floor in front of the screen by the fire. He leaned his back against the arm of the sofa nearest the kitchen and watched the flames slowly die out for almost an hour. When his body finally told him to go to sleep, he got up and unplugged the small Christmas tree having no intention of ever plugging it in again.

He was up before Clair and out of the cabin early the next morning. It was Saturday, December 17, the tenth anniversary of his last night with Julia, the tenth anniversary since he had been accepted into medical school, and the fourth unseasonably warm day in a row. He was actually grateful that he'd traded workdays with a fellow paramedic, so his mind would be occupied with work. His EMT partner was a guy named Morris. He was named after his grandfather, and it was unwise to make a joke in his presence about Morris The Cat, the finicky feline that sold 9 Lives Cat Food. Morris was thirty-six years old and made Lance look svelte. He was, to put it kindly, a "big boy," but he could dress a wound and comfort a patient with unexpected gentility.

The first call of the day was an auto accident a little outside of town on M66 involving teenagers; some minor cuts, a bump on the head, Doc and Morris didn't even take those involved to the hospital. The only other call of the day was a slip-and-fall in the IGA grocery store's parking lot. It involved a sixty-one-year-old Hispanic female who had a torn ligament and a fractured ankle.

When his shift ended at 6:00 p.m., he left the fire hall, climbed into his Jeep, and headed over to the Portside Marina to see if he might catch Farren there. He didn't really expect to, but at least he'd be able to tell Clair he'd made the effort at another contact. As he suspected, when he drove down the lane with the tall Leland Cypress trees on either side he could see the large square gravel lot was empty except for one Honda Accord SUV and a shadowy figure walking from the sandstone veneer marina store to the storage barn. As his headlights crossed the figure, he saw that it was Gus hoisting a snow shovel over his shoulder.

"Ah ... just what I need, some young muscle," he said, as Doc slowed to a stop with his driver's side window down. "Park that thing and c'mere for a second, will ya?"

"Sure," Doc replied. He parked the Wrangler, then walked over to the older man who was wearing a long tan nylon coat with a hood. "What's up?"

"Oh, I locked my keys in the storage barn. Left 'em on the workbench. I do it about once a year. I can't lock the other building or drive home without 'em."

Doc reached for his cell. "Want my phone to call Farren?"

"Naaa. I try not to bother her when Charlie's home. Give 'em a little space, y'know?" Despite his Sperry Docksiders, he began to trudge through the melting, but still shin-deep, snow heading around to the back of the building.

"C'mon," he said, still lugging the shovel.

Since it was already dark, Doc pulled the small flashlight out of the narrow pocket on the arm of his coat and clicked it on. "Where are we going?"

"Most of the barn floor is concrete, but there's a little ten-by-eight piece of floor that's wood," Gus explained, as he pushed the brittle remnants of waist-high weeds aside. "Underneath the wood floor is a root cellar that my daughter, Jackie, had put in when they built the barn. She envisioned doing canning and storing fruits and vegetables there but never got around to it. Anyway, it's got a stairway and a trap door that leads up to the wooden floor of the barn and there's an entrance back here that's a storm-cellar entrance." He paused. "Get ahead of me and shine that close to the wall."

Doc rattled through the overgrowth and stepped ahead of his companion.

"How will I know when I've found it?"

"Even with the snow, you should be able to make it out. It's two doors that swing open close to the ground. Once opened, they lead down a flight of stairs to another door that goes into the root cellar."

"Are the doors locked?"

"Nope. Never have been."

"Isn't that a security issue?"

"You think somebody's gonna squeeze a cabin cruiser through a trap door?"

"Good point," the younger man agreed. He aimed the light on the ground ahead of him and saw the snow covering a large square on a slight incline. "I see it," he said. He traded implements with Gus. He handed him the flashlight, took the snow shovel, and then started to scrape the snow off the metal doors.

"Good thing we've got this warm spell," Gus observed. "The hinges won't be frozen." He stomped his feet to shake off the fact his Sperrys were now soaked. "So, what brings you out this way?"

"I haven't seen Farren in a few days and thought I might try to catch her here," he said, filling the shovel with snow, and heaving it aside. "But I kind of figured she doesn't work the weekends."

"Not many. Especially since she got married and it's off season. But as I say, I don't mind. I know she and Charlie are apart all week."

"Commendable attitude considering you said you didn't like the guy much."

"I don't. But Farren wants the marriage to work, so I respect that."

Doc just smiled politely, scraping more snow off the doors.

"I still haven't figured out *your* story, though," Gus said, pointing the light on the doors to assist his companion.

"You mean, do I like Farren as a friend, or do I have other intentions?"

"Well, yeah. Now that you mention it."

He finished cleaning the snow off the doors, then stuck the shovel into a pile of tossed aside snow and tried to pull one of them open. "I'd be lying to you if I said I didn't think she was attractive. But, she *is* married, and there are rules about that."

"I'm glad you feel that way," Gus said. "Not that I'm defending Charlie. But, the institution."

The storm doors didn't budge. "I don't think the hinges are frozen," Gus said. "Just a little rusted. Bang on 'em with the shovel." The suggestion sounded reasonable to Doc, so he grabbed the shovel again and did so while Gus held the light on one of the three hinges each door had.

"What about you?" Doc asked.

"What about me?"

"You're a good-looking mature guy who seems fit. You ever date?"

"There's a lady I see in Boyne City every so often, but it's just gin rummy, beer, and conversation with a woman of my generation."

"What generation is that?" he asked, banging on the second hinge. "What time frame we talking about?"

"The Pre-Boomers: Nat King Cole, the Cold War, Gary Cooper in *High Noon*. In 1952, I was nineteen years old and had it all figured out, man."

"I sometimes wonder," Doc said, moving on to the third hinge, "if those bygone days were as interesting as people make them out to be."

"No time was ever as interesting as people make it out to be," Gus answered. "The only *real* interesting time is now, and what you're going to do with tomorrow. Today is the first day of the rest of your life and all that."

"Pretty prophetic for a Saturday night."

"Yeah, well, I've got kind of a new outlook on life these days."

"How's that?" Doc asked, standing the shovel in the snow again.

"Remember that day I saw you at the hospital, and I said I'd just had some tests done?"

"Yeah?"

"Those were actually a second round of tests; X-rays and an MRI. A first set of X-rays revealed some suspicious shadows. I figured maybe it was the beginning of the end. But, it turned out to be a false alarm.

Nothing. I'd just gotten the news minutes before I ran into you."

"That's great. Congratulations. So you're feeling pretty positive about things these days, eh?" Doc concluded.

"Yeah. I finally caught a break," Gus nodded. "You want a hand with the door?"

"Sure."

They both leaned over and tugged on one of the storm door handles. With a squeaky complaint, the metallic door finally gave way and opened.

Past the storm doors were six steps leading down to another metal door that led into the root cellar. Gus held the light while Doc descended the stairs.

"So after Farren's folks died, you were made her legal guardian?" he asked, brushing old cobwebs away.

"Of her until she was eighteen, of the business until she was twenty-one, then the property reverted to her. We lived together in Jackie and Paul's house on West Upright until she was twenty-five, then she had to spread her wings, and bought one of them Earl Young homes."

Doc turned the handle of the root cellar door, nudged it with his shoulder, and the door opened.

"She has a mushroom house?" he asked, pausing.

"You didn't know?"

"No. She never mentioned it."

"Didn't you drive her to Traverse City on Tuesday?"

"Yes, but we rendezvoused downtown and she left her car."

Gus descended the stairs. "If the bulb's not burned out, there should be a light switch on the wall to your left."

Doc felt the concrete wall, found the switch and flicked it on. A sixty-watt bulb illuminated an empty root cellar, empty except for two sets of homemade wooden shelves. There was nothing on the shelves, only more cobwebs.

"Nice décor," the paramedic observed. "Very Addams Family."

At the end of the room were six more stairs that led up to a swing-open trap door. "Careful," Gus warned, as he turned off the flashlight. "On the other side, you'll find yourself near the prop of a couple of tons of boat sitting in a storage cage. You won't have much clearance. You'll have to crawl out."

Doc wondered how a man in his seventies thought he was going to move all that snow, open rusted storm cellar doors, and then wiggle around under a boat in a storage cage before he had happened along. But then he recalled how most people rarely took their age into consideration so long as they felt good. Within another minute, the keys had been retrieved off the workbench and Gus wanted to thank Doc by buying him dinner at the Crow's Nest Bar & Grill. He passed on dinner, having no way to call Clair and figuring she might be cooking something, but agreed to a quick beer.

Despite the fact there was a pretty good dinner crowd at the Crow's Nest, there were available stools at the bar, so Doc and Gus crunched their way across the peanut shells on the floor and sat down while Peggy Lee sang a breathy version of "Jingle Bells" on the jukebox.

"What're you gonna do for Christmas?" Gus asked, after they'd settled in and ordered drinks. "Stay in town? Go see family?"

"I'm not sure yet. I've got Christmas Eve and Christmas day off if I wanted to go see my folks in Ann Arbor. But I don't know. I mailed my gifts off today at lunch, so I'm covered either way. How 'bout you?"

"The past few years I've made a big turkey at my place, and Farren has come over and opened gifts. But, now that Charlie's on the scene, I'll probably go over there. If I'm invited, that is."

"Of course you'll be," Doc said, as their beers arrived.

"To my rescuer," Gus said, picking up his longneck and toasting his companion. "Well done."

"My pleasure," Doc smiled, clinking bottles with Gus.

They both took sips of their drinks, then Gus eyed his young friend while rubbing the stubble on his chin "As I recall, you were askin' about angels the last time we were here. Do you believe in God?"

"Well, a lot of my patients do."

"That's not what I asked."

The paramedic chuckled. "That's usually my line. Yeah, I do. I wasn't sure for the longest time—years, in fact—but, yeah. Absolutely."

"What changed your mind?"

"Meeting your granddaughter, for one thing."

Gus raised his eyebrows. "How did meeting Farren help you believe in God?"

"I see how she gives to others and the inner light she has. That, and some other recent events, has made me reassess things."

"Simple as that, huh?" Gus asked, analytically.

"No. But that's a sound-bite answer over a beer. How about you? You believe in God?"

"Ah, well, that's one for the ages," Gus replied, taking a swig. "When

I was your age I wasn't much of a believer, but assumed I'd figure out the answers by the time I was an old man. Now, I'm seventy-eight, and I still don't know Jack."

"So, since you were nineteen and had it all figured out," Doc recalled jokingly, "you've been getting progressively dumber, eh?"

"Yeah," the elder responded, "I guess I have." He smiled and took another sip of beer.

"Well, you've got *my* respect. You've cultivated young minds at Central Michigan, became both mother and father to a teenage girl, moved here so she wouldn't have to deal with losing her parents *and* her surroundings, learned a whole new trade—" he stopped in mid-thought. "Where were Paul's parents during all this?"

"They divorced years ago and both remarried. His father's down in Costa Rica and his mother has lived in Texas with her second husband for nearly twenty years. They keep in contact at birthdays and Christmas, and Farren even went to Texas a few times to see her grandma at Thanksgiving. But, she's always wanted to stay pretty close to Charlevoix. Besides, me being her legal guardian was specifically stipulated in the wills." He chuckled. "Guess Jackie and Paul never figured anything would ever happen to them, huh?"

"Or, maybe they just picked the right grandparent for the job," Doc observed. He looked at Farren's grandfather with a sincere eye. "You've done good, Gus. Real good."

The older man rubbed his chin again and was more appreciative of the compliment than he let on. The more time they spent together, the more they realized the things they had in common. Neither one was afraid to ask pointed questions, both considered a married woman off limits—at least, usually—both were bachelors, both had wondered about the existence of God, both didn't like Charlie, although Doc had never admitted his dislike to Gus, and both wanted to keep Farren from harm.

By 7:10 that night, Doc had said his goodbyes and was heading out of town. Shortly after he made the turnoff onto Boyne City Road, heading for the pothole-filled lane leading down to his cabin, he noticed the headlights of another vehicle coming up fast behind him. The headlights sat a little high off the pavement, like they belonged to an SUV or pickup truck. Figuring that whoever it was, they wanted to pass him, he tapped on his brakes and slowed down to let them go around. In another few seconds, the vehicle passed him, but then abruptly braked, squealing to a stop in front of him. This forced the Wrangler to also brake, swerve, go off the road, and skid to a stop on the shoulder. Considering the wet weather conditions and potential slickness of the pavement, it was a downright dangerous maneuver.

Instead of road rage, once he had his vehicle in park, Doc assumed something must be wrong with the driver of the SUV. He saw it was a white Cadillac Escalade and quickly concluded these weren't kids out joyriding or some good ol' boys who'd had too much to drink, but rather it must have been someone who had a seizure. Maybe it was a senior citizen who simply misjudged the passing distance when they cut him off. In either case, his expertise might be needed. He hopped out of the Wrangler and ran over to the Cadillac to see if he could be of assistance.

He approached the dark tinted glass of the driver's side door and knocked.

"Hey! Jeff Gordon. You okay? I'm a paramedic."

The door suddenly flew open and into Doc, knocking him backward to the ground. By the time he caught his breath and looked up, he saw two beefy men quickly moving toward him. One was wearing a lightweight North Face jacket and loafers with tassels; the other was carrying a baseball bat.

Twenty minutes later, Clair was in the kitchen standing over an overdone meatloaf and shaking her head when she looked up through the window over the sink. She noticed a pair of headlights bouncing down the lane en route to the cabin.

"Well, *finally*," she said, with a heavy breath. She put oven mitts on her hands, opened the oven door, picked up the pan of meatloaf and slid it back in. "It's going to be tough as leather," she sighed. "But at least it'll be warm."

She closed the oven door, took off her mitts, adjusted the temperature, and saw Doc's Wrangler roll to a stop out in the turnaround, although she noticed it was at a peculiar angle. She was wearing her Charlevoix Yacht Club white sweatshirt, jeans, and black slippers. She turned and inspected the already set table for dinner, then rounded the corner and went into the living room. She checked the fire to see if it needed another log, then went over to the CD player and radio on the bookshelf and turned on some Christmas music. Next, she turned and walked over to the glass gun case, checked her hair in the glass' reflection, then returned to the kitchen. She calculated Doc should've been walking through the kitchen door about the time she re-entered the kitchen and was surprised that she didn't hear him kicking the snow off his feet against the log walls outside.

"What's he doing?" she muttered to herself. "Getting firewood?"

She walked to the window above the sink and looked outside. The Wrangler's headlights were still on and the driver's side door was open.

Puzzled, she walked over to the kitchen door and opened it. When she did, the pulverized body of Doc Reynolds collapsed into her arms.

"*Doc!*" she yelled, in surprise. The weight of his body folded her legs until she was on her knees, and his head was in her lap. His blue nylon coat was dark stained with blood, his swollen face was a smear of red disfigurement. His hair was wet and stringy from lying in the snow. His lips were twice their normal size and his right eye was grotesquely swollen shut. A few soggy leaves clung to his wet, black pants. His hands were chapped red and he was barely conscious. Blood trickled from his left ear, nose, and mouth.

"What happened?" she asked, intensely concerned.

It took all of his strength to muster a barely audible answer.

"N-n-n-no goo deee…hose unpunishsh." He smiled a little, as if attempting to be funny, then passed out.

Although it would have been babble to most, she understood what he was trying to say. It was an old adage: "No good deed goes unpunished." It meant he had tried to help someone, but had paid a price for doing so.

She assumed it was the work of either Bartholomew or his men but wasn't sure. She looked through the open door at the abandoned Jeep, ignored the wind blowing inside, and put her hand gently on his forehead. She closed her eyes and waited quietly for a few seconds, as if her palm was a supernatural sensor making a scan of his body.

"Fractured skull," she whispered, "shattered eardrum…two broken ribs…bleeding kidneys…bruised spleen … broken jaw … broken nose … hairline fracture in the right femur…" she opened her wet green eyes and her shoulders slumped.

"Oh, Doc," she said, as tears slid down her cheeks, "I'm so sorry. I'm so very, *very* sorry."

PRIVATE TALK

It had been years since Wyatt "Doc" Reynolds had had dreams that were so pleasant he didn't want to wake up from them. But this particular night, he did. They were wisps of scenes that drifted into his mind, lingered for a while, then slowly dissolved into something else like a cloud changing shape. One moment, he was opening a Christmas gift at his parents' house. The next, he was walking on a sandy white beach while watching a beautiful sunset. The next, he was reunited with his dog, Barkley, who died when he was thirteen. After that, he dreamed he was waking from a long sleep and Farren was there, leaning over him and smiling when he opened his eyes.

Twelve hours after he had collapsed in his kitchen doorway, and on the morning of the tenth anniversary of Julia's passing, he did open his eyes. But the only thing looking down at him was the old ceiling fan of the guestroom. The room was exactly the same size as his bedroom, except the walls weren't knotty pine paneling. They were bead board painted light yellow. The bed was a double instead of a queen, and this, combined with the lighter-colored walls, made the room appear larger.

He slowly brought a hand to his forehead thoroughly expecting a wave of pain to engulf him, but it never arrived. His fingers gently felt his right eye. Amazingly, it wasn't swollen, and he could see out of it perfectly. Next, he touched his lips. They seemed to be their normal size and uncut. He touched his left ear. His hearing was normal. He didn't understand. He vividly remembered the beating he had received the night before. He remembered a loud ringing after the baseball bat had struck him squarely on the left ear. He remembered lying in the snow and cringing while the bat came down on him again and again. He remembered a foot kicking him in the jaw and someone taking his wallet. After what seemed like an eternity of pain upon pain, he remembered a man's voice saying, "Dude, he's half-dead. That's enough!" But now, inexplicably, his wounds seemed to have evaporated like his dreams.

He slowly pulled back the covers and noticed he was naked. Just as he was climbing out of bed, he heard the quick movement of footsteps going into the bathroom that connected the two bedrooms together. This was followed by the sound of vomiting. He looked over at the closed bathroom door. He knew that sound very well. Clair had gotten nauseous again. Probably earlier that morning she had morphed into an animal and had just changed back. Vomiting frequently followed transformation into human form. He knew there was nothing he could do for her at the moment, so he plucked some clean jeans, underwear, and a rugby-style long-sleeved shirt from a stack of clothes that he had moved from his room into the guestroom, then headed for the half-bath off of the kitchen.

Once he was in front of a mirror, he could see how undamaged he was. It was like the attack never happened. He stared at himself for a long time in the mirror knowing that Clair had restored him with her angelic power. In truth, he knew it wasn't Clair's doing at all, but rather God's. At the moment, though, that was too much for him to process. It was too vast. So, he limited the miraculous accomplishment to Clair. Even there, though, her abilities gave him goose bumps. For the past two weeks, she'd been so fragile at times, so sick, so fascinated with the simplest of things like the weather, or making snow angels, or fires in the fireplace. To see this other side of her—the powerful life-force-changing-side—required a major adjustment in thinking.

By the time he came out of the bathroom, his houseguest was in the living room huddled up in a corner on one of the leather sofas with the quilt from her bed wrapped around her. There wasn't a fire in the fireplace, so the room was chilly. She looked pale and weak, and a few strands of golden hair hung limp over her face. She looked anything but powerful and celestial. Seeing her exhaustion, he silently went over to the refrigerator and poured her a small glass of Vernors.

"Good morning," he said, approaching with the glass.

"Hi," she replied, taking it.

They both asked, "How do you feel?" at the same time. She smiled weakly, said, "You first," then took a sip of her ginger ale.

"Why didn't I wake up dead?" he asked. "Or at least in the ICU?"

"I absorbed your injuries?" she replied.

"Absorbed?"

"I couldn't take you to the hospital. I have no driver's license or ID. How would I explain myself, not to mention what happened to you? So I absorbed your wounds."

"What does that mean?"

"I took the damage out of your body and put it into mine. I'm stronger. I heal faster. But, it *does* take a toll. Think of it as a type of healing by the laying on of hands."

"You laid hands on me?"

"In a manner of speaking, yes."

He raised a suggestive eyebrow. "All over?"

She looked at him straight-faced. "Don't make me sorry I did this."

"Sorry," he smiled. "Are you going to be okay?"

"Eventually, yes," she said, taking another sip. But, I wouldn't go in my bedroom until I've cleaned it up."

"Well, thank you, Clair. You saved my life. I wish you could've absorbed your own wounds."

"Regeneration *is* absorption," she clarified. "What happened last night?"

He sat down on the sofa opposite her. "A Cadillac ran me off the road. At first, I thought maybe the driver had suffered some sort of attack. But it wasn't that. Two guys purposely ran me off the road then jumped me. One of 'em had a baseball bat."

"Do you think it was Bartholomew or people that work for him?"

"They took my wallet, but that could've been just a smokescreen to make it look like a robbery."

She thought for a moment while sweeping the hair off her face. "I think you're right. I think it was a smokescreen. Doc, you've *got* to warn Farren. Tell her about Charlie. I don't think we've got the time for subtleties anymore."

"You sure?"

"I don't think Charlie liked you going to Traverse City with Farren. He probably sees your friendship as a threat and wanted you sidelined because he's about to make his move."

"You think?"

"I do. You should see her today."

"It's Sunday. I ... I don't even know if Charlie leaves town on Sunday night or Monday mornings."

"Usually it's Monday mornings. But I don't think we can afford to wait. Let's just hope whatever rapport you've established with her is strong enough for trust."

He nodded, then rose and went over to the desk. He opened the drawer and pulled out the Smith & Wesson snub-nosed revolver he usually carried in the Jeep, but removed when it went into the body shop. "I'll have to report my wallet being stolen," he said, clicking open the weapon to make sure all five chambers were full.

"What're you doing?" she asked, eyeing the pistol.

"He's *not* going to hurt Farren, Clair," he replied with conviction. "I won't allow that. Look what he did to me."

She set her glass down on the wood plank coffee table, rose, still wrapped in her quilt, and walked over to him. "You taking a life is not part of this scenario. God doesn't need you to kill for him. Just warn Farren."

"But—"

"Do as I ask," she said, extending her hand for the weapon. "Just have faith."

When her hand was extended, the quilt separated slightly, and he could see that all she was wearing was a pair of panties. But, this wasn't a sexual observation so much as a familiar one. It struck him as incredible that he had been cohabitating with an angel for more than two weeks. They had eaten together, shared the same bathroom, he had held her forehead when she was sick, they'd taken walks, watched movies, discussed God, cleaned house, he had cared for her, and she had cared for him. In a very real way, he regarded her as he would his own sister in North Carolina. He looked at the handgun, then spun it around and handed it to her butt first.

"If you say so," he relented.

"I say."

Having studied Farren's life and routine before coming to Earth, Clair knew a few things about her charge. She knew that she liked to visit the bookstore on Bridge Street every Monday to check out the new titles that had arrived the previous Friday. She knew her usual hours at the marina. She knew the places she was likely to go for lunch. And she knew that she usually went to the 11:00 a.m. mass alone on Sundays at St. Ignatius. Charlie slept in on Sundays, and Gus almost never attended mass. So on this particular Sunday, as Father Ken was standing by the front doors saying goodbye to parishioners leaving after the service, Doc came up behind her knowing she'd be alone.

"Hey," he greeted.

She turned, a little surprised. "Hi ... I thought you didn't do church."

"I need to talk to you about something. Can we go somewhere private?"

She hesitated. "Uh, Charlie's waiting for me at home."

"It'll take just a couple of minutes. Please, Farren, it's important."

"Okay," she said. "Hang on." She went up to the priest, who was still chatting with parishioners, excused herself, and asked him something. He dipped his hand under his vestments, produced a set of keys, and handed them to her. Then she returned to Doc.

"Let's go across the street to the social center. Tess Groom happened to mention she lost her iPod the night of the dance, and I promised I'd double-check the coatroom. Might as well do it now and we can talk, too."

She was wearing a skirt with high heels, and as they walked across the street, she stepped carefully over the puddles in the pavement. It was yet another unseasonably warm day, about forty-eight degrees, and the occasional patch of grass could even be seen on nearby lawns.

"If this is about what happened in Traverse City," she said, as she navigated a puddle, "I know the whole story. It was a simple misunderstanding."

"Charlie selling a book behind your back given to you by your mother that belonged to her mother? Telling you he flew to Milwaukee out of Traverse City, when he didn't? How are these misunderstandings?"

"We're friends," she replied, taking his arm as they stepped around some more water, "but this is between me and Charlie, okay?"

"Okay," he agreed, "I won't mention Traverse City again."

"Good. Thank you," she said, as they approached the social center.

Once inside, Farren checked the closet that served as a coatroom for the dance while Doc wandered into the main hall of the center and looked around. It hadn't changed much since the Christmas dance and auction, although, in the light of day, the place looked older and more worn. The linen-draped tables and folding chairs had been put away, and the DJ equipment was gone, but the choir risers and unplugged Christmas trees on either side of them were still in place as was the large wreath hanging on the wall.

"No luck," she said, coming out of the closet after a minute. Her navy pea-style coat was unbuttoned, and she carried her gloves in her hand. Her heels echoed slightly on the gray linoleum floor as she walked over to him. "That's the oddest thing. A couple of people have mentioned they lost one thing or another that night. Anyway, what's up?"

He had an idea about what might've happened to the missing articles but let it pass. There were more important things to discuss. He unzipped his WWII-style bomber jacket with the wool collar and took a moment to find what he hoped would be just the right words.

"There aren't a lot of things in life we can count on one hundred percent. Some say, the only permanent thing in life *is* change. Most of the time, that's true. But there are exceptions. Your relatives will always be your relatives, the stars will always be in the sky, and your spouse always owes you the truth."

"Doc!" she protested.

"I'm not talking about last week. I'm talking about something you deserve. Honesty between partners should be a given. You can't base a marriage on lies, Farren, and you *know* this. You *know* it's true!"

"People make mistakes."

"Yes, they do. And you made a big one when you married Charlie Huffman. Long before we ever met, didn't Gus's instincts tell you something? Have you ever met Charlie's parents? His siblings? Anybody he works with? Bet you haven't, have you?"

"You'd better stop right there, Doc."

"You said it, yourself. You got starry-eyed. Impulsive. You moved fast because you knew what loss felt like. That's not bringing up Traverse City, by the way. Technically, you said that on the highway miles from Traverse City."

She looked at the gloves she held, then tossed her head back and brushed her dark bangs aside. Her immediate inclination was to be angry, but she also wanted to hear where he was taking this. "So, what're you saying?"

"I'm saying Charlie isn't what he appears to be. You shouldn't trust him. You're caught up in something—"

"You don't want me to trust the man I married?" she interrupted. "You want me to listen to *you*? Someone I've known for, what, two weeks?"

"I want you to listen to your heart. Listen to your soul, Farren. I know you had questions about Charlie before you even met me. I know you've prayed about your marriage. What has God been telling you?"

She looked at him as tears welled in her brown eyes. "Where were you when I was free? When Charlene wanted us to meet? Where were you all those years when I got dressed up, fixed my hair, came here to the Christmas dance and prayed that maybe somebody different, somebody good would find me?"

"I was coming."

"You're late," she said tersely. "Too late. We can't be friends anymore, Doc. I think we're both frustrated because we wish this could be something more, and we know it can't."

"Is that what we wish?" he asked, catching that she had revealed private desires.

She held up a hand. "I've got enough problems with my marriage already. I'm not going to throw temptation onto the fire."

"Pretend I'm not a guy. Pretend I'm a girlfriend who *doesn't* find you incredibly attractive. He's going to hurt you, and I don't mean with just lies. I mean physically. I think you're in genuine danger."

She pointed a finger at him and started walking backward toward the door.

"We can't be friends anymore. Stay away from me."

"Farren."

"If you like me, Doc, like me at all, stop now!"

He fell silent in frustration as she turned and hurried away, her heels clicking on the linoleum masked the sound of her sniffles.

AGAINST THE ODDS

Farren didn't wait for Doc to come out of the social center. She left the keys in the door and, as he came outside, called over her shoulder for him to return them to Father Ken back in the church. This he did, explaining to the priest that Farren had to hurry home. He also reported that they had found nothing in the closet, and Father mentioned that, he, too, had received a couple of complaints from people saying one thing or another had disappeared from their coat pockets the night of the dance.

Once again, Doc was tempted to say something about Charlie, but didn't. As he walked back to his Wrangler, he wondered if remaining quiet was a mistake. It seemed the time for polite silence was over. People had attacked him the night before, and although he couldn't prove it, he was 99 percent sure Charlie was behind it.

As he climbed behind the wheel, he wished he hadn't been so roundabout with Farren. He wished that he had told her straight out that her marriage was a scam, and her husband was planning to kill her. But how could he prove it? Say that an angel told him so? Show her wounds from a beating that no longer existed because they'd been "absorbed?" He sat behind the wheel clutching it and not knowing what to do next. If he returned to the cabin, Clair would just tell him that his warning hadn't been emphatic enough. Maybe he could follow Farren home, but then he realized he didn't know where she lived, only that she lived in a mushroom house. Finally making a decision, he started up the Jeep and headed for the fire hall.

As he drove through town on Bridge Street, he looked out across East Park, past the city marina and noticed the ice on Round Lake had puddles of slushy water on it because of the warm spell of the past several days. This was only his first winter in Charlevoix but he had already read up on the unpredictability of the area's bodies of water. It was very rare for Lake Michigan to freeze completely, but, on occasion, it had. Notable years for this were 1962, 1976, and 1979. Usually, ice just formed for miles along the shoreline like a frosty white ribbon that extended out dozens, and sometimes hundreds, of yards into the lake. Because of its smaller size, Round Lake frequently froze but, oddly enough, not always, despite the sub-zero temperatures. Then, there was Lake Charlevoix that had certain parts of its upside-down Y-shape freeze, but not others. Some sections froze solid enough to accommodate fishing shanties and snowmobiles, while other parts remained liquid, black and foreboding. It all depended upon the severity of the winter.

Walking into the fire hall, he was surprised to see Lance wearing jeans and a sweatshirt, sitting on the perpetually shiny floor where their ambulance normally sat, assembling a large birdhouse. Beside him, the four city fire trucks sat in their usual bays with their waiting open doors, and two firemen were also in the garage, stacking hoses onto one of the trucks.

"Hey," Doc said, "what's going on?"

"Christmas gift for Charlene's dad," Lance explained, glancing at an open set of instructions. "If I assembled it at my place, Charlene would get all excited and blab it to her father. She wouldn't mean to, of course. But she would."

"It's a great birdhouse."

"Thanks. What're you doin' here?"

"I have no life," Doc shrugged. "I'm just seeing what's going on. But since you're here, you can probably answer something for me. Do you have an address for Farren?"

"I can't give you a street number, but I can give you directions." Lance put a small plastic bag of washers down for the feeder and climbed to his feet. "It's not very far from here, maybe not even a mile. What do you want it for?"

"I lent her a book and wanted to see if she was finished with it."

He nodded, accepting the answer and walked over to a black cordless phone mounted on the wall with a chest-high writing surface bolted into the cinderblock. There was a pen and a pad sitting there. He picked up the pen and started to draw a map.

"Where's our ambulance?" Doc asked.

"Morris and Joe got a call about an injury near the cement factory. It didn't sound too serious on the radio, though."

"Good."

"How'd it go with Morris yesterday?" Lance asked.

"Fine. Good guy. But, he doesn't know anything about James Bond. The only Q he knows is Barb-B-Que."

Lance smiled, appreciating the compliment, then ripped off the paper from the pad and handed it to Doc. "Make sense?"

Doc looked at the paper. "Yeah. Thanks. You're right. It isn't far. But what's this name and number on the bottom."

"That's Jeff Motto's number. A good therapist I want you to call."

Doc looked at his partner, not understanding. "Therapist?"

Lance leaned in and lowered his voice. "You know, for that ba-aa-aa-ad problem you've got?"

Doc looked at him, puzzled. "What are you talking about?"

"What we were talking about the other day, right here in this very garage."

Doc thought for a moment, trying to recall. "Y' know," his partner continued. "when you were in the back of the ambulance and had just juiced up the electronics. You said you didn't know how it all started, but you hadn't done anything yet?"

"What did you think I was talking about?"

"Doc, c'mon, man," the larger man leaned into him, confidentially. "I saw you and that walking sweater in the parking lot last Saturday. I was watching from a distance. You even said something about it wearing jewelry, for God's sake."

Doc's eyes widened as he realized his wiry-haired partner had seen him with Clair when she was a sheep. Then, his eyes got even wider when he realized that Lance was implying bestiality.

"Oh, oh, that's wrong. That's really, *really wrong*! And gross! No. *No*! It was absolutely *nothing* like that!"

"But, I heard you talking about taking the animal to bed, man."

"You've also heard me say to patients with broken legs, 'So I guess we're not entering the rumba contest Friday night, huh?' Lance, that's what I *do*. I say quirky, unsettling things. Whatever you *thought* you heard me say, it wasn't real. It was just me being me."

Lance sighed, visibly relieved. "Wow, that's, that's *good!* I was really worried about you, partner ... and really disgusted. But, I didn't turn my back on you."

"No, sir. You sure didn't," Doc smiled, appreciatively.

"So what *were* you doing with a sheep? Where'd you get it? Why was it wearing jewelry?"

Doc stared blankly at his friend for several seconds. "It's ... it's a ... a Christmas gift a patient of ours asked me to keep so his kid wouldn't find out about it."

"What kind of kid wants a sheep for Christmas?"

"Uh ... a 4-H member?" Doc suggested.

"Who was the patient?" Lance pressed.

"That's the wrong question," Doc stammered. "The sheep's irrelevant. What you should be asking is: Who was I talking about the other day?"

"Okay. Who were you talking about the other day that made you feel so guilt-ridden?" A moment later, his green eyes flew open and his jaw dropped as he figured out the answer. "Oh my God. You've developed a thing for *Farren?*"

"C'mere," Doc said, taking Lance by the arm and walking farther away from the two firemen on the other side of the garage. "If I told you something that was kind of hard to believe, something I couldn't absolutely prove, but had *really strong* suspicions about, would you do something to help me? I know you're going to say 'yes' 'cause you want to know what I'm talking about. But, I *really* need you to believe me, Lance. This is like one of those moments in a James Bond film where Bond goes against all the odds and acts on his instincts."

Lance stared at his partner intently. "Like, in *Octopussy* when Kamel Kahn and Bond are playing a dice game, and Bond said he didn't play the odds?"

"Uh, yeah," Doc replied, having no idea what scene his partner was talking about.

WHAT'S OWED

Charlie and Farren's mushroom house was so compact that it required some furniture rearranging to accommodate a Christmas tree. Because it was shaped like a teardrop, from an overhead perspective, all the exterior walls had a curve, while the interior walls that made up the rooms in the back half of the house were built at slight angles to guarantee each room had its own unique shape.

Normally, a thirty-two-inch flat-screen TV sat in front of the usually drawn living-room curtains in between the wooden front door at the narrow end of the house and the fireplace with the mantel holding old family pictures on the other, more-rounded end. But this time of year, a Scotch pine with short, prickly needles sat in front of the living room window with the curtains pulled open. To accommodate the tree, the TV was sitting oddly against a curved piece of wall in between the far side of the front door and the entranceway into the black-and-white check kitchen. Meaning, if someone were to be sitting on the sofa, directly across from the front window and curtains, they'd either have to turn their head to the left to watch TV or sit on the floor in front of it. A Feng Shui enthusiast would've shuddered, but it was better than sticking the TV in one of the two small bedrooms.

Charlie lay on the sofa with his head propped up by pillows watching the Red Wings play St. Louis. He occasionally took a swig from a Sam Adams he clutched while wishing he'd put some money on the game. Meanwhile, Farren was in the kitchen putting the last of the dinner dishes away. It was now 7:30 p.m. on Sunday evening, and she was just about ready to tackle the laundry.

"Do you have any jeans you want washed, honey?" she asked, passing him, as she went through the living room to their bedroom. She was wearing jeans, a white turtleneck, and her K-Swiss boots.

"Yeah," Charlie replied, not taking his eyes off the TV. "In my duffle."

She shook her head that he'd been home since Friday but hadn't emptied his bag yet. She wondered if he intended to leave on Monday, or if he was going to look for work closer to home now that she knew he was unemployed. She assumed he'd do the latter, although they hadn't really discussed his next steps in any detail. She figured she'd broach the subject with him as soon as the game was over, which it almost was.

The bedrooms of the mushroom house were even smaller than the ones at Doc's, but Farren had done her best to make the master bedroom space efficient by putting a small dresser in the closet, then wall shelves for clothing were above the dresser. Charlie's duffle was jammed in between the closet door and the bottom drawer of the dresser. She picked it up, unzipped it, then turned and dumped the contents onto the white comforter of their made-up queen-sized bed. As she picked through work shirts and Fruit Of The Loom boxer shorts to get to a pair of Wrangler jeans, a small bright red foil packet fell out of the back pocket of the jeans onto the comforter. She picked it up and looked at it. It was a condom, the kind one would buy from a vending machine in the men's room at a truck stop. She looked at it for several seconds not understanding. She already had birth control patches and there was no need for Charlie to have such a thing. But a few seconds later, her naivety evaporated and she understood all too well.

She sighed with heartbreak, then bit her lower lip, determined to fight back the tears. She turned and sat on the edge of the bed, her posture sinking like a wilting flower. She supposed her husband would have an explanation. She was beginning to realize that he was very good at explanations—too good, in fact. After the better part of a minute, she straightened up with resolve, wiped her wet eyes on one of his shirts, and rose with the red foil package in hand.

It was only a ten-foot walk out of the master bedroom, past the bathroom and guest room, and into the living room. But, as her courage mounted to confront Charlie, she didn't realize that there was an odd medicinal smell and a shadowy figure lurking as she passed the doorway of the darkened guest room. Just about the time she paused and realized Charlie wasn't on the sofa anymore, a large hand holding a white washcloth came around from behind her and clamped itself tightly over her nose and mouth like a vice, so forceful it almost broke her nose.

Farren's eyes flew open as she tried to scream, and her body jerked in reaction. Her hands frantically reached behind her and slapped at the face of her attacker. It was a chiseled face with a couple days' worth of stubble that she had felt a hundred times before. The oddly placed TV with the hockey game on it suddenly seemed as if it were in a tunnel—a tunnel that was expanding longer and longer into blazing white light. The sound of the crowd and the play-by-play announcing got more distant and vague. Her arms fell limp and the heels of her boots squeaked across the wooden floor as she was being dragged.

When she opened her eyes again, she didn't know how much time had passed. She wasn't even sure where she was, at first. But, she did know she had a tremendous headache. She also knew she was cold. She blinked her eyes hard a few times as if each blink would make her better understand what had happened.

Before her was a man who was floating horizontally with his arms extended in front of him like some sort of flying superhero. He wore a tan cape. As he floated, she heard the sound of a jet engine. But, with another couple of blinks, she realized it wasn't a superhero, it was Charlie standing with his back to her, wearing his tan fabric coat with the corduroy collar. And he wasn't floating, he was standing on an A-frame ladder, and she was looking at him from a tilted-over position on the ground. And, his arms weren't extended because he was flying, but because they were doing something with a battery-powered drill above his head, a drill that whined a little like a jet engine.

Within another thirty seconds, she realized a number of other things. She was cold because she was lying on her side on the concrete floor of the marina's storage barn. She was also now wearing her red down vest. She also realized she was lying in one of the barn's two empty storage cages. Charlie was on a six-foot ladder doing something with a drill involving one of the tracks of rubber wheels that normally held the hull of the boat in the upper cage. As she looked around, and her senses became sharper, she realized the thirteen-foot Pro-Line Bay Boat that was supposed to be in the upper cage had been removed by the marina's forklift, but the boat was just barely out of its cage. The lift with its long rubber-sheathed arms cradled the suspended boat some ten feet to the left and above her. Its stern was just a foot or so from the beginning of the cage's tracks and the engine shaft was raised. Next, she noticed her hands were bound behind her back, her ankles were also bound and there was something stiff and sticky—tape, she realized—over her mouth. It was gray duct tape. Tape was also holding her wrists and ankles. The drill stopped whining, she grunted a little, and Charlie turned to see her awake.

"Hi, honey," he called, just as normally as if he had come in from running a Saturday errand, "bet your head really hurts, huh? You've been out for about four hours. Just in case you were wondering, that was chloroform." He came down the ladder with the drill. "I got it and a couple of other things from some guys I know in Flint."

He looked at her, sighed a little, then set the drill down and approached. It was at this point she noticed the clear, skin-tight white latex surgical gloves he was wearing. In between her head throbbing and the cold, she calculated that, if four hours had passed, it must be around 11:30 Sunday night.

"I'm afraid I've got nothin' but bad news for you, babe. But, the good news is, I *do* think enough of you to tell you the bad news. I think you're owed that."

He stooped down and helped her sit up. Then, he pulled the red foil condom out of his coat pocket and held it in front of her.

"Yeah, I kind of forgot about this until you were already digging through the laundry. Her name is Margo. She lives outside of Traverse City. Those couple of times that you called Miller Construction trying to reach me you were actually calling a toll-free line set up at her place. She's my 'old switchboard friend.' If it's any consolation, I've known her since before I met you, so it's not exactly like we got hitched then I started to fool around."

He sighed again from all the work he'd been doing and sat down on the floor facing her. He put the condom back in his coat pocket then pulled out a Beretta 9-millimeter pistol. The same pistol Bartholomew had given him to kill Daniel with in Mt. Pleasant. Upon seeing the gun, Farren's eyes became noticeably apprehensive.

"See, the thing is," he continued, scratching his head with the barrel of the gun, "our marriage was never about you and me. It was never about love. It was about business. Settling a debt. I'm not exactly the guy you think I am.

"I like to gamble, gamble a lot, actually, and a while back, I got myself into debt with a man in Flint named Bartholomew. This is *not* a guy you want to owe a lot of money to, and I *did*. But, oddly enough, he didn't want money. He wanted land. This land. It's a long story, but the bottom line is he's some sort of nut about Charlevoix and fancies himself a real estate mogul who could make a fortune if he built condos right about where we're sitting. He already had this location picked out before I was even brought in. So you see, darlin', you were someone who had to be dealt with. Played. Remember how I urged for us to draw up wills right after we got married? I'm afraid there's going to be an accident tonight, and you're going to be the star. What we're talkin' about is literally your life for mine. You gotta understand, these guys play *rough*! They already took my toe as an incentive. Like I said, I felt I owed you an explanation because," he paused with a certain fondness in his voice, "…well…you *have* been very accommodating in a number of ways, not to mention, positions."

Her brown eyes drifted away from his, processing everything he had said. She wondered if what was happening to her now was somehow connected to a query a local real estate agent had made about the marina approximately a year earlier on behalf of an "unnamed, but interested party." She was hurt by what she had just heard, but surprisingly, not as devastated as she thought she might be. No doubt her having questions about Charlie for some time had something to do with it. After several seconds, she looked down at the tape over her mouth and grunted, wanting him to remove it.

Understanding, he put the barrel of the Beretta under her nose. "One scream, Farren," he said, seriously, "even if you raise your voice, you'll get whacked upside the head. Whacked hard. We clear?"

She nodded in agreement. He slowly peeled the gray duct tape off her face. The action was painful causing her to whimper a little. When it was finally off, she flexed her sore facial muscles for a few seconds then looked at him with genuine regret.

"You know what's sad?" she observed, quietly. "If you had really loved me, I would've given you the land to settle your debt. I fell in love with you, Charlie."

"You fell in love with an illusion," he corrected. He rose and looked at the storage cage above them. "Here's how the accident's gonna go: you were working late and sweeping out the floor of this bottom cage, when the tracks holding the boat above you suddenly collapsed. I really have worked on a construction site or two, so I know how to handle a forklift and how to stress bolts to their breaking point."

He pointed to a brown bottle and a white washcloth sitting on the floor near one of the forklift's tires. "A little more chloroform, I untie you and position your body just so with a broom, then I slip the boat above back onto the loosened tracks. A few seconds later, five thousand pounds of hull comes crashing down. They'll call it a freak occurrence, but a very fatal one. Don't worry though, honey. You'll be out cold. You won't feel a thing."

She looked at the suspended boat, then at him. With each passing second, the flames of her love for Charlie were quickly being extinguished.

"You don't have to do this."

"Yeah, actually, I do."

"You'll never get away with it."

"Actually, I will," he disagreed. He slipped the gun back into his coat pocket, and then went over to close the ladder. "I don't have any life insurance on you, so there goes motive. And what bad things are people going to say about our relationship? That I bought you flowers every week when we were dating? That I helped you with social functions at church? That I made outrageous bids at a charity auction on your behalf, or gave you presents in restaurants?" He carried the aluminum ladder out of the empty cage, maneuvering it around the forklift, then leaned it against a back wall. "Yeah, I sound like a real animal."

"My grandfather knows I don't work weekends," she reminded. "He'll contest the will, too."

"Even there, babe, we're talking paper legs," he said, heading back to the storage rack. "I'll just say we had our first little spat as marrieds, you left the house in a huff and wound up here to cool off. People already know Gus never liked me, so folks will conclude any bitching he does is sour grapes. If he makes *too* big a deal out of things," he shook his head and ran his fingers through his short blond hair, "well, the ol' guy could be headin' for a meltdown, y' know? I mean, he's outlived his wife, his daughter, now you; the strain of losin' all his women might be just too much for him."

"What're you saying?"

"Who knows?" he shrugged, picking up the drill. He put it to his head like a gun. "Maybe he'll want to check out."

"You mean, you'll kill him too, but make it look like a suicide," she concluded.

"This is business, Farren. I've already killed once this week—some college kid in Mt. Pleasant to prove my resolve to Bartholomew. I wasn't crazy about it, but you do what you've gotta do to survive. Like I said, sweetie, it's your life for mine."

He walked outside of the storage cage, set the drill aside, then picked up the brown bottle and white washcloth off the floor.

"Alrighty then," he said walking toward her, "now you know what's what. For whatever it's worth, I am sorry. But, in life, some people are victims, and some are natural survivors."

"And, some are going to prison for the rest of their lives," a voice suddenly announced.

Charlie and Farren turned simultaneously to see Doc appear from behind the bow and boat trailer that held the thirty-six-foot Carver yacht named *Joyride*, the same boat where Farren had fixed him lunch.

"You get all that, Lance?" he asked, holding one of the city's shiny new black walkie-talkies with the improved transmitters and receivers. He'd had his finger holding the talkback button for several minutes.

"We got the general idea," Lance's filtered voice responded. "Me, and about half the police department."

Charlie suddenly jammed his hand into his coat pocket.

"He's got a gun!" Farren yelled.

Doc turned and quickly disappeared just as three rounds spat from the Beretta. They slammed through the Carver's fiberglass hull and blew through the other side, sending little pieces of fiberglass flying in all directions and missing the paramedic by only centimeters.

"*Shots fired, shots fired!*" Doc yelled into the walkie-talkie, as he raced down the starboard side of the yacht. Charlie rounded the bow coming after him and got off three more shots. But since handling a gun wasn't his forte, all three slugs missed, and Doc rounded the stern and disappeared into the shadows, taking advantage of the barn's poor light. Meanwhile, Farren tried to get to her feet, but with her hands and ankles bound, it was difficult.

A few seconds later, Charlie rounded the back of the yacht by its painted name and paused, trying to determine where Doc had gone. There were two filled storage cages to his right about eighteen feet away, a detailing area where boats were sanded and polished to his left, and in his immediate foreground was a vintage teak wood Chris-Craft touring boat, circa 1960. It sat on a trailer with its stern angled toward him.

"Hey, Ambulance Boy!" he called, peering into the dark corners. "How come you're not in the hospital? How'd you get away from my boys last night?"

"The game's over, Charlie!" Doc's voice called.

Thinking the sound came from around the older Chris-Craft, Charlie pointed the gun toward it and fired. Glass exploded out of the driver's side front windshield sending shards of glass trickling down the recently varnished wooden deck of the bow.

"Maybe so, partner," the blond-haired man answered, not knowing where his opponent was. "But it would sure be nice if you weren't alive to be declared the winner."

He took a step toward the boat, then stopped, hearing the approaching sirens. He thought for a moment, then decided to break off his search.

"Doc, I gotta run. But I guarantee I'll be seein' you and Farren again." He began to back up toward the door near the workbench and metal shelves. "Now, remember," he called, as he went, smiling slyly, "you behave. She's a married woman."

Just before he reached the door, he turned and kicked aside the wadded up comforter he had taken from their spare bedroom. He had used it to roll up his wife, then he lugged her on his shoulder to her car and brought her to the marina.

***

Farren's car was a 2003 mustard yellow VW Beetle. She liked its fuel efficiency and lighter weight in the snow. She also liked the idea of a rear engine car. 2003 was the last year Volkswagon made the Beetle with a rear engine, and she figured if she held onto it long enough, it would become a classic. It wasn't exactly the kind of vehicle Charlie would've wished for in an escape, but it was all he had. He bolted outside the barn, climbed into VW, and fired it up.

His original intent was that, after Farren had been crushed by the boat in the cage above her and he verified she was dead, he'd simply leave her car in the lot, then walk home carrying the comforter while keeping to the shadows. But Doc had put a stop to all that. Gravel flew in the parking lot as he slammed on the accelerator and headed for the street. But he never got there.

A dark blue Charlevoix police cruiser with its red and blue bubble lights piercing the night suddenly appeared and skidded to a stop at the end of the lane leading into the lot. Charlie couldn't go around the cruiser because of the thick rows of Leyland Cypresses on either side of the lane. The newest and youngest member of the police force—a thin, short, twenty-five-year-old named David Wright—hopped out of the cruiser, drew his gun, pointed it over the open driver's side door and yelled for Charlie to halt.

But, what Officer Wright hadn't paid attention to was that, in his haste to put his cruiser in park, turn off the engine, get out of the vehicle, and draw his weapon, Charlie had also slammed on the breaks, skidded and turned his wheel, causing the VW to slide sideways at an angle where the driver's side window was now facing the cruiser. The window was already down by the time the young officer could take a firing stance, and Charlie blasted off two rounds. One lodged in the cruiser's open door, but the other hit the policeman in the upper left arm, causing him to stumble backward, land on his rear end, and drop his revolver.

Charlie quickly hopped out of the Beetle, walked toward the downed cop with his Beretta aimed at him, and repeatedly pulled the trigger. Killing was quickly becoming an easier thing to him. But, the Beretta's ten-round clip was empty. He briefly thought about grabbing Wright's pistol, finishing him off, then stealing his cruiser, but was interrupted when he heard more sirens coming down East Dixon and approaching fast.

Beginning to panic, he ran back to Farren's car, climbed in and circled the lot, looking for an escape route. He couldn't drive overland because the empty boat trailers, sitting just off the parking lot, blocked his way, and trying to make a run for it on foot didn't make much sense to him, either. Suddenly, he got an idea. He turned the car toward Round Lake and looked at it. He remembered seeing snowmobiles on parts of Lake Charlevoix the weekend before. He'd also seen pictures from years past of cars actually sitting on Round Lake belonging to ice fishermen who drove out to their shanties. While he sat there wondering about how light a Beetle was and weighing the considerable risks—and he knew they were considerable—there were a series of pops behind him and the rear windshield exploded. Officer Wright was back on his feet and fired repeatedly at the VW. Suddenly, it was no longer a matter of choice. Charlie gritted his teeth and floored the accelerator.

A minute earlier inside the storage barn, Doc cautiously came out of the shadows carrying a small and heavy piece of pipe about the length of a yardstick. He found it on the floor near a back wall and traded the walkie-talkie for it figuring he might need a weapon. Hearing a car churning up the gravel outside and assuming it was Charlie, he ran back passed the large Carver yacht to Farren who had finally just gotten to her feet.

"Are you okay?" he said, out of breath.

"Yes, except for a splitting headache."

"I don't have anything to cut you free," he said, feeling his blue jeans.

"There's a pocketknife on the workbench over there," she said.

As he ran over to the bench and set the pipe down, she asked, "How'd you know I was here?"

"I've been watching your house since about two this afternoon."

She looked at him with a furrowed brow, as he returned with the knife. "I know," he admitted, "it's a fine line between concerned friend and creepy stalker. But I just had a bad feeling about today and a suspicion that you were in danger. I figured, sooner or later, Charlie was going to say or do something that would be incriminating, and I needed other people to be witnesses."

"You don't hear me complaining," she said, as he cut her ankles free. Then, she turned her back to him, so he could work on the tape binding her wrists.

"How'd you get in here? Wasn't the door locked?"

"The root cellar," he replied.

They heard a series of gunshots in the parking lot and a car rapidly accelerating. They ran to the door, cracked it open, and when they saw the flashing lights of the police cruiser, figured it was safe to go outside.

As they did, two more police cars came down the lane one behind the other. Officer Wright was leaning against his cruiser trying to put another clip in his gun but was fumbling with it. Lance and his poker-playing buddy, Michael, arrived first. Lance hopped out and ran over to the wounded cop, while Michael, carrying a shotgun, ran across the parking lot toward Doc and Farren. He was a well-built guy about six-feet-two. Meanwhile, the cop in the other cruiser behind Lance and Michael ran over to Lance to see if he could be of assistance with the injured man. While all of this was going on to their right, Doc and Farren then looked left. Out on the icy lake, past the three concrete docks of the marina and about a hundred yards offshore, the VW had come to a halt.

"Oh my God," Farren said, concerned. "The lake isn't frozen all the way across anymore. The ice will never hold the weight of my car."

"I think Charlie's just figured that out," Doc noted, observing the bright red brake lights on the car.

"You two all right?" the arriving officer asked, breathlessly.

"Yeah, Michael. We're okay."

The cop looked out at the Beetle. "Damn fool! That car's gonna fall right through the ice."

Almost at the exact moment Michael said this, there was a loud crack out on the lake, and the back wheels of the VW sunk in about five inches of water. Moments later, the driver's side door opened and Charlie got out with both hands raised.

"I quit, I quit," he called. Three seconds later, there was another loud series of cracks, and the ice gave way under his feet. All of Charlie and about half the VW were now engulfed in icy black water.

"Charlie!" Farren screamed, empathetically. She ran across the lot to the water's edge.

Doc and the big cop looked at one another. The paramedic knew instantly what he had to do.

"Shhhit," he sighed, under his breath.

He took the cell phone off his belt and dropped it to the ground, while he started to run full out across the lot toward the lake. "Flashlights, rope and blankets," he called over his shoulder. "And call the emergency room. Tell 'em they've got two incoming hypothermia cases."

"Don't do it!" the officer yelled, following behind him but stopping at the shoreline.

Farren turned and saw Doc race past her and out onto the slushy surface of the ice, his footsteps causing little explosions of water as he ran.

"Doc, no!" she likewise called. But he didn't respond. He kept running, just as she knew he would. Even if Charlie had tried to kill them minutes earlier, he was in trouble now and needed Doc's help. That's what paramedics did. They weren't supposed to judge people, just try to save them.

With a large gurgling sound, the back of the VW disappeared completely into the water causing the lighter front of the car to point straight up into the air like a gigantic yellow bobber. The beams of the headlights shot up into the starry night—the first truly clear night in several evenings—then the rest of the car quickly slipped below the icy water. Oddly, but fortunately, the headlights continued to stay on as the car disappeared, illuminating the water, similar to lights in a swimming pool and allowing Doc to the see the silhouetted figure of Charlie treading water. As he neared him, he slowed down and took off his bomber jacket.

"Charlie," he called, getting on his hands and knees, then crawling toward where the ice was broken, "I'm going to toss you the arm of my coat. Grab it when I get near enough."

The con man heard him and even nodded, but had too much to contend with to make a verbal response. His clothes and boots were heavy in the water, chunks of ice the size of small boulders were bumping him in the head and shoulders, and the frigid water made him dizzy and disoriented. Doc was only five or six feet away when he flattened out on his stomach and made his first toss.

"Grab the sleeve, Charlie," he urged. "C'mon, man. You can do it."

Struggling to keep afloat but making the effort, Charlie grabbed at the jacket sleeve. But, the instant he did, Doc heard a series of loud cracks underneath him.

"This is going to suck," he moaned, just as the ice gave way under his chest. A second later, he spilled into the water.

"*Nnnooooo!*" Farren screamed, seeing Doc's shadow-like figure slide away. She couldn't believe that another lake was swallowing up people she cared for. Reacting on pure adrenaline, she bolted toward the lake, intending some form of impromptu rescue. Michael caught her by wrapping a strong arm around her stomach that literally lifted her feet off the ground.

"Whoa!" he urged, "We don't need you out there, too!"

She realized a second later that he was right and relaxed her stiff body. As Michael released her, they both stared out at the lake. What was once a sheet of dark white in the night was now several broken-up pieces of dark white and pitch black, except where the headlights still eerily illuminated the water.

By the time Doc's head broke the surface, his jacket had been lost, and a panicked Charlie Huffman was on top of him. Coast Guard rescue swimmers are taught that, when civilians are distressed in the water, they'll sometimes cling onto their rescuer using them like a life preserver. Problem is, this drowns the rescuer. That's what Charlie was trying to do now. It was just a pure survival instinct driven by panic, but it meant Doc was in trouble. In an instant, Charlie tried to pull the paramedic down and use his shoulders as a step to climb out of the water and onto the ice. But there wasn't any solid ice to climb onto anymore—at least, not within a several-foot radius.

Meanwhile, back on shore, Lance and the other cop had tucked Officer Wright into the cruiser closest to the street, and the other officer was backing down the tree-lined lane to take the gunshot victim to the hospital. As soon as they were away, Lance ran across the lot toward Farren and Michael, while the well-built cop used the police radio on his belt to have the dispatcher alert the hospital as Doc had instructed.

"Where's Doc?" Lance asked, running up to them.

"Out there," Farren answered, distraughtly, nodding toward the water. "Charlie tried to drive my car across the ice and didn't make it."

"So Doc went after Charlie," the EMT concluded. He turned to Michael.

"Get a cruiser down here with a spotlight, *now!*"

"Right," the cop nodded. He started to run toward Officer Wright's car.

Back in the lake, the struggle for survival continued. After already having escaped a frantic Charlie once, Doc was under the water again, and, this time, Charlie accidentally kicked him square in the Adam's apple. When he got away from the frightened man and reached the surface, he felt like he had swallowed a raw potato whole, and it had stuck in his throat.

He'd no sooner gotten some air into his lungs through his nose when Charlie's hand came around from behind and grabbed his forehead. This time, though, Doc was ready, and he elbowed Charlie squarely in the face with all his might. He heard the snap of the Charlie's nose, then his hand released Doc's forehead. When the paramedic turned around, the blond-haired man was leaned back in the water with his eyes closed, apparently unconscious, then he slipped below the surface.

Doc quickly reached out to grab him, but missed. He tried to reach out again, but now *his* instincts kicked in, and his hands went immediately to his injured throat. It took several seconds, perhaps ten or fifteen, before he was able to draw even a partial staggered breath through his mouth. Meantime, he was treading water with only his legs and fighting off hypothermia.

Just a few feet below the surface, Charlie opened his eyes as he felt something tug on his right shoe. Through the water still lit by the headlights, he looked down to see a thin man in a long black overcoat with a hand upon his foot. The fingernails on the hand were long and curved inward, and his white hair was likewise long, thin and floating around his head in every direction like Medusa. His eyes were slightly slanted, but wide and bright yellow like a lit Jack-O-Lantern, and his hollow face looked like it had been washed with a cheese grater.

Dozens of little fleshy stubs floated every which way from his forehead, chin and cheeks, and thin long streams of what looked like blood and puss oozed out from the stubs. Looking down at this horrific sight, Charlie Huffman opened his mouth and screamed. When he did, the freezing water of Round Lake poured into his lungs. The man in the black overcoat smiled, revealing putrid pointed teeth, then sank down to the depths, taking a flailing Charlie with him. As Charlie sank farther away, the lights of the VW, now perhaps thirty feet beneath them, flickered, then went out.

Just as the stabbing pain in Doc's swollen throat seemed to somewhat subside, a hard piece of ice smacked him in the side of the head. A trickle of blood ran down his soaked temple, and, momentarily dazed, he slipped below the water's surface. When he tried to break the surface again a few seconds later, a large piece of floating ice had shifted its position and closed off his access.

"I don't believe this!" Michael yelled, as he stuck his head out of Officer Wright's cruiser.

"What?" Lance called.

"Dave's keys must be in his jacket. I've got no way to move this thing!"

Farren and Lance looked at one another. Michael's cruiser—parked behind Wright's—couldn't maneuver around because of the Cypress trees lining both sides of the lane. And while Wright's headlights were on, and the vehicle had a spotlight attached to its hood, it was too far from the water to be of much help.

"Lance, *do* something!" Farren urged.

He looked at the sandstone veneer building next to them. "Do you have the keys to the store?"

She felt her pockets. Charlie had intended to put them in the pocket of her red down vest, but his plan never evolved that far. They'd gone down with him in the lake.

"No," she said.

"Mike!" he called. "Everything we need's inside: flares, rope, wetsuits, PFDs, but she doesn't have the keys!"

Instantly understanding, the officer pumped the shotgun once then ran toward the store's locked front doors.

Kicking his feet and feeling his way submerged in pitch black, Doc's fingers probed the ice above him looking for an opening. In a way, it reminded him of rock climbing; chalked fingers feeling for the smallest crack or ledge to latch on to. After several seconds, and just about the time he thought his lungs were going to burst, he found the edge of the ice. His head broke the surface with a loud, contorted gasp. He was getting only about half the air he needed because of the injury to his throat. He told himself to calm down, close his mouth, and breathe normally through his nose.

After a few more seconds of just breathing in, then out, he looked around. To his surprise, his position had shifted in the lake. He was now twelve to eighteen yards from where the Volkswagen had sunk. He also noticed that the car going through the ice had started a domino effect. Chunks of ice both large and small were breaking up all around him. He might be able to grab onto one and maybe pull himself out of the water, but there was no large section of ice anymore that he could crawl onto, and then walk back to shore—at least, none that he could see from his vantage point.

He suddenly heard something echo across the lake like a gun, a shotgun, maybe. He looked toward the marina and saw the silhouettes of Farren and Lance run toward the slight A-frame store. Seconds later, lights went on inside. He stretched out a trembling hand and tried to call out to them, but a weak, whispery "Aayyy" was all that came out. His voice box had been damaged when he was kicked, and nobody was going to hear him. Just then, another piece of ice slammed into the back of his skull. Instinctively taking a gasp of air, Doc slid under the surface, and the ice shifted once again, cutting off his access for a second time.

This time when he was under the water, he thought he saw something in the depths below. He thought he saw two small, faint yellow lights. He didn't know what they were, but he knew they weren't from Farren's car, and they seemed to be coming up toward him. Figuring his mind must be playing tricks because of his weakened condition, he started to scissor-kick and probe the ice with his fingers like before. Ten seconds went by, fifteen, thirty, about the time he started to panic and was slamming and cutting his hand against the jagged ice, his hand found another opening.

He broke the surface and drew in a shivering fresh breath, but couldn't get his bearings this time. He didn't recognize any of the landmarks or buildings on shore. He couldn't feel his feet or legs, either. He'd now been in the water for over three minutes and knew that hyperthermia was taking its toll. There was a large piece of ice a couple of yards away, perhaps five by eight feet, big enough to support him if he could just grab onto it and pull himself out of the water. He made an exhausted swim, then reached for it, but missed. He tried again, and this time, got a hold of it, but was too tired to hang on, let alone pull himself up and out. As the last of his strength gave way and his hands slid off the ice and plopped like hammers back into the water, Wyatt "Doc" Reynolds realized he didn't have much longer to live.

No longer knowing whether or not he was still treading water or even capable of it, he straightened out his back and began to float on it.

Looking up, the sky was full of stars. He could see the constellation of Aries although his vision was now fuzzy. Then he found Orion. Then, near the left foot of the hunter, the long winding constellation of Eridanus. "I'll miss you all," he whispered in between chattering teeth. He heard something stir by his feet like a fish jumping.

Glancing down the length of his floating body, he saw a hand with long curved fingernails come out of the water and wrap itself around his ankle, an ankle he could no longer feel. Even though Doc had never actually seen the thin man in the long black overcoat with the slicked-back white hair, he *knew* it was him. He didn't know if he was a demon or an angel. He didn't know why some trauma patients saw this particular figure, while others claimed to see a long tunnel of light and still others had out-of-body experiences. He didn't even know if this was real or imagined. But, he did know he didn't have the strength to move anymore, and his feet, then knees, then waist were disappearing below the water. He wasn't scared, angry, repentant, peaceful, or any other emotion. He was just tired.

Moments before the water covered his face, Doc closed his eyes. There wasn't anything to see anymore, anyway. His arms dangled lifelessly and haphazardly raised above his head. Lower and lower he felt himself descending, until, suddenly, something warm grabbed a hold of his right wrist. Then he felt a tremendous surge of water swirling around him that seemed to push him upward. He felt the surge again, then again and again. He opened his eyes and looked up to see two, large, white glowing wings, one on either side of him, moving up and down and bringing him out of the depths. The two wings extended together must've had a span of eight to ten feet. They were attached to the back of a golden haired woman, a woman wearing a long white robe with a golden cord around her waist. It was Clair surrounded by an aura of majestic light. He looked down at his feet. Not only was she pulling him up, but also the man in the long black overcoat, who was still clutching his ankle. His slanted yellow eyes were angry as he shook his head to and fro in disagreement. He opened his mouth with its pointed teeth and screamed something at Doc. But being underwater, it was indistinguishable.

As soon as Doc's head broke the surface, the man in the long black overcoat released his grip and made a terrible howling sound as he sunk like a stone back into the depths. Once Doc was completely out of the water, Clair scooped him up into her arms like a baby while the steady whoosh-whoosh-whoosh of her powerful wings seemed to instantly dry her robe, hair, and send ripples racing across the water. Loose and smaller pieces of ice also skittered everywhere. Fluttering over the lake, she looked tenderly at the barely conscious, bleeding, and shivering paramedic. As one of Doc's arms hung helplessly, she drew him close, then looked down at the black water below and murmured something:

"Not today, you son of a bitch."

SLEEP

From Doc's perspective of trying to stay afloat in the mind-numbing icy water of Round Lake, it must have seemed like an eternity when Farren and Lance left the shore and ran into the marina store. But, in fact, they were back at the water's edge in about two minutes.

Lance was now wearing a diver's wetsuit, complete with a hood that covered his stiff hair, ears, and outlined his chubby face, as well as gloves and high-top neoprene boots. He had hurriedly stripped down to his boxer shorts in one of the aisles of the store, right in front of Farren and Michael and couldn't have cared less about it.

Michael grabbed three fifty-foot ski ropes and tied them together. Farren grabbed two Coleman WD Waterbeam Flashlights, a personal floatation device, or PFD, and a flare gun with flare.

When they all arrived back at the shore, Farren pointed the flare gun toward the sky over the water and fired while Michael secured the ski rope around Lance's thick waist. With a sudden pop, then hiss, the flare illuminated the lake. Under its bright yellow glare, they could see that the VW had caused a chain reaction of breaks and floating ice chunks out toward the middle of the lake that was now as big as a football field.

"Oh my God," the cop gawked. "Ice is moving everywhere."

"I don't see them," Farren said, turning on and pointing one of the flashlights to where she approximated her car went down.

"If they went below the surface in one place, they might've had to come up another," Lance observed. "The ice is shifting around pretty good out there."

"*If* they came up," Michael added.

Lance picked up the other Coleman flashlight, turned it on, and started to walk carefully out onto the slushy ice. He was on a section large enough to take him about a dozen yards beyond the ends of the docks.

"No," he disagreed, moving the light to and fro out on the lake, "they're both pretty fit. *Doc?*" he called. "*Where are you, bud?*"

Michael looked at his wristwatch while he doled out sections of ski rope for Lance and the flair began to fade. "It's gotta be over five minutes since they went into the water. That ain't good." He eyed the EMT. "Careful, Lance. We don't know how stable that ice is."

"What's that?" Farren suddenly chirped. She pointed to a dark figure on a large piece of ice about twenty yards off shore and to their extreme right. The figure was approximately forty yards to the west and eighty yards inland from where they had last seen the two men in the water.

Aiming her light, Farren's jaw dropped in disbelief. "It's Doc!"

"How the hell did he get way over there?" the policeman asked.

Lance started running across the ice toward Doc and causing explosions of water under his feet like his partner had earlier. The two men were on separate fields of ice separated by a six-foot fracture, but with surprising agility, Lance jumped the watery void, landed, then tumbled and rolled onto the same piece of frozen water that held Doc. It was miraculous that he made the jump and even *more* miraculous that the ice didn't split apart from the sudden weight of his landing. Quickly crawling over to the paramedic, he saw that his skin was pale, and his lips were blue. But, more importantly, he also saw that he was breathing. He was unconscious, but breathing.

"We're going to need some blankets here," he yelled.

Farren turned and ran back toward the marina.

Pleased that his fast thinking had gotten them the tools they needed and that he was the first one to reach his friend, the EMT couldn't help but raise an eyebrow and say quietly to himself: "Vale. Lance Vale."

Two hours later, Gus looked out at the night through open Venetian blinds with a cup of coffee in his hand standing in the light beige waiting room of Charlevoix Area Hospital. Nobody else was in the room but him. Although it was still clear outside, the temperature had started to drop again.

He zipped up the front of his sweater and thought about how he should've moved down south a long time ago, like he wanted to. But then he remembered that line from the John Lennon song "Beautiful Boy"— "Life is what happens to you while you're busy making other plans."

Michael the cop rounded the registration desk interrupting his thoughts. He'd been in and out of the hospital since Doc had been brought in. The big-shouldered man looked beat. It had been a long night for a lot of people.

"Hey, Mr. Cooper."

"Officer."

Michael looked around, "I…I was looking for your granddaughter?"

"She's sleeping in one of the treatment rooms. Can I help with anything?"

"I just wanted to give her an update. The Coast Guard has had men out on Round Lake for well over an hour and have come up empty-handed. The Chief's sending 'em home and calling off the search. I think it's fair to say that Mr. Huffman has been lost."

"Good," Gus nodded, taking a sip of coffee.

The cop looked at him a little surprised.

"What?" Gus asked. "You want me to shed crocodile tears for the son of a bitch. He tried to kill my granddaughter."

"Yes, sir."

"And one of your own, too. How is that boy, anyway?"

"I'm told Officer Wright is going to be just fine."

"Good."

"Anything new on Doc?" the cop asked.

"Still in the ICU and they still won't let anyone see him. And, Farren won't leave until she can." The older man thought for a moment. "That doesn't sound exactly right for a woman who was just widowed, huh?"

"I understand," the big man smiled. "After all, Doc was the one who figured out her husband was up to something. You might tell her when she wakes up that a warrant's been issued in Flint for this guy named Bartholomew. Apparently, he's no stranger to the authorities down there."

"Does that mean Farren's out of danger?"

"I don't think Mr. Bartholomew is in a position to make a move against anyone. He's a conspirator to commit murder, an accessory to do great bodily harm to Officer Wright, and he's implicated in that other murder Mr. Huffman confessed to in Mt Pleasant."

"Thank God," Gus sighed with relief.

Meanwhile, upstairs in a private room of the Intensive Care Unit, a gentle hand with long slender fingers touched the throat of a sleeping Doc Reynolds. A few seconds later, his eyes fluttered open, and he saw the smiling face of Clair standing over him. She was wearing the same clothes that she had excitedly modeled for him that one night at the cabin: a long-sleeved red silk blouse, pleated black slacks, black leather shoes with slight heels, and a shiny wide black belt. She was also wearing the other purchases Doc had gotten for her: the dark green overcoat, gold earrings and gold necklace that she had worn the night of the dance.

"Hi," she said, softly. "How're you feeling?"

He looked around the room and opened his mouth to speak, but she anticipated him.

"You're in the ICU of the hospital. No one's supposed to be here. I snuck in."

"Ch ... Charlie?" he asked, struggling to speak.

She shook her head. "Charlie's where he's supposed to be. But it was very noble of you to try and save him. You demonstrated great character."

"I...I," he shook his head and put his hand on his throat, not being able to express his thought.

"I know," she said, understanding. "Your throat got really hurt. But it's going to be remarkably better by morning. I promise. I can't stay long. I just wanted to come by and say thank you. You did good Wyatt Gabriel Reynolds. *Very* good."

He looked at her shoulders. "W...wings?" his voiced creaked. "And a robe?"

She smiled and shrugged. "I was who you needed me to be."

"You're leaving?"

"Shhhh," she said, stroking his forehead. "Rest now. Go to sleep."

He didn't want to sleep. He was afraid Clair was leaving and he'd never get to see her again. He was also afraid the next time that he awoke, she would be erased from his memory. But when she stroked his forehead, it was like a soothing tranquilizer and he fell back asleep in seconds.

Seven hours later, he opened his eyes again. It was now Monday morning, December 19. The first thing he saw was the dimpled smile of Farren sitting in a chair next to his bed and watching over him. He looked at her with a sense of déjà vu.

"Hi," she said, rising. "Welcome back."

"I dreamed this," he replied. His voice now clear, and the pain in his throat gone.

"What?"

He put a hand to his throat. "My voice...it's okay."

"Did you lose it last night," she asked, not understanding.

He looked at her and smiled. "Doesn't matter. Have...have you been here all this time?"

"I wanted to make sure you were okay," she said, warmly. "I wouldn't even go to the police station to give my statement. They had to take it here in the cafeteria. But they wouldn't let me see you until about an hour ago."

He looked at her gratefully, then he thought of her husband. "I'm sorry about Charlie."

"So am I, in more ways than one. How did you ever suspect he was going to..." she paused, then continued, "to hurt me."

"I told you, his deceits were pretty major. I just figured there had to be something more to them. But I had to wait until he admitted them out loud."

"You'd make a good cop," she observed.

"Waiting could have been very dangerous," he noted. "I think someone else besides me was looking out for you."

They were silent for a moment. Then, he slowly reached out and touched her fingers. She opened her palm, and they held hands for several seconds. She had a couple of calluses on the inside of her hands from years of working at the marina, but, to him, calluses had never felt so good.

"You okay?" he asked.

"No," she answered, letting go of his hand to wipe her moist eyes. "I feel violated, betrayed, embarrassed, my heart is in pieces ... I feel anything but okay."

He looked at her, compassionately. "I'm a medical professional. I can fix that."

She chuckled nervously, dipped a hand into her jeans, pulled out a wrinkled up tissue and dabbed her eyes.

"I'm going to need time to heal, Doc," she said. "I don't know how long that'll be. But I ... I know you have a history of moving around. Are you going to stay?"

"Yeah, but only three or four more decades. Then I want to retire to Sedona."

She bit her lip, fighting back more tears and smiled. As an afterthought, and knowing that it was far too soon to talk about the future, he added a qualifier. "I mean, if I live that long. Since we've met, I *have* wound up in the hospital a bunch."

She laughed a little more loudly, and then she remembered something.

"Will you be up to a couple of visitors later?"

"Lance and Charlene?"

"No, your parents."

"My parents?"

"You're not the only one who can do deductive reasoning. How many lawn-and-garden nurseries do you think there are in Ann Arbor?"

"You tracked them down?"

"Got a hold of your dad about a half-hour ago. They'll be here later today. I hope that's okay. You saved my life, you're in the hospital, and I thought they might want to know."

"Yeah," he said, impressed that Farren would be so thoughtful considering everything she'd been through. "You told my dad what happened?"

"I did."

"What did he say?"

"He said that he really appreciated the call, that he was proud of you, and that he'd *always* been proud of you. He also said I was the first female friend of yours that he'd actually spoken to in—well—in a long time."

"You mean, since Julia."

"He didn't mention anyone by name."

He looked at her sincerely. "The ghost of Christmas past is gone, Farren. I'm only interested in the present and the future now."

She smiled again, then looked at her wristwatch and rose. "Right. Now that I've seen you, know you're going to be okay, I'm going to go home. I need a hot shower and a nap before your folks arrive. You should try and get some more sleep, too."

"All right."

She picked up her red down vest off the back of the chair she'd been sitting in and stepped over to the door. Pausing in front of it, she turned, walked back to the bed, leaned over, and kissed him gently on the lips. It was a simple thing, but her round warm silent lips spoke volumes. Afterward, they looked at each other briefly. She almost asked if her impulsive action was okay. But she could already see in his eyes that it was. So, she walked back to the door, opened it, smiled slightly while brushing her bangs aside, and left.

BETTER DAYS

Marion and James Reynolds were both native Michigan residents and originally from Ann Arbor. Being born and raised in a Big Ten college town, the Reynolds were a bit of a walking contradiction. In one way, they were liberal old hippies. Marion had dark brown hair with several strands of gray, was lean and fit, favored ankle-length denim skirts, listened to the Grateful Dead, and had a tattoo somewhere on her body that her children had never seen. Similarly, James had salt-and-pepper hair, liked to camp, was a little pudgy, and had once gotten high with the members of Pink Floyd when they played Hill Auditorium at University of Michigan in the 1970s. In his youth, he had a penchant for growing pot and this was actually the beginning of his green thumb that led him to own a lawn-and-garden nursery.

On the other hand, the Reynolds also had their very pragmatic, Republican side. Being an accountant, Marion was bottom-line oriented and pushed her children to financially succeed. Even before Doc had been accepted to medical school, she calculated his probable annual income in five-year increments and dreamed of her son being a prominent U of M physician. James, meanwhile, loved what he did, but wished for his children to accomplish more than help landscape other peoples' flowerbeds. Consequently, they never understood how their son could lose interest in medical school after Julia died and were vocal about it to the point of bullying. To them, Doc was using her death as an excuse because he was afraid of failure. There was more truth to this than he wanted to admit, but Doc also saw no point in pursuing his mother's dream for him to become a prominent physician if Julia wasn't there by his side. A large part of this was plain simple guilt, because he was going to go on and have a life, and she wasn't. Marion and James saw this as a form of morose self-punishment and suggested counseling. Doc refused and started to drink instead.

After things reached a boiling point, and Doc moved away, Marion and James never stopped loving their son, but they kept him at arm's length until he was willing to, "Grow up and get on with life." When he announced he was moving back to Michigan, they hoped that part of his reasoning was to heal the breach and were very pleased that this was apparently the case. So, when the call came from Farren that their son was in the hospital after having foiled an attempted murder, Marion and James dropped everything.

They arrived in Charlevoix mid-Monday afternoon, spent several hours with Doc, then stayed at his cabin, which Lance and Charlene were happy to show them. They went back to the hospital first thing Tuesday morning and remained with Doc until he was released Tuesday afternoon. Then, they stayed at the cabin a second night to make sure he was going to be okay.

Farren accompanied Doc home Tuesday afternoon with his parents, and, even though she had arranged for Father Ken to conduct a short prayer service for Charlie on Wednesday morning, she still insisted on cooking everyone dinner at Doc's Tuesday night. It was clear to James and Marion—but especially Marion—that this young woman's gratitude toward her son might be more than mere gratitude. It was in the way Farren looked at him when he was being wheeled out of the hospital to go home; the way she approved of his cabin and how he maintained it; the way she spoke of his bravery when trying to save Charlie.

During dinner on Tuesday night, James had casually mentioned what a shame it was that Doc never went to medical school. Kindly, but pointedly, Farren reminded him that there were lots of people like George Pratt, Austin Redman and herself who would disagree. Considering these observations, Marion wasn't surprised at all when Doc suggested that he'd like to stay in Charlevoix for Christmas, if she was okay with that. He promised to drive down the following day, and she responded that would be fine. When everything was said and done, all Marion and James Reynolds wanted was for their son to be happy.

To his great relief, Doc did remember Clair and everything they had shared, but he hadn't seen her since she visited him in the hospital and concluded that she must have returned to the hereafter. Although this saddened him because the last time he saw her he was feverish, hurting, and groggy, he didn't have much time to think about this disappointment because of his parent's visit. His mind was also diverted with more news about Bartholomew.

He was arrested Monday night in Flint, and, even though he took his incarceration in blustery stride and pontificated to the arresting officers about the clever attorney he had, an incriminating portfolio was also seized. It contained artist renderings of a condominium complex to be built in Charlevoix. The complex's dual views of Round Lake one way, and Lake Charlevoix the other, plus three familiar-looking concrete docks in front of the building—one of which even had two Shell gas pumps—seemed to more than corroborate Charlie's story.

On Wednesday morning, December 23, Marion and James returned to Ann Arbor, but before leaving, Doc once again promised to see them on December 26. In an odd but real way, his being hospitalized helped to bring him and his parents closer more quickly than any schedule he could have mentally outlined. He also didn't go to work that day on doctor's orders, so he spent the day canceling credit cards and getting a temporary license. Since he had Christmas Eve and Christmas day off, then the weekend, he could look forward to five whole days without anyone bleeding, going into shock, needing CPR, or seeing a scary-looking guy in a long black overcoat. The war against that guy would continue, but Doc now had a deeper appreciation of the battles yet to be won, and even lost.

On Christmas Eve morning, it started to snow lightly, and Doc had lunch with Lance at Sadie & Jake's Gallery & Cafe on Bridge Street to give his partner moral support about the ring he planned on giving Charlene later in the evening.

"What if she turns me down?" Lance asked.

Doc responded that would be like a 007 film without Bond bedding a woman. It was an impossibility.

Lance also brought up the subject of the sheep, but Doc simply reiterated that he was sheep sitting for a former patient who was going to give it as a Christmas gift and that he was sworn to secrecy.

Normally, the ever-curious Lance would have never accepted such an answer, but because he was so preoccupied about his pending engagement, he let the subject go for the time being.

Farren liked to go to midnight mass on Christmas Eve, and this year, she invited Doc who unflinchingly accepted. She hesitated to invite him at first because she was worried about the gossip. She was already the talk of the town when the story about Charlie and his scheme broke in the paper, and all the attention and fuss made her very uncomfortable. But Gus helped to calm her fears. He advised the best thing she could do was to demonstrate that she wasn't going to be destroyed by Bartholomew's con and to get on with her life. He even volunteered to attend church with her for moral support and host a Christmas dinner at the family homestead on West Upright Street. She gladly accepted, if she could include one other person at the dinner table and Gus didn't mind the addition at all.

Promptly at 11:00 p.m. on Thursday night, Doc's red Jeep Wrangler pulled up in front of Farren's quaint mushroom house behind Charlie's pickup. It wasn't snowing anymore, but a few flakes sprinkled the air here and there. Since it had been snowing for most of the day, a fresh blanket of sparkling white covered everything in the Charlevoix area. The temperature was back to normal for the time of year, a balmy thirteen degrees, and Doc watched his step as his dress shoes slid a little, and he made his way up the sidewalk. The plan was he'd arrive at 11:00, share a glass of wine with Farren, then they'd hook up with Gus over at the church. About halfway up the sidewalk, he paused and looked back at Charlie's dark blue F150. It had a "For Sale" sign on the front windshield.

The front door opened and Farren stuck her head out. "Hey, mister, you lookin' to buy a truck?"

He turned and smiled at her, then came up the remainder of the walk. "Since your Volkswagen is now a man-made reef in Round Lake, I thought maybe you might want to keep the Ford."

"I don't want any reminders of the past staring me in the face every day."

"In that case, I'm not interested in the truck."

He stepped inside and looked around. The Christmas tree was beautiful, a fire was burning brightly in the fireplace, and a CD featuring the Vienna Boys Choir was playing in the background. "So this is a mushroom house, eh? Very charming. I like the higher ceilings."

"They make the rooms appear larger than they are. Here, let me take your coat."

He slipped off his coat revealing a black dress shirt, black pants, black shoes and socks, and a dark red tie. The same tie he had worn the night of the parish Christmas dance and auction.

"You look very handsome," she noted.

"Thanks, but I need more dress clothes. I feel like a wise guy in a Martin Scorsese film." He looked her over while she went to the closet and hung up his coat. She was wearing an off-white cowl-neck dress with a wide brown belt and matching shoes. She also wore dangling gold earrings. It was a simple, but elegant ensemble.

"You look great, too. Better than you have any right to, considering the week you've had."

"The week *both* of us have had," she corrected. "Would you like some wine?"

"Please."

"Make yourself at home," she said, stepping into the kitchen.

He dipped his hands into his pockets and wandered farther into the living room. "So how long have you had this place?"

"Four years," she called. "It gets a little cold in the winter, but it's nice and cool in summer. Tourists even come by in the summer and snap pictures."

"How old is the house?"

"It was built in the '60s. It's shaped like a teardrop. The front door is at the most narrow part, then the end of the living room and master bedroom to the right are at the widest."

"I love that fireplace," he noted. "I don't ever think I've seen one or a mantel that actually curves inward like that.

"Thanks. That was a big draw for me, too."

He strolled over to the fireplace, looked at the flames, then he glanced up at the mantel. There were several old family photos on it in nice frames. His eyes moved pleasantly from picture to picture until they suddenly froze on one in particular. His mouth slowly opened as he leaned in to a three-and-a-half-by-five-inch framed photo. It was a black-and-white picture of a young Gus. He was in his early twenties, dark-haired and handsome and sitting on a porch swing. It was the kind where the chains came down from the ceiling of the porch and attached into the arms. Sitting on his lap was an infant.

Sitting next to the infant was a young woman in a small flower-print sundress with long blonde hair in large curly ringlets. She had a high forehead, long fingers, and was curvaceous like Kate Winslet was in *Titanic*. But it wasn't Kate Winslet. It was another familiar face. It was Clair. Doc didn't know how long he stood staring at the picture, but it must have been longer than a few seconds because he wasn't aware of the angelic voices of the Vienna Boys Choir in the background anymore or Farren coming up behind him.

"Beautiful, wasn't she?" she said, holding two glasses of red wine.

"Unbelievable," he said.

"That's my mom's mom. My Grandma Clair. It was her book you bought back for me in Traverse City. She died really young. She was only twenty-five."

He took a glass of wine from her, and turned back to the picture. "What happened?"

"You remember that TV show, *M*A*S*H?*"

"Sure."

"Well, it was kinda like that. She was a nurse in the Army Reserve. They were doing weekend exercises over at Camp Grayling, when an incoming chopper had a mechanical failure. The chopper crashed, there was a fireball, and she was in a surgical tent with two other nurses. Including the pilot, there were four deaths in all."

"That's horrible," he said quietly. "Such a tragic waste."

"Her death almost killed my grandfather. They used to have this thing where they'd end every phone conversation by saying 'I love you.' But, the night before she died, she called him from a phone booth on base and forgot to tell him. I'm not sure why. That always bothered him. It's been over fifty years and he's still angry at God, although he won't admit it to anyone. He doesn't go to church, except for maybe Christmas and Easter, and even then you've got to twist his arm."

Doc looked at the picture and exhaled a heavy breath. "What year was this?"

"1956. They eloped to Petoskey, just like me and Charlie. Weird coincidence, huh? But I never thought about that until I saw how upset Grandpa was afterward. My mom was just fourteen months old when Grandma died, so she obviously didn't remember her. Grandpa raised Mom by himself. She wasn't really active as a Catholic, either. But that changed after she met my dad."

He looked at another picture of her father, Paul, on the mantel and saw the resemblance to Farren. "So, after raising Jackie, Gus did it again for you, huh?"

"Yeah, in my teens," she chuckled. "The worst years of all. How'd you know my mom's name was Jackie."

"Gus told me."

She nodded. "He's always joked his life has been filled with beautiful women, just not the way he wanted it to be."

"I knew he was single," Doc said. "But I didn't know why. I figured he was a widower, but I also assumed he'd lost his wife in more recent years."

"No. He moved out of town a couple years after she died and got a teaching job at Central Michigan."

He shook his head and smiled self-deprecatingly. "No wonder we get along. In many ways, we've been down the same road."

Everything made sense to him now. He remembered that first time he ran into Gus at the Crow's Nest Bar & Grill. Doc had said something about how tough it must have been for him to lose a daughter and son-in-law, and Gus responded it wasn't his first roundup with loss. He also now realized why Clair used old-fashioned expressions like "neat," "woo," and referred to blue jeans as "dungarees." It explained why she knew Vernors and older songs, singers and movies but showed less interest in newer things like microwaves and laptops. It explained her interest in his medical books. Clair being Farren's grandmother even explained why he never developed any feelings for her other than friendship.

"Let's have a toast," Farren said, raising her glass. "To better days."

"To your grandmother," he suggested, instead. She smiled, nodded in agreement, and they clinked glasses.

By 11:26, they had rendezvoused with Gus and were at St. Ignatius Church. They were seated on the left-hand side about ten rows back from the altar, but right next to the center aisle. The choir started to perform at 11:30 on the two steps leading up to the altar and would conclude at midnight with mass beginning immediately after. While they sat there listening to a splendid version of "Carol Of The Bells," Doc thought about all the stories involving angels he had heard throughout his life. Like, how an angel appeared to Zechariah to inform him he would have a son, even at his advanced age, and that this son would grow up to become a great prophet called John The Baptist. He recalled the story of how an angel appeared to Mary, the mother of Jesus; how an angel announced the birth of Christ to shepherds in the fields, and how an angel awaited visitors in Jesus's tomb.

Then he thought about all the songs he had heard involving angels, from old southern spirituals about Jonah and the whale to Martina McBride's "Wild Angels."

While he pondered all of this, he happened to look up and to his right. Across a sea of seated heads, over in the crossbeam part of the crucifix-shaped church, in the entranceway to the hallway that went behind the confessionals and eventually led to a stairway and the basement, stood Clair. She was dressed as he had last seen her, wearing her dark green overcoat, red silk blouse, and pleated black pants. She looked at him, jerked her head toward the hallway, then turned and went into it.

Understanding, he turned to Farren. "Will you excuse me for a few minutes?"

"Sure," she said.

He rose, walked down the center aisle to the back of the church, then wentaround the last row of pews to walk back up the far right side, turn right and head toward the hallway. Watching him go, Gus leaned into Farren.

"He okay?"

"Yeah, bathroom break," she figured.

They turned their attention back to the choir, giving the matter no further thought.

As he descended the stairs leading into the basement, Doc saw another parishioner coming out of the ladies' room. The men's and women's bathrooms were on the right side of the hall and back to back of each other. She came through a push-open door that squeaked and smiled at him as she walked past. To the left, across from the bathrooms, was a small meeting room with two collapsible tables that were set up and thirteen chairs positioned around them. The room also had a podium, a coat rack and a nickel-colored floor lamp with a knob rheostat on its pole standing in a corner by the open door. The fluorescent ceiling lights were off, but the floor lamp was on, and its rheostat was turned partially up, giving the room an ethereal look.

Glancing around, then looking into the half-lit cinderblock room, he saw Clair waiting for him. She was standing next to a framed photo of Pope John Paul II on the wall. He stepped into the room, glanced over his shoulder to make sure no one else was coming down the stairs, then closed the door.

"I thought you might have …" he pointed his finger upward.

"I'd never leave without saying goodbye," she smiled. "But, it *is* time for me to go." She stepped forward and unbuttoned her dark green coat. "I wanted to thank you, once again, for everything, Doc. Taking me in, the food, the clothes, the makeup, and jewelry. I especially appreciate your confidence."

"You're welcome. But, why didn't you tell me you were Farren's grandmother?"

"It wouldn't have made a difference about her needing help. Besides, some things you had to learn for yourself."

He folded his arms and looked at her as the choir upstairs began, "O Come, O Come Emanuel."

"Why you?" he asked. "Why weren't one or both of her parents sent to help?"

"I'm a generation removed. I could be more objective. Also, I suppose, because I never got to be much help to my family in my married life."

He continued to look at her, his mind working overtime. "None of this was an accident, was it?" he realized. "You running into my Jeep, the extent of your injuries, convalescing at my place, it was all supposed to happen like this, wasn't it?"

"Actually, I didn't lie to you when I said your vehicle hitting me wasn't part of my plan. But you're right. I think everything was supposed to happen the way it did. My granddaughter needed to be saved, you needed to put Julia's memory in its proper place, and even though it's been years, I needed to come back and say goodbye to my Gus."

"That's why you were daydreaming that first night when you were a deer running through the woods," he recalled. "You were going home, seeing family."

She looked down and smiled a little while he figured out something else.

"That's where you've been since Monday, isn't it? With Gus."

"I've also been watching Farren, too," she confirmed. "She looks so much like her dad. They don't see me like you do, but I think they feel my presence. Especially Gus."

"And your healing touch," he added, putting more pieces together. "Gus' first round of X-rays really *did* reveal a problem, didn't they? When I danced with Farren at the Social Center, she said Gus had things on his mind. I assumed she meant Charlie. But, it was his health, wasn't it?"

"Yes," she admitted.

"That's where you went the night of the dance," he continued, "to his house. You absorbed his illness without him knowing. That's why you had the animal relapse and got sick later that night. Like you said, 'it takes a toll.'"

"Farren was right," she observed, "you *would* make a good cop."

"How could you know she said..." he began. But then, he remembered what she had just mentioned about watching over people. "Right. Angel," he reminded himself.

"I also visited Austin Redman the night of the dance," she said. "It would've been too inexplicable for him to have made a complete recovery, but I *did* have permission to help him considerably."

"Good."

They were quiet for a few moments. She stuck her hands into the pockets of her overcoat, while he slid his hands into the pockets of his black pants.

"I'm sorry, Clair," he finally offered.

"For what?"

"Things had to be proven to me before I believed. A better man would've simply believed."

She smiled again. "There once was a guy named Thomas. He was doubts, too, and things had to be proven to him. But he turned out okay. You might, too," she quipped.

Hearing the beautiful soprano voices of the choir upstairs, she turned her eyes toward the ceiling then briefly closed them, savoring the music. "There are so many wonderful things here that I'd forgotten about: snowflakes and crackling fires in fireplaces, the smell of the pines, hot showers, the wind on my face, homemade soup, and music. Especially music. It was a very special gift to be allowed to come back. I'm going to miss our evenings by the fire and drinking hot chocolate."

"Me, too," he said sincerely. "There are only about ten-thousand more questions I'd like to ask, but I'll settle for one: If Gus was sick, why heal him? Why not let nature take its course? After all, then he'd be with you."

"A logical question, but he's been granted more time. He doesn't know it, but he's still got something important to do. He's also got some much deserved happiness coming his way—enjoying his great-grandchildren, for one thing."

He paused. "Uh, would that, by any chance, happen to be Farren's and *my* children?"

She grinned playfully. "You said *one* question."

He nodded. "You're right."

She looked at him warmly with her bright green eyes. "God bless you, Doc Reynolds. I'll be seeing you."

"Well, not *too* soon, I hope," he joked. "What's the ol' saying? 'Everybody wants to go to heaven, but nobody wants to go tonight.'"

Just then, he heard someone coming down the staircase. He turned and looked toward the closed door.

"Shh," he whispered. He leaned his ear toward the door and heard the approaching click-click-click of a woman's high heels. Then, he heard the squeak of the door opening across the hall as the parishioner entered the restroom. When he looked back over his shoulder, Clair was gone. He looked around the room, surprised at first, but then smiled faintly, slowly opened the door, and turned off the rheostat on the floor lamp.

By the time he returned to Gus and Farren upstairs, the choir had just begun to sing, "Joy To The World."

"You okay?" she asked, after he had sat back down.

"Fine," he whispered.

She looked at him, smiled her dimpled smile, then turned back toward the choir. Gus leaned slightly forward in his seat, looked at Doc, then across the crowded church to the entranceway of the hallway. There, he saw a blonde-haired woman in a dark green overcoat smiling at him. At first, he assumed she was looking at someone else. But as he glanced around, he realized she wasn't. She bore an astonishing resemblance to his late wife. They looked at each other for about five seconds, then she quietly mouthed the words, "I love you."

Before he had time to react, some people obstructed his view. They walked down the center aisle to take seats others had been saving for them. When the people in the foreground finally cleared his line of sight, the woman was gone. His brown eyes darted here and there trying to find her. His arms were a sea of goose bumps and his legs felt weak. He positioned his feet as if he were about to spring up, but then paused. He decided he must be mistaken. He concluded his old eyes were playing tricks on him. Then again, he *had* been feeling something unusual the past couple of days—a presence, a closeness to his old love that he couldn't explain. Maybe it was just the emotional time of the season.

Gus slowly settled back into his seat figuring he already had everything he wanted for Christmas. His granddaughter was safe, his instincts about Charlie had been proven right, and his health was good. He told himself that whoever that young woman was, it was just a coincidence that she looked like his Clair. Still, she did seem to say, "I love you." Maybe he'd look for her after church. If he didn't see her, maybe he'd start attending mass regularly to see if he might spot her again.

As for Doc, he watched the choir, glanced at the Intended One sitting next to him with the pixie haircut and freckles on her nose, then turned his eyes up to the ornate chandelier hanging in between the first row of pews and the steps leading up to the altar. As the choir sung, "Let heaven and nature sing. Let heaven and nature sing," his eyes drifted from the chandelier to the large crucifix hanging behind the altar. He thought about his Christmases of the past decade. They hadn't been particularly happy ones. He had worked through most of them, didn't pay much mind to the meaning of the day, and he always went home to an empty house.

This year, however, he believed things were about to change. He looked over at Farren again, then back at the altar. Touching her hand, he felt more optimistic about the future than he had in a long, long time.

Timothy Best is a writer, producer, Creative Director in the advertising business. He works at one of the largest ad agencies in the south and has written for some of the world's best-known brands. The recipient of over 180 advertising awards, he also teaches copywriting at the University of Alabama. He is also the author of *The Intended Ones*, which is both a prequel and sequel to *Substitute Angel*. A Michigan native, Tim now lives in Birmingham, AL with his wife, daughter, and two rescue dogs. You can follow his blog by looking up his author page on goodreads.com

Cover design & illustration by R. Brannon Hall. Photography by Trey Tomsik.

Made in the USA
Lexington, KY
29 June 2014